CW00521676

SIGHT OF THE BEAST

SIGHT OF THE BEAST

The Dark Chronicles
Book 1 (Limited Edition)

TM. MCGEE

T.M McGee Publishing

Author's Note

Be forewarned that this story is intended for mature audiences—it contains dark, demonic imagery, racial slurs, gore, infant death, murder, strong language, and sexual content.

This work is a book of fiction. Any similarities to that and real situations and people are purely coincidence.

For Better Understanding
The structure, grammar, and syntax of this novel are written using conversational form and creative liberties. You will see purposely misspelled words, slang, and verbiage unique to the characters and author's own interpretations. Demons – Fae – and other supernatural beings mentioned in this novel have been changed—altered and creatively reimagined to fit the narrative of the story

Copyright

Contents

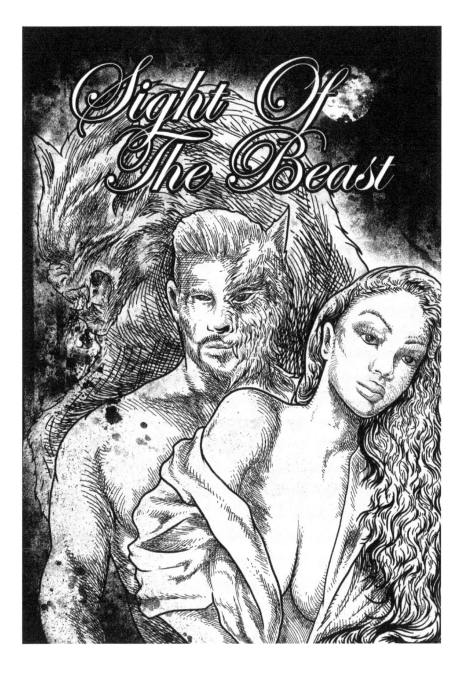

Chapter One

Please have your boarding passes ready. Flight number 957 arriving at terminal 2-A.

The luggage area was overly crowded and noisy. People scurried to and fro like ants. Tiana slouched forward, rubbing her temples, trying to ease the building pressure in the back of her skull. The elderly man, a few seats down from her, smelled like mothballs, and... she couldn't think of the smell... what is that? rotten cabbage? His odor conflicted with the overly sweet scent of morning pastries from the airport bakery a few stalls down. Everything about the airport was nauseating. Her nerves were getting the best of her, and a migraine was about to rear its ugly head.

She grabbed her cell phone from the pocket of her denim jacket and pulled up her itinerary. Current time: 10:53am. Check-in, 12:00 pm. Schedule free until 5:45pm, medical conference dinner. Tiana did a once-over on a few work emails, then cast a tired look in Tao's direction.

Tao was slumped over like a wilting flower. A red White Sox cap sat low on his head. He stood with his hands folded in front of him.

That's weird–

Tao was normally the stoic type, a stickler for proper posture and poise. But today, well... Tiana's assistant was taking a page out of her book.

Looks like I'm not the only one, she thought... The tension radiating off Tao was palpable, even from where Tiana sat near the luggage claim.

"When we left O'Hare, all our bags were accounted for; please look again, sir!" Tao growled as he leaned into the concierge desk, staring aggressively at the prune-faced concierge.

"Yes, yes ve Find yes Ve finds," replied the concierge that kept tapping away on the keyboard, barely paying Tao any mind.

His distinct Japanese features hardened as his eyes narrowed at the airport concierge. Tao's jaw kept clenching; he was normally the peaceful one between them, the lover and Tiana... well, she was the fighter. To see him minutes away from losing his temper was unusual. Tiana chuckled. It was rare for anyone to get Tao this worked up.

Tiana's mind drifted back a few years when a 6'3 muscle-bound Asian had come strolling into her office, persistent about interviewing with her. Tiana was taken aback by his appearance. He looked every bit like those yakuza types from her fantasy novels. He was totally her type since Tiana had a thing for handsome, mysterious men.

His dark hair was cut short on the side with a bit more length left at the top, almost like a Mohawk but not quite. He had seductive, slanted eyes and tattooed, muscular arms. Tiana assumed he was there to interview for the security job posted on Linked IN. Despite her assumptions, Tao blew her away during the interview. Turning the Japanese bad boy into her paper pushing assistant. After a few weeks of working with him, Tiana discovered Tao was the complete opposite of everything she had preconceived.

He was a stickler for calmness, punctuality, and respect. It was like working with a monk, martial arts instructor, and life guru all in one. Probably why he and her bestie Yolanda, the vegan nut, hit it off so well.

Tiana's amusement was short-lived. The longer she continued to watch their interaction. The more anxious she became. Whatever the concierge was saying to him couldn't be good. She reached into her purse, fumbling around a few minutes before finding her Excedrin.

She was quickly regretting this last-minute trip to Berlin. The moment they had landed, they were met with snarky glances and hushed whispers. Sure, her chocolate complexion and his slightly brown skin were rare in this part of the world. But this shit was getting old pretty quick; being here was like stepping back in time. She could have sworn she saw a few men still rocking the Charlie Chaplin mustache.

She sighed for what seemed like the hundredth time since arriving. Her hackles rose as she watched a security guard approach the concierge Tao was talking to.

Tiana shook her head as her fingers danced over her phone keypad as she dialed up her best friend. She had promised to let her know they had arrived safely. The phone barely had enough time to ring before Yolanda's soft, husky voice came through.

"Hun, have you made it safely?" Yolanda asked. "It's nighttime here. So I'm guessing I should tell you good morning... so what's it like over there, anyway?"

Tiana smirked. "That's like five questions in one breath. You may have set a record."

"I'm hyped up on caffeine, Sorry!"

Tiana sat forward on the uncomfortable airport bench and clutched her purse strap. "Well, it's different here. They look like they still throw their hands up and shout, *"Hail Hitler!"* The security personnel's suspicious stare turned toward Tiana as she rose from her seat.

Tiana strolled around the luggage area, looking for the least crowded place. Beside the concierge desk were two doors labeled *Mannlich* and *Frau*.

"What was the app that translates words from German to English again?" Tiana muttered into the phone.

"Tiana," Yolanda hissed, "I told you to download the Google translator app before you left. If you weren't so busy running out of here, you would have been better prepared."

"Yeah, yeah... I'm sorry. You know I had to hurry and get out of town. The College Alumni Board kept hounding me about giving that graduation speech."

Tiana's fingers twirled through her long, kinky coils. This wasn't the smartest of decisions she'd ever made. But she couldn't see herself speaking to thousands of people. Jumping on a plane at O'Hare and flying halfway across the world to Berlin just seemed like a better option in her introverted mind.

"Yeah, I bet," Yolanda fussed back. Tiana shut her eyes and imagined her best friend, her cinnamon- skinned, high cheek-boned face, all puffed out and pouting. She was probably standing in her kitchen with her Betty Boop robe (she looked *exactly* like her) and leaning against the countertop while boiling some vegan sea moss concoction.

In a fake, motherly tone, Yolanda replied, "No, you are not sorry, missy. You did what you wanted to do. I couldn't have stopped you. You know how you get whenever any social interactions are required. But I'm still mad at you, heffa. You knew I needed you to help me paint the salon this week. But no, Dr. Tiana just had to run off to some fancy-shmancy maternal health conference in Berlin."

"I mean, really. Who would have thought my CHD job would come before our friendship?" Tiana chuckled. "I'll make it up to you. I'll be done with this conference in a few days, and I'd be back before you know it."

Yolanda clicked her tongue. "The salon will be painted by then. So you'll owe me a spa date."

"A spa date.... you sure? What if I promise to eat one of your weird vegan casseroles again instead?"

Yolanda giggled. "Come on, Titi. The last eggplant casserole I made was sort of good."

Tiana snickered as she idly kicked her sneaker against the adjacent wall. "You know, doggone well, it was nasty!"

"What I do know is that you aren't slick, trying to change the subject!"

"Oh, whatever do you mean, my dear friend," Tiana replied.

"You know exactly what I mean. You picked Berlin over giving the keynote address at your old university. Plus, you left me to paint all by myself!"

"Uh-uh. Lay it on thick, why don't you." Tiana leaned against the wall, clutching her purse strap, her phone resting against her left ear. She looked back over to the desk, where Tao still seemed to be struggling with the concierge over their baggage.

"Yoyo," she said. "You know I hate any type of social situation. This conference is smaller. I couldn't even imagine standing there before thousands of people, telling them their futures are all set out before them like everything they'll face after graduating will be smooth sailing and easy. When the truth is, they'll be lucky to land a damn job in their field, and those hundreds of thousands of dollars spent on that pretty Ph.D. won't mean shit if they can't find a damn job!"

"Well damn, tell us how you really feel... Alright, alright. I gotchu. I'm going to look for someone else to help me paint. It's just a—"

The sound of surprised gasps and a crowd gathering caught Tiana's attention. "Yoyo, I have to go now. They've messed around and pissed off Tao."

"Tao pissed? They better leave my My-Ty Alone. I'll fly out there and kick su—"

Tiana hung up before Yolanda could finish. She pushed her way through the small crowd gathering around the concierge desk. With a bit of force, she was able to squeeze her way over to Tao's side. The stocky pale guard was talking to the concierge in German, pointing at the luggage on the floor. Tiana hesitantly walked over to the luggage track and whispered to Tao, "What's the problem here?"

Tao's jaw clenched once again, as if he had to take a moment to compose himself before speaking. Tiana wrapped her hands in his as she looked up at Tao's face. She noticed the lack of shine in Tao's dark eyes, and his hands felt clammy.

"Tao, are you alright?"

"Why, yes? I am."

Because of Tao's raised emotions, his Japanese accent was showing a bit more. He gave Tiana a reassuring nod.

The hell you are, she thought to herself. Tao withdrew his hand from hers and pointed to the luggage beside them. "I don't get what the delay is. He's been checking the same screens for over fifteen minutes. But don't worry Tiana, I'll sort it out."

The guard standing behind the desk stepped forward. His murky grey eyes rolled over Tiana's face, lingering a bit too long on her chest. The guard cleared his throat. His perverted gawking was cut off by Tiana, folding her arms across her chest.

He gestured at the three bags—one brown Gucci hard-side bag with spinner wheels that held her files and documents, a red laptop bag sitting on top — and one blue rolling suitcase, with its white tag still attached to its side handle.

She quickly counted the luggage, noting that they were missing one piece: one large green travel bag. The bag that held all her clothes, makeup, and toiletries. "You have to be fucking kidding me!" She yelled. "You lost my damn bag?"

"Ja, Ze bag will be returned upon finding, yes?" The guard's smug face smirked, finding pleasure in their unfortunate circumstances. Tao removed his hat and ran his large hand over his face. Tiana rubbed her temples, praying this wasn't karma biting her in the ass for not staying in Chicago for that goddamn speech.

"Ja, it will be found," said the guard. "Of course, yuh vil be staying at a BHH, no? Ve can keep you updated if somesing is found?"

Tao worriedly looked over at Tiana. He knew Tiana was a spitfire. In the last three years working for her, he had to play fireman on plenty of occasions.

"So my bag is not in there? It's out there somewhere, lost or stolen or something?" Tiana looked at the guard, impatiently waiting for someone to tell her something. "You keep looking at me? What seems to be the problem, sir?" "Vi need to zearch bag, ma'am."

"What bag?" Tiana looked at Tao, who also looked just as confused as she was. The guard repeated himself, still not making a lick of sense. The guard's heavy accent reminded her of a bad Arnold Schwarzenegger impersonator, the way his heavy tongue fell on each vowel like a hammer.

"Ze bag on yur showdur ma'am."

"What does my purse have to do with my missing bag? Are you fucking kidding me right now? We are Americans; we already passed through customs. Are we a risk right now because we're mad about the luggage you lost?" Her tone was short and clipped. "You need to start searching all over Germany for my missing bag, not asking me about the bag on my shoulder."

"Tiz iz pour-seizure." The guard's smug face was pissing her off the more she looked at it. Tiana shook her arms, attempting to shake off her rising temper. No wonder the ordinarily cool-headed Tao was at his limit. In less than ten minutes of talking, Tiana felt like she would end up in some German prison for assaulting an airport security guard.

Their little skirmish had gotten the attention of quite a few people. When Tiana looked their way, the small crowd began to disperse. Another guard stood near the *Frau* and *Mannlich* door, which on closer inspection were probably the bathrooms. *Duh*, Tiana said to herself.

She took a deep breath and put on her professional smile. "Look." She pointed over to the older white woman a few feet down behind the glass barricades. "That lady over there issued a stamp on me and my assistant's passports. Our papers were already verified, which I'm sure you already know." She waived the stamped passport in his face, making sure he saw the very bright fluorescent stamp.

"Ja, zo it zeems yes." His narrowed eyes scrutinized Tao before motioning to his colleague standing a few feet away.

"Diese braunen verdammten Affen müssen sich beeilen und gehen. Die Taschen werden gefunden, wenn sie gefunden werden. Bring sie einfach aus meinen Augen."

Tao's eyebrows rose as he stared at his Samsung note, silently nudging Tiana to get her attention. Her eyes widened as she looked at his screen. The Google translator app had just installed, unbeknownst to the guard:

Google Translate: "these brown fucking monkeys need to hurry and go. The bags will be found when they are found. Just get them out of my sight."

Tiana was about to say something when Tao grabbed her shoulder, shaking his head.

He held the phone up to his mouth as he spoke rapid Japanese, then extended the phone out to the guard for him to read.

Google Translation: "Alright, no problem. If this fake fat ass wannabe Arnold Schwarzenegger here wants to check your luggage, he can. He's not aware that we understand his racist remarks or that you are a doctor that probably makes 500 times more than he ever will in a lifetime. So let's just play nice before we have to call our contact at the local embassy and report this back to his superiors."

By the look on the guard's face, Tiana assumed Tao had written something that put the guard in his place. She smirked at Tao. *That's my boy.*

Tiana placed her hands on her hip, demanding answers. The concierge looked at the guard, and they both nodded. "Zill ve one moment ja, zill gets the supervizor?" Finally, someone was calling the higher-ups.

A few minutes later, two female representatives entered the luggage claim area. The shorter blonde wore a fashionable black hat, red lipstick, and a uniquely styled shirt dress; the other taller woman was dressed plainly, donning regular everyday office attire. As they approached, their heels clunked on the shiny, cream vinyl floor. The woman wearing red lipstick spoke first: "Tee-anha McGur-e?"

Tiana nodded in reply, but Tao quickly corrected her. "It's Doctor McGuire, ma'am."

"Ah I see vell, aud ur hur gurd?" The woman narrowed her eyes and looked him over.

The door on the adjacent side of the room opened, causing Tiana to turn her head. A tall, attractive man wearing an impeccably cut blue business suit stepped out, followed closely by two guards.

Tiana couldn't help but steal a few glances at him as he stood to the side of the desk, reading over some documents. Something about him was mesmerizing. The woman with the bright red lipstick must have been looking, because her reply was cut short. Tiana raised her hand and cleared her throat. "Yes, that's me, Dr. McGuire."

"Ve aur from de ale port sick-urity organization," she said. Her lipstick smudged her two front teeth as she forced a smile. The attractive man in the corner gestured for her to step over. She hurried to his side, leaning in close to hear him. Tiana couldn't make out what he said because he spoke to her in German. She glanced over at Tiana, and then her eyes roamed over Tao, slowly narrowing with every other word spoken by the man in the suit. With a shrug, she straightened herself and walked back over to Tiana and Tao. The man shot Tiana a sly wink, causing her to blush.

The representative stopped halfway to whisper something into the ear of her female companion. After a firm nod, the second woman finally spoke.

"They vunt to check the purse you carried on during the flight. But don't vurry, it will take only a little time."

"I'm only missing one bag—a big green one with all my clothes, and you know everything I would need. My purse is the least of your concerns," Tiana responded in her best, nice-nasty tone. The second woman's English was easier to understand. But no one explained why they wanted to look through her things. It was her bag missing, not theirs. Tiana rubbed the back of her neck; the migraine was throbbing full force now.

"Tiana, please!" Tao pleaded. "We're both tired; let's just let them do this so we can hurry and replace the things they lost. They are wrong. There's no question about it. But we can't keep going in circles. I need to get you checked into the hotel as soon as possible and ready for your presentation at the conference."

Tiana pushed down her anger. If it wasn't for Tao looking under the weather, she wouldn't have given in. But Tiana knew this wasn't a battle worth fighting, at least not with their energy tanks on E.

Tiana nodded stiffly while handing her bag over to Tao. It was a petty move, but she refused to hand the purse over to them herself. As they poured the contents of her purse on the counter, her cell began vibrating in the pocket of her denim jacket. Tiana reached in her pocket, garnering the attention of the two blondes. She shot them a smug look before answering her phone.

"Yoyo, Sorry about hanging up on you—"

"What's going on out there? Is Tao okay?"

Tiana walked away from the desk, shooting a look at Tao to make sure he kept an eye on them as they went through her purse. "Well, it looks like I'll be presenting at the medical conference in some jeans and a denim jacket."

"Don't tell me they lost your luggage? O-M-G, girl, okay, let's look at the bright side. You can just have an international shopping spree, courtesy of your employer!"

Tiana smirked at the way her friend could find the silver lining to any messed-up situation. "Have I ever told you that you would make an excellent counselor?"

Yolanda laughed. "Umm, you tell me every time we talk, call it a trick of the trade hairdressers just give off those therapeutic vibes."

Yolanda was right. The bag was gone, so there was no use sitting around waiting for it to reappear. "It's inconvenient, but you're right. I'll just buy a few things before the presentation. I'm here to do a job. The quicker I present, the faster I can come home."

"That's my girl, you got this. Shake that negative energy off you. You were chosen to do this presentation because you're the best in your field. Doctor McGuire, you've helped thousands of pregnant women and children get their lives on track, your booty is big, and your edges are flourishing; remember who the Hell you are!!—"

Tiana smiled.

"Don't let those British fuckers mess with you, alright?"

"It's Berlin, Yoyo. Not Britain."

"Oh." Then after a beat, she added, "Well, same shit, different name. Have you seen any Nazis?"

"They don't have Nazis anymore — well, at least I don't think they do."

"Um huh, you ain't seen those TV shows about them, have you? How they are everywhere now, even in the good old United States of A."

As Tiana talked on her Phone, Tao watched the guard slowly probing the contents of Tiana's purse. He was struggling to stay in control. Despite all his meditation and training, he had reached his bottom line.

"You've done your search and found nothing," Tao said. "So we are free to be on our way, correct?"

Tiana could hear the anger in Tao's voice. There had only been one other time she'd heard Tao raise his voice. That night had concluded with her bonding him out of a cook county jail for breaking the nose of a guy that wouldn't take no for an answer when Tiana refused to dance with him.

"Yoyo," she said, "I'm going to have to go again."

"What?" Yolanda says. "Be careful out there and don't get locked up in a Berlin jail cell. My money is long, but it can't reach you there."

"Later." Tiana hangs up and walks back to Tao's side.

Tao gives her a slight nod.

"How is your head feeling?" He reached down, cupping the back of her neck, applying just the right amount of pressure. Tiana leaned into his embrace. A hug was exactly what she needed. Because of her five-foot stature, he practically dwarfed her.

But right now, she just needed some comfort. Tiana wrapped her arms around Tao and looked up. He was looking better, less pale and more his usual self. "The healing power of hugs, huh?" Tao smiled down at her. Like Yolanda always said –

"The power of positivity," they said in unison, releasing each other from the embrace.

"We shouldn't be delayed any further. They've finished their search and should allow us to be on our way soon." Tiana peeked over at the two women. Both seem to be glowering at them with disapproval. *Is physical touch frowned on in this culture?*

"Ten men-nuts, at the most," said the plainly dressed woman, as Tiana returned their gawking stares. Tiana's eyes once again drifted to where the man in the suit stood. The two guards were now speaking to him as well. By the looks of it, they were being reprimanded by their superior. A few moments later, they both returned to the concierge desk with new attitudes.

The guard that was standing by the bathroom asked something in broken English, "Ve ur zory fur the mis-undo-stands kave vu zelt safe since kuming her? Caz hun-eone zrethens vu?"

"Uh-uh. Of course not. My bag is missing. I'm scared I might go missing, too, if I stay here any longer." Tiana gestured at Tao. "Along with my hunky assistant here."

The guards smiled awkwardly. "Superb. Ur vree to go now."

Only the word 'superb' is pronounced as *Siuperb*. Tiana tried to smile, but the attempt fell flat. She walked away slowly and stopped just at the edge of the cubicle, where she waited for Tao to grab their luggage.

Just as Tao grabbed the last bag, the blonde with the red lips stepped into Tiana's path. "Ve got off to a poor start, no? My name is Charlotte Wagner." She introduced the other female as Corinna Schmidt. Their heels clacked against the floor with every step as they escorted Tiana and Tao out of the luggage area. Tao looked down at his watch—12:45pm. He huffed as he quickly made a mental note to adjust Tiana's schedule.

Tao waved his large hand in the air, flagging down a taxi. A car quickly pulled up, and the driver hopped out to help load the luggage. As Tao helped the driver place the suitcases in the back seat, Tiana opened the car door. Corina was the one to step in her way this time. "Ve have made provisions to make up for the zelay aund loss of the package, Dense You've ur not be used to German efficiency—"

Tiana took a step back. "What the—"

Tao quickly made his way to her side in time enough to grab her elbow, lightly restraining her.

Charlotte caught the irritation in Tiana's voice. Charlotte quickly interjected, "Oh, Fraulein. No, she duz not mean it that vvay. You must forgives our use of English. Zoon, you'll be meeting with the odors ove zur Amerikan, kind yes? I as-cure you; you vill be spared any further disasters, ja."

Subconsciously, after a few deep breaths, her shoulders softened. Tao gave her a quick nod. He hustled back to the trunk to make sure the driver loaded everything in.

Charlotte opened a bag, produced a large brown envelope, and extended it towards Tiana.

"A gift from our organization, zumething to comp-in sate for the delay ja." The woman flashed a smile.

"What's in there?"

"Vou'll see." Charlotte flashed that toothy grin again, creeping Tiana out for what she could only pray was the last time. Tiana timidly took the envelope and felt around it before passing it to Tao, who opened it and extracted a cash voucher. He turned and showed it to Tiana.

"Oh, and just when I thought Berlin lacked class," Tiana crassly responded.

Charlotte cleared her throat. "Aund de car ride is on us too."

The car ride was uneventful, and Tiana was grateful for the brief reprieve. By the time the taxi parked in front of the Berlin Honors Hotel, most of Tiana's tension had melted away. Tao had been silent for the entire ride. Which wasn't surprising since they were both jet-lagged and in need of a good rest? Before Tao could even help Tiana out of the car, a young bellhop appeared beside him to help take their luggage into the hotel.

Tao held out his hand, gently guiding Tiana to the curb before directing the bellhop where to place the luggage. Tiana took the time to stretch her back and take in her surroundings. Tao's phone rang. He shot a quick nod, excusing himself off to the side.

Tiana paid him no mind as her eyes darted about in admiration. *Well, this is nice!* The hotel was richly decorated; warm tones and brass adornments were placed strategically throughout the lobby. Two enormous chandeliers illuminated the foyer, crystals sparkling as Tiana walked beneath them. Everything was posh, from the gorgeous gold and black ceramic floors to the canvases lining the walls.

Tiana slowly made her way to the front desk. A small line was forming; quite a few tourists were also standing around, admiring the paintings. So far, the hotel was everything the tripadvisor website said it would be. Things were looking up.

Tiana inhaled deeply. There was a citrus fragrance lingering in the air, but it wasn't unpleasant. Tiana yawned as she finally reached the front of the line.

The sound of movement behind her caused Tiana to look back. A woman walked in dressed in a long sapphire gown. A man in a tuxedo escorted her.

"*There must be a ball here tonight,*" Tiana uttered to herself. They walked past Tiana, turning their noses up as they glanced over at her attire. Without sparing her a second glance, they stepped into the elevator, out of sight.

She glanced down, suddenly more conscious of her clothing—she wore a stylish but comfortable denim jacket. Her curly blackish-brown hair had a life of its own, with some form-fitting jeans.

Oh well, not much I can do since they lost my bag. Tiana placed her purse on the front desk, waiting for the concierge to check them in. The hotel lobby hummed with a cacophony of tongues—bad to moderate English, bad to average German, French, and a couple of other languages too obscure for Tiana to place. A regular-looking man, who Tiana assumes is the concierge, stared at her but made no effort to approach. *Maybe he's doing something for another guest?*

"Have you checked in yet?" Tao inquired. "Sorry I took so long coming in. I had a personal call." Tiana slapped his shoulder playfully. "Had to check in with your bae, huh?"

"Come on, stop that." Tao chuckled while hoisting the satchel bag higher onto his shoulder. Another person stepped in behind the desk, so Tiana waved her hand to get the female's attention. The girl's face froze when she saw Tiana.

"Entschuldigung, haben Sie sich verlaufen?" the girl asked.

Tiana shrugged and asked, "English? Do you speak English?"

"Excuse me, are you lost?"

Tiana looked at Tao, her lips parting slowly. Tao scratched his jaw; his eyes looked bloodshot, like he needed some quality sleep.

"Did she just ask if I'm lost... is this déjà vu the airport all over again?" Tiana asked Tao, who nodded, his shoulders slumping with defeat. "Yes, it feels like the twilight zone—" Tiana thought it best to remain silent. But the girl asked the same question again, thinking Tiana did not get it the first time. And this time, the girl asked more slowly and with plenty of condescension in her voice.

"Sind Sie im falschen Hotel?" she said. "Are you in the wrong hotel?" Tiana looked at Tao, praying for him to intercede on her behalf.

He said, "No, we have a reservation here."

The girl looked at Tiana, then back to Tao. "One moment, please." The girl quickly left the desk area. A tall, well-dressed male took her place. "Good day to you, Mister and ma'am. How may I help you this evening? Perhaps you have a different hotel in mind?"

Tiana gasps. "Well, goddamn..."

The man didn't bat an eye. Like sending them away was an everyday occurrence. His icy blue gaze was sharp and penetrating. His stare appeared to favor Tao with a more favorable light than Tiana. Tao stepped to the desk, resting his elbows on the counter, lowering himself to be eye level with the pompous front desk staff.

"Check the computer for a reservation right now," said Tao, "it will be under the name Tiana McGuire. Dr. Tiana McGuire."

The concierge's face fell slightly, his lips parting as if he wanted to argue his rebuttal. However, Tao could be quite an intimidating force. With a huff, he glanced back down at his computer screen, glancing up every so often. His brown eyes throw some not-so-subtle shade off Tiana's way.

"Eva!" He called the girl from earlier back to his side. "Please check the name. It must be a... er... mix-up somewhere." He coughed and tried to lower his voice. "Dr. McGuire is a speaker at this week's conference in the main ballroom. Please find their reservations."

Tiana smirked at Tao, who nodded his head back at her. "It's a shame I have to drop my credentials to get better respect around here."

Tiana stepped back from the desk, allowing Tao to handle the stuck-up front desk staff.

Meanwhile, Tiana took a few moments to people watch. From the sounds of the various conversations in the lobby, there must have been a large mixture of American, German, and French guests in the hotel. Tiana's ears perked up as she listened to a French couple discussing one of the paintings in the lobby. French was a bit more pleasing to her ears; it sounded romantic. Her lips moved and wrinkled in an amusing little smirk at the act of a man holding his—wife, or maybe girlfriend? — Around the waist, his lips falling and rising in enunciation; it was like watching music play instead of hearing it.

"Excuse me, ma'am?"

She turned and met the concierge's eyes. He sighed and said, "I am so sorry very much. I misjudged you for a different guest of ours from the States. You share a strong resemblance. To make up for the inconveniences you've experienced, I have upgraded your suite to a better and bigger one. Now, if you follow me, I can take you to your suite."

Tao signaled a hotel assistant who was standing with their luggage. Together, the procession followed the concierge.

"I have just received word about the incident at the airport. I'm sorry about it," the concierge continued.

"Will they find the bag?" Tao asked, his deep voice echoing through the richly decorated hallway.

The concierge clicked his tongue in disgust. "Berlin has many great things. Our airport is not one of them."

Oh, we are painfully aware of that little fact. But out loud, Tiana said, "I can imagine."

The concierge stopped at the elevators, pressed a button, and the doors slid open. Everyone stepped in. The elevator numbers flickered 1-5, finally stopping at the fifth floor.

Tiana gasped. The hallway itself was a view, very picturesque; one side of the wall was lined with more paintings, some grotesque, abstract, while others looked like original works of art. She made a mental note to take a closer look at them when she has settled in. Art history was one of her favorite electives during university, but she could never find the time since taking the CHD job.

The concierge stood before a door at the end of the hallway. Beyond that was a hallway leading to another stairway. "And here we are," he proclaimed, as he deposited her luggage in the middle of the suite before swiftly making his way out the door.

Just as Tao grabbed the door and attempted to shut it, the concierge stepped back in. "One last thing," he said. He removed a card from his breast pocket, opened it, and placed it seductively in Tao's hands.

"Please, as a compliment from us, for your troubles." Then he whispered, *"My number is on the back."* The man bowed and left.

Tao cringed.

"What is it?"

"You've just been offered a pool pass, and wait—" Tao's slanted eyes opened wide, his mouth hung open.

Tiana snatched the card from his hand and gawked at it; her face began to replicate the expression on her assistant's own. "Oh, wow!" She looked at Tao and shook her head. "The pool is probably crowded, with you know people..." Tiana shivered. She had already surpassed her limit for social interactions.

Tao's expression quickly switched from an excited grin to a frown. He said, "Oh no, you don't, you need to unwind; it's been a long day, Tiana. It's just free shopping for a bathing suit. It's nothing really."

"Shut up, Tao. You expect me to trek down there and get a bathing suit. You've already seen how unwelcoming they are." Without another word, Tiana turned and scurried away from Tao before he could refute her. She quickly called up Yolanda to give her the latest tea.

Yolanda answered with a yawn. "You know it's midnight here, right?"

"Yep, and I know you're wide awake watching people eat food or some other weird ASMR thing."

Yolanda couldn't help but laugh. "Gahhhh, you know me so well. I can't eat meat, but watching other people do it is so fascinating."

Tiana related everything from the beginning again, her lousy fortune at the luggage check-in the airport, the hotel welcome downstairs, and how Germany seemed to have some serious racial discrimination.

Tao rolled his eyes, flopping on the couch with a thud. His eyes began to shut as he watched Tiana paced back and forth while on the phone.

Yolanda yawned into the phone. "So make sure you get a bikini, something that flatters that banging cornbread fed body of yours."

Tiana growled, "Uh-uh, Yoyo. I'm not going out to the pool. I'd rather walk around and look at all their exclusive art pieces; it's the main reason I had Tao book this hotel. Plus, they aren't too welcoming of our kind here. I'll just sit in my suite and eat sweets until the dinner reception tonight. That way, I can fake a stomach ache and worm my way out of it—"

She looked around the place. There was a complimentary pile of chocolates in three baskets in the middle of the carpet; red drapes covered the wall from the ceiling to the floor, but a gap was left open, leading out to a small balcony. A quaint chunk of Berlin was visible from where she stood.

"Girl, you can't do that to yourself," said Yolanda. "Go downstairs and do some shopping. Get a bikini and dip in the water. You're a big girl. Stop letting your social anxiety dictate your every move."

"Uh-uh."

"Right, so tell me, what are you gonna do, Tiana?"

"I just told you, Yoyo."

"Nah, I meant about the vouchers and things, the pool pass," Yolanda clarified. "What are you going to do about them? Throw them away?"

Tiana glanced at Tao, his head lolling as he started to doze off. She told Yolanda she'd probably have Tao go down to the pool to represent her or something. Tao gave her a seditious glare, as if it would take Buddha himself to move him from the couch.

She chuckled. And whispered to Tao, "I'm joking; get some rest."

"Girl, I'm going to curse you out if you do that," said Yolanda's singsong voice.

"Okay, okay. You want me to do me; I'll do me."

Tiana dropped the call and sprawled out on the nearest couch. Closing her eyes as the stress of travel slowly weighed her down.

Tao sighed, then grabbed his laptop from his shoulder bag; he'd been carrying it since they left Chicago. Once again, Tiana was amused by his efficiency. The rim of his cap cast a shadow over his eyes and nose. But he looked a lot better than he did at the airport.

He tapped and tapped, then said to her, "You should take Yolanda's advice. Your calendar is free the whole of the weekend; the dinner isn't mandatory, so we can scratch it off." He smirked as Tiana did a short, little happy dance on her side of the couch. "You don't have any mandatory engagements." He paused. "Until Monday, when you're expected at a small meeting before the main event itself." He finished and looked at her.

Tiana nodded, happy to have at least one ally on her side. There was no way she was mentally ready to wine and dine with the international medical conference members tonight. She'd had quite enough of the pretentious, snotty types.

Tao added, "As your assistant and a best male friend, I endorse the swimming pool."

"Have you seen the pool?"

"Nope," confessed Tao. "Neither have you. You want me to check it out for you?"

"Nope. I don't trust your judgment. You are as much a part of the conspiracy as Yoyo."

Tao grinned. He was tired too. Plus, his girlfriend texted him, and he had yet to respond. He quickly dismissed himself, telling Tiana that he'd like to check his own suite out, while she took her swim.

As the door closed behind him, Tiana stumbled over to the balcony. Sucking in the crisp late summer air, she peered down at the street. Taxis from the airport dropped more people off. The bellhop teetered up and down the steps, carrying luggage.

Tiana looked across Berlin's skyline: the red roofs of Gendarmenmarkt, the horses on Brandenburg Gate and a section of the graffiti-ridden Berlin Wall. She smiled at the sight of one of the cities that shaped

Europe for a quarter of a century. She exhaled, imagining the rich history of this place. How much tragedy and mourning this city had endured because of outlandish ideologies of sociopathic men and their brutality. With a history so deep-set in prejudice and anti-Semitism, today's events shouldn't surprise her. Despite the current times, there were still people like the Nazis living among us. Just look at how things had been going back in America. In her own country, hate was brewing something even worse; racism wasn't just in Berlin; but in every corner of the world, every state in the United States, and every neighborhood.

Tiana shook her head, ridding herself of the dark thoughts, and drifted back into her suite. She pulled off her denim jacket, revealing a white t-shirt pulled tight over her ample bosom that was decorated with the cartoon head of sponge Bob Square Pants in all his yellowy glory. Then she removed her form-fitting pair of blue jeans and white sneakers. She glances at herself in the gold inlay mirror in the suite's entry while giving herself a pep talk. *They want me to shop for a bikini, and shop for a bikini, I will.*

The hotel's mall covered most of the ground floor in the back. The pool was the size of half a football field and teaming with people. From here, the water looked crystal clear, with wispy white clouds reflecting off it. Beach chairs were set on one side, with people laying out enjoying themselves.

Well, isn't this great? It's a whole sausage fest out there. She regretted leaving her room. Most of the pool goers were men: there were old guys, middle-aged sugar daddies, young muscular jocks, and flabby hairy-chested men.

Tiana was introverted, but she enjoyed the beach like anyone else. It was only the people and unnecessary interactions she didn't like. She'd been everywhere, from Bali, Spain, Dubai, Hawaii twice with the girls and once in Sao Paulo on an office retreat. But this was her first time in Berlin.

About ten feet from the sunbathing area, Tiana saw the sign: Pool Shop. With a deep breath, she forced herself to walk in, her sweaty hands squeezing the voucher in her pocket.

The young woman behind the counter smiled at her as she entered. Tiana nervously presented the voucher to the woman at the small desk by the entrance. The woman smiled again before asking Tiana. "French? Or English?"

"English." Tiana replied with a smile.

"Okay, great," the woman looked at the voucher, "you are entitled to a five-hundred-euro worth of purchase. You can split this spending over the rest of your stay. Or you can do everything now." She smiled again and hands Tiana back her voucher. Her face was flushed, as if she were more nervous than Tiana. The woman's warm smile and chipper attitude was probably the first genuine interaction Tiana had experienced since arriving, helping to put her more at ease.

"So, what would you like to purchase?"

"I'd like a... er..." She hesitated. Tiana quickly glanced around the large place before pointing to the female clothing section. "A bikini."

"You like to swim, yes?"

"Yes, I'd like to swim."

The woman gave Tiana's figure a quick assessment; her eyes roamed over her large chest, then fell to her hips. Even on the trip down, the security guards and bellhop ogled her.

After the woman was done looking at Tiana's figure, she nodded her head then took off towards the back of the shop. Her flared skirt flicked every time the woman's stubby legs turned a corner. She looks like she may be thirty at the least, but her dirty blonde hair and warm smile made her look younger.

Tiana stood before the racks of bikinis, at a complete loss. There were hundreds of them, in every type and style. She hesitantly walked into the rows. A sea of colors and materials. It felt like a maze. The woman extended her hand, inviting Tiana to step forward for a better look. "With your shape, anything will look good. Ring me if you need me."

She glanced back as the woman walked away. Tiana smiled. *Well, she was lovely.* She made a mental note to herself to inquire her name later;

hopefully, she could leave her an excellent review. But For now, she had to find a bikini.

Ten minutes later, Tiana had it narrowed down to two. But the one she truly wanted ended up being a bit too small. Her eyes narrowed on the blue velvet Fendi bikini. It was pricey, but cute. Tiana placed the bikini against her body and stood before a long mirror on the wall. "Okay, I'll admit this would *look wicked on my body*," she murmured to herself. She stretched the material checking to see if it would fit her wide hips. As much as she loved her body, it was hard finding clothes to fit her coke- bottle figure, especially in international sizes. Tiana looked around to make sure no one was looking before turning to check out her own ass. She could hear Yoyo's voice in her mind:

You'd make a straight girl change her mind!

She giggled while checking the bikini one more time to make sure there was nothing better. Tiana looked around and notices a few other women prowling the racks of clothes... As she made her way to the changing room to swap out her jeans and t-shirt, a bright orange Nike sports bag and a light blue kimono swim robe caught her attention.

The pool seemed even more crowded than before as she made her way out of the shop. People were having a merry time, laughing, talking, and clinking glasses, half-filled with drinks. Tiana looked up. The temperature was hotter now. The late afternoon sun burned low, hidden behind low, floating clouds.

Tiana rummaged around in her purse, pulling out a pair of dark shades while exiting the shop. She looked up and down the narrow passageway, toward the private baths. The stucco floor was gritty under her bare feet. " *should have purchased some flip-flops. Hopefully, I won't fall and embarrass myself.*" She strolled on, reminiscing about last year in Ibiza. The beautiful private beaches and warm, clean sand. Her favorite thing about the trip was that people kept to themselves.

She stopped at a vending machine and selected a drink that had a picture of a strawberry on it. After a quick sip, she soon regretted it. It tasted more like strawberry seltzer water than actual pop, but it would have to do for now. The kimono was pulled snug around her waist. Despite her best efforts, it did little to hide her ample bosom. She walked forward, a can of soda in one hand and the bags in the other.

The sound of water splashing caused her to look over to the pool area. Everyone seemed to be trying to escape the heat. Folks were sitting, standing, and talking beside the pool. She looked around, trying to find the least congested area, spotting a few vacant lounge chairs on the deep side of the pool.

She quickly made her way to the vacant seats; no one seemed to notice her scurrying along. Only a few heads turned when she reached the chairs. Picking one in the middle of a collection of five, she dropped her bags and made herself comfortable.

Tiana jumped, roused out of her shallow rest when she heard the laughter of a young girl. She looked to her side, where a teenage girl with milk-colored skin jumped off the side of the pool. A lanky-armed, prepubescent boy cheered her on. She smiled.

The innocence of youth.

A moment later, two women and a man strolled over to where Tiana lounged on the chair. They waved a quick greeting. As the women sat down, they began removing their bikini tops and slathering each other with suntan lotion, with a bit more intimacy shared between just friends.

Okay, gone with your bad selves.

Tiana couldn't help but steal a few glances before leaving the women to their privacy and heading towards the pool.

Oh yeah.

She blushed, slightly embarrassed at having to circle back to remove her shades. Tiana also removed the kimono and grabbed a towel from the rack stationed behind her. Her white towel was fluffy and warm, crested with the hotel's insignia—a purple lion, its tail curling underneath the initials BHH, for Berlin Honors Hotel. She quickly made her way to the edge of the pool, her thick thighs jiggling with timid steps.

Shiiiiiit ouch ouch. The hot concrete under her bare feet was just a few degrees away from unbearable. Just as she dipped her toes into the water, the catcalls began.

"Oh gosh," "look at how big her bum is," growled someone from behind.

And just like magic, the heads started to turn. She looked down the side of the pool and was bombarded by squinting eyes, open mouths and lustful gazes—most of them from men, though there were a few admiring smiles from women.

Dammit, I should have stayed in my room. She was acutely aware of eyes on her butt and thick thighs.

What *the fuck? The actual fuck?* Tiana's eyes widened at the sight of the bulging erection stretching the shorts of a nearby man. She shook her head.

Nooooo Nope, this isn't gonna work. She was no prude, but there was a difference between attention you want and unsolicited staring. Just as quickly as she came, Tiana hightailed it back to her chair. She quickly picked up her towel and wrapped her body. She took the kimono and tucked it away in the bag before walking to the bar. A few men huffed out disapproving groans and grunts.

Tiana ignored them and pulled up a stool. The bartender was a young, broad-shouldered stud with sandy brown hair. He placed a fruity cocktail before Tiana and put a plastic straw in. She gave a weak, grateful smile. From her peripheral, she could see a man standing to her side, idling by, hoping to get her attention. She purposely avoided his gaze, concentrating on her drink, sucking it slowly. Tiana wasn't ashamed of her body by any means, but introverts just weren't big on attention.

"Yoyo, you were wrong. I shouldn't have listened to you."

When people stared, expectations were heightened, forcing Tiana to become super self-aware. Just like in Ibiza last summer with Yoyo and Laura, Tiana had confined herself in her hotel room following a failed attempt to enjoy the water when some couple kept soliciting her to be their third because her husband liked her chocolate skin. *Tiana remembered that night like it was still fresh in her mind.*

"I mean, come on, Titi, it could be seen as a compliment, and you aren't

upset by that, right?" Yoyo had asked Tiana as she stomped through the sand, away from the beach.

"And why not?"

"You have a body—" Yolanda stumbled after her, "You have a body that many girls have to go under the knife to get. At top dollar, if I may add. Wait, Titi!"

"No, I'm going back to my room."

Yolanda got a hold of her hands and tried to pull her back. Tiana reluctantly let her. They stood in silence for a bit, letting the anger simmer down.

Yolanda took a deep breath. "Titi, you can't just run away from everything that makes you uncomfortable."

"What do you mean?"

"You can't live shut off from the world forever. You spend all your time trying to heal this world of shit, but you won't take even the slightest piece of it for yourself. You won't meet someone—"

"Well, apparently, meeting people isn't an issue. Hell, a couple just asked me to be their ebony fucking fantasy."

"It's the way of the world, Titi. You're fine as Hell; it's fun. Come on, you go on like you ain't got the body. Girl, you are attractive as fuck, and it's not like you this is your first rodeo..."

Yolanda smirked." You got a little freak in you. I know you better than most."

Tiana had sighed.

Her shoulders slumped. "I just can't do it, Yoyo." Yolanda had looked back at the spread of clear Blue Ocean, the dots of people scattered throughout the beach, bikinis and bare-chested men in colorful shorts. One of those men had asked Yolanda to have dinner with him that night, and Yolanda had already said yes. He was a sexy black marine, too. Yolanda bit her lower lip, not wanting to abandon her best friend over a free meal and a sexy one-night stand. Maybe they'd have sex by the end of the night, perhaps not. But she was prepared to take the holiday and make it something memorable.

Yolanda looked at her friend and wondered what Tiana wanted to make of it.

"Alright, let's go," Yolanda said finally.

"What? You need to go back. Your dates' going to be looking for you soon—"
Yolanda dipped her hand in the corner of her tight bikini, showing Tiana a piece of paper with a number scrawled on it. *"I can call him."* She winked.
"I don't want to make you do this. I'll manage on my own."
Yolanda slung her hand around Tiana's neck. *"Shut up, Titi. You've made me do worse shit, you bitch. Let's go on up and get high and drink wine—"*
"And watch old movies and eat cake—"
"And mope about how your life is such a bore—"
"While doing nothing about it—"
"Except maybe, make trouble with the hotel attendants—"
"Or we can go wake up Tao and make him play some cards with us."
They both smirked. *"Sounds like a plan—"*
Tiana was so deep into her memory that she didn't realize she was flicking her straw with her tongue. Her tongue worked the straw in her open mouth. Flicking it round and round, she hadn't noticed two men sitting across the bar, enthralled by her performance. Tiana was lost in thoughts of her luggage and fretting over parts of her speech during the conference on Monday.

The burly middle-aged man sitting across from Tiana carefully laid his bottle of Sternberg on the bar top, his lips slightly parting, his tongue licking dry lips. His lustful gaze roamed over her as he leaned forward. His companion swallowed some of his beer, sat back, and spread his legs open, granting Tiana a view right up his shorts.

She choked on her drink as she hurried to avert her eyes.

Are those his balls hanging—?

After an exchange of awkward stares, Tiana pushed her drink away. The younger guy left his place at the table. His friend gives him an encouraging nod. He slowly made his way to her side, pulling up a stool to sit beside her. Tiana said nothing, not wanting to give him the impression she was interested.

Tiana now understood what she'd done. In her head is a picture of her twirling tongue—it must have looked like an open invitation. She rolled her eyes, angry at herself for not being aware of her surroundings. A bitchy sneer ruffled her lips. She averted her eyes as he waited for her to look at him. He gripped the bottle of Stenberg in his hands. He looked German or some European mix; maybe Nordic, sandy brown hair, soft blue eyes. He was not very attractive. His face was too long.

"Having a great time schwarze schonheit?" he asks with a toothy grin.

Tiana shrugged and replied that she was trying her best. The man nodded and smiled at her.

"I'm just here to check the scenery and enjoy some time alone," she said.

"Berlin is a beautiful place, isn't it?"

Tiana glanced around. "Yes, one could say it is. Beautiful."

"You are, indeed," he said.

Tiana looked at him and tried to fight back a gag.

"I mean. You are gorgeous, drop-dead gorgeous. That's how they say it in English, yes?"

Tiana nodded uncomfortably, looking for a way out of the conversation.

"And you don't say much either. It is good. Where I'm from, a smart woman says less."

"And how much does a smart man say?" Tiana said, trying to mimic the man's peculiar inflection.

"A man says his mind, I guess."

"Does a woman say hers?"

"Of course. She's free to." He leaned towards Tiana, adding, "But mostly not with her voice, if you know what I'm talking about." He winked, and for a moment, after a tiny microsecond, Tiana felt flirtatious. But she feigned ignorance, refusing to meet his probing eyes, "I don't know what you're talking about."

"Umm, I could show you, better than tell you."

Tiana's eyes widened at his bluntness. She shook her head. Pushing her drink further away, she then grabbed her belongings from the adjacent stool, leaving him at the bar by himself.

He will rather show me. Tiana shakes her head, slowly chuckling to herself.

She took another route on a whim, meandering through wide hall-ways, passing hotel staff and other tourists. Her ears perked up as she picked up on the conversation between two men on her way to the ele-vator. "Excuse me."

The French guy said, "Ja?"

"I don't know much French or German, but it sounded like you both were talking about a steam room or sauna?"

The blonde middle-aged man replied first, "Yeah, it's a cool place. You should see it."

"If you have a voucher, you don't pay," said the younger male in clear English.

Tiana fingered the side of her kimono. Her voucher is not there. She panicked for a second, before remembering that it was in the bag with her clothes. She nodded at the two men and stepped back from the door of the lift.

"Thank you."

"Ja. No problem. Go to the steam room, you will love it," the older guy advised again.

Tiana nodded, stepping further away from the elevator doors, and opened her bag. She picks out her voucher and turns it over in the yellow light of the hotel lobby. It said nothing on it about a steam room. The French guy said her voucher would get her in. She pushed the voucher back in the bag and glanced around the expansive lobby. It was not as crowded as earlier.

The concierge from earlier was out of sight. Tiana stared at the new female working at the front desk. Making her way to the line, she posi-tioned herself behind an old, rich-looking woman.

"How may I help you, please?" the girl asked when it was Tiana's turn.

"Is there a steam room here?"

"The sauna?"

The girl's eyes narrowed as she pointed to the left of the lobby, to-wards an archway. "That way, please."

Tiana thanked her and started that way. She stopped at the archway entrance and dropped her bag on the floor. She placed her ear pods in, her fingers quickly swiping to her YouTube playlist. Chris Brown's *Indigo* filled her head as she walked down the long hallway. She looked back when a glimmer of something moving dashed past the corner of her vision.

She removed one earbud, cautiously looking around for a few moments. After a few seconds of silence, she placed the earbud back in and continued walking, tapping the side of her thigh to the rhythm of the music.

At the end of the hallway, there were giant, golden double doors. She looked back the way she came, still unable to shake the uneasy feeling from before. But there was nothing there.

The hallway was well lit, no one lurking about. Tiana shrugged it off as she pushed the doors open and stepped inside.

Entering the sauna feels like stepping into a different world. The room is enormous, bigger than any steam room she's ever visited. It was humid with a faint sulfuric smell. The scones cast an eerie blue light throughout the room. There were no guards or security, no one was working the check-in desk. She shrugged it off and kept walking down the short streak of concrete steps. The room appeared to be empty. She surveyed the sauna and instantly liked the solitude it provided.

The polished wooden seats, spanning three sides of the room, beckon her. Tiana's knees wobble; the day's fatigue is finally wearing her thin. A puff of steam rose from the middle of the room. The temperature was at least eighty-five. She set her bag on the floor. She took off her kimono and wadded it into a ball. She chose a space in the sauna's furthest corner. She placed her rolled kimono beside her and flopped down, wincing when the hot wood seared her soft brown skin. Once her skin adjusted, she sat back, closing her eyes as Chris Brown's song, *Sex you back to sleep*, played softly in her ear. The steam rose all around her as her mind drifted off.

She imagined what would take place come Monday morning. She was scheduled to meet the maternal health council of Berlin's CHD chapter.

Tiana took a deep breath praying her research topic would be well received amongst her international peers. She succors herself with the thought that her community health plan could address the health disparities plaguing the women of Berlin.

As always, her mind haunts her with the faces of the women and children she had failed to save years prior—broken faces, bloodshot eyes, quivering lips, and mournful cries. She squeezes her eyes shut, praying to shut it all out in the gloom of her mind's eye, willing away the negative thoughts.

"You can't save them all, Tiana, you can't save them all."

Her eyes crack open the tiniest bit at the sound of sucking and slurping. The room is filled with steam, white mist rising from the center to the roof. The wood walls are shiny with perspiration. Something moves again. Her eyes squint as she tracks the movement in the shadows. The sound intensifies.

Tiana removes her earbud. The sound of hushed voices comes through clearly now. She frowns, mourning the loss of her solitude. As she peers through the steam at the blurry image to her left. Tiana's mouth drops open as her eyes adjust to the suffused light. The tendrils of steam disburse, revealing the naked forms of three people...

Aren't they the people from the pool?

The blonde that waved earlier is sitting on the man's face, grinding her pussy on his mouth while the other's head bobs up and down on his penis. Tiana gasps, dumbfounded, looking around to make sure it wasn't a hallucination.

What the Hell... let me get out of here?

Tiana quickly and quietly gathers her things. As she reaches down to grab her bag, she and the man lock eyes.

His eyes are a fierce green, stark against the sea of white. It is like gazing into the eyes of some green abyss. The girl with her mouth on his cock moans; her eyes are shut tight as his fist grips her blonde hair between his fingers. Her naked plump breasts dangle as she works the man's shaft with both hands.

The slurping noise fills Tiana's head, and she takes out the other bud in her ear. The second female rises off his face, only to taste herself on his lips. Her short blonde hair tousles wildly as she bites and nibbles the man's lips. Her fingers grip the man's spiky black hair with her thin fingers. Her eyes shut suddenly as dark veins start to blotch over her skin, her complexion turning from creamy white to a sickly grey parlor, but her kisses seem even more possessive and forceful. She hungrily drives her tongue in and out of his mouth.

Strange as it is, Tiana can't seem to look away. The man's eyes never leave hers. The girls seem oblivious to Tiana's presence. Both were enthralled with bringing him to completion. The man's cock grows longer, thicker, stretching the girl's mouth wide. Dribble foams around the corners of her mouth with every thrust of his enormous cock. The girl's mouth hardly fits, and she chokes but keeps sucking.

Tiana feels her lower limbs quake, her core clenching with arousal. She licks her lips, unable to look away from the trail of spit dripping down his shaft. The man slouches; his chest rises and falls as he breathes fast, matching Tiana's labored huffs. Her eyes stay on the sucking movement going on between the man's thighs, then move from over the dark shiny pubic hair. Tiana's eyes drink in the man's body. His abs were solid blocks of pure muscle. His dark brown nipples were hard and pointed. She bites her lip, her pussy fluttering to life.

How long has it been since I had a good lay?

Her own hands start to drift towards her breasts, her fingers sliding slowly into the bikini, tweaking her hard chocolate points.

The man's finger mimics her own, aggressively rubbing on the woman's tits, twisting them between his thumb and forefingers. His green unblinking eyes never stray from her, as if hypnotized. Every move the man made mirrored hers. Tiana's gaze falls back to the woman sucking his cock, whose tongue glides over the fat mushroom head of his throbbing member. She gyrates hard against the bench, seeking relief from the building pressure; the sexual noises keep drawing her into a lust-filled haze. Tiana is trembling, sweat trickling down her body. She opens her thighs, needing something, missing something. A lustful hunger is growing deep within her.

She looks down at the bathing suit; it feels suffocating... restrictive. Her chest heaves up and down frantically. Her body is on fire, and flames are erupting from her panties. Her hands cup her crotch, hoping the pressure will relieve the ache, but it worsens. She whimpers. Tiana looks sharply across the sauna; the man's eyes are still on her. Tiana recoils in anger.

This man... he's done something to me.

She shakes her head, attempting to shake off whatever this is... *I don't want this...*

She tries to get up to escape from the prospect of being taken down. But her body won't move. Betraying her no matter how much her mind screams for her to flee and leave. She just sits there, unable to escape the man's trance. Her clit throbs in sync with her pumping heart; her bikini bottom is soaked.

This isn't right! No... I have to go!

But no matter how hard she fights, her body is completely overtaken by the strange force emanating from his unblinking, glowing green eyes.

"This is such a pleasant surprise," he says. "Do not fret my heavenly chocolate noir; I will save you for last."

At those words, his lips widen in an inhuman grin. Rows upon rows of dagger-sharp teeth extrude from bloodied gums. Tiana attempted to avert her eyes, but her face whipped back to face him.

"It is impolite not to look your dinner date in the eye, Mona me," he grunts out, forcefully pulling the dark-blonde girl's head towards his gaping maw. Brutally crushing her face into his. Spearing her soft flesh against his shark-like teeth. Her body convulses as he eviscerates her flesh from her skull, his serpentine tongue tugging her lifeless body deeper into his gullet.

With a sudden movement, he swallows her whole. Slowly slurping on chunks of flesh and innards stuck between his jaws.

Tiana feels the bile rise to her throat, burning. Her body shakes uncontrollably as he continues to pick the blonde hair from in between his jaws. The other woman still bobs her head up and down his shaft, blissfully hypnotized, unaware of their dire circumstances.

2

Chapter Two

His spit struck the pavement, the *splat* echoing through the alleyway. Ishtan, well, the fellows have been called many names over the... years? Or would the correct term be centuries? These days he goes by the nickname Bounty.

With a quick swipe of the back of his hand, he rids his mouth of the foul taste of fae.

Puh.. Yuck, by the Gods, those fuckers always taste like sugary shit sacks. He growled in frustration, his hunger barely sated by such a small hunt. Berlin had always been prime hunting ground, and there's excitement in the air tonight. His eyes flash momentarily, his inner beast pressing close to the surface.

Simmer down, boy; you'll get your turn.

He utters a short incantation and blue flames erupt from the concrete, melting away any remnants of the dark fae's corpse he left behind. Bounty strides from the alleyway casually. Pedestrians halt in their tracks, allowing him to pass. His dark olive skin and pale greenish yellow eyes stick out like a sore thumb. But it was his ruggedly handsome face and near seven-foot height garners everyone's attention. Humans always lusted after his kind, like moths to a flame. He paid them no mind. His attention was laid solely on the hunt.

His nose twitches as his long, muscular legs stride across the road. The faint scent of salty air and sulfur lead him along. He walks up the steps and strolls past the bellhop. The young boy freezes for a moment, fascinated by Bounty's sheer presence. He clears his throat; the bellhop lowers his head and bows, quickly opening the door for him to hide his embarrassment.

The lobby was crowded with tourists and locals alike. Bounty inner ears twitched as he listened closely, opening his ear beyond the human norm. He took in everyone's sound and voice. Five conversations caught his attention. Five different distinct languages: French, Polish, Swahili, English, and Portuguese. He speaks them fluently. But none of them seemed like very good leads. The hair on the back of his neck rose, and his beast pushed again. His teeth lengthened, then snapped back into shape.

Calm your shit pup, the scents in the air again. He bristles from the pungent smell of dark fae, beast, and demon alike. *Jackpot!* He ambles past the grinning concierge down the hallway in the far left of the lobby without being spotted. Not that it mattered to him if anyone sees. It's not like they could stop him. Yet, it intrigued him how much he could get away with it.

The putrid smell of rotted fish and mulberries was enough to make a powerful demon like him sick to his stomach. He slows his pace. His hell-hound pushes to the surface once again, causing him to shift partially. Bounty pinches the bridge of his nose, resenting his heightened smell.

"What the fuck has you so riled up, beast?"

He pulls back, refusing to let his beasts take control. Bounty is determined to stay in the lead. Most demons can't master their inner beings. But he takes pride in his mastery, refusing to let his split nature dominate him—especially not his wolf side. Bounty lives on his own terms. Never again will he allow another to control his destiny. He took responsibility for his own actions, unlike some of his kind.

Aurone, Bounty's grandfather, the chief instigator of Bounty's every woe—if it wasn't for that bastard, who knows how different life might have been. He blames that arrogant son of a succubus for everything shitty he and his siblings experienced. Well, not just him... his trollop of a mother, too. To spite her father, the mighty Cerberus, the great Hound of Hell, she committed the greatest offense: bedding and spawning three half-blood pups with a low-ranked beta lycan. Tainting the bloodline. Condemning her offspring to centuries' worth of misplaced wrath and contempt. Aurone was a master of manipulation, capable of poisoning and controlling the minds of anyone against him. But he'd failed to keep Bounty and his siblings under his control for long. Where Aurone fell short with them, he succeeded in winning back his daughter. Following his deadbeat father's adulterous betrayal, her progenies became curses of a memory she rather be left forgotten.

Ria, his mother, the Keeper Demon of the Darkness of Hell, was even more of a pain in the ass than her old man. She assigned him the shitty cases no other demon hunter wanted to take. Ria's wrath was mostly directed towards Ishtan; because he resembled his lycan father the most out of the triplets. But a Cerberus and lycan union was doomed from the start.

"Unacceptable, extremely unacceptable! You insolent cunt," Aurone roared. Spittle hung from his muzzle. "They're a blight on the bloodline — abominations! I will not allow them a place in my domain."

"But father, I have nowhere else to go. He left me with nothing." Ria cried, throwing herself upon her father's paws.

Bounty had been a little sniveling half-demon when his mother left the human realm. He spent his days lurking through the caves and corners of Hell, scavenging the fire pits for a hiding place, far from the brooding eyes of Aurone. It was his resilience and independence that allowed him to survive.

As a teen, his tenacity and perseverance were well known throughout the lower levels, allowing him to cross paths with some of Aurone's demon warriors, those who eventually trained and molded him into the ultimate killing beast. But Bounty wasn't fit for true battle; he fought dirty with animal-like savagery. Not with the refinement of a warrior, plus that title class was only for the pure-blooded demon kind.

So Aurone simply hid him, Keanu, and Stacia into the hunter's lower ranks,

where both he and Bounty's mother Ria would see less of them. Ergo, Ish-
tan, and his siblings were forced to become hunters. Hunting down the rogue
demons and fae of the human realms and in-between—Beings who threaten
the balance, the peace treaty between Heaven and Hell. And both sides were
itching to kick off the Great War. Sadly, it was mainly the demon kind that
constituted the greatest threat to this agreement. Bounty had rarely encoun-
tered an angel or light bringer breaking the treaty.

In time, Bounty poured all his anger into his work, hunting down the most
sinister, gluttonous, psychotic prey, hurling them back through Hell's gate, to
the pits where they suffered a punishment worse than what awaits the humans
Gabriel sent down. But despite his accolades, or his sibling's accolades, their
existence was frowned upon. There was no hope of ever being accepted by Ria
or Aurone.

Bounty's thoughts drift back to the present. He shakes his head to clear his mind. This isn't like him. He refocuses his energy and empties his thoughts. He stands before a slightly open door; that fishy sweet smell is stronger now. Bounty's inner beast lets out a low growl, rumbling in his barrel of a chest. He puts his large hands on the door and pushes it open slowly.

He walks in and shuts the door behind him, making hardly any sound. Stealthy, walking down the steps, quietly approaching the sauna that swirls with steaming vapors. Bounty doesn't feel the heat; this place is as cool as an Eskimos abode compared to Hell. His pulse quickens, adrenaline coursing through him, pumping him for battle. But a strange throbbing echoes beneath it. The scent leads him directly to the demon sitting towards the back of the room.

It's a Mer-Demon. A male mermaid
. They used to be rare and hardly ever stepped out of the hot caves of the ocean. This, however, is the third in the past few weeks.

These fuckers are up to no good. The demon is in the middle of a feeding. Its scaled body is arched, the skin of its back stretched over its spine. It snarls, exposing blood-stained teeth. The demon is crouched over the body of a dark-skinned woman. In the room's corner are the remnants of a body.

The demon has chewed off the women's eyes, nose, and lips. White bones protrude from her mangled corpse. He feels nothing for the dead women. No apathy, no scruples. The demon growls in frustration, pissed his meal was interrupted. He crawls off the body of the untouched woman, and Bounty's eyes dim in surprise.

He clearly sees the naked black woman's body through the steamy mist. Her heavy breasts are full and supple; her dark areolas are like large saucers stretched over the sweetest chocolate skin. His beast whines, pacing back and forth within the confines of his inner mind.

His eye roams upward. Her heart-shaped face and chubby cheeks are balanced out by her full pink lips. Her eyes are dark and lifeless. Conscious, but bewitched by the Mer-Demon. She is frozen in time; her glazed eyes stare sightlessly into space. Her perfectly shaped lips part as she pants one labored breath after another.

Bounty's eyes roll down to what the woman is doing with her hands—her bikini bottoms are pulled to the side, her fingers rub vigorously on the pink nub between her puffy fat lips. Her other hand spreads them wide. She moans, jerks, lost in the hypnotic trance. Bounty's gaze goes to those breasts again, the beads of sweat glistening off them like a sugary glaze.

"Mine..." Bounty rumbles.

The Mer-Demon snarls at him, but Bounty lashes with unnatural speed and the demon is hurled against the side of the sauna. The wall cracks, denting the wood. The demon drops on all fours. It draws forth its powers, intensifying the swirling steam. Bounty moves fast. Shielding the woman on the floor with his large body, his beast comes forth, enlarging his form. His muscles bulge and pop, his nails become razor-sharp claws.

Bounty sneers, massive, deadly wolf-like fangs shine and glint off the blue lights. His beast growls possessively. The Mer-Demon must not know who Bounty is. Perhaps he has only heard of him, or he would have sought to escape instead of trying to do battle with the Bounty hunter of Hell.

The Mer-Demon lunges again. His fists connect with Bounty's shoulder. His fists crack and the demon's bones splinter. Its arms flail as it screams, a screeching whine like a mourning banshee. Bounty snatches the Mer-Demon's neck and smashes him against the polished wall of the sauna. The demon fights back again. The woman on the floor whimpers. Bounty can smell the venom of the Mer-Demon coursing through her veins.

"Let me go, you bastard!" the Mer-Demon hisses.

"You dare harm her!"

Bounty tightens his grip, choking the life force from the demon's neck. Bounty's knuckles whiten as he clamps down harder. Bones crack, veins burst, the demon's neck leaks green fluid. Its eyes pop from their sockets, and its black serpentine tongue falls limp to the side.

"I banish you now, Mer-Demon," with the whisper of an incantation.

"I banish your soul with the death of your flesh. Your iniquity is paid in full with your life here in this realm!"

The demon in his grasp shudders, jerks, and goes limp. Bounty flings the body to the side and kicks it into the rear of the sauna.

Fuck, just what I didn't need. The Berlin police will be called. Things are bound to get messy now.

He swivels on his feet, turning to the woman who seems to be waking out of her trance. Her big brown eyes widen. She bites her lip; dual looks, confliction and passion fill her face. But the smell of her sweet-scented pheromones still lingers in the air, revealing her true desires. Her hands pet at her breasts and vagina.

Bounty licks his lips, drinking the image in. Tiana springs forth with inhuman agility and hurls herself on Bounty, the incubus' aphrodisiac trance numbing her inhibitions.

He yelps in surprise and falls backward in a swirl of shock and other emotions like fascination, rising curiosity, and a sprinkling of rage.

"Get off me!" Bounty grumbles. But his inner beast howls–mate... mate.

"You know you want me," Tiana purrs, descending on him. She rips his shirt open and gasps at the sight of his thick, muscled chest. His body is enormous, rippled with corded muscles. His abs are deeply etched and pulled taut.

Bounty squints at her face and shakes his head. "You are not yourself, woman. You have been cursed."

"Oh, it's been too long. I know exactly what I want. Let me show you just how much I want this."

"No, wait—" Bounty protests.

Tiana kisses the words out of his mouth. She runs her vagina over his crotch, the coarse fabric of his jeans grating on the lips of her vagina, making her press harder into his thick outline. Tiana sucks his tongue into her mouth, her eyes shut tight. Her breaths fill Bounty's nose. She smells like mulberries and spiced cider.

She smells like home.

He tries to stop her, contemplating tossing her like a rag doll across the room.

That would probably kill her.

Bounty's beast had already laid claim on her. Humans shouldn't be able to withstand or retain their sanity after being entranced by a mer-man, at least to his knowledge. No one had ever exhibited symptoms like this. She was so ravenous, but deep down, it pleased him.

He keeps trying to resist her, to push her away, telling her she isn't in her right mind, but her strength is unnatural. He looks her over through his beast eyes and still finds no trace of fae or demon lineage.

Tiana's shaky hands find the zipper of his fly. She coos. His nether regions are hot against her hands. She slips her fingers into his boxers, and she grips his thick cock. Her small hands can barely close around it as she pulls it out. Her jaw drops open at the sight of his huge honey-colored penis and she caresses it lovingly. Tiana pulls the fly all the way down. She smiles at his balls; they're huge, round, and hairless. She's never seen a bigger ball sack in her life.

Bounty tries to get up. Tiana strong-armed him with such force that the wind rushes from his chest. She puts her palm flat on his abs and pushes him back into the steam. Bounty tries to grab her hands and Tiana resists him, her eyes glowing slightly as she stares him down.

"Mine," she breathed.

Her sweet, heady smell fills Bounty's senses like a drug; he lets himself observe her. She positions Bounty's cock towards her mouth, studying it, trying to determine the best angle of attack. He smirks, knowing that no human woman had ever handled his massive cock.

Tiana starts off by kissing it, from the balls to the bulbous mushroom head, before swirling it slowly into her mouth. It only gets about an inch into her mouth, and no more. He's too huge and thick. Bounty throws his head back, his jaw muscles clenching tightly–

Her mouth feels better than any cunt I've ever fucked.

She takes her mouth off. "It's so thick." She swallows. "You taste so good." She relaxes her throat and tries again. This time, Bounty's cock goes all the way to her throat. She chokes, her eyes pop open wide. Bounty looks at her with astonishment, rising to his elbows for a better view.

Tiana's eyes bulge and redden, tears running down her smooth caramel face. She begins to move her head slowly. Her mouth is stretched to its limits. Saliva dribbles down her chin and the sides of his juicy, thick cock. Up and down. She does it till Bounty starts to move his hips, too.

Tiana stops. She removes the penis from her mouth and glances at him. "What are you doing?"

He growls, "What are you doing?"

"Who says you can enjoy this?"

Bounty cocks his head to the side, befuddled by the question. Before he can say another word, his balls are in her hands. She applies just the right amount of pressure, shuffling them around in the sac. Her head goes down slowly and Tiana takes the balls in her mouth, the one and then the other. Bounty closes his eyes and leans back. "Aaah," he coos, his inner alpha beast quivering like a frightened lamb.

She stops abruptly and slaps the erect cock. The dick pendulums around before pointing up again. Tiana tugs on his jeans, forcefully pulling them down while turning him over. He passively resists, but this tiny human continues to overpower him.

"Woman, I do not wish to take advantage of you. Let us stop for now until you are in control of your senses."

Bounty lies on his belly now, his inner beast howling in alarm. Tiana grunts at his remark before kissing his waist, then his muscled butt cheeks. Bounty's body quivers. She slaps his bottom and a red handprint blossoms forth. "Be still!"

She pulls the crack of his ass apart and stares at the tight crevice between his cheeks.

Taste him, urged a voice deep within her. Tiana feels her core throb as her tongue slides across his forbidden place.

Show him your pussy's power, says the voice. Tiana hisses, her mind and body overpowered by the potent aphrodisiac.

Bounty swings his arm back in alarm. But she moves quicker, folding it tightly against his back. Tiana straddles him into submission while dragging her womanhood over his lower thighs, all the way to his upper back. She closes her eyes and moans, pleased with herself for marking him with her scent.

"What are you doing?" Bounty moans

"Silence," she barks back.

Tiana spreads his ass again and lowers her face into it. Flicking her tongue over his asshole, she then plunges it deep inside. Bounty tenses. Unsure of how to react or feel. This is something he's never experienced. Her soft tongue on his forbidden hole triggers his inner beast. Waves of intense pleasure shot up his spine, then traveled around his lower pelvis area, making his balls feel heavy and tight.

He grunts in defiance, his ego crumbling before his very eyes. His voice spills out, sounding like a young lass losing her purity on prom night. His inner mind calls forth the strength of his Hell Hound. But the beast has been lulled into a submissive calm. His claw digs into the concrete floor as his cock weeps pre-cum. The moment lasts a few seconds—but Bounty will remember this for years to come.

He looks around the floor of the sauna, momentarily lost in his daze. He feels Tiana's presence behind him, sees the withering body of the

Mer-Demon, the faceless body of the woman to his right. Then his eyes narrow back to her. Bounty smashes the floor with his fist. "Stop!"

He jumps to his feet, quickly yanking up his jeans. He glowers at her as he pulls up his fly, stopped by his engorged and veiny cock.

She's actually fucking smirking! Frowning at the uncertainty of his emotions, part of him feels emasculated; the other wants to bend her over and place his seed deep within her womb. He slips his rod into its place and rolls the zipper all the way up.

Tiana's hand falls to her vagina again. That lustful leer still clouds her face, her eyes faintly aglow as Bounty studies her closely...

Dammit, there must be a way to stop this.

He wrings his hands hesitantly before slapping Tiana across the face, with just enough bite to knock her down without breaking her jaw. Tiana lets out a small yell of pain and falls to her knees. She covers her temples with her palms, as if suffering a blinding headache. She opens her eyes and gazes around. She sees the bodies and Bounty and falls on her butt.

"Who are you?" she stammers. "What happened to me?"

"To you?" Bounty shakes his head.

He continues gazing at her, secretly amazed by the transformation that comes upon her after she recovers from her bewitched state. He steps to her and stretches out his hand.

Bounty grumbles, "Come with me."

Tiana gets up quickly, her reflexes on high alert. "Mister, I don't know who you are, or what you are. I thank you for helping me, but we need to call the police?"

"And what will you tell them?" Bounty growled. He gestures at the corpse of the Mer-Demon. "Will you tell them a demon attacked you?"

"A what?"

Tiana looks at the gruesome scene before her, her steps faltering. His eyes roam over her figure. She blanches, noticing her nakedness. She quickly puts on the kimono, tying the sash before grabbing her bag. "I need to go. Get out of my way!"

"You have seen. What you can't unsee."

She frowns. "What are you talking about?"

"This, here." Bounty twirls around. "You've witnessed our kind; you know too much." He huffs, buttoning his shirt with impatience as if she should already be aware.

Her mouth moves, but words cannot come out, so Bounty continues. "You might be in danger. I can keep you safe."

"I'm not going anywhere with you. Who the Hell do you think you are?"

"I am—" Bounty stops.

He realizes she doesn't seem ready to accept the truth. He shakes his head and steps aside; Tiana walks past him, her fragrance seducing his senses. He struggles to stop himself from grabbing her hand.

I could do that, he thinks. *Take her here, on this floor, unravel her and fill her with my essence, own her completely.*

"You're the killer," Tiana whispers while stepping into the hallway. "Not me. And you better remember that little fact when the police ask!"

"And just who are you?" he asks, stepping closer to her, crowding into her space.

"Ti... Tiana McGuire," she whispers, sidestepping his domineering stance.

Bounty says nothing. He only stands there, staring at her. Fear lingers in her eyes. She stumbles away from him and runs up the stairs, refusing to look back.

3

Chapter Three

Tiana enters her apartment panting, adrenaline-pumping through her veins. Her back is to the door, hoping that was enough to secure it firmly. Her bag drops aimlessly to the floor...

She shakes her head frantically. "This can't be real. I must be dreaming!"

She bolts across the living room, snatching the curtains back, fearfully glancing down to the street below. The street is empty. Nothing seems out of place. Berlin is business as usual. A dusky mist rises against the lowering sun. She pulls the drapes slightly, fearing that he may have followed to her room. The movement of a black Jeep catches her attention. It pulls to the curb and idles. No one gets out. Tiana's eyes narrow as paranoia sets in. For a minute, Tiana thinks it might be the guy from the sauna, sitting there, waiting for her to leave so he can kill her for what she's seen.

Tiana hurries to the nightstand, pulls out her cell and dials the hotel lobby privately. A female's voice squeaks in her ear.

"Verlin Honors Hotel," says the voice in German. "How may I help jou?"

"There's a dead body in the sauna." Tiana quickly hangs up and tosses her cell on the floor, afraid to even touch it, as if they'll call back.

****

A clanging bell startles Tiana awake. She sits up in bed and gazes at the wall. Unease crawls up her spine. *When did I fall asleep?* Tiana rubs the sleep from her eyes. She sits up and surveys the room. The feeling of being watched has subsided. There's nothing here, though the painting across from her bed freaks her out. It's a portrait of a man with a three-headed dog on a leash. *Hercules and Cerberus,* she recalls from her studies of ancient Greek artworks.

She clutches herself. The room felt cooler since it was nighttime. The sound of church bells chime from a church nearby. She checks the bed-side clock and lies back down, before pulling the cover snuggly under her chin.

"Thank you, God, for saving me..." she whispers a quiet prayer as she lays back and closes her eyes, wishing herself to sleep.

Her mind wandered to earlier that night when Tiana watched from her bedroom window as the police stormed inside and wheeled out a body on a stretcher... She shook her head, certain that there had been three bodies, two of them women. She couldn't recall much, except the fear of dying.

From her window, Tiana watched as the police questioned the lady from the lobby. She looked hysterical. Tiana looked away, guilt invading her thoughts.

She breathes out slowly, her nerves getting the best of her.

What if they find me? What if he finds me? Am I an accessory to murder? Oh my god, I'm going to jail if I get caught! No, it's alright; it's just one of those weird and terrible things that happen to good people. I'll be alright. Besides, it's not like in the movies. Technology is advanced, but it should be pretty hard to find me.... Right? But wait!

She bolts upright.

In the movie Taken, the father found the perps by tracking them on their phone. Aren't Hollywood guys always doing these things in movies because they can actually be done in real life?

She flips over and buries her head into the pillow, screaming every imaginable curse she could utter.

The next morning, Tao comes into her suite wearing a black sweat-shirt and pants. Perspiration darkens the front of his shirt. His thickly corded muscles show through. He grips his laptop firmly to his side.

"Boss, I have good news, but we may have an issue."

Tiana freezes as she exits the bathroom, realizing that she'd been found out despite her countless prayers.

"The hotel may be on lockdown after some drama that went on last night. Do you want to look at some of the venue changes? I also have your missing bag."

Tiana blinks slowly, her shoulders loosening.

"Are you alright?" Tao asks.

She bobs her head slowly, extracting the bag from his outstretched hand.

"When I woke up from my nap, I couldn't find you. And when I checked the pool, you were gone."

"I had to leave."

Tao frowns. "Did something happen?"

She tenderly walks to the sitting area, her lady parts unusually sore. She bends down, grabbing a handful of chocolate cream candies from the bowl near the couch before plopping down. Her long hair is a mess of black and brown coils. She gets some chocolate on her red sweater but ignores the blotch.

"I'm alright," she says.

Tao says, "You look spazzed."

More than you would ever know.

Tiana notices that Tao's skin is once again taking on the pale, sickly hue. "The question should be, are you okay, Tao?"

He shrugs, and his eyes blink suspiciously. "I'm okay, but something with you is definitely off."

Tiana stops scooping chocolate cream and thinks about Tao's re-mark for a moment. One of her greatest flaws is that she wears her emo-tions on her sleeve. Last night her dreams were filled with gruesome images. She couldn't tell if they were figments of her trauma or genuine memories.

There were shadows lurking, shifting shapes, incoherent faces, whispering voices, blood, and many naughty things. If she took the time, she could probably decipher the dreams' meaning; it was her body's way of coping with the traumatic events.

Trauma, she muses. But to Tao, she says, "I'm fine. What have you got for me?"

She puts her chocolate bowl away and joins her assistant. Together, they plan for the conference for the following day.

4

Chapter Four

The main hall is packed to the brim. It seems all the expecting and postpartum women of Berlin are in attendance. The event is slated for two hours, the main topic being maternal health and Postpartum Psychosis. It follows the usual routine of all the previous conferences, with authorities in various fields publicly discussing the breakthroughs in treatment and disparities women still face.

Tiana looks back over at Tao. He's standing to the far left of the stage with the rest of the assistants and organizers, silently cheering her on. She's set to present next, her topic being: **Miscarriage and Postpartum Effects.** The speaker before her steps on stage to present her research. Tiana shakes her head at key points she found intriguing and well delivered. The older woman finishes her speech, and the host applauds her off. The hostess this time looks about fifty-year-old, plump in the middle; her suit jacket neatly cropped and fluffed out. Her lush white hair is tucked into a neat school teacher bun, and her glasses hang from the tip of her nose.

Tiana giggles. *All she needs is a red hat–Good day, Mrs. Claus.*

The host rises as she announces that it's time for Tiana to step out. "Ladies and gentlemen, I want to welcome to the stage one of the foremost researchers about women's welfare from the United States: Dr. Tiana McGuire, of Chicago University."

The conference hall roars with applause. Some of the women stand and wave at Tiana. She glances at Tao as she gets to the podium. Her assistant nods. *You got this.*

Tiana hopes the audience doesn't notice the dark shadows under her eyes that her makeup failed to hide. She shyly smiles at the audience, her heart racing with every person she makes eye contact with. She draws in a deep breath, hoping to compose herself.

Her nerves feel frayed, and her back and body ache with a dull pain. Even her vagina was tender when she woke up last night. She thought nothing of it. Maybe her fingernail scratched her labia during the lewd dream she had last night. *There was a man... I was riding him hard. His sharp claws dug into my hips as his hot semen shot deep into my womb...* It was a short, bittersweet dream, but its intensity still affects her.

She silently stacks her papers on the podium, smiling to herself. Even now, she can feel moisture in her panties.

Get yourself together, girl, and present your topic!

"Hello, Berliners—," she begins, "and all the other women in attendance today—"

Tiana scans the faces as she talks, her voice inflecting into the microphone and resonating from the speakers hung up in the ceiling. There are so many faces, mostly women, of different shapes and shades of color, all listening with rapt attention as Tiana speaks.

There are a few men in the audience. Some are university staff, or members of the studies' supporting fields. Her eyes move over the audience to the rear, where most of the men are.

Then she notices something strange.

At first, Tiana thinks it has to be the light from the stage, causing her eyes to play tricks. Or maybe it's the dim lighting in the back. Sitting between two men is the figure of someone.... *something* dressed in a grey tweed jacket, like the appearance of most of the men in the hall. But his head is shaped oddly, like a pumpkin. Tiana squints, but continues to speak. She tried to avert her gaze away from him, but she can't look away.

The man sits forward, giving her a clearer view. His oddly shaped head contains two sinister green eyes. A mocking grin splashes across his face, exposing horrid fangs. One of the green eyes winks at Tiana. The mouth doesn't move, but Tiana hears a cackling croak.

Well, blow me hard. You can see me, can't you?

Tiana breaks her speech to ask, "What—?"

The word leaves her lips before she realizes the voice had been in her head. Mocking laughter follows: *Ha, ha, ha.*

"—I er, um, so, as I was saying." She struggles to continue her speech about data that debunks the long-held belief about stillbirths and weight gain. "Our research shows that—"

Shut up, bitch, no one cares about this shit. Just drop down on all fours, will ya? Like the good slut you are! Ha-ha, ha-ha!

Tiana gasps. She smiles at the crowd, tearing her eyes from his taunting gaze. She inhales and exhales, trying to get control of her breathing.

You can do this. It's all in your head. Come on, it's the trauma. That thing isn't real, can't you see? How come no one else sees it or hears the voice?

She looks away from him and directs her gaze to the left. An Asian woman is walking up the side of the aisle wearing a white business suit. She turns to look straight at Tiana with greenish glowing eyes, blood-red lips, and—*Oh God!*

Where the woman's nose should be, there's a dog-like snout with several reddish-brown tendrils flailing out. The more she stares at them, the more they writhe. The woman looks away and continues up the side of the hall till she enters a row, then asks a woman carrying a baby to scoot over, and she sits. When the woman looks up again, the tendrils disappear out of sight.

Tiana clears her throat and continues her lecture. Tao is grimacing where he stands in the corner of the stage, hands wet with nervous sweat. One of the organizers called Hans sidles to him and asked, "Geht es ihr gut?" *Is she alright?* Tao only needs to look at the almost pink face of the man beside him to see everyone's anxiety mirrored there.

Tao nods. "Yeah, she'll be alright." He looks concernedly at Tiana, whose stand just ten feet away. Her hands are gripping the podium as if it were the only thing that could save her life.

She turns her head and coughs off-mic, then quickly adjusts the beret tilted to the side on her curly fro. Tao wrings his hands, trying to believe what he just said to Hans.

Tiana barely finishes her presentation. Sweat dampens her furrowed brows. Surprisingly, the audience stands up and claps; the hall is filled with the roar of many hands coming together to thank a strong woman for her efforts on their behalf.

She smiles weakly, waves at the women and promises to make her new book, **Disparities and The Wounded Mother**, available in stores around the university and Berlin soon.

As she walks backstage, she glances towards the back row seats. The man in the tweed jacket is still there, but his face is now that of a very handsome man. He grins; flashing a perfect row of teeth, then blows Tiana a kiss.

When Tiana reaches Tao, she crumbles against her assistant. She looks around the corner of the stage as the woman who is hosting the program goes on stage to wrap things up. Tiana sees the Asian woman wearing a white business suit. She joins the audience in clapping. Her creature-like appearance is also gone, replaced by the short snub of a nose.

"Tiana?"

She turns sharply and looks in the face of Tao and Hans. The German asks in English, "What happened out there?" But Tiana shrugs it off, quickly composing herself while handing Tao the book in her hand. She glances around the side of the stage and scans the audience again for anything unusual. She thankfully sees nothing. Tao and Hans look about as well; both men are even more confused now than before.

"What are you looking for, Tiana?" Tao asks.

"There was someone—"

But how does she even begin to explain what she'd seen? Who would believe her? Hell, she doesn't even trust her own eyes and memory anymore. Somewhere in the dimly lit place in her mind, she knows the truth, but it all feels so unreal.

Can this really be happening?

"Did you see someone you know?" Hans asks, while wrinkling his nose.

"No. I was mistaken. But it's okay now."

Tao gives Tiana a curious look, but says nothing; Tiana smiles, knowing what her assistant is thinking about. The situation diffuses, and Tao brightens again.

The conference hall is filled with the resounding chatter of women's voices gossiping, talking and encouraging one another. They swarm around Tiana, requesting her email address, autograph, and other maternal advice. Soon, a dozen women encircle her, some begging that she visit them in their homes or attend privately hosted brunches. Tao politely declines for her, stating that they will head back to the States within the next flight.

Tiana steps out of the hall, leaving Tao to his plight. It's late summer, but it's starting to look like fall outside. The blooming flowers hang drearily from the trees in the street.

This is such a picture-perfect sight.

Tiana takes several photographs with the women in attendance. After several minutes, she looks for Tao but can't find him. Tiana stands by the street curb, declining invitation after invitation for dinner from the group of young single mothers surrounding her.

Tao walks out of the conference hall, hand in hand with a tall, beautiful Asian woman wearing a fashionable pink gown.

Tao smiles brightly. "Guess who I bumped into?"

Tiana's smile falters in surprise before she raises her hands up to wave. "Inyoku..." she calls out.

"Tao, you didn't tell me Inyoku was coming to Berlin," Tiana scolds her assistant.

"Oh, that is absolutely my fault," says Inyoku, bowing in greeting.

Tao's girlfriend continues to explain. "It was an emergency, actually. The agency sent me here on brief notice to replace another model for a shoot. I wanted to surprise him." Inyoku praises Tiana, confessing that she loved Tiana's presentation, and insisting they all have dinner tonight.

Tiana reluctantly agrees. Inyoku bends again before grabbing Tao's hand and leading him off. The feeling of unease pebbles her arms with goosebumps. Her eyes focus on the couple walking across the street. She watches as they pick a table and have a seat. Tao still looks haggard, still not quite his usual self...

Inyoku's hand crosses the table, her fingers intertwined with his. Something flickers behind Inyoku, causing Tiana to rub her eyes. She thinks it must be an optical illusion created by the glass, the mild sun's glare, and the traffic passing by. Tiana frowns and tries to look harder, but Inyoku turns and glances at her across the street. She waves. Tao looks up and waves, as well.

"Doctor Tiana?"

She turns and faces Hans, the one from the conference. "Oh, Mr. Hans?"

He smiles. "A group of women will like to demonstrate their appreciation for her work. They are waiting in the hall."

Tiana takes one last worried look at Tao and Inyoku across the street before turning to go back in.

****

On the ride back to the hotel, Tiana gives a reassuring nod in reply to Tao's question. "It wasn't him, I promise you."

She pats his leg to calm his nerves. Tao's eye narrows in suspicion, still not sure if Tiana's ex-boyfriend is to blame for her skittish behavior.

Raj Budden was a rich Arabian man that didn't understand the word *No*. Ever since their break- up a few months ago, he kept adamantly trying to win her back. Thankfully, Tiana didn't want him. Tao had grown tired of the phony submissive act she flaunted around him.

Tiana is a spitfire, a female dragon among men, but she would turn into a docile cat with him. Tao couldn't stand it. It went against her true nature. The dude sent gifts every weekend, popping up on her without an invitation. He'd even called on the flight here, upset she hadn't told him about the trip.

"Raj, stop talking to me like we are together," Tiana blurted out.

"You act like I don't deserve a second chance, Ti."

"Because you fucking don't."

"Well, I disagree," said Raj.

"And the answer is NO. Go be with the slut you cheated on me with." Tiana *simply dropped the call and switched off her mobile phone. Looking at Tao sitting beside her, she added, "Tell me why I ever dated that guy."*

Tao chuckled. Raj Budden was nothing more than a spoiled rich kid with a man-sized ego.

That was days ago. So seeing Tiana this worked up had him on edge.

"We're still on for dinner with Inyoku tonight?" she asks.

"Of course," replies Tao, giving her hand a tight squeeze.

Tiana gives him a side glance. The flesh over his hands is so pale that his veins show through. She sighs, deciding to keep her concerns to herself.

5

Chapter Five

Detective Jürgen is confused. He looks at the dents in the wall, then back to the floor, the deep gashes in the cracked concrete. The place where the body of the woman had lain is marked with placement placards. Nothing adding up. He pulled out a notepad, rereading the autopsy results.

The female's face and body had been chewed off by an animal.

He reads it over and over, but each time it makes less sense. There has to be something else. Jürgen crouches lower to the floor, looking over the evidence sample found near the body. He nods to the two cops that responded to the emergency call from the hotel desk.

"Die Haut sehen?" *See that skin?"*

One cop has a hairy dark blotched birthmark under his left eye. He nods and says, "It looks like the skin of an onion that's gone bad."

Jürgen agrees with this assessment. He reads another line of the autopsy report: *And it's been almost a day, yet, no smell. The corpses are not rotting.*

Jürgen goes down to the desk and meets the concierge. He asks to see the manager, but the concierge tells him that the manager is not available. Jürgen raps his knuckles on the desk and smiles. "Pass the message: avoiding me stops nothing from happening.

"I need access to tapes, register, and to ask your guests questions as soon as possible," the Detective orders. "If the people who were here when it happened leave before I question them, I will have you arrested for the impediment of my case."

The concierge nods. He makes a call on the spot, right there in the lobby. He claps his phone in his hand, bows, and asks Jürgen to follow him. They walk up the steps and out of sight.

Ten minutes later, Jürgen emerges from a small security office, where a fat guard monitors the cameras. The Detective tells the concierge he wants all hotel guests that checked in the day before the incident to be delayed for questioning. Jürgen also tells him to provide the list of all who visited the sauna that day. The concierge gave him a serious look and said, "I'm sorry, but our guests just go down there whenever they want to."

"There are no cameras in the sauna, I get it," Jürgen says. "But how can you not have cameras in the hallway that leads to the sauna?"

"Perhaps, you can take up that query with the management, Detective."

Jürgen nods. He supposed he should. He says, "I'd like to see the registers for the names of those who checked in the day before and at the time of the crime."

The concierge agrees to show him.

Later that night, Tiana walks to an Italian restaurant not too far from the Berlin wall; Inyoku had raved that this chef was Michelin gold star rated. Throughout the day, the couple was nauseatingly lovey-dovey. Inyoku can never seem to keep her hands to herself. Tiana just hopes the food is good, because being with them left a bitter taste in her mouth.

Berlin is a beautiful city at night. The hanging lamps burn with yellow electric fire, cobblestone streets giving off a medieval vibe. City folks walk past, all minding their business.

"No litter, no gangs, you would think this place had no crime," she observes as she walks with Tao. "This place is really different from Chicago."

He doesn't answer immediately; submerged in his own thoughts.

"Is there something wrong?"

"I don't know, maybe I caught a bug," he says, worry lacing his voice.

"You have seemed a little off; I'm sure you'll be feeling much better after dinner."

Somehow, even Tiana doesn't believe her words. She pulls the collar of her jacket up to shield her neck from the evening breeze.

Inyoku sees them approaching and waves excitedly from the front of the restaurant called *Rizzo Steaks* on the street called Wiesbadener. Tao tries to pronounce the name without success.

She's wearing a long grey coat with big black buttons running down the length of the front. Her blonde hair is held inside a black beaded turban. Her skin looks flawless; she looks even prettier than the last time, younger even. Tiana shrugs it off, thinking that the lighting or her dress must be responsible.

She kisses Tao on the lips, embraces him passionately then offers Tiana a loose embrace. Tiana detects a hint of Inyoku's perfume—a thick, almost oriental fragrance laced with some spicy flavor. Beneath that scent is another moldy undercurrent. As Inyoku lets go of her, Tiana feels a weird jolt, like an electric shock. But the moment passes swiftly.

While they wait for their food to come, Inyoku talks nonstop about her family's company. A dairy manufacturer in Boston, Chicago and Japan. Then she mentioned something about pursuing a merger here in Berlin.

"Berlin?" Tiana asks. "Why would they want to do that?"

She shrugs. "Dairy is cheaper in Europe. Factories will probably move here. The cost will be cut across board, production and all."

"And jobs will be lost back home?" .

Inyoku looks at Tiana oddly, smiles, then adds, "It's a dog-eat-dog world, Tiana. Whether it is my modeling agency or the family's business, I just do what I'm told."

When the server finally returned with their food. The table fell into an awkward silence.

Tiana grinned hard, forcibly showing her teeth, despite inwardly cringing through the meal. Tao sat slouched in his chair, sitting beside Inyoku. He stared at his Caesar salad; his Adam's apple bobs up and down like he's about to barf. Tiana starts to ask Tao if he's alright again, when Inyoku beats her to it.

Inyoku quickly puts her arm around Tao and kisses his lips. Only at that moment, Inyoku's lips look more like a muzzle: she even has dark red whiskers sticking out of her face. She whispers rapidly in some language. It's not English or Japanese, nor is it any language Tiana understands.

"Inyoku?"

The females' head turns slowly, her face resembling that of a fox.

"Yes, Tiana?"

Tiana sucks in air sharply. She gasps. "Um, er—"

"Tiana?"

She looks at Tao, who is also staring at her, frowning.

"Are you feeling alright?" Tao asks.

Tiana looks from her assistant's face to his fiancée's, quickly trying to determine the best escape route. "Can you? Tao, can you—?" She flounders, stammering over her words. Her eyes bouncing from one face to the other. The couple stares at Tiana with anxious eyes.

Inyoku remains in her monstrous form; Tao is unable to see it. Tiana worriedly looks around the restaurant.

I can't be the only one seeing this! No, I can't!

She starts to hyperventilate. *I can get through this. Just don't look her way.* She tries to keep her head down and look past her, but her curiosity keeps forcing her to look Inyoku's way. After what seems like an eternity, the evening finally winds down.

There's a fucking monster at my table. God help Tao, and I get through this safely.

Tiana silently prays. The server saunters over and smiles, with a face that looks like a bear mixed with a crocodile. Tiana clutches her chair, forcing herself to look down at her plate.

"Is everything alright here? Do you like the food?" she asks again with a heavy German accent.

Tiana almost flips her plate of food in the air. She pushes her chair back, heaving and gasping for air. Tao jumps up instantly, coming to her aid.

"Tiana!"

She squeezes her eyes shut, refusing to look anyone's way. Tao grabs her face and puts his forehead to hers.

"Tiana, tell me how to help you."

She takes a deep breath and opens her eyes, only making everything worse. Inyoku, the server, and across the restaurant, four tables away, sits a man with half his face missing, the other half festering with maggots...

My god, I have schizophrenia.

"I want to go back to the hotel—"

"Yeah. Come on, Inyoku, help Tiana get up," Tao says, hurriedly waiving down the server to clear their bill. Inyoku's arms feel like anvils as they wrap securely around Tiana's waist. Nine bushy red tails twist and slither over her arms.

Tiana bites the inside of her cheek, drawing blood in an effort not to scream. If I act like I can't see them, I can get away to safety. But she feels herself losing strength, as if Inyoku's hands are sucking the life out of her.

Tiana wants to push her away, but she is afraid Inyoku may attack. A rancid smell of death and decay fills Tiana's nose; Inyoku's body exudes heat like a furnace.

Tiana stumbles away from her into the street. Tao catches up with the two, hails a taxi, and they all jump in. Tiana begins to feel better the further away she moves away from Inyoku. When they arrive at the hotel, they swiftly run Tiana inside.

Tao deposits Tiana on the suite's sofa, then runs to get a spare blanket from the closet in the bedroom. Inyoku busies herself making coffee. She pours a cup and brings it over. Tiana takes the cup but refuses to take a single sip.

Inyoku's face is a mask of concern. "Will you be alright alone? I want to make sure Inyoku gets to her room safely. Tiana flashes him a weak smile, whispers goodbye, then watches them leave the room. Tao is only gone for what seems to be a few minutes. Rushing back to Tiana, fearing that he shouldn't have left her alone.

"Do you think it was the food?" Tao asks, while propping her feet into his lap to massage her calves. Tiana takes a deep breath and grabs his hand. "No! It is not the food!"

"Then what is it?"

She ignores his questions as she asks her own question back, "How are you feeling, Tao?"

"What?" he chuckles. "I feel great. Why?"

Tiana whispers, "No, you don't. You just don't know what's happening to you!"

"Now that's it.... that's it. I'm taking you to the hospital in the morning, ma'am."

"Can't you see, or are you pretending you don't see!?"

"See what?" Tao asks, his face taking on a reddish hue.

Just then, there is a rap on the door. Tiana jerks in the door's direction. Tao frowns at her reaction. He rises and cautiously goes to the door. Tao opens it, but there is no one there. He peers in the hallway, right and left. There's no one in sight.

"There's no one out here," Tao says in a puzzled tone.

"But you heard it, right?" Tao stands at the door, confused.

"What's your point?"

"Do you trust her?" Tiana asks again, anger in her tone.

"Who? Inyoku?"

Tiana nods.

Tao shrugs his shoulders wearily. "What does she have to do with anything?"

"You've changed... since you've met her. Can you feel that?"

"Now you're confusing me, Tiana," he says while sticking his hands into his pants pocket, avoiding her gaze. "Try to get some sleep. If you don't get better in the morning, it's the hospital for sure."

When Tao leaves, Tiana gets up and locks the door. She places the key under her pillow in the bedroom. Then shuts and locks the doors to the balcony, even locking the window, too. Before going back to the couch, she grabs the coffee Inyoku made and tosses the contents in the trash, even the cup, too.

Tiana inspects the kettle from top to bottom to ensure it hasn't been sabotaged or tampered with before brewing herself for a cup of tea.

There's no way my black ass is sleeping tonight.

Tiana contemplates calling room service. But she can't risk it. Anyone or anything could come up to her room.

"No hospital tomorrow, Tao," she whispers at the wall, "I have to get home."

✳✳
✳✳✳✳✳✳✳✳✳✳✳✳✳✳✳✳✳✳✳✳✳✳

Tiana spent the rest of her time packing. She is ready to leave right there and then. She doesn't stop moving until the sunlight filtered through her room. She wants to call Yoyo, but knows her friend wouldn't understand what was going on. Plus, Yolanda is so deep into the occult stuff that it is bound to get out of hand after long.

When Tao comes to the room early that morning, he still looks worse for wear. He uses the excuse of staying up all night editing the recorded audio and video from the conference the day before.

"Our flight isn't until later tonight," he says, "a little before dawn, but I don't feel right leaving you alone, especially after I heard about the incident."

Tiana asks, "Incident? What do you mean?"

"You know what I mean."

"You still think I'm worked up over Raj? He's not in Berlin. This isn't that." She throws a blanket over her feet. She keeps getting cold. She drinks what feels like her fifth cup of hot chocolate. "I'll be fine, Tao."

"You seem subdued. And you have this look like—" Tao doesn't finish his thought. He sighs.

I look like I'm going crazy. Tiana exhales, too. *Maybe I am going crazy.*

Tao reluctantly leaves again after she insists on being alone. The inner room is now lit by a single lamp near the couch. The mid-afternoon sun doesn't reach her from here. Tiana pulls out her Kindle, hoping a good book will keep her mind at bay. Her fingers quickly book up her favorite book, *White*, by SJ Sanders. She enjoys the way Sanders depicts her scenes, painting vivid imagery.

The room is cloaked in semi-darkness. One half-lit by sunlight, the other dark as night...

Tiana lost track of time. Not budging from her seat at all. *Have I even eaten today?*

She looks at the clock. 9:30pm. Their flight is scheduled for 4am. Fatigue begins to wear at her. She goes one more page, engrossed in the story, when movement catches her eye.

She turns her head to the door area, where she sees the silhouette.

It's so long, reaching all the way to the floor and across the carpet. She raises herself on an elbow, heart pounding in her chest. She follows the outline of the shadow to the balcony door, which she deliberately locked.

Fight or flight, bitch. Fight or fucking flight.

Someone is on the balcony, standing there, watching her and probably waiting for her to fall asleep before they pounce. Tiana clenches her leg together; her fear making her so nervous she has to urinate. She looks around the room for a... *Weapon, cellphone, anything.*

There are two telephones in the suite, one on the table by the door, the other hanging from the kitchen wall. Plus, the cell in the purse by the balcony door. She doesn't think she'd reach them before whatever it was attacked

"Our father who art in heaven" She whispers her prayers, before her voice shakily calls out, "Who's there?"

No answer.

Wide-eyed, she peers at the shadow on the wall. It doesn't move. She slinks off the couch and crawls towards her work bag, which she had dropped on the floor by the other couch. Mid crawl, she stops, realizing she's now in full view. *Oh shit.*

"I have a gun!" she warns.

The shadow remains static, thick, and foreboding

She scooches faster, back out of view. Behind the couch, Tiana is now obscured from the view on the balcony.

You have to move, bitch. Alert Tao! Move!

Tiana shoots forward again, her bare knees and palms scraping the soft carpet, her breath pumping in bursts from her nose. She looks at the balcony as she goes by, out of fear more than necessity. Her eyes widen at what she sees.

There's no one on the balcony. It is empty. It is just the dark Berlin night out there; a halo of city lights lay beneath a smog cloud of gloom. She gasps and backs away from the balcony.

Am I going crazy? There's no one standing there.

Tiana keeps staring at the spot, unmoving; she can taste bile rising up her throat. The world turns and spins as her belly knots around her abdomen. She clutches her stomach, unsure if she'll make it in time to the bathroom.

Once again, a shadow flickers, moving from one side, then deeper into the room.

Oh, hell naw! Tiana rushes for her bag, rummages in it without taking her eyes off the floor.

She finds her work phone, grabs it and tries to make the call. But her hands shake so terribly that she can hardly hold the phone.

The shadow stretches further and further into her room. So close now that it's just a few steps away. She picks up her phone again, but this time she places it against her ear. But it's too late.

"Taoooo!" she screams

The shadow splits in two, then three, four, surrounding Tiana with tall shadows. Not even a moment later, the door flies open so hard it damn near breaks the hinges; Tao busts in, flipping on the switches before rushing to Tiana's side.

"What happened?" he asks, with wide eyes, his chest heaving as he looks about the room for the source of her fear. Tiana weeps like a young baby, panting, unable to get the correct words out.

He stomps around the room, checking to make sure no one is inside.

Tiana sits on the floor sobbing; her eyes are the size of saucers. Tao collects her blanket and picks her off the floor. He carries her out of the suite to his own one door down the hall. Tao's suite is smaller, less lavish, but it's cozy enough. There are no paintings on the wall, and it's well lit.

Tao deposits Tiana on his bed and tells her to give him a moment. He goes back to secure Tiana's suite, checks the balcony and the kitchen too. He finds nothing, so he hurriedly grabs her bags, locks the suite, and leaves.

"You'll be alright. We check out in a few hours."

Tiana nods slowly, feeling, at last, somewhat safe. She drops two capsules of aspirin on her tongue and chases them down her throat with a glass of water. Tiana's eyes are bloodshot red, her lips dry and cracked from thirst.

"There was something in my hotel room, a shadow," she says with a level voice, "I saw it as clearly as I see you now, Tao."

Tao comes to her and sits. "Who was it?"

"You won't believe it if I told you."

"Raj. It's Raj, I know—"

"No, it isn't," says Tiana with a sudden force.

It's something worse than Raj. Something —

She frowns. Her trembling hands tighten on her empty glass. Could it be that guy from the sauna the other day? Is he back to silence me? Tiana's frown deepens as she contemplates the possibility.

"A scare tactic to silence me!" she says out loud.

"A what?"

"The shadow, maybe someone, is trying to scare me. That guy from the sauna—"

"What guy? Tiana, you're not making sense right now." Tao gets up from beside her. He digs his hands in his pockets and gives Tiana the *elder brother* look.

"What is this? I don't get it. At the conference the other day, you zoned out; it's almost like... this is not you."

"I knew it; you think I'm crazy."

"Knew what?"

Tiana puts the glass on the table before her. "Don't worry about me, Tao. I'll be fine."

She holds the blanket tighter and walks into the bedroom. Quickly jumping on the bed, covering herself from head to toe. "You take the couch tonight, alright—"

"Yes, ma'am."

"And Tao—"

"Yeah?"

"Watch me."

Tao stares at her, mildly shocked. "You don't even have to ask that." He nods and goes to the couch.

Tiana opened her eyes, knowing instantly something was off, but she couldn't place it. She swiftly made her way to the bathroom, urinated. Wiping the gunk off her eyes before stepping into the shower.

The quick shower felt good, but it didn't help. She approached her reflection in the mirror. Her dark-coily hair looked dull and ashy. She stretched her shoulders. Her joints felt stiff, like they were gummed together with Gorilla glue.

The cup beside the bathroom sink is quickly filled with water. Tiana popped another aspirin in her mouth and got back in bed. It was still dark outside. The only source of illumination came from the living room, where Tao is resting. But Tiana could feel it. She knew she wasn't alone.

"Who are you?" she asks. "How did you get in here?"

The man's face is lost in the darkness. She can only make out some of his body, from the torso to his thigh, where the bed covers the rest of him.

Tiana sits up, pushing the cover aside.

"Tao, please tell me it's you?"

But she already knew Tao wasn't that tall or as big. The closer the man moves, the more the moonlight reveals his image. He's dressed like a Neo-Nazi—black, shiny leather jacket and hat. The man's outline moves to the side of the bed, and two glowing eyes tell her all she needs to know. Tiana tries to scream, but her voice is snatched from her throat. A dry croak is the only sound that comes out.

"Shush. Now lass, it's time for us to play."

She tries to yell again, but her voice remains trapped. With the flip of the demon's hand, the covers float off her body and she levitates into the air. Tiana flounders and thrashes around as she struggles to get back on the bed, but the harder she tries, the higher she floats to the ceiling. The entire room is levitating; the bed sheets, armories, the liquid from the coffee cup strings floats like big black beads. The nightstand hovers just beside her. She grabs for it, misses, and instead hits the hot floating spill of coffee.

His glowing eyes follow Tiana as she rolls in the air, her mouth opening and closing in a silent scream for help. The distance from the bed to the ceiling seems to stretch forever. The room feels like it's expanding. The curtains float off the windows and flutter slowly towards the ceiling like capes.

She grapples to catch hold of something but keeps coming up short. The more she struggles, the worse the spinning becomes. She squeezes her eyes shut, only to open them to find razor-sharp teeth snapping. Closing her arms over her head, Tiana utters her last soundless scream of terror before she wakes up sweating. The alarm clock on her phone blares out Moonlight Sonata. It was 2:00am.

It was a dream...

Oddly, Tiana feels great despite the nightmare. Like she's recharged.

Both their bags are packed, so it takes no time for them to step out. Tao informed her that Inyoku left earlier, because she had to see to family business back in Japan.

Tiana takes a gander at Tao, who is walking ahead of her.

"Tao, there's something I wanted to—"

Tao stops and looks at her, waiting.

She says, "You know what, never mind."

Tao doesn't argue. He turns his pale face away, and they walk on.

****

On average, the concierge welcomes two hundred guests every day into the Berlin Honors Hotel. He can't memorize every face, but some-how, he recalls Tiana's. Her dark skin, thick kinky hair, and her overly curvaceous shape. This morning, Dr. McGuire is wearing an oversized hoodie, a pair of blue jeans, and Nike sneakers. The concierge looks her up and down and frowns.

"Chello, Mizz... I mean Dr. McGur," he calls as Tiana walks by. She's with Tao Ikeda, her assistant; they both look miserable, dragging her luggage behind them. A taxi is waiting on the street for them. Tiana looks at him hesitantly, as if she's expecting to hear bad news.

"Yes, sir."

"Would you mind if I took a little of your time, please?"

"Yes, I mind very much—"

"Call me Matthew.

"There is a matter that requires that we delay our guests a little. If you would follow me, please."

The concierge gestures towards a corner of the lobby, which seems like a conference space has recently been created. It houses a table and two chairs. There's even a pitcher of water on that table, besides which are two glasses.

A man is sitting on the chair; he looks too formal to be a guest. Tiana glances at the man and tries not to show alarm, doubting that it worked.

The concierge introduces Tiana to the man, "This is Detective Jür-gen." The Detective gets up but keeps his hands stiffly beside himself. In a deep baritone English voice, he asks Tiana to sit.

Tao interrupts. "What's going on here? What is this about?"

"Who are you?" Jürgen asks Tao.

Tiana replies, "He's my assistant. Our plane leaves in a few minutes. We must hurry this along."

Jürgen gives Tao a long, hard look, eyeing him with his opaque blue eyes. His eyes stay a little longer on Tao's tattooed arms and neck.

Tiana tells Tao to wait for her, so he reluctantly stomps off. "I'll wait for you in the taxi outside."

She nods, then glances at Detective Jürgen.

"Tell me, Detective, what the problem is."

"I am aware you went down to the sauna the day before yesterday," Jürgen says softly. "That would be Saturday?"

"I did. Yes, Saturday, I guess."

"Tell me what happened down there."

Tiana tilts her head to the side. "What happened? It's a sauna, Detective. What's supposed to happen there?"

"There's no need to be so defensive—"

"I'm sorry, I'm just tired, and seriously, I want to get back home."

"You are tired?" Jürgen asks with a raise of his eyebrows.

"Uh, huh?"

"According to the information I have, you are in Berlin to attend a conference. Are you not?"

Tiana shuts her eyes. The headache is back. When she opens her eyes again, a wave of heat flushes over her face.

I must be coming down with a fever.

"Detective, are you here to accuse me of something, 'because it's sounding like it?"

"What would I be accusing you of?" asks Jürgen.

"I don't know. You tell me. I was on my way to America. But here I am with you and your Gestapo shit, asking me these weird questions about the sauna. Wait, did something happen down there? Someone died, they got electrocuted, drowned? Did they tell you I was at the pool too, where I was ogled and cat-called? Tell me, Detective, why are you asking me all these questions?" *Fuck it. Play the race card; get yourself out of this mess.* "Why am I the only guest you questioned? Is this because I'm black?"

Jürgen gets up suddenly. "That will be all, Miss McGuire; I know it's still early morning but have a good day. I will be in touch."

Tiana shakes her head, gives the concierge hovering nearby a scathing glare, and walks out of the hotel lobby.

"What happened?" Tao asks as the taxi pulls out of the curb.

"I went down to the sauna; they just had some questions."

Tao frowns and continues to type on his mobile phone. Tiana calls her friend Yolanda and tells her she and Tao are on their way to the airport.

* * * * * * * * * * * *

The Concierge looks at the Detective. "So vhut now?"

Detective Jürgen shrugs his broad shoulders. "It is difficult to know. I can't keep her without a court order." He nods at the concierge, then walks out.

Something seems off about Dr. Tiana McGuire.... Something big happened in that sauna, something beyond the ordinary. The Doctor knows something, maybe not about the bodies, but there's definitely more to her.

By the time the Detective gets back to his precinct, Dr. McGuire will be out of his jurisdiction.

6

Chapter Six

Yolanda stares curiously at Tao as she serves out her favorite gluten-free cookies. Tao picks a cookie and wolfs it down.

"Hmm, this is good. Very good. There's a bit of ginger in there, right?"

"Umm Huh, now you eat a few more, okay?" She glances at Tiana, and they both share a look.

Upon returning, both women briefly spoke about Tao's diminished figure. Tiana had insisted for Yolanda to bring them back to her place after leaving Berlin. Tiana hadn't dreamt of monsters at all. Nor has she seen any, thank God.

She thinks it best to keep these things from Tao. She knows Yolanda would at least try to understand. Only now, Yolanda seems too preoccupied with Tao, her motherly tendencies kicking in. Yolanda scoots up a chair, joining the two at the table. A platter of ginger cookies and plain yogurt is spread out on the platter before them. Tiana fills Yolanda in on everything that happened in Berlin, but leaves out the dreams and things that she saw, unsure of how to explain it or where to start.

FYI, demons and monsters are real, and I'm an accomplice to murder. Surprise!

Tiana opts to keep her recap brief and monster-free for now. After taking a sip of water, Tiana looks over at Tao; he's deep in thought, half a ginger cookie still clutched in his hand.

The ladies clear their throats, causing him to look up at them. He puts the cookie down and ruffles his hands through his hair. "I know, I know. I have not been myself lately."

"Are you taking medication?" Yolanda asks.

"No."

Tiana questions him next. "Do you have any idea why you look twice as small?"

"What? What do you mean I look smaller? Well, maybe I've slacked off on my workouts and training a bit."

"You never miss your workouts," says Tiana. "Even in Berlin, you trained three hours a day as usual."

Yolanda cuts in, "Let's be real, Tao; you never miss workouts. What's going on? You look like you're on something, like, do we need to have an intervention or some shit?"

Tao glares at them for even suggesting such a thing. "I don't do any drugs; it goes against my beliefs."

"So it's Inyoku then?" Tiana blurts out.

Tao stares at Tiana, sighs. "I. I... I don't know what you are talking about."

Tiana leans forward, tired of tip-toeing around the subject. "Yes, you do."

"Tiana, I don't. Inyoku and I....... no, it's you I was afraid for."

Yolanda looks at her friend. "Titi, what's Tao talking about?"

Tiana averts her eyes, hoping to drop the subject since it's now about her. "Whew! Well, if you don't want to talk about it, I won't force you."

"I think you should see a doctor, Tiana." Tao glances at Yolanda and then back to Tiana. "Tell her, tell her about the dreams, the hallucinations."

Tiana's face fogs; she looks down to the floor. A feeling of dread rises in her.

What if I look up, and two of the three people I love are monsters too?

She squeezes her eyes shut. Too much of a coward to look at them now. She retreats deep into her mind. She sees green glowing eyes, strong muscular arms and.... suddenly a deep voice fills her consciousness: "Mine!"

This isn't the first time the stranger from the sauna has plagued her thoughts. Hell, anytime she is alone, her mind thinks of him. Even this morning in the shower. As the warm water cascaded down her body, she shut her eyes tight and rubbed herself raw. She imagined herself sitting on the man's face. His thumb plunged deep in her asshole as he sucked on her clit. The orgasm that hit was powerful enough to make her slip in the shower. Even now, just thinking about it makes her want to be alone.

"Tiana?"

She looks at Yolanda sharply. "What?"

"Fess up; why are you sitting there with your eyes closed?"

"The fuck! I can't tell you even if I wanted to, alright!"

Yolanda raises her hands. "Oh okay, okay." A look of hurt and surprise blankets her face.

Tiana pushes her chair back, quickly making her way out of the kitchen into the living room, where she sits and buries her face in her palms.

Tao bends down in front of her, attempting to pry her hands from her face. She peeks up and looks into his stern eyes.

"Taooo?" Tiana whines.

"Whatever is happening to me," Tiana says, "is happening to you, too."

Yolanda appears at the kitchen door, hands folded across her boobs. Her eyes center on both Tiana and Tao.

Tiana ignores Yolanda and whispers, "Do you have—weird dreams? Do you see—?" She thinks about the word *demons* but changes her mind. "Strange things? Monster faces, bad people?"

"There are bad people everywhere."

"These aren't bad '*bad*' people. These are worse than that. I'm talking about really ugly looking people, glowing green eyes—"

She stops talking when she notices how Tao stares at her. She asks him, "Do you think I'm crazy?"

"I would not say that, even if I thought so. You're my boss... but also my friend. Hell, I see you as I would a little sister."

"You know, you two are freaking me out now," Yolanda shouts from the kitchen. "What the hell are you guys whispering about?"

Tiana gets up. Dragging Tao after her and heads for the door.

"Yoyo, we have a convention to prepare for."

And Tao has a few truths we need to discuss.

Without so much as a goodbye, Tiana drags Tao to the car. Tiana throws the car in gear, but guilt causes her to look back. Yolanda didn't deserve that. But she doesn't know how to explain any of this. Tiana looks over at Tao while once again lost in thought, then back to Yoyo's door. Yolanda still stands there, anxiety stenciled across her face. She presses the brake and then freezes. Tiana's eyes wander to one of the windows above Yolanda's flat. She gasps when sees him standing there...

Tiana rubs her eyes and looks again... but no one's there.

7

Chapter Seven

Things have practically gone back to normal since coming home. Instead of demon-filled nightmares, her dreams are now filled with lustful encounters with her mysterious stranger.

Tiana stretches her back, sore from yet another night of tossing and turning in the sheets. She shuffles through her work bag, double-checking to make sure she had the right number of flyers and printouts for the Midwestern SIDs Convention. Before settling down at her desk in her study, Tiana goes around the loft, making sure all the lights are on, doors are shut and blinds are drawn.

I should double-check the locks.

She sprints over to the door, checking the locks. She stares at it for a few moments then rechecks it again. With that complete, she settles down to prepare for her lecture. This would be a smaller event, just a few pre and postpartum mothers from Bronxville and Grand Boulevard.

Tiana has always been passionate about her job, but disliked dealing with Sudden Infant Deaths cases the most. Despite the lower national statistics, Chicago is recording more cases, almost half the regional average. Most of the women attribute the phenomenon to unknown forces.

Unknown forces. Tiana grips her desk. Before the trip to Berlin,

maybe she would have found that amusing. But now... could other fac-
tors be at work? Without collecting more data, Tiana cannot delve
deeper. Nobody drops funding into anyone's lap these days, so she has
to make these presentations stand out.

When Tiana looks up again, the day has slipped away. It's already
night.

-Thud-

She turns around swiftly. It sounded like something falling. Tiana
gets out of her chair and backs further from the door. She parts the curtain and peeks out. Rain patters the cars and the sidewalk. Neon signs
flicker on and off in the windows of TEA 'N BISCUITS, the 24-hour
café on the opposite side below.

She quickly picks up her cell from the desk and begins dialing 911.
The knob turns, she freezes. Her body is pressed flush against the window; her heart pounds so hard it's practically jumping out of her chest.
The scent of evergreens and rainfall waft in from the other side of the
door. She frowns at the familiar fragrance.

The door swings open, the knob hitting the drywall so hard it breaks
off the door. Tiana lets out a faint whine as her eyes drink him in.

He stands motionless, the living room light eclipsed by his massive
size. The tips of his spiky dark hair are visible as he ducks his head lower
to walk inside. He's dressed like he was in Berlin, in a gray button-down
leather jacket, and ripped jeans. His yellowish-green eyes glow faintly.
He walks slowly, like a wolf approaching its skittish prey. Every part of
her is screaming, but not for her to get away.

She swallows the lump in her throat and asks, "You followed me all
the way from Europe?"

He folds his massive muscular arms and leans against the door
frame. "I couldn't help it."

Her core quivers just listening to his deep voice. He walks into her
office like he owns the space.

She quietly looks him over; even though it's raining outside, his
clothes aren't wet, nor do his shoes leave puddles on the floor.

"What do you want?" Tiana asks, surprised by her own sudden calmness.

He smirks with his rugged five o'clock shadow and full, thick lips.

"I want to return the favor," Tiana whines again, her lady parts betraying her even more. Tiana has already typed 911 on her cell. Her thumb hoovers over the red SEND button, but the will to press it is now overshadowed by curiosity to hear more.

He stops in the middle of the room. "I go by the name Bounty these days; you can call me that."

"I don't want to call you anything. Please go!"

He walks to her wall, casually pursuing her portraits. "Don't you wonder? By now, I thought you'd have questions—"

Tiana raises her phone. "I'm calling the police now. Leave—"

"Oh, don't be naïve!" he growls.

Tiana struggles between actually calling the cops and squeezing her thighs tighter together, so he won't be able to see her wetness. Her clit is swollen, and her pajama shorts apply just a touch of pressure to her core. His nose twitches, as if her smell has given her away.

Bounty roves his gaze over her body. Her nipples point through her white t-shirt, her shorts exposing her smooth caramel skin and hips that can't be hidden.

"In Berlin, you were unfortunately attacked by a demon that bewitched you; before that fishy fucker died, he cursed you. Most mortals would have gone crazy by now."

He turns to face her head-on. "But you.... you're different."

He takes a few steps toward her.

"What... what do you mean, different?" Tiana asks, unsure she even wants to know

Bounty doesn't answer; his blazing greenish yellow eyes hold hers.

The forgotten memory flashes before her, fragments of Berlin appear, and she gets a snippet of the memories lost deep within her mind. She sees herself, naked, her thighs wide open, her insides stretched by the girth of his massive penis. Her head is thrown back, the halo of her dark coils in disarray.

"Was our lovemaking that forgettable? You've summoned me to fuck you so many times that your cunt should be molded to my dick by now," he growls. As His large finger tugged on a wayward coil of her hair.

"No other woman has ever done... that to me."

Tiana cackles a mocking laugh. "Me?" she asks, blown away by the very notion, "I fucked you? In Berlin, you're saying we fucked, as in we had sex? Where exactly did we, you know, do this thing?"

He drops the strand of her hair and backs away, unamused. "You remember what happened. You are the one that instigated everything.... every night."

"Every... every night? No, I don't believe you," she lies, deep down. She always considered their late-night encounters just to be dreams.

"Then let me remind you. Let me do to you what you do to me. Only, let me do it to you better."

Tiana raises her phone. "No! Get out of my house! You are not—" Bounty grabs her shoulder.

His touch feels so right.

Her resolve crumbles. Bounty's mouth snatches her lips as his large hands snatch the phone from her and toss it on the desk. He pulls away abruptly, finally allowing her to breathe; her lips are swollen, chest heaving in soft pants.

In one swift motion, he lifts her off the floor and slams her back against the wall. Tiana's arms wrap around his neck, as if this was an all too familiar dance. Bounty whispers something, and the lights go off. Lust has taken over her senses; the will to stop him is nonexistent. Bounty's hands are all over her body. His clawed hand tears the shirt off her chest and the shorts from her butt, his long thick fingers snaking around her body, looking for holes to explore.

"Your body was made for me. You want me to fuck you senseless, don't you?"

Tiana bites her lip, drawing blood. Her inner ego is revolting, but her need for him matters more.

"I want your fat dick inside me—!" she gasps.

Bounty kisses her while her plump behind sits in his hands. He carries her to the living room. The lights magically cut off as Bounty walks past. He settles her onto the couch. Her beautiful naked form is presented before him as her head lolls from side to side, delirious with the rapture of the past. Her memories come flooding back like visions. She sees everything that happened between them. Her large, round breast bouncing and swaying, her panties moved to the side, his cock glistening with her essence.

She sees another foggy memory of Bounty lying beneath her, a smug expression on his handsome face, hands folded behind his head as he watches Tiana fuck him, her thick chocolate thighs bucking against his muscular frame.

"Yes," she growls. She wants that again.

On cue, Bounty dives on her and spreads her wide. His tongue scrapes the top of her mound and grates against her clit. But his tongue doesn't feel like an ordinary tongue; it's forked like a snake, each side moving in rhythm with the other. Tiana's body raises from the cushions as Bounty's tongue probes her hole. One hand spreads her lips wide as he nudges her clit with his nose.

His other hand curls around her face. His thumb pushes forcefully against her neck.

"What are you doing to me?"

Thwack! He slaps Tiana on her face. Her head is knocked to the side.

"Claiming what's mine!" he growls.

"Fuck you!" she moans as her body pushes closer to his face. Her core clenches as his two fingers enter her. So thick and long, they feel amazing. She feels him dig deep, tickling her womb, prowling, probing her tight, wet walls. He pulls his fingers out of her and pulls her face up to his. She pushes his fingers into her mouth. He watches as she licks them clean, sucking off every bit of her own essence.

"What do you want from me!" she moans in his face.

"Give me what's mine, give me control!"

"What difference does it make if I fuck you or you fuck me?"

"I'm the alpha; you are mine to take charge."

Anger flashes on Tiana's face. Her dominant nature takes reign. "Get off me—!"

With surprising force, she pushes him off of her and rolls away from the couch.

She stands before him naked, arms folded, lips puff in a pout. He growls as his giant cock juts out. He grabs a fist full of her hair from behind and forces her against the wall, spreading her ass crack before thrusting himself home. She instinctively raises her butt, arching her back ever so slightly so all of him can get in. His cock thrashes her, as his balls smack rhythmically against her bum.

"Yes..." she roars." Fuck me—" His clawed hand grips the upper wall as he thrust feverishly into her.

"You're so fucking tight."

"Yes, daddy."

Bounty pauses. *Daddy?* A shiver rakes over his spine. He pushes his cock in deeper; her gushing core tightening so much it clamps down. Tiana gnashes her teeth and squeezes her eyes shut at the twinge of pain. She bites her lip, forcing herself to be silent, not wanting him to know she is now under his domain.

"Oh no, you don't. Let me hear your passion."

His engorged penis pushes deeper into her sheath. She whimpers into the bend of her arm as he continues to pound her cheeks.

"Fuccccck... I can't take it. I'm hurting..."

Bounty leans toward her ear, his breath blowing hot, "But it's the good kind of 'pain; yeah, do you want me to stop?"

Her eyes water as her body relaxes in submission. His inner beast pushes forward and takes charge. His warm breath caresses her neck. His palms cup her heavy breasts as his clawed thumb and index twist and tug at her large, dark nipples. His touch is gentle now, but his cock remains ruthless. His deep, slow strokes open up places inside her no other cocks have ever reached. He knives her with it, deep. His heavy balls slap her clit.

He can feel her greedy cunt's orgasmic convulsions, seducing him to part with his seed. Bounty grunts once and thrust forward, filling

Tiana with an eruption of his essence. Tiana falls backward and faints in sweet exhaustion, fully sated with zero feelings of regret, even as her body topples into his hands. His shaft knots deep within her.

He looks down at her, perplexed but not surprised. He had already claimed her as his. His inner beast is making sure it has solidified the bond. He carries Tiana, gently crawling onto her bed. She stares at his tall figure through groggy, sleep-deprived eyes. A part of her mind already struggles to store this moment. She'll likely have aches come morning, and once again, she may not remember why.

8

Chapter Eight

Tao Ikeda lives in a terraced house near Palos Hills. For the most part, he enjoys being alone; at other times, whether he likes it or not, his four younger cousins are usually invading his home. Tao's mother's family was close-knit, descendants of Japanese wine merchants that immigrated here after Tao was ten; Tiana remembers him telling her about how he and his mother were cut off from his father's side.

He comes from old money but lives a simple life. Despite his bad-boy style, Tao's a perfectionist, especially with regard to honing his body and skills. He runs 8k almost every morning, works out in the local gym, and sometimes even teaches karate or Kenpo to the younger children.

Tiana knew she had to talk to Tao. Besides being her assistant, he's like the big brother she never had; she called him several times that morning, fearing the worst, she drove over to his house.

She arrives and parks in the street. She looks up at the lit house and at the balcony where she often sights her assistant doing his karate thing in his thick black keikogi, as Tao likes to call the karate uniform.

He's not on the balcony practicing his Kata. Tiana considers calling him again to see if he'll answer. She bites her lip. *I'm worried about him.* One glance at her mobile phone and she decides not to call him again. She already called five times.

Tiana walks up the drive, looks back, double-checking before just walking into his home. The homes here are set far apart up the road; the block is quiet except for a few kids riding their bicycles around. A guy in a black hoodie and skinny jeans rolls along, checking out Tiana's blue Corvette.

Tao's lawn is freshly cut. She hears the crunching blades of grass under her Vans sneakers.

The garage is open. His Camaro is missing, the floor is oil-stained and some tools are scattered about—it means Tao is alone, and his cousins are probably out joyriding. She knocks lightly. She doesn't want to startle him if he's asleep.

"Tao?"

The house returns Tiana's knock with a hollow echo. Tao loved minimalist decor. The house is an open space floor plan, with a few chairs and tables here and there. White walls and elegant Japanese paintings adorn the walls. Sculptures hang from the walls in the corridors, and the smell of herbal tea faintly peppers the air. The living room is empty; she sees a cup of tea on the table near the couch, and behind that is the painting of a Japanese Pagoda on the wall.

Tiana continues to walk around to the side of the house. She finds Tao stretched out on a sofa on the screen porch. A magazine sits crumpled on the floor, near a smashed cup. The carpet is soaked red near his head.

Alarm tears at Tiana's heart. Just as her anxiety reaches its peak, Tao's hand lifts and scratches his stubbled jaw. He yawns and drifts back to sleep, head thrown back, mouth open.

Tiana exhales and frowns. Tao looks even worse. He's bare-chested but has on grey running pants. Tattoos decorate his shoulders—dragons—on his arms and chest. On his belly, there's a samurai with a skull and Katana.

Tiana taps the glass door with the edge of her cell phone. Tao's eyes flutter open. He sits up and looks across the porch at her.

"Tiana?"

"Fuck's sake." Tiana sighs, "Come get the door, will you." He quickly staggers forward to let her in. "And here I thought I was the one who needed a doctor. Have you looked at yourself in the mirror lately?"

"Every day, of course."

"Uh huh, and what do you see?"

"I see me, Tao, the firstborn son of the Ikeda."

Tiana shakes her head. "I'm serious, Tao. Cut the shit, you know there's something wrong."

Tao returns from the kitchen with two cups of ginseng tea. He hands a cup to Tiana and sips from the other. He joins her on the porch. Sunlight begins streaming in, and the warmth refreshes Tiana's as she drinks Tao's brew.

"Will you be honest with me?" Tiana pleads.

"Sometimes I—" He breaks off and says, "Maybe I'm just tired."

"Uh huh, tired of your life forced being siphoned out."

Tao shrugs it away, not mentioning another word as they prepare to head out to the lecture.

9

Chapter Nine

Bounty's usually able to blend in. He's walked the human realm millions of times. His experience taught him countless things, helping him hunt down rogue fae and demons. He chants a small incantation while walking, somehow contorting his body to average size. His massive, muscle-bound 6'8 body now looks about 5'8. He hurriedly blends in with a group of students from the University as they cross the street.

As he crosses the intersection, Tiana's blue Corvette turns the corner and heads toward the parking garage. With a snap of his finger, he transports himself to the presentation hall. The elevator chimes as Tiana and an Asian man walk past him. His inner beast growls. *Simmer down. She's ours.* She glances his way. He quickly turns, hiding from her sight. Tiana notes the back of a guy in the hall, dressed in a grey jacket and plaid trousers, but absent-mindedly shrugs it off.

Bounty continues onward, stopping at a red double door. Tens of voices hum behind it. He smirks as he pushes the door open and steps into a large hall of people waiting for the presentation to begin. He growls and scans the crowd, throwing out his scent. A few heads in the audience snap his way. A few lesser demons spot him by the back entrance. He settles down in the back row, between two staring emo girls and a nursing mom. Three demons leave their seats quickly and walk out. To their luck, he makes no move at them. Not now, not today. Today, his only care is Tiana.

****

Tiana glances at Tao, her nose turns up as she sniffs the hall. It smells like moldy cheese. "Do you smell that?" she asks Tao.

He stops walking and looks up from his phone. "I smell a faint chemical smell, like the floor's been freshly waxed." She shakes her head. The nearer they get, the more anxiety she feels. Tao catches the strange look in her eyes. "What's wrong?"

Tiana looks at him in disbelief.

He really doesn't smell it!

Tao pushes the door open, and they enter the hall where about fifty delegates from WHO, UNESCO and several other local non-profit organizations turn to look at them. Tiana's seat is reserved in the hall's front where other members of the CHD community health unit are waiting. She counts five women and one man.

Of these six people, only Dr. Christy Marlow is familiar. When they make eye contact, Christy's deposition lights up. Her caramel hand caresses her short-cropped hair as she tidies herself when she sees Tao. Tiana muffles a giggle as she watches Christy primp and preen. Tao doesn't even spare her a second glance. He really was all about Inyoku, despite Christy's attractive looks.

As they approach, Christy Marlow scoots over and pats Tiana's hand. "You are right on time. They just announced that today's session is cut in half."

"Why didn't you shoot me an email, Christy?"

"I'm sorry, Tiana. But you know how it is with these things." Christy swipes a hand at the waiting audience. "Give the board an inch, they take a mile."

"Well, it better not be more than the original time allotted—"

"They requested an hour from us, and then the second session will break off into small groups."

Tiana shoots a smug look at Christy. The woman's pretty Latin lips pucker as she shrugs. Tiana looks away, suppressing her irritation for the last-minute change. As she turns her head, the moldy smell rushes by once more. She risks a quick glance into the audience. It had been days since her last sighting. She was grateful for the reprieve.

There are two sets of female participants here, pregnant women and mothers grieving a loss. The difference between the two is unmistakable. The dark ring under their eyes from sleepless nights and tear-stained cheeks. Tiana sighed; she hated this topic the most. She wasn't good with death. And grieving the death of a child must be unimaginable.

It was her turn to speak now. She stepped to the podium as Tao concluded the distribution of flyers and print outs titled: UNDER-STANDING SIDs—A GUIDE FOR SAFE SLEEPING PRACTICES.

Tiana gazes at her audience appreciatively. A few women hastily open the paper and begin peering at the words she painstakingly put together the other day

"Good afternoon—," she begins.

Bounty sits forward in the hell-forsaken auditorium chair. The surrounding women keep eye-fucking him, hoping that he'll give them a go. But his sights are only set on her. To his surprise, she has more than just a killer body. He finds his mate to be quite intelligent.

Mate... I like how that sounds.

His chest puffs out as she finishes her speech, frowning soon after, as the tall, muscle-bound Asian follows her off stage. At times, he became worried. He could sense her sadness over the topic of dying infants.The women in here reeked of death, heartbreak and grief. This event was like a buffet for any demon that fed off human emotions.

Bounty made sure to keep a watchful eye on the higher demons that had refused to leave when he entered. They foolishly believe that he can't see past their half-assed fae glamours. There's one slouching in his seat in the front. A Mer-Demon, probably hunting for his next meal. Those filthy fuckers only ate women—well, most male demons and fae usually do, but Mer-Demons are just irritating as fuck. The fuckers always leave shit behind that Bounty has to clean up. They have a nasty habit of playing with their food, fucking their prey and killing them during coitus.

The demon tries hard to conceal his presence, practically sweating bullets, hoping Bounty doesn't look his way. Bounty chuckles softly; the Mer-Demon must think him some low-rank hunter. Bounty furrows his brows. Telepathically sending a warning the Mer-Demon's way.

"You insult me, Mer-bitch. I'm especially coming for you."

Bounty rises and drifts down the aisle, ignoring the stares that follow him. Even with his less attractive glamour, his attractive, dominant nature shines through. A few female students nearby are instantly smitten by his gruff bearing. A few give him the look of interest, but he ignores them.

Mere shells, unworthy of my beast or me.

He stops and looks down the row. The demon locks eyes with him.

"Hi," the boy starts.

The girl whose cunt the Mer-Demon has been furtively touching through her short-pleated skirt asks, "Brian, you know that guy?"

"Yeah, umm, we go way back."

"Brian, huh, that's the name you're going by?" Bounty asks telepathically. The girl smiles at Bounty. The demon frowns. Bounty asks, "Oh, why the frown? Are we not having fun anymore?"

His putrid, fishy smell strengths the angrier the Mer-Demon becomes.

Bounty scrunches his nose. "You fishy fuckers are the worst!

"Alright, Brian. Time's up; you need to go home." Bounty's voice rumbles from the end of the row.

Brian doesn't get up. "What do you want? Why don't you go fuck yourself, hunter?"

"Right... now get up!"

"Whoa." The girl chuckles, her unknowing eyes wandering from one man to the other.

Bounty groans silently; he knows he is drawing attention, attention Brian is deliberately setting the pace for. Meanwhile, Bounty couldn't give a flying fuck. Without saying a word, he ambles to the front and stands before Brian*.

Brian's glamor is fashioned after a college jock. Sandy commercial worthy hair, full lips, and square jaws. The type of look that usually lands him any willing slut. He looks like he surfs when he's not fucking women in dark alleys and eating their guts.

Bounty leans close. "How many now?"

"What?"

"Your body count. Tell me, are your kills disposed of, or do you swallow them whole?"

Brian sneers, "I'm not stupid."

"You are neither a coward, I give you that," Bounty growls, "But you know I don't give a hoot one way or the other, So, get up!"

The girl sitting beside him retorts, "The professor will be here any minute. He has to attend to get credit.... But umm," she leans forward and whispers, "Do You sell weed?"

"You sure know how to pick 'em." Bounty laughs, before leveling the girl with a sizzling stare, and her jaws magically snap shut. He swivels toward the Mer-Demon once more. "I will fry you where you sit, your choice!" The Mer-Demon gets up quickly; he grabs Brian and drags him away. Brian struggles to wrest himself free from his firm hold. Bounty overhears someone in the murmuring crowd say they think Bounty is probably a DEA agent.

The door leading to the docking area bursts wide into the sunlit sky. Bounty hurls the Mer-Demon against the wall. Brian's fine features ruffle on edge. His skin shimmers as his strength to maintain the glamor wears thin.

"What's happening, Bounty Hunter, huh? You getting desperate—"

Thwack!

Bounty punches the demon's jaw, ramming his head into the concrete bricks. He shrieks in laughter. Bounty picks the demon by the neck and pins him to the floor. "There are a lot of you here today! What gives?"

"Nothing—" the demon wheezes. "Were just thankful for the easy meal."

Bounty sticks his hand in the demon's belly. His claws slice through the fake human skin, past the scaly flesh straight into his innards—the demon squeals.

"Shut up and give me what I want, or I'll make it worse than hell itself!"

"Okay, okay!"

"Spill it!"

The Mer-Demon convulses, unable to endure the pain. He reluctantly confesses the locations where he's killed numerous girls on the Southside. Bounty growls in disgust. These fishy fuckers always make his job ten times as hard. His nose twitches, catching a whiff of Brian's friends close by. Three – sniff – no, make that five. Five of them, two boys and three girls — plus the one whose cunt stench still lingers on Brian's hand. Bounty growls, mad about having to speed up his kill.

That shit-for-brains whore would have ended up dead in an alley tonight if I didn't step in.

A few minutes later. The group passes by, but all is quiet. There's no sight of Brian or the weird guy. They shrug it off and keep searching. Bounty steps from the shadows and cracks his knuckles, pissed that he couldn't torture that fucker longer. With a quick snap of his neck, he kills him. Scorching his remains, not even a speck of ash left behind. Bounty lazily strokes his scruffy beard.

Hopefully, I can retrieve those bodies before the Chicago police department connects the dots.

Back in the conference hall, the last presenter rounds off their speech for the first half of the conference. Christy Marlow stands and declares it's time for a break. A few other women are invited into a smaller conference room down the corridor for their group session.

With the first part concluded, Tiana can't hold it in much longer. She rushes out of the conference, with Tao on her tail. She bounds to the ladies' room, retching from the horrible smells, fish, wet dog, mold, must and beyond. Tiana sucks in a few deep breaths, then splashes her face with cool water from the sink. She looks herself over. Her black pinstripe jacket sits awkwardly on her shoulders; she fights the urge to take it off. The shoes are uncomfortable, too. The Gucci heels hurt her toes.

And who says I can't come to these conferences dressed in jeans and a tee? She sighs. *The department says.*

"Ma'am?" Tao calls from outside the door.

Tiana grabs a paper towel and wipes water off her face, happy that day is halfway over.

"Get it together, girl!" she whispers to the woman in the mirror.

Ever Since Berlin, Tiana no longer feels like her normal self. Her senses—all five of them—feel enhanced and overpowered. She's even begun to write out a few theories, deciding to tackle the phenomenon using logic and research. From her understanding, the odors could mean two things. She was able to smell people's pheromones and sometimes even perceive their emotions. Something similar to an Empath. Inyoku smelled moldy, like putrid, rotten flesh. Tiana has the foreboding thought that maybe this explains Tao's weakening, much as how prolonged exposure to certain gases can cause gradual death.

"Tiana?" Tao calls again.

Christy Marlow's voice asks, "Is she in there?"

Tao replies, "Yes."

The door opens slowly, and Christy appears behind Tiana. "Hey, Tiana, are you alright?"

Tiana pivots, replying that she's fine. Together, they come out of the ladies to see the women leaving the conference hall on their way to the group session.

"You look pale, Tiana," Christy hints. "Are you sure you don't want to take some time off? I could arrange for the ladies to come tomorrow."

"No, it's okay."

Tiana stares into Tao's gaunt face. Her heart breaks. He looks worse even now. As they walk, Tiana asks him, "Is Inyoku back from Japan?"

"Yes. Inyoku came back last night."

"Have you seen her?" she asks further, dreading the answer.

Tao glances at her before nodding. Tiana clenches her fist.

She's killing Tao somehow. I just don't know-how.

Tiana stops suddenly. Her eyes square on Tao. I know deep down *he suspects it, too.* She holds his hand and opens her mouth, but her words fall short. A bitter stench comes from him. Tiana assumes it must be Tao's confusion. She can read it in his eyes. When he doubts what he thinks, he knows. Instead of questioning him, she steps forward and wraps him into a hug. His body stiffens at first, unsure how to take her sudden outburst of affection. But as they make contact, his color deepens to a warmer pinkish hue, the prior stench vanishing.

Yes, that's it!

With a burst of loving energy, Tiana let him go. Christy looks on with a bit of jealousy before darting her eyes to an amused-looking Tao.

Tiana opens the small conference room door and steps inside. The smell of what she could only describe as death almost forces her back. With a hard swallow, she steadies herself and marches forward.

"Hello everyone, I'm Dr. McGuire; I'll be sitting in during your session. Please feel free to carry on."

A small table was reserved for her, outside the circle of chairs where the ladies are grouped together. Tao has also laid her bag and belongings on the table there. Eight mothers are present, minus Christy Marlow, who is attending this session as a moderator, since most of the women are under her care in the SOUTHSIDE WOMEN'S CLINIC. The women all smile at her in greeting. A chorus of praises ring out that they appreciate that she's trying to help their cause.

Walking to her seat, Tiana feels as though her legs are attached to a heavy iron chain. She focuses on breathing through her mouth as her stomach roils with the stench of remorse, regret, and—*death?*

The emotions are so high that, for a moment, Tiana is actually able to see a blue and black haze hovering around the women; a bitter taste coats her tongue. It's as if this is the physical manifestation of each woman's grief.

Not only can I smell it... if the emotions are strong enough, can I also see it?.. Humm is this similar to the way dogs perceive fear...?

Tiana looks sharply at each mother's face, each at a different stage of mourning, a varying assortment of young and old. Christy told her a mixture of married women and single mothers would attend. Tiana looks in some of their eyes and recognizes the depth of their despair.

"Alright, ladies. Let's begin." she smiles. "We should begin by stating our names. That way, we'll feel comfortable sharing stories. Today is about healing and overcoming the loss of a child—"

She gestures at the woman closest to her on the left side of the table.

"You, ma'am."

"Trish Johnson—" The addressed woman's face unfurls into a sweet smile, with her big, pearly white teeth.

"Emily Landers—" She has an opaque stare on her squinting face, and her composure betrays a shy and unsure personality.

"Aretha Bannerman—"

Tiana leans to the side to look at the woman but sees nothing, because the woman happens to be leaning too far back, and her face is blocked off by Emily's. But there's something else. Aretha oozes the smell of pure death and raw sewage, so strong a wave of nausea washes over Tiana. She strains to sit upright. The hair on her arms tingles when she hears the sound of a faint baby's whine.

Tiana frowns, leaning forward in morbid curiosity in an attempt to see the woman's face, but she's shrouded in a dark mist. Of all the women in the room, Aretha's is so thick it's practically black. Christy tries to get Aretha's attention with a kind, prodding smile.

"Aretha, are you, okay, honey?"

Tiana looks around the room, trying to determine if she's the only one that can hear the baby crying. Aretha finally leans forward, the mist parting just enough to reveal an entity clinging to her breast. Its figure shifts and reforms like smoking vapors.

Oh God—isn't anyone else seeing this? Am I finally going insane? Is this fucking real?

The entity has a vague shape of a baby whenever it solidified enough for her to see its true form. It has an odd-shaped head, its malformed eyes are rolled back, and its cleft lip is drawn over snapping fangs. The skin is pale and membranous, with club-like feet and paws...

Tiana stares in horror as the entity splits its form: *1... 2..4.* The infant-like phantasms cling to Aretha Bannerman's neck, arms, and waist. Another looks old enough to be a toddler; it sits near her feet on the floor.

"I've been through too much, you see..." Aretha sniffs. "I've hardly left my house since... our loss. I'm sorry."

She mops her pale skin with a white handkerchief. Tiana breaks out in a cold sweat when one of the entities suddenly shrieks like a nursing babe hungry for its mother's breast. The cry is haunting and ear-splitting, yet no one hears it but her. Tiana's eyes go to Tao, where he's seated beside Christy. Tao's face is screwed in a questioning expression, as if trying to figure out what's wrong. Tiana shakes her head—*No, no, nothing. I will get through this, but...*

She turns back to face the screaming entities, her hands shaking where they are placed on the table. Tiana watches as Tao leaves his seat and walks around to her side.

"You are not looking good, Tiana. Should I get you some water?"

"No..." she says through pinched lips

"Are you sure?"

"Go back to your seat, Tao, go back now."

If anything, Tao himself is the one in need of fresh air and water. His skin looks shallower with each passing day. Christy and a couple of the other women stare at Tiana, not with worry but with shared empathy.

They think I'm sorry for Aretha Bannerman?

Aretha rises. "I would like to tell you my story. Hopefully then my child's soul can rest." The other women encourage her with a round of applause. She applies the handkerchief to her dripping nose, looking over to Christy, who nods her support.

Tiana's brain struggles to accept what's playing out before her. Aretha casts doleful eyes at her and begins, "His name was Caleb, and he was fourteen months when he passed. He was everything my husband, and I wanted, so when he died, I... I..." She sobs into her handkerchief again.

Emily Landers puts her hand around Aretha's shoulder and squeezes gently. Aretha Bannerman says that her child was diagnosed with dwarfism and died at fourteen months in his crib from medical complications.

"Could you... tell me about these complications, so I can place them in my report?" Tiana's throat is dry and tight, her eyes riveted on the phantom babies clinging to the woman's side.

Aretha blinks. She looks around the table at Christy, as if waiting for approval to continue. Christy nods. Aretha says in a shaky voice, "Hydrocephalus—that's what the doctors called it. Fluid buildup on the brain. They gave my son about a year and a half. He died in his crib, in his sleep, there was..." her voice breaks, as she sobs miserably.

"He had this, this, thing coming out of his ears, and nose—"

"Brain fluids?" whispers Tiana, a bit more bite in her voice than she could contain.

Aretha glances at Tiana and nods. Her eyes are gauzed in mock desolation. Tiana sees through the haze of blackness. "Go on, Aretha."

"Yes, brain fluids, that's what the doctors said, too. They think it was a complication that my Caleb should have lived longer."

As Aretha continues to speak, pouring her heart into the room and forcing those fake crocodile tears, the baby-like phantasms around Aretha begin to shimmer and morph. They shake and bubble; the skin boils and pops as their festering flesh begins to ooze. This metamorphosis takes only a second, but watching it is enough to make Tiana want to barf. It is a miracle that she can hold it together. Tao looks her way in concern. His hands are on the armrest of the chair, ready to charge to Tiana's aid should there be a need. But she holds strong. She keeps swallowing back the thick glob of bile crawling up her throat.

Aretha Bannerman finishes her tale. She leaks more tears and wracks a few sneezes. A few of the other women cry along with her too. Christy is won over by the heart-wrenching tale, but Tao's attention remains fixed on Tiana.

The apparitions solidify again, turning their greenish glowing eyes her way. As if summoned, they start climbing down Aretha's body, writhing and squirming as they get on the floor.

Tiana watches in frozen horror. The bigger one disappears for a moment, then reappears once more, its club-like limbs crawling unsteadily. They make sloshy sounds that no one but Tiana hears, as their decaying flesh *splats* against the floor, slowly approaching her side of the table. Terror grips Tiana as the first of the entities reaches her feet. She flinches, yells and almost falls over her chair as she staggers away from the spectral entities.

"Tao!" she whispers.

Tao is on the move. He grabs her as she hits the ground. Tiana gasps for breath, eyes wide as a dawning realization hit her: the horrific truth about the infant-like apparitions.

"Don't you see, Tao? Look!" she points.

"What, Tiana? What?"

Tao follows her gesture to the point on the glazed tiles near Emily Lander's feet and chair. He sees nothing but tiles.

Distressed, Tao whispers, "Tiana, there's nothing there. What's going on?"

"Buh, but, but it's there—"

"There is nothing there, Tiana!" Tao hisses.

The women begin to murmur, expressing their concern. Aretha Bannerman cries even more, thinking Tiana is on the floor because of the distress she feels for her story. The entities begin to mewl at Tiana, tears trickling from the corner of their eyes. They tug at her feet and she bites her lip, forcing herself not to cringe.

She takes a deep breath and prays silently as the sensation of the first entity grabs her shin. A zap of energy rushes through her, forcing her to open her eyes. She sees clearer now, as if a haze has been lifted. She looks down; the little creatures are not what she thinks they are. They are not demons, nor are they evil entities.

"The truth," Tiana mutters, "they want to show me their truth."

The *children* gather around Tiana. Their haunting gazes lock on her horror-stricken face. With a trembling hand, she grabs Tao's wrist and whispers in his ear, "They are sitting right in front of me. Do you see them?"

Tao looks into her eyes, follows her gaze to the spot on the floor where he is supposed to see *something*. He sees only a crescent blotch.

"I see a stain, a coffee stain," Tao confides. He smiles wearily.

"Oh..."

"Yes, Tiana. It's tiles, coffee stain, and nothing else." He puts his hands around her and prepares to lift her off the floor, but she resists.

The bigger one reaches for her, its malformed limbs outstretched as if for a hug.

Do they want me to carry them?

Tiana senses their pain, their hopeless yearning to *live and be loved* fully. Their lives were cut short.

Do you seek closure? Are you some soul tethered here to the realm of men?

She takes a deep breath and looks at them. Not with fear-filled eyes, but with eyes yearning to understand. Her eyes sweep over them, taking in and studying each one. Oddly shaped skulls, clubbed hands, with various malformations and mutations. The biggest one seems to be the least mutated, but it's dwarfism is still recognizable. They look at Tiana, their glowing green eyes growing fainter the more she unravels the truth.

My God...

As she silently assesses their appearance, the truth sets off like a bomb in her head. Tiana weeps uncontrollably. Her mind is bombarded with visions. Through their eyes, she lives out their pain, as if the broken cord that dangles from their ruptured navels is alive again and tethered to her memories. She reaches her hands out to them, pulling them all to her chest in a loving embrace.

Her tears spill even more because the babies feel it too. They see into her heart, her soul. They *see* that she knows how they came to be, and how their innocent lives were taken. With that, they slowly begin to fade away from the grip of Tiana's tear-stained fingers. It's like watching a puddle of water in the desert vaporize in the heat of the sun.

Aretha approaches slowly, hovering over Tiana on the floor. "I know my story is heartbreaking. This is not the first time my story has brought others to tears. Thank you for grieving for me. Together we can get through this."

Tiana stops crying as anger rushes forth. She wipes a trail of snot from her nose.

"Help me up."

Tao takes her by the arm and supports her.

Christy Marlow appears beside Tiana and offers her a motherly smile. She beams. "The women appreciate you even more now. You understand their grief—"

Aretha Bannerman is smiling, basking in everyone's compassion and shared pain. "Everyone, we are lucky indeed to have such an empathetic woman such as Dr. McGuire here to assist us," says Aretha, as her soft dimpled cheeks pull back in a pretty smile.

"Such pretty lies!" Tiana snaps.

"Huh?"

The room is suddenly plunged in silence. All heads turn to Tiana as she returns to her table. She removes a piece of tissue paper from her bag and dabs her wet face. She adjusts her jacket on her shoulders properly and glares at Aretha.

Of all the monsters I've encountered, you are the ugliest one.

Tao steps into her line of sight. "Tiana?" he says, his tone questioning yet apologetic.

"I got this, Tao." Tiana brushes him to the side, reassuring him with a pat on the hand. Her eyes divert back to the woman whose appearance is once again coated in a miasma. Smelling like putrid rot and... fear.

Her blue eyes look towards the faces of the other women, confused. Tiana leans forward so that only she could hear. "I know the truth, Aretha," Tiana says simply. The woman stumbles backward, realizing she's been caught in her lies.

The vision of those innocent beings drowned in the tub, suffocated with pillows, or left to starve, replays in Tiana's mind over and over again. Aretha was pure evil. Her children never knew a mother's love. She's not some grieving woman, but evil made flesh, a depraved mother who killed her own children due to their malformations.

How long did she starve each of her babies? How long did they fight for just another breath as she suffocated them mercilessly as her drugged-out husband slept in their bedroom next door?

Tiana shudders as her mind replays the vision again. It's as if she is there experiencing it herself; she can smell the garlic on Aretha's breath that morning, the sound of the alarm blaring in the bedroom next door, feel her lungs filling with the scalding water from the tap. Aretha killed them. Murdered every single one.

"You wanted a perfect baby?" Tiana mumbles.

"I, I, you—"

"You hated that they were abnormal, but they were made that way due to you; you were warned that you carried that gene and still punished them!" This is all too much. Tina feels her insides rolling, and she dashes for the toilet, covering her mouth. Perplexed and concerned gazes follow her out.

Tiana patters down to the end of the corridor and bursts into the toilet, pushing the door of a stall open without making sure anyone else was inside. She falls on her knees and vomits into the bowl, her breakfast of eggs, bacon, and coffee. Her head is swimming as the vision starts to fade from her mind. Feeling some strength return to her feet, she stumbles out—colliding with a solid mass of muscle standing between her stalls and the sink.

"Bounty?"

"Tiana, are you okay?" He practically looks her over from head to toe. His beast frantically pacing with concern for their mate. She looks at the door and then at Bounty. "Why are you here?"

The door suddenly pushes open, and Tao bursts in. He balls one of his hands into a fist, and his feet spread apart as he readies himself in a defensive stance.

"No, Tao, stop—!"

Bounty grabs Tiana by the arm, snatching her closer, his possessive nature getting the best of him. "She's mine." His beast pushes to the surface. Hackles raised from that all too familiar scent.

"She's what? Let her go!"

She's already claimed... Bounty's beast projects telepathically.

Tao's eyes glow faintly but quickly revert to their natural hue. With a quick shake of his head, he returns to his fighting stance. Tiana raises her hand. "No, Tao, it's okay, it's okay."

"You know this guy?"

"Yeah."

Tao drops his fist, but not his hard expression. Still uncertain about the situation, he asks Tiana what he should say to the waiting women in the conference room.

"Do and say what you deem best; I'm counting on you," she says.

Tao nods and backs out of the room reluctantly.

Tiana turns to Bounty, a familiar heated look in her eyes. His beautiful emerald eyes fall to her face. Her teeth are clenched down tight on her plump lower lips. Bounty's large hand pulls gently on her chin, granting its release. Tiana shivers at his slightest contact; he looks striking, utterly divine. She suddenly jumps into his arms, seeking the release only he can give. She inhales him: evergreens and spring rain.

He rubs his stubbled chin across her jawline. His inner beast grunts and his testes grow heavy with seed. He pulls away, suddenly taken aback by her new smell. her scent was more complex and richer now. His beast pushes forward, desperately yearning to mount his mate. He pushes him back; his claws partially shift as Bounty reins back control. He cups her face with his one unshifted hand.

"I need to be inside you," he says.

Tiana smirks, her mind silently thinking the same.

"Then, take me home."

10

Chapter Ten

Tiana can't bring herself to go back to the conference. So she doesn't. Christy calls repeatedly, but Tiana's phone hums endlessly in her bag in the living room. The sound of slapping flesh and lust-filled moans echoes through the bedroom.

Bounty's powerful thrust has already broken the frame. The wall behind the headboard was cracked and splintered, the paint chips falling into Tiana's hair. Her back arches as Bounty's powerful grip tugs on her curly hair, Tiana's ass jiggling with every thrust of his hips. He abruptly pulls out of her and pushes her on the bed before dragging her through the river of rumpled sheets, over to the edge, where he turns her on her back.

"Grumpy, are we?"

"Shut up!" he growls.

His veiny, rock-hard cock dangles over her as Tiana hangs upside down off the side of the bed.

"You want to fuck my face, big boy?—"

Bounty grabs Tiana's face and shoves his bulbous cock into her throat, smiling at the bulge in her neck as his huge cock rams into her face. His head falls back as she gags and chokes while he fucks her mouth.

Who the fuck was that guy? He was trying to take what's mine? She's mine!

"You like me fucking your face?"

"Guck, umm-mm—" Tiana gags.

"Can he do this to you?" he grumbles. "Does that prick ass Asian fuck you like this?

Tiana's eyes widen, recognizing the source of his sudden burst of anger. She wants to stop and correct him, but hell, it feels too good. He pulls out of her throat and growls; his cock pulsates before her eyes. Tiana rises from the bed to a sitting position.

"That Asian has a name. It's Tao."

"I don't care."

Tiana shakes her head. *He's kind of cute when he's mad.* "He's my assistant, hell more like a brother slash friend, there's nothing between us."

Bounty climbs back on the bed, his massive body dripping with sweat, boner standing tall, reaching well past his navel. She watches as his muscular, veined thighs flex and ripple. He picks her up. "Mine," he rasps. "Mine!"

He turns her around on her belly—boobs down, ass up — again, spreading her legs apart with his large hands, tautly tugging her ass cheeks so his penis can slide back in. He begins to smash her furiously—all fourteen inches, stretching her to her limits.

"Yes! Yes!!" Tiana screams.

Bounty groans as he pulls out swiftly and descends on her puckered hole. He runs his nose over her naughty entrance, scenting his newfound mate. Her rich fragrance, enticing him to release his seed. His forked tongue shoots out, slowly licking and poking its way into her tight little brown hole. He soon replaces his tongue with his forefinger—in and out it goes.

His cock inches back into her dampness. Tiana's body clenches, orgasming from the tandem assault of pleasure and pain. His semen explodes deep inside her as Bounty bellows Tiana's name.

His beast pushes fourth unexpectedly and it catches Bounty by surprise. His eyes spark with fire, his hair flowing past his back. His muscles quake as his beast's cock grows larger. Tiana is taken aback by the sudden tightness, causing her to look back. What Tiana sees causes her to scream and move away.

He looks twice his size, maybe nine or ten feet now. Much longer black claws extend from each black-tinged finger. His face is shaped similarly to a wolf but with more humanistic features. His eyes spurt tendrils of fire, and his teeth are razor sharp and long. Her wail titters to a silent scream, and she cringes against the headboard.

His beast whines like a wounded puppy. Bounty fights back to regain control of himself, hurrying to change back to his human form. Steam rises from his back, his chest heaving as his beast resists the turn. Bounty's height slowly stabilizes. He staggers onto the edge of the bed, his body racked with pain.

"What are you?" Tiana whispers.

Bounty's eyes roll in his head, and they fight to focus on his woman hiding behind the sheets in her hands, her eyes wide with terror.

"I am the same person I was moments ago."

"What the fuck!" she says. "You know what I mean?"

"Don't ask me shit, you already know!"

He sits up with his back to Tiana. His hands ruffle his spiky dark hair in frustration.

"Look, I'm not like them... I am a Bounty hunter. I hunt those of my kind—"

"I can't do this!" Tiana limps off the bed, body against the wall. She wearily watches him as she stalks away from him. He turns around slowly and looks at her.

"I would never hurt you." He gets up, his hands outstretched in surrender, still naked, damp with sweat.

She snaps and goes on the defensive. "Stay away from me! Please!" She points at the door, and the sheet falls off her naked body. "Get out!"

"I refuse to leave my mate."

Furious and frustrated, Tiana's lips tremble, his words warming her heart but also filling her with dread. She feels deceived, but deep down, she's always suspected. His true form was hidden from her eyes.

"Tiana, I can feel you. You take over my senses; even from miles away, I'm aware of you. Your smell," Bounty confesses, "You feel the same too!" His tone was not questioning, but stating.

No! This is absurd! This can't be happening to me! I suspected he had powers, but I've fucked one of those things...

"I don't fucking want you around me! Get out now!"

"Tell me you don't feel it, Tiana!"

"I don't!" she screams. "I can't be with a demon!"

"You are mine."

Tiana's hands clamp down over her ears as she shouts, "Stop saying that! I don't want to hear it!" She closes her eyes tight and grits her teeth. Tiana feels his hand on her shoulders. She lashes out in a fury, pushing him with all her might. Surprisingly, Bounty is shoved aside just an inch. Tiana escapes past him and runs into the bathroom, where she locks herself inside.

When Tiana finally steps out of the bath, Bounty is gone. She steals across the bedroom, picks her jeans and pulls them on. She finds a random t-shirt from the floor near her closet and tugs it over her head. The door to the living is half-open. She listens stealthily, making sure he was no longer there. When she is certain, Tiana walks into the kitchen and picks a knife off the rack, then returns to the living room. She sighs in relief, flopping down as she covers her face.

Why me? God, why me? I went from fuck boy to a demon...

She wipes her eyes and scrunches herself into the fetal position at the end of the couch; a knife carefully placed beside her in case Bounty shows up again. The image of his demon form plagues her thoughts. She shakes her head.

I've fallen for a demon... How am I supposed to appear in church after

this? What do I tell my friends or Nana? Oh, lord... Nana.... I got a man...
but he's also a demon —

Tiana sighs, buries her face between her knees, and weeps.

11

Chapter Eleven

Tao tries to talk himself into going to the hospital. Perhaps he really is coming down with a bug. Or worse, some debilitating disease yet to be diagnosed. He stares at the reflection of a stranger, no longer able to recognize his own face. He's naked from the head to his waist.

He is exhausted. His face is sunken in, cheeks hollowed with patchy skin. It's just as Tiana has been complaining. Even the guys at the Dojo say they can sense it, too.

I'm so tired.

Tao doesn't want to face it, wishing for it to remain hidden away. But it just won't go away. Like a dull pain under his skin, a tumor growing silently, where the light never reaches. His phone begins to ring, and he answers it. Inyoku, a soft voice, issues from the other side.

"Baby, our plane is about to land," she says. "Will you come to get me?"

Tao tries to smile. What he sees in the mirror stuns him. "Of course, I'll come to get you."

"Be seeing you soon."

Tao goes back to staring at his own face in the mirror. That smile isn't his. It's a shadow of what used to be him.

Am I dying?

He couldn't even execute a proper jump kick today at the dojo. That foreboding feeling begins to consume him. Tiana's voice replays in his head: "Do you think your illness is related to Inyoku?"

He shakes his head as he silently readies himself to go.

****

Temperature in Chicago is forty-three degrees. A stiff, biting breeze blows across the airport. The sun glows like a low energy bulb from behind a white, gauzy mass of clouds. It is early afternoon when Tao arrives at Midway airport. His black Camaro sits idle in the parking bay.

He sighs, preparing himself mentally to meet with his girlfriend.

Inyoku embraces him tightly, kissing him lightly while holding hands as they make their way to his car. Her single carry-on bag hangs from his opposite hand. Inyoku likes to travel light; anything she needs while traveling, she prefers to buy. He waits to hear her remark on his appearance as he drives, but it doesn't come. They chitchat about her family in Japan.

"Otosan wishes you visit more often," Inyoku says in reference to Tao's dad.

"He wishes many things."

"And you should; the family wishes to reconcile," she says, and glances at him. Tao looks at her too, hoping she says something about his sickly appearance.

"What have you been up to?" she asks.

"You know the same routine; work, dojo, and books. I'm grading next week; you'll come to see me?"

"Are you alright?" she asks.

"What do you mean?"

Inyoku's eyes rove over the outline of his face. "You sound subdued. Are you feeling overworked? I'm sorry I have to travel so much lately—"

"It's okay. You told me why you had to leave."

She sighs, visibly aware of the awkwardness between them. Tao holds back his own exhalation. Unease settles over him. The thought of marrying this woman in the next few months leaves him feeling weary. He can't even talk freely with her without feeling awkward or judged. And Inyoku doesn't see what everyone else sees.

She really doesn't see me, or does she simply not care?

"Are you worried?" she asks abruptly.

"Worried? About what?"

"You know, coming back to Japan after all this time, meeting your Otosan again, mine and your other kin. I know it's a lot to take in all at the same time. Which is why I'm recommending you visit Japan again in advance before the wedding—to cushion the patch up. This marriage will strengthen both our clans."

"Patch up, huh?"

Tao looks at her and almost shakes his head.

I wonder, does she even love me, or is this all duty?

"That's why you want me to visit before the wedding?"

Tao feels her gaze on the side of his face, probing. Those large, slanted eyes always have a way of making him want to kiss her; he checks to see if he still feels this way now. But he isn't sure. There's something else that he's been feeling when he's with Inyoku, an alien vibe he cannot put a name to.

He makes two turns and drives up to his home. Tao retrieves his girlfriend's small travel bag from the back of the car and watches Inyoku stare at the house.

"Are you alright?" he asks.

She turns and chuckles. Her eyes don't smile. "It's been a while since I was last here, that's all." She looks around again, as if she sees something out of place. Tao thinks of questioning her about his appearance but decides to leave it be.

Inyoku waits patiently for him in the foyer. She seductively removes her clothing as Tao comes in with her bag. He's struck by her beauty: her small perky breasts and slender waist enticed him. The small tuft of smooth black hair over her sex makes his mouth water.

Any other time, Tao would have tossed the bag aside and fucked In-yoku right on the spot. But things were different now.

He smiles at her. "Looking great, as always."

"Is that all?"

Tao drops the bag and walks to her. Inyoku hesitates at first when Tao kisses her, eyes wide open. She yields when his thick tongue slides into her mouth. He lifts her off the floor and up to the lounge, overlooking the top of the house and the street below. The room smells like jasmine. The shag rug and jade plants give off a warm, homey feel.

Tao undresses slowly, still expecting Inyoku to say something about his smaller, less muscular frame. She says nothing. Her eyes are focused solely on his dick.

Inyoku takes his twelve-inch erection in her hands, caressing it and gently placing it in her mouth. Her mouth feels damp and cold, like sticking his prick in a jar of Vaseline. Tao struggles to keep his erection. With foreplay out the way, she takes him into her.

A few deep strokes later, Tao seed drips from her core. They lay side by side, staring at the white ceiling, each person riddled with their own thoughts.

Inyoku sighs. "Something is not right."

Finally, maybe we can salvage this thing that's crumbling.

"What isn't right?"

Inyoku turns her head. "Us. It's cold, not fiery like we used to be."

"You think?"

"Yes." She adds, "I know I haven't been as available as I used to. My main residence is in Japan now. And you won't come home. I understand why. But maybe before the wedding, we can discuss you moving back. Your family's elders wish to make up for past grievances against you and your mother. What do you think? We extend an olive branch by you moving back home?"

Tao feels a short flash of anger inside him. Here he thinks In-yoku is thinking about him, and she doesn't even notice how sick he's become. Her only concern is what the family wishes. Tao starts to question himself:

Do I even want to marry her? Her loyalty is to the family, not to me.

"I'll think on it."

She is looking at him. "You will?"

"Uh huh, yeah."

"Good."

So mechanical.

Tao gets up, gently taking her hand, and leads her to the bathroom. Warm water sprays over their naked bodies. Tao's erection performs long enough to convince the suspicious Inyoku that he still loves her. She had a kink for shower sex. The sensation of the jet of water beating against his body distracts Tao from how much his love for her has diminished. He runs his tongue from the nape of her neck down the length of her back. She lifts one leg and places it on the edge of the tub so that Tao can eat her out.

He flicks his tongue in there, dragging it through her labia flaps. Inyoku spreads her labia and water streams down his face as Tao sucks her clit. She rubs her vagina all over his face, marking him with her essence, then pushes him down on the floor and begins rolling her hips. Next, she's on all fours, the river of her black hair clinging to her body like inky tendrils. Her small butt arches, granting him full access to her core.

His throbbing member is fully erect and aroused. Tao gets up behind her and pushes his dick in deep. Planting his hands on the shower floor, he attacks her from behind. Inyoku grits her teeth. Her core tightens, but Tao keeps pounding, making her orgasm several times till she falls from exhaustion. Tao watches his dick slide in and out of her tiny cunt until he screams, once again giving her his seed. They kiss under the shower, then Tao winds it all down by gently bathing her and shampooing her hair.

12

Chapter Twelve

The meeting with the Pfizer executives has just concluded. Tiana walks down the clinic's corridor building, her stilettos clicking and clacking on the hardwood floor. She turns her head, quickly glancing over her shoulder. The feeling she is being watched has her paranoid. But there's nothing, just a bunch of grad students talking by the elevator doors.

She exits the building, the sunlight warming her back despite the frigid breeze. The walk took all of ten minutes from the grounds to the faculty lot. A whiff of evergreens and spring rain lingers in the air. She shivers.

So familiar, so right....

She stops and glances back the way she came. Nothing but students erupting in laughter. The sound of their banter fills her with memories from her time as a grad student. From the lot, she catches Christy's sight: a new guy she heard the others calling Topper (real name Charles Toppence) and the Community Health Division's new head, Aaron Lett. They all wave her way, and she waves back. The strong breeze tries to snatch Topper's hat, and he presses it down.

Tiana places her work bag on the top of her corvette. Quickly changing out of her stilettos to her favorite flats. She opens the door, throwing the heels in the back, and settles in.

"How was your day, sweetheart?"

Tiana jumps, her heart lurching out her chest. Sitting comfortably reclined in the passenger's side is none other than her beast.

"How the fuck did you get in?" Tiana reaches for the door, but Bounty grabs her hand. His scent is saturating the car; her nostrils greedily inhale.

He's so close.

His warm breath washes over her face. His eyes hold her with intensity, making her want to give in, despite the truth of him being a demon.

The locks on the doors all go up—*clunk*—snapping Tiana out of her daze. She turns and lifts her feet in the air, ready to fight if he won't let her go free.

"Simmer down and be still!"

With those words, she kicks him. "Let me go! Get off me!"

He pins her against the door. She bites and scratches his arms, struggling to wriggle free. She tries to look out the window, hoping that someone will look their way.

"They can't see us, Tiana."

He calls her name. Her heart quivers, slowly losing her resolve to fight. He gazes deeply into her eyes.

Why does he have to be such a handsome demon?

They sit in silence, staring at each other.

He's not a demon now. Most of the time we're together. His monster form is hidden away.

She looks him over quietly, assessing the pros and cons of their pairing. *It's not like we haven't already had sex...* She rolls her eyes at her own stupid way of justifying it. *I've never been with a man that can handle me sexually. Maybe it would be fun to make a demon my bitch...*

"What are you thinking?" Bounty asks. "That look in your eyes is creeping me out!"

She blushes and pushes him back, adjusting her clothes and her hair as they both settle into their seats.

Bounty growls out, "I want to start over. My mortal name is Ishtan Rustivich."

She silently listens as he continues on.

"Maybe if you see me as Ishtan rather than Bounty, perhaps you'd be more comfortable with this whole ordeal."

"Uh-uh." She nods her head and folds her arms.

He grits his teeth in annoyance. "Look, I'm not used to asking or playing nice. It's usually my way and nothing else." His large hands ruffle through his dark hair, flustered by his little human's feistiness.

Tiana simply starts the car and begins to drive out the lot. He looks about in confusion. Not sure where her actions will lead.

"Where...?" He looks at her, a faint smile tugging at the corner of her lips.

"Somewhere where I can fuck you."

His beast growls as his penis becomes hard and thick. Tiana drives for a long time, not knowing where to go now. It would be uncomfortable to take her demon home. She goes past Washington Park, where there's a colony of trees, then back onto the expressway. Unable to find a place where they could be at ease. About thirty minutes pass as she travels further south away from the city.

"Stop. Park."

"What?" She looks in the rearview mirror. "Here? There's nothing but forest preserves for miles?"

"This place is as good as any."

"It's the fucking broad daylight and—"

His finger stops her lips. "Be silent!"

A rush of anger snaps forth as she bites the finger pressed near her face. But he doesn't flinch. If anything, he looks more aroused. Tiana steps on the brake, and the car comes to a screeching stop on the shoulder of the road. She grips the wheels nervously. Visions of him balls deep in her core flash before her eyes.

"What now?"

"Get in the back," Ishtan commands her.

"You're fucking kidding. Not in my corvette?"

"I don't kid."

One glance at his face, and she knows he means every word. She climbs in the back seat. Bounty steals a glimpse of her black lace panties through her skirt. With the whisper of a short incantation, he shrinks down a tiny bit and joins her. It's like watching a lion trying to cram himself in a birdcage, but somehow, he fits.

Without further instruction, his hand goes up to her thighs immediately. But she quickly grabs his hand for him to stop.

Oh God, he knows how to get me. She shuts her eyes as the wetness pools between her legs.

"Look, if we do this, there needs to be an understanding."

His nostrils flare. "Can this wait till after I fuck your tight cunt?"

She rolls her eyes, then hands him a manila folder from her workbag. He sits up in confusion, slowly flipping through the papers, half-assedly roaming over the words. She reclines in the seat, heart-pounding, unsure of what he'll think after reading her proposed contract. Without a word, he tosses it to the car floor. Tiana clicks her tongue in a pathetic attempt to calm her rising irritation.

"You expect me to abide by this?" Bounty chuckles. "I'm no weak-ass lesser demon, I'm an alpha, your mate, your man!" Power ripples through him as his words drive-through her heart and mind.

"I am owned by no one. I'm not some animal, nor am I a demon. You can keep that alpha macho shit to yourself. That's half the reason I'm single, I refuse to submit. I do so at my own volition, not yours. So promise me you'll never force me to do anything outside of my own will. No magic eyes, no magic spells!"

His beast didn't like it.

She's his woman. It's his right to lead. Anything he does to her is for her own good. His beast paces back and forth in irritation, unwilling to submit. A smug look creeps over Bounty's face as he sits back, pondering her list of demands.

"You want me to be your bitch?"

A shiver racks through Tiana. The thought of dominating him makes her lady parts sing. She can't even hide her excitement as her eyes dilate and sweaty palms grip the back seat. Bounty's beast whines, half fearful of his tiny little mate.

By the Gods, she really means it. Bounty's eyes widen as he watches the perverted gleam in her eyes.

Tiana can sense his discomfort, so she clarifies her desire for him to better understand. "I'll admit that you're a pretty good lay." Bounty's chest puffs out as the words inflate his ego even more. "But... if I do this with you, I need my safety net. If you can go against your nature and submit, that shows me I can be safe with you.... I guess."

Even she knew half of that is complete bullshit. The perverted part of her brain just really wants to tame him. Bounty looks at her begrudgingly, unhappy to say the least.

"As you stated, it is against my nature." he pauses.

Tiana sits forward, licking her lips in anticipation.

"You will have to agree to a switch." He folds his massive arms and looks down at her scrunched-up chocolate face, morphing from pouting to anger then back to sad.

By the gods, this woman has some faces.

Before she can even accept his terms, she finds herself once again spread out under his perusal.

"Didn't we just talk about this?"

"Yes, ma'am. Now order me to fuck you."

"That's not how it wor...."

Her words die off as his fingers find her wet pussy. His thick digits fumble and twirl her sticky entrance. He slowly retracts his hand, smelling and licking his fingers. "Fuck—" Tiana pants out, her breaths becoming raspy as Bounty sucks every drop of her dew from his hand.

He brings his lips to hers, wanting her to taste herself off his tongue. She eagerly kisses him. She instinctively parts her thighs for more touching. Bounty opens her thighs wider and pulls her panties to the side.

He frowns at the black lace barrier between him and his prize. "This is a nuisance," he grumbles. Quickly burying his face between Tiana's puffy wet lips, he squeezes and sucks her swollen clit. She holds onto the back of the seat and tries to stabilize herself against the window of the door. Cars speed past outside; a truck rolls by so close Tiana thinks maybe this isn't the smartest of ideas.

"We could go get a room in a hotel?"

"No."

He delves deeper; tongue-fucking her into silence. His tongue reaches all the way to her cervix. Bounty licks frantically, wanting to leave his mark on every wall.

Several orgasms later, Tiana's skirt is around her neck, breasts pressed against the window as he grinds against her. His cock is thrust deep inside her. The tip of her womb poked with each hard prod. Tiana reaches down between her legs, gripping his heavy sac. His beast howls his elation as they both find their release.

It was a quiet drive back to the city. Tiana is not quite sure how to go about all of this. She likes to keep her social interactions to a minimum, and small talk with a demon was definitely out of her league. She squints at him, unsure if her question should be asked.

"Do you go back and forth, I mean, from here to hell?"

He looks her way, then shakes his head. "You're not ready for that answer."

Before she can reply, Bounty vanishes from her car.

****

Tiana thinks it best to keep her demon boy-toy to herself. Even as she finds herself getting chewed out over text:

Yoyo: You and Tao are really funny acting these days. It's been damn near two weeks, and I haven't seen you guys since–Heffa, refund me my friendship!

Tiana: Nooooo. Don't throw me away!!! Are you home? I'm headed over now.

****

Yolanda watches excitedly as Tiana marches up the steps to her apartment. Her smile widens as they embrace. Tiana feels Yolanda's fresh aura envelop her, squeezing tighter, hoping to absorb some of her positive vibes.

Yolanda is seeing a new guy, and she is eager to share the news. "So, there's this guy," Yolanda begins. "He works as a day trader, by the way. He used to be a car sales associate in Orland, making a thousand dollars every week. Now he makes that in about an hour. Isn't that something?"

"Yeah, it definitely betters Jamal from last year, the street pharmacists."

"Yeah, baby!" Yolanda laughs, slapping the table with mirth. After a beat, Yolanda looks at her sideways and asks, "So, are you ready to spill the tea?"

Tiana squirms in her seat. "What do you mean?" She takes a sip from her orange juice, looking at Yolanda over the tip of her glass.

Damn, she figures out everything. Yolanda always has a way of knowing things without actually knowing things.

"So who's been knocking the dust off your box?" Yolanda asks. "Spill it, I want the deets!"

Tiana grins, placing her glass on the table, and closes her eyes. "Tao told you."

"Uh-uh, you bet he did."

"I'm firing him right now, and it's your fault."

"Nobody gets fired, Titi. Fess up, come on."

But where does she start? Tiana thinks. Should she begin with the sex his size both up here and down there? The thought of it makes her shiver and leaves her tingling between her thighs.

Nope, Titi, that's done. He vanishes, and we haven't heard from him since.

Yolanda shrieks and slaps the table. "I was only playing. O-M-G, you whore, you really did let him hit!"

Tiana flushes as she bites her lower lip. There is no hiding something like this. She can't hide who Ishtan Rustivich—or Bounty, whatever his name is—for long. But it's not just the effect he has over her. Just thinking about him is enough to piss her off, while making her smile from ear to ear.

Yolanda keeps laughing, wanting to know all about Tiana's mystery guy.

"So, what exactly did Tao tell you?"

"Not much," says Yolanda. "You know how cryptic Tao can be. Just that he's big, like, a really big guy. And that he's seen him and you around a few times, and that he picks you up from work—"

Tiana glares at her. "Picks me from work? What the hell, no, he doesn't, and no, Tao didn't tell you that!"

Yolanda giggles. "Nah, I'm just messing with you. I made that up. But come on, what is he picking you up? It ain't a bad thing, is it? Now tell me—" Her voice drops to a whisper. "How is he down below? Is he as big as he is tall?"

Tiana softly laughs. "Let's just say he stretches me past my limits."

Yolanda replies with a moony look in her eyes, "What I'd give to have a man fuck my shit up with something like that. I'm happy for you, Titi, especially after Raj."

Tiana holds her hand up, mimicking Raj's short penis size. Both snort in laughter. Tiana's phone rings. She glances down. Tao is calling.

"Tao?"

"Inyoku is here."

"Whoa, hey, that's great." Tiana smiles wearily.

"And she'd like to meet you again. Dinner? Later tonight, tomorrow, whenever?"

Tiana notes the tightness in his voice. "Tao, is everything okay?"

"Why, yes? Everything's great, what do you say?" he asks.

She confirms for tomorrow. Worry fills her mind as she ends the call with Tao. Yolanda stares at her, a questioning expression on her face.

"What was that about? Is Tao alright?"

Tiana exhales. "I think Tao might be in trouble, but I'm not sure at this stage."

"Trouble? From who?" Yolanda sits up, fear causing her voice to come out with more of an edge.

"His past... that Yakuza shit?"

"No, not the Yakuza. He cut ties with all that." *Something much worse.* "I think maybe he's sick with something."

"He did look kind of fucked up last time I saw him."

Tiana looks lost for a moment. So many things she is unable to tell her best friend these days.

Yolanda gets up and announces, "While you're here, let me wash and clip your ends."

13

Chapter Thirteen

Tiana walks into Ramsey's Steak Bistro alone wearing a purple and brown sweater fitted ripped jeans, and some sneakers. She is grateful that Tao told her tonight would be casual. No need to throw on a dress. By the large round wall clock hanging on the wall inside Ramsey's, it's a quarter past seven. Beige walls and polished Rustic mahogany make up the interior decor, arches leading from one room to the other in the large place. Tiana has never been here, but she's been dying to try it from reading all the foodie reviews. Most of the tables are taken already.

That should be a good sign; she can't attack us with such a large crowd.

Tao catches sight of Tiana and waves her over. At first sight, Tiana notices Tao's color has improved. But his cheeks still look sunken, and his shoulders gaunt and lean. Inyoku's dress catches her attention; a kimono-style flowered dress accentuates her straight, narrow form, her long inky hair held in place by diamond-studded pins.

Inyoku smiles awkwardly. Tiana stops in her tracks, attempting to suppress the fear of once again seeing Inyoku's monstrous form. She barely just misses a server carrying a large tray of food when she walks toward the table again.

Unlike in Berlin, there's no monstrous fox demon with its long sinister tails. Tina exhales, praying the dinner will end without Inyoku switching forms.

Inyoku steps forward to Tiana, placing air kisses on both sides of her cheeks.

"I regret never having enough time to be friends with you, Tiana,"

"Oh, it's quite alright, you're a busy woman." Tiana waves her hand dismissively. Tao clears his throat. As Inyoku's eyes snap his way, Tiana looks around the room for the nearest exit.

"Family is the most important. Our family resides in Japan, our culture believes in staying close knit," Inyoku chips in.

Tiana nods. "Yes, family is important. It makes sense that you're often away."

Thankfully, a server appears beside Inyoku, interrupting the awkwardness. He asks what they want to eat. Inyoku takes the big menu book and peers at it. Tiana glances at Tao and sees there's a film of perspiration on Tao's forehead. He wears a red and blue checkered flannel shirt, buttoned to his neck and tucked tight into his jeans.

It's been around thirty degrees all day; now, but feels colder than that. Tiana frowns and starts to ask Tao if he is feeling sick when Inyoku announces out loud: "Fish & chips." The server turns his bearded face to Tiana. "And you, my lady?"

Tiana takes a brief glance through the menu and says, "I'll take the veal shank and sweetbreads."

Tao says he'll eat what Inyoku's having. The server leaves, and the dry conversation resumes. As Inyoku holds the wine menu, Tiana notices an engagement ring; she looks at Tao, who smiles.

"I have an announcement to make," Tao exclaims while leaning forward towards Tiana. Inyoku grins from ear to ear. "I proposed to Inyoku. You know, to make it more official, more than just a family promise. I wanted to solidify our bond with a ring."

"We both prefer privacy, so why make it public?" Inyoku cut in. "You know, social media has a way of overdoing things."

Tiana smiles weakly, her appetite fading as dread for her friend's sets in.

"Yeah, we are having the wedding in Japan. And we want you to come," says Tao.

Inyoku announces that she wants Tiana to be one of her bridesmaids. "It's only appropriate. Since you are like a sister to Tao that also makes you family in my eyes." Inyoku giggles.

Tiana's smile falters as darkness begins to creep over Inyoku. Her eyes begin to morph, stretching and slanting across her face. Her ears elongate and sprout thick red fur. As they shift from the side by her neck to the top of her head. Her nose and mouth now have a more canine appearance, sharp fangs and all. Tiana avoids looking into her glowing green jade eyes.

The sound of someone approaching offers Tiana a chance to look away. Their orders arrive on trays carried on massive trays by two servers. Tao begins tossing his chopped fish around the plate with his fork, his forehead shiny with sweat. He looks as if he is slowly wasting away.

Fuck, she's sucking his life force. Tiana loses her appetite instantly.

Inyoku eats her food with slow gusto, chewing deliberately on each piece. Her monstrous eyes glare at Tao as she struggles to get the prongs of his fork into fish. With a bit more effort, he shoves it into his mouth and slowly starts to chew. His every movement looks mechanical, like Inyoku has him tethered to a puppet's string.

Tiana braces herself and looks toward Inyoku. "Do you guys have a date set?"

"Yes," Inyoku replies, face glowing with mock happiness.

Tiana glances at Tao, unable to swallow the wad of meat in her mouth. She pushes it to the side of her cheek as she looks worriedly at her friend. "Tao?" Tiana calls.

"Huh?" He looks around the table as if he's just come down from a dream. Tiana asks her question again. "Oh, yeah. In a month," he replies dryly.

"I'll de-clutter our schedules before then we can maximize our time in Japan."

He looks at Inyoku; his Adam's apple bobs up and down as he licks dry, peeling lips.

Inyoku smiles and continues eating her food. The rest of the dinner flows by like a silent movie; Inyoku acquaints Tiana with random facts about Japan, her family business, and a little about Tao's father's side, too. Tao remains passive and silent, only replying when needed.

I have to get him away from Inyoku.

Tiana now understands the aberrations she sees, the humans who aren't exactly what they seem. She knows Inyoku is a demon; from her research last night, she must be similar to a nine-tailed fox.

The tails are long and covered in scales and fur, and each rises into the air from under her dress, crawling all over Tao as she silently eats.

The dinner ends without incident. Tiana feels a greater resolve to save her friend. Tiana promises to drop by Tao's place before Inyoku leaves Chicago again. With a wave, Tiana heads for the parking lot towards her car, then abruptly turns around. "Don't forget Tao, I'll need that doctor's note saying you are healthy enough to attend work this week. I'm still worried about your condition!"

Tao looks at her, confused. Unsure of what she means. Tiana watches for Inyoku's reaction. Her phony, friendly face is now upturned in a scowl.

Take that bitch. I'm not giving you Tao without a fight.

The trip back home takes less than ten minutes. Tiana prances through her condo door, running straight into Bounty, Ishtan Rustivich's hard chest. His hands are deep in the pocket of his corduroy pants, his lips wrinkled in a nasty snarl. The dim lights from the foyer cast shadows on rugged features. Tiana opens her mouth but says nothing. She glances at him again before firmly shutting her door. Ishtan waits for her to turn around, then tugs at her clothes with his massive hands.

"Wait—"

"No, I need you now," he growls.

His mouth smashes against hers, swallowing her breath. He rips her sweater off her body and rubs on her chocolate skin as he cups her breasts. He finds her stiff chocolate nipples with perception squeezing and twisting them hard; Tiana loses her resolve to be the dominant, as her body naturally submits. With one quick movement, Tiana finds herself in his arms. He takes no time to reach her bedroom. His lips fall to her breasts as his full lips suckle her nipples. Ishtan slowly lowers her from his arms, then gently pushes her onto her knees. His handsome face stares down at her as he unbuckles his pants and reaches inside.

Tiana protests, "You can't come into my—*humph!*"

Bounty rams his cock into her mouth with great force. Her eyes bulged from the sudden surprise. "Suck me!" he growls. Tiana's head moves back and forth in submission as she gulps on Bounty's enormous shaft.

"Look at me!" he commands. So she does. He pulls out of her mouth, his penis dripping with drool. "Say my name!"

She looks up at him, "Ishtan—"

"And to whom do you belong!"

"Myself—" she coughs.

Her fiery spark snaps back to life, ignited by her defiance. Bounty smirks and rubs his hands together, happy her dominant nature has finally reared its head.

"I'm going to claim you tonight. I'm not waiting any longer. So get your juicy ass up in that bed."

Tiana takes his hand and stands, seductively placing her knees on the bed while crawling on all fours.

"I'm fucking you in the ass tonight!"

Tiana winces at the thought of his cock up her tight, forbidden hole.

Shit, oh no, there's no way he'll fit.

His words cause her to pause. Unconsciously, her hands move to her butt, as if that would be enough to protect her ass from his plundering penis.

"I think not, no, you are not doing that to me," she squeals.

"I am. You will love it."

"Fuck you! I won't." She runs for the bed, towards the door. She turns around and Bounty is standing in front of her. Her lips drop open, terror grips her throat. She gasps, "No, you're too big—!"

"Yes, Tiana. This is the way I must claim you." He rumbles. "I'm fucking you in every one of your holes. Don't resist this."

"Not in my asshole; you're too damn big!" she roars at him.

Ishtan removes his other clothing, his white shirt first, then his trousers. His cock is at least fourteen inches or longer—it's thick with numerous veins standing, pointing towards her. It has an even width from the base where rings of fine hair form a small forest. Tiana bites her lips at the sight of his cock. There is no escaping that pole; Ishtan will only keep coming after her, no matter where she goes.

Nope, can't do it.

She bolts out the bedroom door into the living room. But Bounty is already there, standing next to the couch.

"Did you just walk through the wall? How did you do that?"

"I won't be much of a demon if I couldn't," he chuckles. "Turn around, Tiana."

"What?" she whispers as a shiver makes its way down her spine.

"TURN AROUND," he demands.

Tiana grumbles with a moan, but she obeys, spinning. She feels him coming behind her. His woody smell fills her nose. Her mind revolts against the submission, but her body instinctively reacts as she falls to her knees and points her ass in the air, exposing herself to him.

Oh God, I'm going to hell for sure now. I want him to fuck me senseless.

Trembles course through her body. The thought of his cock ravaging her tight holes frightens and excites her. Her pussy drips in anticipation.

Bounty grips her shoulder, gently, passionately kissing her neck. She closes her eyes, intoxicated by his touch.

Fuck, I can't believe I'm doing this.

He gets on his knees behind Tiana, gently spreading her ass

cheeks wide. Tiana jerks when she feels something crawl across its rim: Bounty's tongues, her tight entrance, slathering it with spit to help him enter with ease. Her core clenches with every flick of his rough-textured tongue.

She feels a tingling sensation dragging its way right up her spine. *Yes!*

Bounty toots her up higher, giving her cunt the same deep kiss, refusing to stop until her body is boneless and pliant. He takes her back to the bed and dips his tongue in her asshole again before placing the head at the rim of her hole. Tiana's breath catches in her throat.

"Oh—" she reaches back and tries to stop him. But he grabs her hand and pushes in. She gnashes her teeth as the fiery bite begins.

"Don't hold your breath, Tiana. Relax and let me in." Bounty's cock pushes in further, the mushroom tip finally passing through the first sphincter.

I feel so full. It's burning.

Tiana's feet jerks up as she pounds on the bed. With one hard thrust, he pushes the rest in. After a few short pumps, Tiana feels her asshole lubricate itself. She can feel an orgasm building.

"Yes, fuck me, fuck me!" she pleads, as his cock pulls out and plunges back into her hole.

"Do you accept my claim?" he blows on her neck. Her chest tightens in anticipation. She moans and arches her back. Her fingers furiously flick her clit in rhythm with his every thrust.

"Answer me, woman, do you accept my claim?"

She whimpers when Bounty pulls out, refusing to please her until she replies to his claim.

"Just fuck me, Bounty; yes, I accept whatever you claim, just keep pumping."

His beast roars in elation, happy to hear his mate accept. He returns to pumping deeply, plunging into her tight hole repeatedly. Bounty can to his power flowing, building up preparing for the claim. With one powerful thrust, he bites her with his beast teeth, sinking deep into her shoulder blade, leaving a deep permanent mark.

Tiana screams as her anal orgasm clamps down, greedily sucking his seed. "Bounty, I can't keep going!"

"We've only just begun."

He pulls out of her ass with a wet pop and shoves it straight into her. Tiana's body spasms, squirting juice on the bed. Bounty groans as he begins to tremble, his orgasm starts to build. Tiana shudders, afraid of once again coming face to face with his true form. His strong hands fall to the sides of her head as he pistons his hips toward her. She wraps her thick thighs around his waist, meeting each thrust he gives. His glowing green eyes look deep into hers as she stares lovingly back at him.

She can feel his body tensing his abs, contracting tighter with every pump. A deep growl rumbles from his chest as he pushes his cock deeper inside her and releases the rest of his powerful seed.

Tiana feels the warmth of his splatter all over her inner walls, causing her to reach her orgasm, too. Ishtan slowly retreats from her sheath and steps away from the bed. His inner beast howls triumphantly as he stands there staring at his beast, seed dripping out of her.

Tiana catches the fluid between her fingers. It is not like any human cum she had ever seen. It's sticky, thick, and golden. She brings her finger to her nose. It smells like him.

"Why is this cum different?"

He sits beside her and stares silently. "That is my beast seed; it is laced with my power."

"Why me?" Tiana still looks at the cum on her fingers, in awe of the shimmering swirls of energy dancing through the substance.

"I'm still finding out."

Tiana sits up. "Ishtan, I need your help."

Bounty looks at her sharply, his green eyes flashing.

"Er... you're not going to like this," she mumbles.

"Tell me."

She breathes in and out. She tells Bounty about Tao. Bounty groans first, a streak of jealousy rising in his face.

"I need help. His fiancée is a demon — ,"

"No."

Bounty gets off the bed and begins to put back on his clothes.

"No, what? What do you mean?"

"I know what you want."

"We need to help him; this is what you do right. You hunt down rogue demons. She's killing Tao. Please, you've gotta help him."

"No."

Tiana shakes her head. "You're still mad about that day. I told you he's only my assistant, but he's also my friend. Do you even understand friendship? Because it seems like all you know how to do is to pop up, fuck, and boom, you're gone again?"

Ishtan says nothing. He grabs his coat and walks to the door. Tiana smirks derisively. "Oh, you use the door after all?"

"I will not help your friend."

She frowns. "You know what? Fuck you!"

"You dare to ask when his scent still lingers on you?"

His lips wrinkle in what Tiana thinks may have been an attempt to sneer or to taunt her. She rolls her eyes and storms to the bathroom. She doesn't hear him leave, but she knows he's already gone. She turns the shower on and the stall quickly fills with steam. She scrubs, vaguely wanting to remove every trace of their lovemaking. She spreads her legs to clean inside her vagina; she discovers there's even more semen.

. *What if I get pregnant... no, we're not even the same species?*

She quickly removes that thought from her mind. The room is a mess; evidence of their passion can be found everywhere. She walks to the bed, rips off the sheets and grabs a comforter from the closet before exhaustion forces her to lie down.

14

⟨∞⟩

Chapter Fourteen

The next day is even colder. The forecaster already warned about a winter weather advisory that would last all morning. Tiana sips her spice cider as she lays several outfits on the bed. Her usual attire, a heather grey dress suit with fitted slacks, just isn't the vibe she is going for today. She loathes formal and dress attire. She's always been a tomboy at heart. Besides, the suit is a red jumper made of thick wool material.

This would shield me from the biting winds. If it wasn't for this damn fur-ringed collar.

The first time she wore it to the office, Christy asked her if she was experiencing a midlife crisis.

Is it really that bad?

She hadn't worn the jumpsuit to the office since then. But today felt different. Today, Tiana was on a mission. She intended to save Tao's life.

She closed her eyes.

Meanie- Mineee- Moe...

Her finger landed on the red jumper.

*****

There are eight conference rooms in the CHD Building downtown, half of them always occupied at any point in time. When Tiana couldn't find Tao in her outer offices, she began to hunt for him from room to room. Christy hasn't seen him, neither has Topper nor the front guard.

She heads down to the library where Tao often spends most of his time researching. The library is full today, with interns and grads working busily on their thesis. Theresa May, the head librarian, sits solving crossword puzzles in the Chicago Daily Times, her reading glasses perched on the bridge of her hook nose. Tiana skips down to the lot to check his parking space, but even that's empty.

She sighs, haunted by images of Tao's body sprawled on the floor of his lounge.

"God dammit Tao, I was hoping to get you alone!" Tiana stomps her foot on the frosted pavement. She quickly jumps into her own car at the edge of the lot and sits to think of another course of action.

"Fuuuuck!" she screams while punching the air. *I can't do this alone.*

With a quick prayer of faith, she dials Yolanda. Her friend picks up on the first ring.

"Hey, honey, what's up?"

"Yoyo, I need you."

"Damn... He dumped you?"

Tiana looks at the phone and rolls her eyes. "No. Now stay focused; remember when we took that trip to the bayou, and you slept with the creole girls, man?"

"Oh shit," Yolanda gasps. "Somebody put a hoodoo on you?"

Tiana busts out in a heartfelt laugh. "No, Yoyo, but we might be up against some supernatural shit." She can hear her best friend getting worked up over the phone. "Get over here now!"

She drives over in a hurry, barely parking her corvette before jumping out the driver's side door. Yolanda was already waiting on the stoop, prepping to hear something juicy.

Tiana drags her inside, sits her down and goes over every juicy detail, leaving out the parts about Bounty. Tiana paces her friend's apartment floor, her hand flying around as she acts out specific parts. Yolanda sits back in total shock, unprepared for the sort of tea Tiana is pouring. When Tiana finishes telling her tale, she slumps down into her seat.

Yolanda chuckles softly, unsure what to make of everything she just heard.

"How do you expect to handle this Tao thing? They obviously love each other."

"I don't think Taos is in love. Maybe he's hypnotized or something," Tiana says, "And besides, Inyoku can't possibly love him, she's a creature—"

"You don't know that; her ass is always far away in Japan. How can you tell?"

"She's killing him, Yoyo somehow some way I know it."

"How do you expect to stop something like that?" Yolanda is in her face, brows raised, waiting for Tiana to reply. "Titi?"

"Let's just say I may have a way to get Tao out."

Yolanda sighs, perturbed by Tiana's accusations. She isn't one to shy away from the occult. She believes in the powers that be. *Could this really be happening?* Yolanda pours them both more orange juice, adding a bit of rosemary to bust the clarity of Tiana's mind.

Tiana doesn't touch her juice. Visions of Tao dying keep replaying over and over in her mind. If not for Berlin, this curse would have never happened. She wouldn't be aware of demons or fae. All this was best left unknown. Tiana glances over at Yolanda. Her friend glows with generous amounts of golden vibes. Even her scent smells like sunshine and flowers.

"You have such a *pure soul*," Tiana whispers, leaning over to grasp Yolanda's hand. Yolanda squeezes her hand back before taking another sip from her glass. With a shrug, she picks up the remote control and turns on the news.

"Chicago should expect a tax increase," says the reporter. Then the screen switches to a report about several crime scenes. "The mummified remains of two male bodies, the sixth occurrence of its kind."

Tiana gasps. She sits up and snatches the remote from Yoyo, turns up the volume.

"Detectives are on the case now," *says the reporter*, "but the preliminary report says the victims may have strangled; similar marks on their necks are believed to be associated with other killings in Berlin, San Francisco, and *several areas* on the *south side of Chicago.*"

The camera zooms into the face of a handsome black guy. There is a brief interview where the Detective speaks about the crime. Then the handsome reporter gestures at the park behind him and says: *"We may very well have a serial killer on our hands until this person is caught; folks should be vigilant when walking in the dark secluded places. The police are adding more patrols to areas that fit the killers M.O. Back to you, John."*

"Oh, he's sexy," Yolanda swoons. She waits for Tiana's reaction to the hot guy, but Tiana looks disturbed. "You okay, Titi?"

Tiana sits back, telling herself it's not possible.

No, it can't—but can it? Berlin, San Francisco, and now here... Could the killer be Inyoku or some other demon? I have to contact Bounty. He's the only one that can tell me for sure.

"Titi, talk to me. Tell me what you're thinking?"

"You've gotta help me, Yolanda. Tao is in danger!"

"I will help you on one condition. I do the talking; I know I don't know her that well, but you're way too deep in your feelings to handle this, Okay? I know you're his boss, but Tao may be deeper into this with Inyoku. After all, he proposed—"

"I think it's only because she made him!"

"Wait; is whatever she is like a witch or something? I thought you said she was some kind of shifter?"

Yolanda runs to her cabinet and grabs herbs, crystals, and sage.

"She's way *worse*. If we don't stop her, she's going to kill him."

Yolanda frowns. "This is why Tao's been looking all sickly..."

Tiana nods as she walks to the sink and rinses their cups.

"What the fuck is she doing to him?"

Tiana says softly, eyes misting softly with tears. "I don't know."

"I guess we better hurry and call him over," says Yolanda. She grabs a small pocket bible and her blessing oil from atop the fridge. Tiana looks at her, puzzled.

"When we don't know what we're up against, a little Jesus never hurts."

15

Chapter Fifteen

Detective Terrance Slaton left the Forensic Pathologist with more questions than answers. The report from the coroner was still clenched tight in his hand. He read it over one last time, then put it away. Captain Wheeler poked his head through the open door. "What does it say?"

"Nothing. I'm back to square one." Terrance throws his hands up in exasperation.

Wheeler purses his thick lips. He pushes the door wider, allowing his protruding belly a bit more room. He picks up the autopsy report and reads over the contents.

"The bodies look like they were microwaved and dropped in the park. And the mark on the neck isn't from strangulation by any known weapon either. "

"So how did they die?"

Terrance says, "Beats me. The cause of death is unknown. They just cooked, like someone stuck a straw in them and sucked the life from them. It's some bizarre shit."

"No leads?"

"I received an email from some English guy in the FBI. Some

similar things have been happening overseas, but not quite like this," says Terrance.

"Well, son, whenever you're done, come by my office. There are a few cases I want your input on before we close them out." With a stiff nod, Captain Wheeler walks out, leaving Terrance to his task. Detective Slaton had worked on some weird cases in the past, but this one tops them all. He reluctantly files the autopsy report when his phone begins to ring.

"Hello."

"Detective Terrance?"

"Yeah—"

It's the forensic pathologist. "You will not believe this, but the bodies are missing... again."

"What the fuck?" The Detective slaps the table, hurries to grab his coat and rushes out the door.

It takes all of five minutes for Detective Terrance to get there. He finds everything the pathologist said to be true: the bodies are missing. *Poof.* Just like the last three. The cops on the scene stand around, stunned by the strange event that keeps happening.

The pathologist is a balding man, hunched back with sagging skin. He trembles as he takes off his glasses to check the compartment where the bodies were. He stammers, "I, I, I don't know how, or what keeps happening. The bodies were just here minutes ago, and I came back to check, and they are gone."

"Why did you come back here to check?" Terrance asks him.

"Maybe I missed some details. I wanted to be sure so—"

Terrance walks away, peering at the cameras in the corners of the wall. He points to them and directs two cops to get the tapes.

"We purposely tripled the manpower, placing cops at every door."

The pathologist shrugs. "You know where they are. The tapes are upstairs in the security office."

Terrance races up to the office, barges in and requests them. He and two cops sit for thirty minutes looking and searching but find nothing yet again. No one is seen coming into or leaving the facility.

"The tapes for inside the morgue?" he asks.

The security guy pulls up the recordings, and they watch. About ten minutes into the tape, a tall guy enters the frame, looks up at the cameras and walks to the closets. He pulls the first slab and then goes to the exact slab where the other body is and pulls it out.

Then, a bizarre thing happens that drops everyone's jaws.

"Look at the size of that dude—" one cop says.

"How the hell did he get in?" asks another.

The man glances up at the cameras again before touching the first body. The camera suddenly blips, goes off for about five seconds. When the picture comes back, the bodies on the slabs are gone. The man looks up at the cameras again and walks out of the frame.

"Where did he go?" Terrance barks. "Where did he go, what direction is that?"

The pathologist stands behind Terrance. "It doesn't make sense; it's the walls. He went to the walls." Terrance turns his head slowly from the screen.

"The walls? Are you sure about this?"

The pathologist rubs his bald head and nods. As he drives away from the morgue, Terrance ponders what he saw on the tapes.

This shit keeps getting weirder and weirder.

****

Tiana thinks it best for Tao to meet her at Yolanda's place. That way, Inyoku is less likely to come along. About twenty minutes later, Tao's black Camaro pulls up to the Yolanda building. He enters the apartment and into the embrace of both his friends. He looks from Tiana to Yolanda, then he drops himself on the nearest couch wearily. He rubs his face, sighs. Tiana and Yolanda sit on both sides of him. A bible in Tiana's hand, Crystals in Yolanda's.

Tiana touches his hand. "Tao?"

"Why does this feel like such a type of intervention?" he looks at her.

Tiana shoots him a weak smile. "There's something I want to tell you—"

"I know, alright. I know what you want to say. I'm gonna see a doctor tomorrow; I already told her." He gestures at Yolanda.

Tiana glares at Yolanda. "The fuck, Yoyo. You talked to him already?"

Yolanda's face breaks in apology. Tiana shakes her head. She holds Tao's hand firmly. "Okay, Tao. Listen to me. What I'm about to tell you will surprise you, and it should. It's about Inyoku."

Some light enters Tao's otherwise dull eyes. Those once bright eyes have lost most of their luster. Tiana stares at him, watching closely for the faintest flicker of green.

Is it even possible to become one of them?

His black eyes hold Tiana's. The smell of sickness and bitterness wafts from him.

"Are you sure you want to marry her?"

Tao looks at Yolanda. He smiles. "What do you mean?"

Yolanda cuts in, "What Titi means is, are you marrying Inyoku because you want to marry Inyoku, or are you doing this out of duty, you know tradition and shit?"

Tiana rolls her eyes at Yolanda. "Yoyo, you just repeated what I just said."

"Uh-uh. With a different tone."

Tiana pulls Tao's hand. She says, "Look at me."

He looks at her.

"Don't marry her. Don't marry Inyoku. She's not good for you; you will never be happy with her. She's, she's..." Tiana exhales. "I mean, look at you, Tao. you've lost so much weight; she's killing you."

"You think Inyoku is making me sick?" he questions.

Tiana nods.

Yolanda's mouth drops open. She wrings her hands between her thighs. Tiana knows Yoyo is bracing herself now for Tao's response, but it's done. There's no going back. Tao's forehead is furrowed in deep thought.

"How do you know this?"

Tiana and Yolanda share a stare again. Tao turns his head to Yolanda. She gives him a trapped look.

"I guess you are just gonna trust us on this," Yolanda says.

Tiana rubs his back. "We are ladies. It's a girl code type of thing. Plus, you're like my brother, I want only the best for you, and whenever I see you with her, it always looks so forced."

The aura in the room shifted. Tiana scooches away as she feels it coming. Yolanda grips the crystal necklace hanging from her neck.

Tao raises his hands in defense. "I know I've been kind of down lately. I haven't been eating well, sleeping well. And I've been training hard for my grading coming up next week. I don't think Inyoku is why I'm not well—"

"At least, now you agree you aren't healthy," Yolanda interjects.

Tiana asks Tao what Inyoku thinks about his present wellbeing. Tao shrugs, purses his lips, searching for a reply. He looks at Tiana and sighs.

"Yeah, that's what I thought," says Tiana. "I know Inyoku hasn't said anything about it; at the dinner, she could have, but she didn't. She's pretending you are alright when you're not. Can't you see Tao? She's not saying anything because she's doing it to you—"

"But how?" he asks vehemently.

"I don't know."

"You don't know, or you won't tell me!" Tao shouts. "Tell me how and what she's doing?"

"I can't, Tao. But one thing I know for sure is that I get horrible vibes from her."

Tao's face remains stoic. The hard edges make it difficult to read him physically, but Tiana can sense his distress. For the first time since she's known Tao, he looks helpless.

Come on, Tao, I know you know the truth.

Tao knows, but the truth is too painful. Yolanda looks at Tiana with a heartbroken expression on her face.

"What are you going to do?" Tiana questions...

Tao buries his face in his palm and shakes his head. Tiana and Yolanda glance at each other over Tao's back, worried.

"You know you can always call the wedding off until you sort things out with her, you know?" Yolanda suggests.

Tiana adds, "Yeah, do yourself that favor."

"I can't, I can't—"

"Yes, you can," Tiana says. "You fucking can."

Tao raises his head. His eyes are bloodshot. "I mean, I can't marry her."

Tiana feels her heart jump. She sees it now; Tao's anxiety is not only about his deteriorating body. He simply doesn't love Inyoku anymore.

"You don't love her, do you?"

He shakes his head.

"You know what—" Yolanda jumps from the couch. She goes to her small collection of wine, gets three glasses. "We can't do this shit sober, I'm not good with heartbreak."

She hands Tao a bottle of fruity wine and he asks if she has something stronger.

"I got brandy.... And a few joints. Take your pick."

Tao downs three glasses of Brandy and even takes a few puffs of the joint. Tiana smiles when she hears the husky rasp of his soft laugh. Even his scent changed. It no longer smells bitter. When all three of them are buzzed, they sit around and begin to deliberate.

"I have never had to do this before. It's gonna hurt her. And our families too. You know those bastards disowned me when I was nothing but a small boy. I just wanted my mother to be vindicated, ya know? I wanted to make her proud—"

"Yeah, families, fuck um, I don't even talk to mine," Yolanda scoffs.

Tiana shouts, "Since you're not close to your father's side. There's nothing to lose right?"

Tao sits in silence, thinking over her words. "Damn, you're right; after he and my mother divorced, I had always just wanted to keep some of my Japanese pride. As the firstborn Son of the Ikeda's, I just thought it was expected of me."

"Well, he cut ties with you, so you shouldn't be obligated to save face for a family that means you no good."

Tiana holds her glass and yells, "Salud!"

Tao shrugs and leans back on the sofa, his cup lifted in his outstretched hand, waiting for it to be filled again. Yolanda pours everyone some more brandy and Tiana puffs on another blunt.

16

Chapter Sixteen

Bounty stands at the top of the Transatlantic Bank building; the vents beside him are filled with pigeons that scatter into the air as he closes in. The stink of pigeon shit and rusted metal fills the air. Eighty feet below, Bounty watches as a man wearing an off-white fedora hat and blazer steps out of a black Rolls Royce. He enters the building. A few minutes later, a woman exits her car and does the same. Bounty walks through the flock of pigeons and they scatter in a spray of wings and coos.

He goes down the seldom-used fire escape and finds a well-lit corridor with office doors on both sides. One of them must belong to the woman from earlier. Her scent is saturated here. By the time Bounty walks halfway down the corridor, the man in the off-white blazer comes around the corner carrying a black briefcase.

Bounty quickly enters an empty office and chants a short spell to conceal himself in the shadows. The man stops at the door, knocks, waits for a response—the door cracks. The woman is there. She smiles, opening the door wider to let the man in. Down the hall, Ishtan opens his own door and listens.

Inside the office room, four doors away, the man in the off-white blazer puts his briefcase on the floor beside the woman's desk. He casually removes his hat and places it on his knees. Bounty smirks.

Oh, this one's a looker.

He's handsome. They are always handsome. Demons are vain in that way. They always set out to appeal to their prey's most basic instinct. And for a mortal, that would be sex. Bounty can't hear the woman talking.

The woman says, "Now, Mr. Jenkins, like I told you earlier, your credit is low, but I'm going to speak with the manager personally. I'll hear what he says, and then we take it from there."

"Fair enough."

"Good. Would there be anything else?" she asks.

The man says, "If it's not too early in the day for a break, I'd like to do that with you."

"What?"

"You heard me."

"Mr. Jenkins." She smiles. "I can't do that."

The woman folds her hands on the table among the arranged files. Her gold wedding ring glints. Jenkins sees it, and smiles. "I know. You're married, but it doesn't matter; there's nothing wrong with having a little break with a friend." He gets up and looks at the door. The woman's smile quickly vanishes from her face. Jenkins goes to the door and locks it.

"I am gonna fuck you on this table."

Her hand drifts over to the telephone on the desk, freezing halfway as the demon locks her in stasis. She trembles, her breasts bouncing with every panting breath. Her terrified eyes follow him as he moves around the room.

"All I wanted to do was fuck you and eat your breasts—" He touches her pretty face with steaming fingertips. "Maybe even chew off your lips, nose, and down there I'll—"

He stops short, startled by a low growl. He looks back. Standing in the corner of the room is a very tall man; his eyes are flaming green orbs, long hands tipped with massive black claws. His lips are pulled back, revealing super sharp fangs.

"Bounty," He-man hisses.

Bounty's voice sounds like crushing gravel, "Get away from her now."

"You are early this time, Bounty. You want to join in the fun?"

The man's steamy fingertip singes the woman's cleavage. She cries out as her flesh bubbles and boils. Her terror triples as she looks from one man to the other. A single tear traces its way down the side of her left eye.

She mumbles, "Please..."

"GET AWAY FROM HER!" Bounty roars.

"And if I don't..... Half-beast?"

"Either way, you die."

"Well, if I must go back to hell. I'd rather burn her alive before I go—" His nails change to steaming blades of water. The man's off-white blazer turns to a black leather vest. His short brown hair turns to long matted Celtic locs, as the Selkie's true nature surfaced.

"Dammit, a Selkie." Bounty growled. These fuckers were ten times worse than Mer-Demons. Selkies are water-based Fae, a hybrid of Fae and seal. The females aren't too bad, but the males are fucking narcissistic sociopaths.

The woman begins to choke from fear, hyperventilating as her neck starts bubbling and reddening where his steam scalding blades touch her tender skin. Bounty's beast growled in annoyance, caught between rescuing the woman from certain death and killing its prey.

The human is the least of his concerns. However, her dark skin and coily hair remind him of Tiana. Bounty shakes the thought of his mate out of his head and makes him gamble. His beast pushes forth as he begins to pace around the room, increasing his massive size double fold.

"You think I care about her? Well, here's what I'd do to you," says Bounty. "After I kill you and send you back to Lucifer, I'll make sure to chant a little spell and keep that pecker of yours stuck here in the human realm. Hell, I might even use it as fishing bait. I hear fish in this realm like little worms."

"It doesn't matter, you fucking mutt. You will always be a half breed. Doesn't matter how many of us you send back down. Brutalize us all you want, but Aurone will never accept you."

Bounty moves across the room and in milliseconds grabs the demon by the neck. His vice-like grip cuts off the Selkie's air.

The demon's hypnosis on the woman is broken; she falls, winded to the floor. Bounty strikes the demon against the wall, and the Selkie begins to shriek as its bone shatters from the impact. But this is no low-level prey. This is a high-caliber demon. The Selkie grabs Bounty's hands, and he bites down on his forearm, secreting scalding acid from his fang-filled jaws. Yet Bounty doesn't feel it. The demon burns Bounty on the neck with his water claws, but Bounty doesn't relent.

"You want to do this?" he asks the demon. "Then let's play nasty!"

Bounty drives his whole arm into the demon's chest. The demon squeals as the blue flames crawl over its body. Bounty pulls his arm out of the demon and lets him go.

The demon falls on his knees, burnt and blackened. Bounty turns when he hears the short scream of the woman behind him. She covers her mouth, struggling not to vomit from the sight and the burnt smell of its fishy flesh.

The Selkie begins to regenerate. The hole in his chest quickly heals. Its body shakes as he gets back on his knees. Bounty knows this spell; it is supposed to make the demon almost indestructible. He becomes as he is in hell, immortal, shrouded in a mortal shell. Bounty chants a quick spell using the words of the ancients, then grabs the Selkie by the neck again before it can go through the full regeneration. With a powerful thrust, the demon's head is pushed into an astral space—and, opening space and time with one hard swipe of his claws; Bounty decapitates the demon, separating its body parts between realms. The headless corpse drops to the door, immobile now that it's been cut off from its immortal master.

Bounty turns to the woman; his eyes are dark pits of blazing fire.

The woman staggers away from him.

She pleads, "Please, don't kill me, please. I, I, I, I have a husband and daughter, a daughter, please."

"She'll live without you; she'll carry on—"

"No, please, please," she sobs.

"It is the strength of your species you carry on, despite tragedy," Bounty insists as he trudges towards the woman. "But your kind weakness you don't know when to shut up."

"I swear I'll tell no one of this, please!"

Bounty looks back at the headless corpse on the floor and sends its partial soul back using Hell's flame. The last shred of it vanishes without a trace.

He turns stiffly back to the woman. "I won't kill you, but I will make you forget." Bounty touches her forehead with the fire of his left forefinger. The woman slumps and falls asleep. She'll awaken with no memory. This entire day will be erased from her mind. Bounty will be far gone by then.

****

Bounty is irritated. Demons and Fae worldwide were getting ridiculously careless. One thing is clear, the water realm demons are standing in resistance. Mer-Demons, now selkies... Bounty was tired. At this point, the only thing he can do is dispose of the bodies before they turned. One bite or scratch and the human would shift the following lunar cycle. The golden rule for all demons lingering in the human realm is either eating your food whole or torching it after you play. Leave too many bodies behind, and the humans start asking questions. Plus, it doesn't help if some of the corpses are reanimated. Bounty thinks Berlin was bad; Chicago was the kicker. With so many rogues running around, he hardly has time for his mate. And that was starting to piss him and his beast off.

Despite Bounty's annoyance, he was getting sloppy, leaving evidence, such as camera recordings of him, in plain sight. Because of it, Detective Terrance Slaton is now looking for a man at least six feet two inches, massive muscular frame, broad-shouldered, probably dirty blonde with square jaws.

Contrary to Captain Wheeler's suggestion, the Detective refuses to declare the man wanted. "We don't want to alert him. He'll run." Wheeler agrees. Detective Slaton is good at his job; he almost always catches his perps. He has the dedication and focus of a sniper, knowing just when and where to pull the trigger.

So, when Detective Slaton sits in front of the monitor waiting for a match on all the cameras in a quarter-mile search, no one questions his actions. Everyone wanted this serial killer taken off the streets, no matter what. The monitor is synced to a network of databases that gets its feed from all cameras in Chicago. The FBI, CIA, and Interpol are all in this arrangement. It took a year and some arm twisting to get the Chicago PD on the network, and so far, Detective Slaton is the only CPD officer to have been able to get five convictions using the new system.

At 1 AM, Detective Slaton's eyes remain bright; sleep for him isn't even an option. He takes a one-minute break to stretch his legs, then comes back with a steaming cup of coffee and stares at the screen unmoving.

He will make a slip.

All perps think they're smarter than everyone else, and that smug confidence is always their downfall. When they begin to fall, they go downhill, rolling to their doom. The image suddenly stops flipping; there is a match. He grins. He sits back and rubs his palms together triumphantly. He picks his cup of coffee and sips. His victory feeling doesn't last, though. He looks closer at the screen, and his jaws slacken. Below the captured face—IMAGE MATCH—proves the most discouraging words: NO DATA.

How the fuck? He chills and tells himself, *Maybe he's an illegal immigrant.* Yet, deep down, Detective Slaton knows better. He jots down the camera's address where the man was spotted and prepares to catch some shut-eye for a few hours before dawn.

17

Chapter Seventeen

Tao's head is pounding. When he left Yolanda's place, his friends were still passed out on the floor. It has been years since they partied that hard. Tao is strict about his martial arts training and the food and substances he consumes, but it was a nice reprieve to just be carefree amongst friends. When Tao finally gets home, he finds it quiet and empty; luckily, his cousins hadn't crashed. He was in no mood to play host.

Tao staggers up to his bedroom. He finds his bed made; the closet sitting open. He checks and sees that his clothes have been arranged. The smell of scallions and soy sauces wafts in. Then he hears the sizzling sound of something frying in the kitchen. Just before he begins to question his sanity, he hears Inyoku call his name. She's standing there naked at the stove, stir-frying some vegetables and rice. She gives him a seductive smile. The rod between his legs stiffens instantly.

She turns to him and says, "A piece of me now, or breakfast first?"

Tao's brain screams, *None of the above*, but his mouth opens and says, "I'd rather eat you—"

He begins to unpack his cock. It dangles before him; from this moment, he seems to feel himself adrift in a dream. Everything gets hazy. Tao looks to his penis and then back to his hands.

Why does it feel like I'm forgetting something?

Inyoku cuts off the stove; Tao looks down, unable to smell the cooking or hear the sizzling sound of frying food. He clenches his hand. He can't feel his extremities. Everything is numb. But he feels Inyoku. He feels his penis inside Inyoku's warm wet walls. He can see that they're on the bed but can't feel it. He knows his waist is moving up and down, yet he isn't pumping. He tries to look around the room, but Inyoku tugs his face back. "Concentrate on me and only me," she demands. Her legs wrap around his lower back, waist bucked up, her core feels wetter and tighter than ever.

"Will you marry me?" she whispers in his ear.

He pumps faster, lost in the pleasure of bliss. "Yes, Inyoku, damn it, yes!"

"Don't ever stop fucking me like this," she whispers on. "Every night, every waking hour, your cock will feed me, Tao—"

She talks and whispers in his ear till her voice becomes an aphrodisiac chant. Tao's mission is to please her, to lick and suck and fill her with seed. Inyoku gets on top of him; her moist sheath swallows his cock whole. She rocks her body to the ethereal song of their lovemaking. The room disappears, the world is gone, but Tao doesn't care. Inyoku's body is his world now, the reason for his existence.

He grabs her waist, bucking her hard from below, screaming from the intensity of the pleasure.

Inyoku looks deep into Tao's eyes and searches for his illicit secrets, ripping his deep fantasy from his mind. She grunts and rolls her eyes.

A threesome—how cliché.

Inyoku makes his fantasy a reality by splitting into two before his eyes. The second Inyoku is slightly different; she appears from the other side of the bed. This one has wide eyes and short hair, just as Tao prefers.

She crawls on the bed and places her pussy over Tao's face, showing him her weeping orchid. Tao licks his lips and dives right in.

Tao is lost in lust. His lips feast on the sweetest ambrosia as the real Inyoku rides him hard, demanding his seed. When sated, the real In-yoku gets up and sits on the corner of the bed, puffing a cigarette, watching as Tao deep strokes the new Inyoku under the sheets.

Tao groggily wakes on the couch in the lounge, his body stiff and weak. His head feels like it's full of static and white noise. Tao staggers to the bathroom and pours water on his face. It helps to make him feel a little better. The fuzziness slowly dissolves as his mind clears.

He hears a melodic voice coming from the adjacent room. He doesn't go to the sound; he knows who it is.

Once again, things go hazy. The feelings of the emotion of love blooms forth. He shakes his head, something isn't right.

Tao lies back down on the couch and tries to sleep off the haze. His mind is full of patchwork-like visions; he can't decipher if they are real memories or just dreams. In one of them, he sees Tiana and Yolanda. Both women are talking, their lips move, but Tao can't hear what they're saying because—the sound of someone singing. Tiana looks frantic, her face full of pain. She screams, but her pleas can't be heard over the singing. It's so loud.

"Listen...." A deep rumbling voice whispers in Tao's ear. The voice contains so much power. It pushes Tao deeper into his dream realm. His mind drops down to the bottom of the strata of sleep and dreams. The lower he descends, the clearer Tiana's voice becomes, the more Inyoku's singing voice fades.

Tiana is asking him, "Do you love her?"

Then Tao sees himself, sitting between the two women, head down, staring at the patch of lonely land between his feet. He hears himself say, "I don't want to marry Inyoku; I don't love her anymore—"

Tao's heart suddenly bubbles with joy, his headache seems to dim, his anxiety lifts. As he experiences a moment of clarity, he knows what has been forgotten.

"You need to tell her," says Tiana.

He watches himself open his mouth to confirm his decision, but something sucks him back from the bottom of that strata to the bed where he wakes, his eyes open and peer into the bewitching gaze of Inyoku.

"You were dreaming, my love. You were thrashing so hard in your sleep. I thought it best to wake you."

"Inyoku?"

"Yes, Tao." She smiles, as she straddles his lap and passionately makes love to him.

Tiana paces Yolanda's living room nonstop, her eyes cast anxiously at her phone. Yolanda peeks through the curtains at the street. Tiana walks over to Yolanda and peers out the curtain too." I didn't even hear Tao leave this morning. Do you think she'll hurt him if he wants out?" Yolanda couldn't give her an answer, at least not one that could calm her friend down.

Tiana's phone rings and they both jump at the unexpected noise. It's an unknown number. Tiana's finger presses the green icon and places the phone to her ear. Bounty's gravelly voice booms through her speaker. "Where are you? I can't sense you?"

She gives a sassy reply, "Oh, I'm busy helping, you know the thing you refused to do—"

Bounty signs off by saying, "I'm coming to you."

Yolanda overhears their conversation and gets excited. "Is that him? The guy Tao told me about?"

"Uh-uh." Her voice cracks with nervousness; he's not the type of partner you introduce to your friends.

Will it be safe to bring him around Yolanda? I didn't even tell him where I was.

Yolanda scurries around the apartment, straightening her crystals, fluffing pillows, and making tea. "He's coming here? I haven't met one of your boyfriends since 2015; this is so exciting!"

Tiana shrugs. Unable to win against her positive spirit.

An hour and a half later, the tea grows cold. Yolanda stopped, checking the window. Bounty is a no-show, and honestly, Tiana is hoping he didn't show. Tiana relaxes after a while, somewhat happy she won't have to explain her ambiguous relationship. The two ladies' curiosities shift back to Tao.

"Have you ever... you know, had feelings for Tao?" Yolanda asks as she clears the table, storing away the leftover snacks. Tiana hesitates and then thinks about how angry Bounty gets about anything regarding Tao.

"Is it that obvious?"

Yolanda giggles and shakes her head. "I wouldn't say obvious, but there's love there; I just never wanted to say it."

"He's a good man, but just not the man for me. Were better off as friends."

Yoyo winks. "So, did you at least taste his fortune cookie?" Tiana slaps her friend on the butt with a disk towel. "No, for real, the most we ever did was a kiss."

"Umm, hum, tell the truth, shame the devil."

Tiana opens her mouth to reply, but her phone begins to ring again. *Incoming call Christy Marlow, Christy sounds frantic; she* asks Tiana if she can transfer research files for a fund bid with WHO. "Christy, it's Sunday Morning."

"Yeah, don't I know? But this thing slipped my mind all week. We still have a window before midnight today. Are you in your apartment, are the files saved to your cloud drive?"

"No, Christy, they're in the office."

"Oh crap, we're screwed."

Tiana sighs and rubs her temples. "I'll go get them from the office. I have my keys with me here."

"Okay, great. You're the best."

"I'll email them to you from there."

The temperature has dropped further since the last weather report. It looks like winter is already here. Tiana drives down lakeshore drive and peers in the rearview mirror. Hope and dread tug at the seams of her thoughts. She parks her car in her assigned spot and walks up to her office, constantly looking over her shoulder for him. By the time she settles and begins to rummage through her computer for the files, the thought of Bounty is a distant thought. She finds the files after looking for fifteen minutes and sends them off.

"Where have you been?—"

Tiana jumps at the voice and turns her head. Bounty stands in the corner of the room, leaning against Tiana's tall shelf.

Tiana gets out of her chair slowly, her eyes glued on him.

"Why didn't you come?"

"I couldn't sense you?" Bounty growls. "Did he hide you from me?"

He steps out of the gloom, looking rugged and handsome. There's a week's growth on his jaw. His body fit so well in his fitted sweater shirt and jeans. Tiana cannot but help a soft chuckle.

He has great fashion taste for a demon.

"Wait, who hid me?"

Bounty growls and comes closer. Tiana glances at the shut door. "Oh no, you don't, not here."

"You smell like him." He steps closer and grabs her hand. "Turn around."

"No, I don't want to do this anymore!"

Tiana stops his hand and stands her ground; she narrows her eyes at him. "I thought we agreed. If we are going to continue to do this, it's gotta be on my terms." Bounty cocks his head to the side like a confused puppy. "My way, or the highway. You can't just pop up and bang, and fuck me into submission. Like I'm some kind of whore! Besides, what am I supposed to tell my friends? I can't even tell anyone about you? What does it even mean to be your mate?"

Bounty isn't even listening; he's too busy roving over the V-shape of her cleavage, her heavy round breasts. His eyes roam further down as his beast yelps, happy to once again be by her side. Tiana bites her lip. She knows what he's thinking.

Who am I kidding? Did I really expect for him to have a relationship talk?

Tiana's pussy throbs at the sight of his dick print. His cock is hard. A thick bulge hangs along the side of his left thigh.

"You are mine!" he barks.

"Oh, really?" Tiana grips the knob tighter. "We'll see—"

She turns the knob and pulls the door; it doesn't open. Her eyes pop out of her face. She tugs harder at the knob, heartbeat racing. She looks wildly around the room. Then he puts her back against the door.

Bounty steps back from her and says, "Come to me. I don't want to take you with force."

Tiana breathes slowly.

"I'm not fucking you if you won't help me?" She lowers her head and pleads. "Help me with Tao. He needs help; his fiancée is a demon." She steps over to the desk and sits on the edge. "From the reference material I was able to find, I think she's a nine-tailed fox."

Tiana pulls her thick coils into a bun atop her head. Bounty silently watches her every move. "She's killing him slowly. He won't live long if I don't intervene."

"He's not my priority."

"Am I?"

"You are mine, my mate."

Tiana doesn't consider herself helpless. She goes to him, places her hands on his wide chest, and pushes him gently against the wall. He doesn't resist. Tiana goes to her knees, unzips his fly, and pulls his thick white cock, slowly stroking it as it thickens in her hand. She kisses the tip, then presses her tongue into his slit. Bounty tenses. His fangs are drawn back in a frustrated scowl. Tiana feels the throb of his pulse from the base of his cock; he dips his hands in his pocket, resisting the urge to grab her and thrust forward.

She starts to suck, hollowing her cheeks and twirling her tongue. She looks him into his lustful eyes. A faint, almost mocking smile curls Bounty's lips. He combs his large fingers into Tiana's hair bun and pushes her head back forcefully. With a dip of his hips, his cock rams forward like a piston in the back of Tiana's throat. Foamy spittle begins to run down her chin. Her teeth scrape on the veins, making him buck faster.

Bounty takes hold of her shoulders and brings her to her feet again. A trickle of saliva stretches down the side of her mouth, splatters on her dress and the floor.

"Look in my eyes!" he snaps. "Grab your cock!"

Tiana does as commanded.

"This is yours!"

She glides her hands all over his shaft, caressing it until Bounty lets out a growl of satisfaction. She twists her spit-covered hands over and under and clockwise. The more she does it, the longer his cock grows... until it sits high in the air, poking at her breasts. Bounty commands her to lie on her back.

"Here, on the floor?" she asks, frowning.

"Yes."

"But the tables right there—"

"On the floor!" he barks.

Tiana lays back and shuts her eyes. Her ego refuses to submit without a fight.

Do this for Tao; just shut up and submit. Win-win...

It still feels strange to Tiana to be ordered around. She hates being submissive. No man has ever been able to tame her, which is the primary reason so many of her relationships crashed and burned. But Ishtan Rustivich is no mere man, despite her reluctance to admit it. Sex with him is starting to become something she craved.

With a deep breath, she cups the back of her thighs, bending them back to expose her tight hole. Bounty steps forward and slowly steers his cock into her tight cunt.

"Awn—",

"Yes!" he hisses. As his hips pump to their own rhythm.

"Harder! Harder!" She grits as her insides break open like a dam, and she spasms. Her core locks onto Bounty's cock. A gush of liquid squirts between her legs. His beast yelps out a cry of pleasure.

"What was that?" he asked her.

She shakes her head. "Did I just squirt?"

"Do it again!" He begins fucking her faster.

"Do it again, Tiana, coat me in your essence!" he pants and fucks her harder; his heavy balls spank her asshole with each thrust.

Tiana tries to concentrate on that feeling, hoping whatever it is happens again. Instead, she cums so hard she pushes out his penis.

He flips her around on all fours, pushes her head down on the cold tile, spreading her thighs, deeply inhaling the combination of their mixed scents. Bounty puts his mouth to her core and rewards her obedience. His inner beast pushes forward, demanding his time with their mate.

Tiana turns her head and sees his true image—not a full beast, but his head and extremities have a wolf-like appearance. His middle portion is still that of a man. She trembles, she clenches tighter, despite the fear icing over her veins. Everything in her is telling her this isn't right, but she is past redemption. She yields to his cock. His claws dig into her waist as his hips piston.

The fur on his legs tickles her thighs. He reaches around her waist and runs the back of his clawed fingers over her engorged clit, sending her headfirst into an oblivion of pleasure.

Tiana collapses, arms splayed out, face and breasts pressed against the hard floor. Her mouth dribbles saliva. The beast doesn't stop there. With his muzzle, he parts her feet and licks her cum soaked pussy. His long tongue fills the hole and his fangs graze her clit. Her eyes water in euphoria. Her fear is long forgotten, replaced by pleasure.

She reaches down and runs her hand over his large, fur-covered ears. The beast growls in appreciation. Pleased to feel the soft touch of its mate upon its true form.

"Fuck me like this forever!" Tiana unknowingly confesses her desires. Her head lolls from side to side as she passes out from exhaustion.

18

Chapter Eighteen

Tao-Sun Ikeda stares at the reflection of a stranger in the mirror. His muscles are barely attached to his bones, and life is leaving him slowly. He can barely run two miles now without collapsing; even attempting pushups leaves him breathless.

Tiana is right.

With Inyoku here, his house felt like a prison. Anytime he attempts to flee, he's once again trained into submission by sex. His whole being is attached to puppet strings, and his life is just a choreographed dance.

Tao cleans himself and puts on something light—a black t-shirt and lightweight trousers. He walks barefoot into the study, where Inyoku sits at his desk working on the computer. He stares at her for a moment, steeling himself to utter the words.

"I don't love you, Inyoku."

As if she misheard him, Inyoku looks up. "What?" she asks coolly.

"I don't love you, Inyoku."

Her mouth drops open, she freezes. The color leaves her face totally, and her fingers hang over the keyboard of the computer.

"What did you say?"

"I said, I don't love you—anymore."

She smiles awkwardly. "Is this, is this, a prank? A joke? Are you doing this because of Tiana?"

"No, this is me."

"No, this isn't you. We just finished making love!"

"That's because you try to control me with sex, Inyoku."

She frowns. She shakes her head in a genuine gesture of confusion. And in this instance, Tao almost believes he did something terribly wrong. Inyoku's face continues to pale out. Her lips tremble, and he looks so helpless that Tao's shoulders slump. She brushes her lustrous hair out of her face and sits up. She folds her legs under and looks out of the window. A single tear treks down the side of her face. He comes to her and sits beside her.

"I'm sorry, Inyoku."

"Since when?" She looks at him. "When did this happen? When did you stop being in love with me?"

Tao swallows with regret, gripping tight at his throat.

"Not long ago."

"So how do you know you are right? What if it's just a phase? Why don't you—"

"No, Inyoku. I know what I feel, and it's not just that—"

She grimaces. "What else is it?"

"I don't know how to explain it."

"Try me. You have to. We've been together for too long—"

Tao shakes his head, unable to voice his reasons out loud. She shakes her head defiantly. "No! This is not fair! We are already preparing for our wedding! Everyone is waiting to receive you back home. Our clans are to be united, and now you will bring disgrace to our families! And shame me! What am I supposed to tell our parents—?"

"Don't worry about Otosan," Tao says. "I'll deal with him."

Inyoku sighs. She takes his hand in hers.

"Tell me where I went wrong, Tao. I'll change. I'll do it, I promise, but please don't leave me." her voice breaks. "I love you, Tao. No one else. I'm not letting go."

There is an unfamiliar edge to her voice. Her tone hardens.

"Is it your friends... do you still have feelings for Tiana?"

"No, Inyoku—this has nothing to do with Tiana or anyone else, okay?"

"I know she doesn't like me," she pouts, "she wants to keep you for herself—"

Tao gets off the couch and puts his hands in his pockets. "Don't bring her into this. No one put me up to this. Look at me, Inyoku; what do you see?"

She gets off the couch, too. "What do you mean?"

Tao raises his shirt, pulls it off, and says, "Look at me. What do you see?"

She frowns. "I see you, your body. What's wrong with it?"

"That's the point, Inyoku. You don't *see*."

"I don't see what? I see you. You are standing right here, I see you, and I love you—"

"I'm wasting away. I'm sick!" Tao bawls.

Inyoku's eyes narrow. They shift as if she is avoiding peering at Tao's body. It is a slight movement of the eyes, almost imperceptible.

"You knew all along—I knew it." He shakes his head.

"So what? Maybe you're working too hard, the grading coming on and stuff."

"No, Inyoku."

"Then what is it?" she asks, her eyes glassy. They probe Tao's, daring him to say the wrong words. Tao puts his shirt back on, walks into the den, and grabs his car keys. Inyoku asks him where he's going.

He says he's going for a ride.

"It's Tiana, right? You are going to see her, right? You still love her!"

Tao shakes his head. "Don't do this."

"No, Tao. You come back inside, right now!"

Her pleas fall on death ears as Tao gets in his Camaro and drives away.

19

Chapter Nineteen

"Gooood morning Chicago, it's a beautiful Monday morning. The temperature remains the same—winter is nigh. Of course, there is music, there is dancing. If you don't have plans to leave your home, just stay in there's a snowstorm is coming later in tonight."

Tiana turned down the radio. The streets are humming with pedestrians, men, and women dressed for the chilly winds in heavy down coats and sweaters; their breaths plume steam as they cross the intersection. Traffic drifts ahead as she passes Stoney Island. Tiana is dressed for the weather, wearing a Burberry sweater, thick jeans, and thigh-high boots. She pumps her horn along with the rest of the drivers when a dickhead barges into their lane. Before long, she finds herself at the **South East Women's Learning Clinic.**

Undergrad interns fill the hallways; they part like the Red Sea as Tiana walks through. A small group of pregnant women awaits her in the small conference room. Tiana peeps through the open door. Eight women peer back. Tiana smiles at them, sensing their positive vibes. They're all happy, but anxious. No one is giving off any foul scents, and there's no miasma of ill-intent hovering around.

Thank God, a normal day, for a change.

"Ladies, I need a minute to get myself together; I'll be back in a jiff."

They shout back a chorus of, "Take your time."

Tiana goes into her office and finds Tao standing by her desk, dressed for work in a flattering tailored suit and tie. Tiana smiles. Her dear friend is looking a bit more like his old self.

Before Tiana can utter a word. Tao yells out, "I did it!"

"You told her?" She hurries in and shuts the door, then grabs Tao, urging him to take a seat and fill her in. He seems just as eager to tell her everything that's happened.

"I had to. And she knows, Tiana. She knows." Tao wears a dual expression of victory and apprehension.

Her heart lurches. "She knows what?"

Surely he didn't tell her about the few times they had gotten hot and heavy. That was ancient history.

"She knows about my health." He pauses awkwardly and looks away from her eyes. "She chose not to say anything about my sickness. I asked her last night, and she confessed to it."

"And where is she now?" Tiana's heart is beating fast, fearing the warpath headed their way.

"I left her in the house—"

"Oh no, do you think she'll go crazy and trash your place?"

"What?" He smiles. "No, Inyoku's not that type of person. There is nothing to be worried about anymore. We are both done now; I made sure of that. There will be no wedding she didn't really put up a fuss."

Damn right, she's not a person at all. Fuck, she's going to come after us...

"Wait, did you say, she didn't make a fuss?" Tiana puzzles. "You mean she just accepted, she didn't put up a fight?"

"Of course, she tried to talk me out of it."

"Don't go back home."

"What?" He frowns. "Inyoku isn't the spiteful type. We came to a responsible understanding."

"Tao, trust me, a calm heartbroken woman is way worse!"

Tiana's office door opens. Without knocking, the head of the community health division, Aaron Lett, steps into the room. When he sees Tao, he nods in greeting. "Am I interrupting anything?"

Tiana sighs at the intrusion. "No, Aaron. How may I help you?"

His stiff grin barely meets his eyes. "The women are waiting. Did Christy tell you they're from the Lactating Mothers Support Program?"

"Yes, she did. Is there anything extra we should know?" Christy didn't, but Tiana covers for her long-time friend. "Did she tell you the Vatican sponsors that organization? And that this clinic has become a beneficiary too?" Tiana picks up a pack of files and whispers to Tao, "We'll talk about this later."

****

Across the city, Bounty follows three men along an abandoned factory road in Whiskey Row. He stealthily follows at a good distance, about half a mile or so back, so the three men can't sense his presence. The stocky bald one in the middle appears to be running the show. He's the most dressed of the three.

He turns his head once, pale white skin, glowing green eyes, then sits over a saggy wide mouth and a double chin.

No shit, an ugly demon. That's something I haven't seen in a while.

He's wearing a rumpled black tweed blazer. His fat belly hangs over his bow-shaped legs. His companions are dressed alike—oversized hoodies, baggy jeans and sneakers. One looks Hispanic, the other a few shades darker. He keeps his hoodie pulled down low.

This must be a drug deal.

A squad car buzzes by the old factory, and Bounty turns to see if the cop will come closer. The cops didn't even look this way. The area is lined with decaying husks of factory buildings, out of use for over a decade or more—the perfect breeding ground for criminals seeking to take possession of the desolation.

Bounty zaps across to the other side of the road and vanishes into the shadow of an adjacent dilapidating structure. Through a broken sky glass on the roof, he observes the deal from above.

The floor is blackened with ancient soot from processed iron ore. The place has the putrid odor of a rusted, dirty mop. The fidgety, hoodie-clad Hispanic guy covers his nose and grimaces.

"What the fuck is that smell, cuz?"

His companion pushes back his hood, his dreadlocks falling over his tattooed riddled face. He sniffs the air as his eyes narrow. "Smells like dead fish."

"Come on, fellows," says the white guy in a deep Italian accent. "Don't embarrass our friends."

Figures appear from the dark corners of the factory. Four men dressed in black suits, their skins white as parchments, the skin pulled so tight it makes their faces look like cheap masks.

These must be new arrivals. They've barely mastered their human skins.

One of them stands out; he's wearing a dark pair of sunglasses. "Hey, Harvey," the stocky white guy calls out. He throws his hand up, as if the guys they are meeting are actually old friends. "Nice to see you, Harvey. How are you?"

Harvey appears to be the one wearing the dark glasses. The other black suits survey the room cautiously.

"Don't fool around, Snokes; show me what you got." Harvey's voice sounds choked. Snokes glances at the two dealers and gives them a crocodile's smile.

The guy with the locks pulls a nearby metal table over the soiled floor; the legs whine and groan as they scrape across the ground. Snokes flips his briefcase over in his hand, like a magician trying a sleight of hand. He places the case on the table and clicks the buckles, but he doesn't open it. He glances at Harvey.

"Nice, like I promised. Have I ever failed you before?"

"You will if you don't show me the merchandise now."

He pulls open the briefcase slowly. "Here goes—"

The odor that comes out of the briefcase sends the two guys beside Snokes reeling back. Locs covers his mouth with both hands and screams, "What the fuck is that!" His Hispanic friend is bent over, hacking in revulsion.

Snokes laughs while smiling. Harvey strolls over to the table, turns the briefcase around, and gazes upon the two decaying human hearts. The side of his lips moves and he glances at Snokes. "Females?"

"Uh Huh. And just like you like it served."

Harvey smiles tightly. "Yeah. You know me well."

Behind Snokes, his associates are still cursing and coughing. Snokes and Harvey look back.

"And them?" Harvey asks.

Snokes shrugs. "Just met them today—"

"—motherfucker, you said we were dealing coke! That ain't coke!" bawls the black dude with dreadlocks. His friend pulls away. "Come on, Ace. Man, let's dip, these clowns loco."

The guys with Harvey pull their guns out. The two guys freeze. Ace, the black guy, stammers, "Hey, man. We want no parts of this. Snokes here said this was nothing but a drug drop and quick cash-out—"

"Shut up, Ace," Snokes snaps. "Calm down."

"What are you gonna do, man they got their guns on us?"

Snokes says, "Nothing." He removes a gun from inside his tweed jacket. Harvey senses it first. His bulging green eyes scan the room with trepidation.

"Wait, we're not alone." He attempts to state in a hushed tone. The others break their concentration on the two guys and look around, scanning for danger. Snokes is the first to notice the intruder. He looks up. Bounty's dark, smoldering green eyes spark up, and his vicious teeth pull back, baring every one of his sharp fangs.

"Fucking Christ, he's up there!" he shouts. "It's Bounty!"

Bullets fly into the open air, ricocheting off the metal broken roof. Glass shatters, sending a rainfall of sharp spears plummeting down. The two gangsters jump out of the way of the falling glass and run right into the massive body of a man that's wearing dark fatigue pants, a black shirt, and a heavy leather jacket.

Bounty deflects the shots with the help of a protective incantation. He beats each of the henchmen until they are all on the floor, in a crumpled pile of guts and bones. Ace and his friend watch, petrified as the fallen men begin turning into nothing but dust and ash. The smell of burning flesh rises and fills the air. Bounty faces the two remaining demons, Harvey and Snokes.

Harvey scurries and grabs the briefcase containing the rotting hearts and fits it under his arm; his hand trembles with fear as he points his gun at Bounty. Ace and his friend need no further proof that this isn't the usual drug drop. They get up and hightail it out of the factory while the others are distracted.

Bounty turns slightly, watching as the humans flee. "Give the briefcase over," Bounty commands.

Harvey fumes. "Why don't you come and get it!"

Snokes eyes the door as he slowly creeps away into a corner behind a steel pole. There is a corridor there behind a concrete wall. Bounty lets him go. He wants the big fish. His prey tonight is Harvey.

He backs away from Bounty, snarling and snapping his gaping maw. The stretched skin of his face cracks as his mouth widens. He fires, *BLAM! BLAM!* The shots miss Bounty's head by a long shot. Harvey whispers a spell and fires more shots, bringing his hand lower. Two slugs sink in Bounty's thighs. Bounty stops in his forward advance. His eyes irritably roll down, staring at the holes in his leg. His inner beast pushes forward. Smoke bellows from his nose, the faint scent of sulfur misting the air.

"You're nothing but a bitch going fetch for its master! You think you can stop what's begun?" Harvey shouts. The skin of his cheek rips, darkness exposed.

He tries to fire more shots at Bounty, but Harvey's beast spirit pushes the shift too fast. It's too worked up on emotion and rage. His eyes pop from the stretching tension on his whole face. The briefcase drops from his armpit and hits the floor; the two putrid hearts flop out and roll. Harvey no longer looks human. His human skin sloughs off, hitting the surface with a wet *Splunk*. His large hooves hit the metal ground, preparing to charge as its reptilian snout puffs steam in the air.

Another fucking water demon.

The Kelpie kicks the briefcase to the side with its strong hind legs, jumping in front of the hearts on the ground. His skin is scaled, mottled with various shades of black and green. A slimy seaweed mane hangs down its stag-like face.

"I'm not some small-time demon, you bastard bitch."

Bounty growls and flies across the space between him and the Kelpie. He crashes into the horse-shaped monster and the creature smashes against a steel pole. The metal pole bends and groans from the sudden impact. Venom flies through the air towards Bounty as the demon hacks. A vile smell oozes from its venom pockets. Bounty dodges and lands a heavy punch on the side of the Kelpies jaw. The demon is winded; he falls and stumbles.

As it struggles to regain its footing, Bounty grabs it by its long horse shaped neck; with both hands gripped tight, he crunches down with all his beast's strength. The demon yelps raspy screams as Bounty crushes his insides and pulls at vital organs. Bounty's claw digs deep into its putrid black flesh, pulling out the heart with a gross *pop* from his chest cavity. The kelpie begins to disintegrate in Bounty's hand. He tosses the carcass to the side as sirens scream in the distance. Bounty leaps up a steel pole and flees into the shadows.

Two cops respond to an anonymous tip of gunfire heard in an abandoned factory. They enter the dilapidated structure with a look of confusion on their faces. "What the fuck is that smell?" one asks as the other coughs. The other cop gags, nearly puking from the wretched stench. "I don't know, maybe some dead cat or a stray dog."

A strong breeze blows through the fractured space in the roof. Pigeons coo and scatter into the air. Broken glass crunches under the officer's feet as they look into the rafters. One of them tells the other maybe they should find a way up top.

"And then what?" asks his partner. "There's nothing here, just clothes and that dead smell—"

"But look at it." The cop queries, "Don't you see the clothes? There's a pattern. What if someone did these guys in and went up those steps to the other side, huh?"

"There's nothing up there but pigeons, man. Let's get out here. We'll call forensics in."

Bounty watches as the two cops leave the factory. In his right hand is one of the hearts he took from the Kelpie demon. He examines it for a second, then throws it into his spatial bag.

This may be the proof I need for the high council.
********* *

Tiana shakes her head in disbelief. "Tao, you can't be this thick-headed, hanging with me, and Yolanda should have already taught you that a woman scorned is nothing to play with."

By the look on Tao's face, it's clear he thinks she's overreacting.

"Don't be naïve," she hollers behind him. "

As Tao makes his way to the parking lot. He looks back to make sure Tiana is out of sight. He checks his phone. No missed calls or texts. Instead of going home last night, he crashed at his cousins. He knows it was a cowardly thing to do, so he considers whether to dial Inyoku's number, but changes his mind. He feels a prick of conscience, but he shakes it off and heads for the car.

Tiana comes down a few minutes later. Delayed by Topper, who had a question about grant writing. She senses Tao's frustration as she walks towards him. The air around him once again has a bitter smell. She opens the door of her car and lets him in.

"Isn't running away from my place a little too extreme?"

Tiana sighs. *If only you knew.* "You can feel it too, in your bones, don't you? You can see what she's doing to you. Tao, I can't watch this happen to you; I can't watch you die. Come on, get in the car."

The female cop thinks Marcio is raving mad, and she's not hiding it. She reaches for the pen stuck in her pocket above her badge, but stops.

"What did you say?"

Marcio pushes his hoodie off his face. He looks around, as if anyone of the cops in the precinct might become one of those things.

"I'm telling you, ma'am. They're real, those things, El Diablo's, monsters. I saw them with my own fucking eyes—"

"Wait; back up a little to the beginning. Tell me what you were doing out there this afternoon?"

"You ain't listening?"

Marcio sits back and shakes his head. Ace told him they couldn't trust the cops. They might both be arrested once they tell them what happened. But now, he can see the cops have no clue what is really going on in this city. Marcio took a risk by coming; he snuck out of the den after making sure Ace was knocked out by the lean he mixed in his soda.

"I am listening. Let's cut out the part where you saw—demons or monsters. Tell me about the drugs."

"Drugs? Come on..." He shrugs. I told you, me, and Ace. We thought we were making a drop. Turns out—"

She cuts him off abruptly. "Where's this friend of yours now, this Ace?"

A picture of Ace lying on the old sofa, drugged-out, pops up in his head. A tinge of remorse shivers through him.

"I don't know where he is—" Marcio says, "Poof-He ran off."

"Well, now we have no one to corroborate your story—"

"He got so scared he ran off. He thinks they're gonna come get us," Marcio protests.

"And you, what do you think?"

Marcio argues that he knows what he saw. He shuffles out of the police station just as Detective Terrance Slaton enters. Both men brush shoulders as they pass. Terrance glances at the oversized brown leather jacket on the lad's back, the old shoes, the thuggish demeanor. He assumes the guy is just some small-time thief not worth his time.

He asks the policewoman, named Kathrine, "Was he giving you a hard time?"

She shrugs, waving her hands dismissively. "Probably just a small-time drug dealer," Kathrine says. "Seems like he's smoking his own supply."

Terrance glances back at the swinging double doors, but the young Hispanic man is already gone. He sits in the chair the boy just left, closes his eyes and lets out a loud sigh.

"Tired, huh?"

"Yeah."

"Why don't you take the day off?" Kathrine suggests.

Terrance looks around the office floor at his fellow cops. A couple of guys here battle heart diseases, especially the fat ones; no one really understands the stress of being a cop. He sees Romey, forty-seven, fresh off the hospital bed for a heart bypass. Romey stopped smoking after his surgery, but the stress of this job may make him retire early.

He rubs the back of his neck, wondering if this job is really worth it. He slaps his hands on his knees and asks Kathrine, "Let me see that dude's statement." He needs something to keep him busy. Kathrine hands over the form. Terrance's eyes open wide as he reads the guy's description, chuckling. He gives the paperback to Kathrine, who says, "Exactly what I thought, too. Looney."

They both laugh.

* * * * * * * * * * *

Yolanda yells into the receiver. "You can't stop them from being together, Titi. I know you think she's a creature or something, but... you took him to your place?"

"See? This is why I didn't bring him to your place. You'd overreact."

"Me? Overreact? Bitch I would bite you if you took my man away from me—"

"Shut up, Yoyo. Tao is in danger." Tiana added, "I know it."

"What if she reports him missing to the police?"

"Why would she do that?"

"I would if I thought some paranoid bitch took my man. There's a law against that; it's a crime, Titi. Unlawful arrest—"

"Unlawful detention," Tiana corrects her, rolling her eyes.

Tiana and her friend have been on the phone for over ten minutes, and it's been Yolanda, mostly yelling and Tiana trying to get her friend to understand. Things are deeper than she could ever imagine.

I just want this to be over.

She looks out of the kitchen window into the alley below, it's dark down there. A strong breeze blows, shakes the window sill. Tiana pulls the window close. She peeks over at Tao in the living room, working on a new project that Tiana was saddled with the previous day. Another conference is coming up in Luxembourg.

"Did you not believe me when I said Inyoku is a witch?"

Yolanda barks a small laugh. "After that shit in the Bayou with that crazy ass creole girl, I'll believe anything Yolanda giggles."

"But are you being serious right now? Like at first, I thought you might be tripping."

"So we're not up against some mad woman. We're up against a witchy bitch?"

Yolanda chortles and snorts in laughter. Listening to her laugh makes Tiana want to laugh as well. She looks around at the doorway. She hopes Tao isn't listening.

"I know, it's hard to believe. Tao's been to the hospital, and the doctor gave him a clean bill of health."

"Okay, Titi. I hope you are right, for the sake of both of us."

Tiana says, "I'm right."

She hangs up. The apartment is suddenly quiet. Tiana tiptoes out of the kitchen. The living room is empty.

"Tao?"

"He can't hear you."

Tiana turns around and sees Bounty standing behind her, his large hands stuffed deep in his pocket. As he rocks back and forth on the balls of his feet, his presence fills the room. His muscles bulge through his black t-shirt, and his woodsy freshness washes over her. Tiana glances back at the spot where she left Tao working on his computer.

Everything is in its place there: the sofa, the table with her bag on it, a bowl of chocolate candy half-eaten by Yolanda from the last time she visited. She frowns at the spot where she is sure Tao was sitting again. "Tao! Tao!" she calls.

Tiana walks past Bounty and heads for the bedroom. No sign of Tao there as well. When she walks back into the living room, Bounty is gone.

"Bounty?"

"Here, and I told you to refer to me as Ishtan."

Ishtan was standing in the corner of the living room by the window mere seconds ago; Tiana rubs her eyes.

"How d'you—"

"Your Fri.. end.. is here," Bounty growls, "He just can't see you. He's fine."

Tiana looks at the couch again.

"What do you want?" she asks Bounty, even though her thighs begin to tremble at the prospect of having him again.

"You," he says. "I want time with my mate."

He comes to her, takes her hand, and pulls her close. His smell fills Tiana's head with memories of their passionate nights. She shakes her head slowly, frowning as his hands begin to unsnap her jeans, touching around the little sprinkle of hair that trails the land between her navel and her core. Tiana begins to purr, pushing more into his hands as he explores her lady garden.

The thought of Tao being right next door is now *lost* to her. The world falls away as passion takes over. She can see herself float into the bedroom, in the hands of her mate, her demon. Cradled in his hands. She feels safe. All her worries about Tao's safety, his sinister demon fiancée and Yolanda's pinning—all of these have now faded into nothingness.

Bounty stands there naked, staring at her abundant curves, the mounds of her breasts, the chocolate halo around her nipples. He crouches before her wet pink flower and inhales her sex. The delicious, indescribable flavor of sin and sugar.

Everything about her drives me mad.

This was a first for him. He never wanted to become possessive of anyone, mate with anyone, or dominate anyone the way he did her. Bounty would bring down heaven to keep her by his side. He would douse the fire of hell to ensure his cock thrust into her forever.

"Do you know who you belong to?" he murmurs.

Tiana bites her lip, her small finger wringing her dark coils round and round.

"Do you understand what it means to be my Mate?"

"Show me."

So, he shows her, and no artist can paint what he does with her body, no melody can capture it on strings, nor does any writer have the words to describe how he expresses his devotion through sex. His shaft points straight at her core, like the pin of a compass. It goes into her as if he is simply coming home. Tiana's body sucks him in greedily into the flaming passion between her thighs. She screams his name over and over on account of the excruciating sweetness; she claws at his back, forcing him to dive deeper.

The long shaft of his cock digs into her like a spear till she throws her feet in the air, unable to contain the tidal wave that sweeps her under. Bounty pulls out of Tiana suddenly and vanishes from the room. Tiana smacks the bed, demanding that he come back. She trashes around the rippled sheets and pulls at the pillows.

"Come back," she whimpers. "Now..."

Bounty didn't leave. He simply steps behind the veil of this dimension, behind the limited reality of *this* space and time. He watches her throw her tantrum, watches her curse his name, and cry.

She dared to bring him into her home. So close to her bedchamber.

He looks down at his hardness, veins pumping along the stem. The tip pulsates as a bead of pre-cum forms at its head. The V-shape of his lower abs flexes with anger, his groin is on fire, lust for his mate's open pussy on the bed. The beast pushes forward, tired of the mental games Bounty likes to play. Tired of the dialed-down lovemaking he's been engaging in with Tiana, his beast wants to pin her down and fuck her raw. When Tiana opens her eyes, his beast form stands before her.

She gasps.

"You are so beautiful—" she whispers. She has never really looked at his true form without fear. But to look upon him with a clear mind was astonishing.

He is bigger in every way. He isn't all beast. He still retains some of his human-ish features. To truly gaze upon his form is magnificent. His fur is a mixture of black and silver, covering his forearms and legs. The chest and sex remain hairless and bare, still retaining their muscular human shape. His Lycan head is massive but regal.

He almost looks like an Akita... no, he looks more wolfish. The beast firmly slaps her thigh, bringing her attention back to him.

"Get out of that pretty little head of yours."

Tiana's smile fades when she sees that his beast cock has also grown to his larger-sized proportions.

"Oh god, it's huge."

"He won't be the one fucking you."

His cock is still at least fourteen inches, but its girth has almost doubled in width. Tiana shakes her head and crawls away from him. "No, you are gonna rip me apart—no! Make it smaller!"

"First, I'm going to use my tongue," Bounty explains, "and you've taken me in this form before."

He grabs Tiana's leg and pulls her back to the edge of the bed. He takes hold of both thighs and kneels before her. His tongue touches the knob of her clit, and down her labia, he licks. She jerks as the tip of his forked tongue dives in, deeper and deeper, until she feels it in her womb. Her head is on fire. *How is he able to—*the thought is cut short by a sweet stab of pleasure.

Unable to hold her peace, she screams, her body exploding with bliss. "YES! OH, YES!" Tiana sings her passionate chorus, cheering him along with every stroke of his tongue.

Bounty taps her drenched core with the tip of his shaft before pushing himself forward, throwing his head back from the boundless blast of ecstasy. He sinks his whole length into the hilt. Tiana grabs his fur-covered ass and grits her teeth. She screams in pain and pleasure. His Lycan face growls and belches fire as he begins to fuck her fast.

"I don't think I can take it. I'm going to break!"

"You were made for me; I'll always be a perfect fit," he grunts through his thrust. He pulls out of her, flips her over and goes in from behind, pumping copious amounts of seed in her. Marking her womb.

****

Tao checks his watch, rubbing his tired eyes. *I've been at it for two hours.* The chocolate candy in his mouth tastes a bit bitter now. He tries to remember when he even took out the bowl. His mouth feels dry.

"Tiana? You awake?" he calls.

The sound of the shower in Tiana's room is his only reply. It shuts off, and she steps out several minutes later in fresh clothes.

"Whoa."

"What?" Tiana asks.

"Your skin, it's glowing," Tao says. "Don't stop using, you know, whatever it is you're using. Is it some new formula or body cream?"

Tiana laughs and sidles to the living room, where Tao's computer is opened. She checks his work and smiles with satisfaction.

"Are you hungry?" she beams.

"I'm famished."

Tiana breezes into the kitchen, preparing a late-night dinner. Tao continues to gawk at her. Unaware of the dark shadow that passes behind him, out the window into the night.

20

Chapter Thirty Three

Hell.

It's not far. Unlike what the ancient books and time-worn pages of your grandmother's bibles say, the barrier between *here* and the *other* side is as close as flipping the curtains down in Reynold Ashe's basement home. It is as close as stepping into a bucket of water while staring into the eyes of a black cat. Behind the walls of walls, in the heat of heats, there awaits a door, a door that only a few men and women know exists, and even fewer can go through.

The door opens. In stumbles the watcher whom Bounty stopped from attacking his mate The watcher walks through after shedding his human skin. He falls through the void and lands like a ball of fire in hell's charred, sulfuric turf. He has been summoned. By The Guardian of the gate Cerberus.

Down here, the watcher; is called Lecrae, a benign Nephilim whose demeanor is fit for lesser assignment among mortals. He passes through the gates of hell, where higher demons are stationed. Cerberus-Aurone lives among the pillars of Ether Flame, the heat of which is hotter than the sun, hundreds of times over. The great Hell-Hound is surrounded by guard-demons cloaked in embers; their nostrils belch black sulfuric smoke. Lecrae enters into the inner chambers where Cerberus sits at a table. At the table with him are the heads of his guards.

Amaruq, the Great Hell Beast, is there too. Lecrae hates him despite that having the same sire. And the other demon feels exactly the same way about Lecrae, his half brother.

Cerberus raises his head slowly and casts his attention to Lecrae.

"Where are the cursed progenies?"

"Your lordship, I do not have them," the demon says.

"And why is this?"

Cerberus nods his head towards his guards. The hound's mouths leak lava. As they sneer at Lecrae. Within milliseconds, their drool could kill him instantly. Before he had a chance to mutter another word. Lecrae trembles fearful now, wary of his words and actions.

"It was Bounty, my Lord."

Cerberus brings his fist down on the rocky table. Fragments of hot rock fly in the air. He glowers at Lecrae.

"You had a direct order to grab the woman and take the babies from inside her. Now you tell me that half-breed mutt is a match for you?"

"It was the circumstances, your lordship. The humans... Her mother is a Dark Angel but still a light-bringer. The treaty. I didn't want to do anything to upset it. Diplomacy requires—"

"You stand here and tell me about diplomacy!? What nonsense! You cheapen your life, Lecrae. If you value it and hope to keep your place, find the girl, bring her to me. Now!"

Lecrae grimaces, wishing he could just go back to earth, where all he likes to do is fuck, make money, smoke, and sunbathe on the pyramids of Egypt, grinning down at the tourists who can't see.

Lecrae hated Bounty. No, he loathes all three siblings. They kept fucking with the profits of his other business, the one where he harvested human parts for demons and fae too afraid to disrupt the so-called balance. Bounty had hunted and killed most of his buyers. The hunter probably didn't know Lecrae and Amaruq were the top two human harvesters; but he was sure Bounty and his meddlesome siblings were getting too close to figuring it out. That was, until the girl came along. It was a good thing the girl was a distraction for Bounty. Lacrea warned Amaruq to leave Bounty be. but his ass kissing half brother had to run and tell Ceberus everything. As long as Bounty was occupied, their business stayed in the green. So Lecrae had no real intention of bringing her to Cerberus. Lecrae silently cursed the old demon.

Now this pain in the ass. Cerberus wants to take Bounty's mate away... If the girl and the pups die, Bounty would be an unfathomable force.

Lecrae shivered, but quickly regained his composure as Cerberus glowered at him. His claws scratched the stone table as they pointed towards the twisted face of Amaruq, the Great Hell beast. The fornicator, the defiler. Amaruq detests Bounty as much as his half blooded brother Lecrae. After their last fight he owed bounty a thrashing or two. Especially that little bitch of his. When he failed the first time, Cerberus threatened to demote him. And that was unacceptable. Amaruq's life's mission was to sit beside Lucifer himself, and he'd lick Cerberus's lava-leaking asshole to achieve it...

"Amaruq, you have always been one of my most trusted allies. Lucifer recognizes your worth. You will expedite my plans and make sure Lecrae does his job—"

Lecrae mentally rolled his eyes.

So, now Cerberus makes him subordinate to lecherous Amaruq. Great, just great.

"Bounty has committed the same transgression as his father! He taints the bloodline even further. These abominations must be destroyed or tamed into loyal pets! " Cerberus slams the table of rocks again; fire spits from the crevices. The demons around him quake. "Get that girl, now!"

Amaruq rises. He bows and joins Lecrae.

"I will search the west if you head to the east, we will meet up when we find her," Lecrae suggests.

Amaruq sneers and simply nods, not seeking to work with his half brother, anyway.

****

Deep in the caves and crevices of hell, Cerberus comes upon his daughter, Bounty's mother. She's a beast, the very incarnation of darkness. Her form hides behind a thick miasma of dark energy.

Her back is turned to Cerberus. She stands before Jezebel's mirror, watching her children on earth. She hears him approaching, drops a long black veil to hide it.

"Ria?"

She turns around to face his father and questions. "What do you want to do with the girls, pups, when they arrive?"

"We have had this discussion, Ria. I want them destroyed; they embarrass me enough here in hell. Must they also do it on earth?"

"I say leave them there. I don't want the babies here."

"They remind you of your pain, I know."

"Then listen to me," Ria pleads.

"If you bring them here, I don't want to see them!"

"I'll remember that." Cerberus pauses, looks around the dwelling of his daughter. Mangled heads of Wolf-Shifters spoils from the hunts carried out by the mercenary demons under her command. In search of her runaway mate. Ria was obsessed with revenge, a vengeance that Cerberus enjoyed fueling. He cackles at the heads, picking up one of them.

"Found him yet?" he asks his daughter.

"No. But I will."

"It's been almost half a thousand years already since his last sighting, Ria. He's probably already taken his last breath."

"I feel him out there, father. Taunting me, daring me to come for him."

"You will stop him, not by killing him," says Cerberus. "But by taking something, he values."

Ria glances at her father. Smoke billowed from her mouth in rage.

"His present bride and their Halfling child," Cerberus murmurs. "I hear the child has his mother's power. The bride is a direct line of the Lycan demon of the east. Even Lucifer declines to war with the eastern Lycan king—"

"You're saying Lucifer has someone he fears?"

"Not fear, Ria. Respects."

"Then I want to take what Demetri values the most. I will take his wife and child. I will make him watch as I squeeze the breath out of them. I will make him suffer."

"You will have your moment, Ria. You will have your moment," Cerberus growls, but you must tread lightly.

Ria goes back to Jezebel's mirror. She scowls at the image of Bounty hunching over his dying mate.

Something about the woman makes Ria uncomfortable; she frowns then quickly covers the mirror and exits the room.

21

Chapter Twenty

By mid-week, Wednesday, Tiana felt a semblance of normalcy. Tao has been staying at her place for about a week now. Maybe things are really getting back on track. Tiana looks over to Tao in her passenger seat and smiles.

Traffic in the city was low this morning. She had kept them busy this week with the preparations for the proposal meeting with—Pfizer and National Geographic, an unlikely coalition for premature babies' health in sub-Saharan Africa. This is a meeting they can't afford to drop the ball on.

Tao's morning itinerary seems to go on and on. Tiana gives Tao a side-eye as he reads her schedule out loud:

"Before that meeting, you have a short sit-in with the department heads on a different matter. I have you scheduled down for ten AM."

"Tao, what the fuck is going on with my schedule?"

Tao gave her a short smile, then returned to his tablet. After a few minutes, he finally blurts out, "Tiana, I can't stay and hide at your place forever, plus I need things from my house."

Tiana shoots him her infamous puppy dog eyes. "I just don't

want you to get hurt. You've put on weight, and you're almost back to your old condition."

"I hear you, but my cousin went by the place and told me she's gone, plus she was due back to japan a week ago."

Tiana drops Tao off at his house with reluctance, then heads to the office.

****

Surprisingly, Inyoku was still there when Tao walked through the door. Even more surprising, she was in a good mood and being friendly. She was wearing a black robe he hadn't seen before, tied around her small waist with a sash. Printed on the back is the image of his family's dragon. Tao notes that this dragon has several tails. *Strange.*

Inyoku stands by the window, watching as Tiana drives off.

"Good Morning Tao," she said, greeting him with a soft bow.

"Ohayo gozaimasu." Tao dipped his head back.

"Where have you been?" Despite her friendly tone, her voice is laced with accusations.

"Working." Tao makes his way past her and further into the house.

"I know. But you weren't working in the office, were you?"

Tao didn't like her tone. He felt anger rising in him. With a short exhale, he simply replies, "I thought you left already."

"I came back." She tossed a shiny metal key in the air, catching it mid-fall. "Good thing I have a spare key, huh? But of course, there was no way you'd have known if I left or not. Since you run from home like a coward."

She walks to his side and puts her hands lovingly around his neck. "I'm willing to forget what you said to me the other day. I'm willing to give us another try, another chance. I know you still love me, Tao."

Inyoku bends forward to kiss him, but Tao quickly covers his lips with his hand.

"What are you doing?" He frowns. "I meant what I said, Inyoku.

I'm not doing this again. We can't keep going back and forth. I told you I'm done, and I fucking mean it!"

She lets go of him slowly, her nails scratching his neck a bit as she passes. She drops herself onto the sofa and opens her thighs as Tao walks past, stripping off his clothes as he heads to the shower. He suspects Inyoku will come to him there, and if she does, he's not sure his willpower will be enough to resist.

Now that Tao is a bit more clear-headed, something wasn't right about his home. With her here, it felt small and inhospitable. At Tiana's, he could breathe freely without the burden of duty tying him down. For a brief moment, his mind goes off on a tangent.

If I hadn't agreed to work with my clan elders to resolve past grievances, Tiana could be mine right now.

He shook the thought off, knowing it was because of him that they could never be more than just friends. He pulls the door close as he steps into the bathroom and rushes through his bath. He checks himself in the mirror. His muscle mass was returning.

Well, I'll be damned. Look at that — Inyoku stands at the bedroom entrance. Her dark eyes call to him, lips pursed as though she is about to cry.

Dammit, I can't fall for her tricks.

He refuses to meet her eyes and quickly busies himself with getting ready. He combs his hair, dabs cologne on his body, then throws on a shirt and some dress slacks.

"You missed your grading," her seductive voice rasps.

Tao feels his manhood thickening. "I can catch up with the next one," he says quickly as he picks his car keys off the ottoman beside the bed.

Inyoku's robe falls off her body to the floor. Her moon-white skin and the space between her thighs catch Tao's eyes, and he shivers. Between Inyoku's thighs, there is a spring of black foliage. The thin cut of her pink cunt puffs out. Her arousal clings to the skin of her inner thighs.

"See how ready I am for you, my love?" she whispers.

Tao stutters, "I, I, have to get to work—"

"Or you could stay and work me all over."

She sticks a finger in herself and pulls it out slowly. A long string of arousal clings to her nail. Tao's cock pokes at his trousers.

Maybe one more time for old times' sake.

"Leave!!" Something Deep within Tao rumbles. Without a second glance, he flees past her. Inyoku dropped to the floor, sobbing

* * * * * * * * * *

Tiana walks to her office, deep in thought. So much has changed since Berlin, all because of the sauna incident. She sits timidly in her office chair, hissing from the slight pain. Recalling bits from last night's tryst with Bounty. Her upper teeth score her lower lip as she relives the memory.

People are still wandering in when Tiana takes her place at the head of the conference room. The proposal presentation to Pfizer and National Geographic goes smoothly. This presentation will be her championing move. By the looks on their face, her promotion is secured.

Her voice comes out filled with passion and vision, clearly outlining her plan, stopping to take questions along the way. The board members seem excited about the projected monetary benefits of her proposal.

Ten minutes later, her presentation concludes. The board members clap and discuss the parts they'd seek to change. A few minutes more, the meeting is over. Some faculty members leave while some hang around to rub shoulders with Pfizer and NG.

Christy and the head of CHD, Aaron Lett, stay behind too.

The door swings open, the handle slamming into the posterior wall! There stands Inyoku Nikaro in a bright red dress.

She walks gracefully towards Tao but says nothing to him. She walks past the other faculty people. Aaron Lett asks Christy Marlow, "Who is she? Call security!" Christy shrugs and she dials security on her phone. The room is quiet as Inyoku stops before Tiana, where she sits behind a long table.

"Hello, Tiana."

Tiana's gaze never strays from Tao. She watches as he becomes defensive. "And hello to you too."

Tiana shakes her head for him to play it cool. He nods in understanding and rises to stand. Sweat drips from Tiana's brow as she nervously taps the pile of papers before her with the tip of her pen.

"I wanted to see you, Tiana, but Tao tells me your schedule is full."

"Oh, you want to meet with me... like, right now? Is there a problem?" Tiana plays coy, wanting to keep her in the room with as many people as possible. Praying that would be enough to deter her from taking on her true form.

"You tell me," Inyoku says coolly. "Look me in the eye and tell me: are you trying to take my Fiancé away from me? Are you trying to destroy what Tao and I have?"

"Inyoku, I'm not sure I'm following. Tao and I are just co-workers and friends!"

"Stop pretending not to know what I'm talking about!"

Heads turn towards Tao. His handsome face reddens with embarrassment, but he maintains his cool. Tao swiftly plants himself behind Inyoku. "Come on, Inyoku. You should not be here—"

"No, Tao! Let me talk to your boss here!" Inyoku yells, her face red with anger.

Tiana continues to tap the stack of papers. Inyoku's eyes blaze as she slaps it out of Tiana's hand. The pen flies across the room, hits the wall, and breaks in three places.

Aaron Lett rushes over and stands alongside Tao, but is forcefully pushed back by Inyoku. He demands the rest of the people to leave. He whispers in Christy's ear, "We're leaving. Make sure to get security up here."

Now they standalone, exactly what Tiana was fearing.

Inyoku fumes. "I am giving you a warning, Tiana. Stay away from Tao—" She drops her voice, brings her face closer so that only Tiana hears her. "Or else, you'll get what's coming."

Inyoku walks out of the conference room without a word or glance at Tao.

****

The office is abuzz with gossip. Rumors of Tiana and Tao's illicit affair have grown more scandalous as the day goes on. Tiana rubs her temple; there is no way she is getting that promotion now.

"Tao, I didn't mean for any of this to happen; I'm not sure why she still believes there's something between us that ended years ago."

Tao mumbles something and smiles wanly. She watches somberly as he drives out of sight before getting in her car, too. She takes a few minutes to consider the incident with Inyoku and the clear threat she poses. Inyoku is coming for vengeance.

Tiana drives home cautiously, checking her rearview and surroundings. She parks across the street from her loft and looks up to her window. The dash's time flashes seven PM as she shuts off her engine. She steps out and looks around. The foreboding feeling still lingers on.

The sky over downtown is streaked with a wash of orange and grey where the sun went down. A cool breeze blows against her face and ruffles her thick, coily hair.

A few deep breaths later, she finally works up the nerve and goes up to her apartment. Maybe she'll be alright; maybe Inyoku's threat is nothing but a warning for now.

I have Bounty. He'll never let anyone hurt me.... But He also said Tao isn't his business.

She quickly lets herself into her apartment and shuts the door, making sure to secure the door. Her relief is short-lived, though—*What if Inyoku has powers like Ishtan? What if she can go through walls and just suddenly appear?*

"Fuck it... I can't keep living in fear," she snaps at the living room. She begins to strip.

The sound of her phone vibrating catches in her ear.

"Tao?"

"Yeah, it's me. I'm on the street."

"Are you coming up?"

Tao says he's not sure. Maybe he just needs to get away for a while. His voice on the phone sounds choked.

"Do you maybe want to get a drink or something? Maybe... blow off some steam?" Tiana inquires.

"Yeah, that may be exactly what I need."

"Meet me at our place in ten minutes."

Tiana places the phone on the dresser, then hops in the shower for a quick wash.

****

Dirty Merlin is a rooftop bar that they frequent. During cold temperatures, the rooftop can stay open due to its unique glass dome. Tiana cranes her neck over the edge, watching as pedestrians and cars drive past. With a sigh, the weight of today presses down. She loses interest in watching the traffic and smiles at Tao.

"Thanks for meeting me here, ladies." He offers them a bottle of beer.

"Anytime, Tao." Yolanda quips back with a smile.

He twirls his half-drunk bottle of beer and looks at it with interest. Yolanda is talking about some new guy again. This one seems even worse than the last.

"Is dating him really that bad?" Tiana asks

Yolanda scrunches her face as she describes the way he picks the crust off his feet in bed. Tao howls. The girls join him in laughter. The waiter sets more beer bottles before them. Three hours in, Tiana orders steak from the restaurant below. Another hour passes and Tao is on cloud nine, arms splayed across the rooftop pillows.

Tiana's head is over the edge of her chair. A satisfied smile spread across her face. Yolanda is singing *Pick up Your Feelings* by Jazmine Sullivan; an atrocious off-key Tao joins in as they put on a show. Tiana takes another sip of her Modelo, then joins in the singing, too. They're the last remaining customers.

It's midnight, and the night is no longer young. They all have work the next day: more presentations, more panels. With a bit of drunk stumbling, they make their way to the street. Somehow they manage to make it to Yolanda's car. An Inebriated Tao belches and says, "I'm not going home, man. Yoyo, you got a spare room, or maybe I can sleep on your couch?"

"Yeah, if you promise not to pee yourself or vomit all over it." Yolanda giggles.

Tao raises his hands up and begins, "I solemnly swear not to pee—"

"Yoyo, you sure we shouldn't get an Uber?" calls Tiana from the backseat.

"No, I got this."

Yolanda sniffs, coughs into her hand, and puts the car in gear. Tiana closes her eyes and slouches in the back. Her eyes close for what seems like a second.

-Screech-

Tiana's eyes burst open. "W... what was that?"

Tao is looking around from his place in the front too. Yolanda is giggling. She says, "I just hit that Range Rover—" *hick*. She hiccups and laughs while pointing to the side.

"What the hell, Yoyo!" Tao cusses and smacks his hands on the dash.

Yolanda's car sits between two cars, one that looks like a Toyota and an SUV. Behind them are rows of other vehicles. The Range Rover that Yolanda bashed sits directly behind her in the lot.

Tao gets out, surprisingly stable. He goes around and comes to the driver's side door; he shoos Yolanda to the other side and jumps in.

"Come on, come on, come on," Tiana urges him.

She raises her head from the back seat to see if anyone noticed them clip the other car, but the lot is empty. Tao gets the car moving and speeds off. She sighs and slouches back down, the cool sensation of the leather seat presses against her arms. As the car picks up, cold air rushes in, ruffling her hair from the cracked window. She smirks at the darkness. Her eyes grow heavy, and she dozes off.

Tiana wakes up, her thick hair plastered to the side of her face. She looks around and frowns. Her jeans are halfway off, one leg in, and the others hanging on the floor. The t-shirt she wore some hours before sits halfway across the room. She looks down as she gathers her bearings. She's on a couch, but it's not hers or Yolanda's. The wall behind her is grey. The one opposite is glass.

What the hell — a guttural groan is mumbled out; someone is stretched out on another sofa near her: it's Yolanda. She flops back on the sofa and closes her eyes as the world begins to spin.

She groans, "Damn you, Tao," she whispers into the silence of the night

We shouldn't be here, especially in this state.

Tiana overestimated Tao's stability. He ends up bringing them to his place instead of Yoyo's. Yolanda throws her hand over the side of the couch and snaps at an imaginary maid for a bottle of water. Tiana looks at her friend and wonders how she isn't passed out drunk. Despite her condition, her ability to sense fear isn't dulled. Her heart races.

Her paranoia was no match for her drunkenness as her head once again lolls, and she silently slips back to sleep.

Tao's laid outstretched like a starfish, his face hidden under pillows on the bed. He was a wreck. He rarely drinks more than two bottles of beer. To Yolanda's urging, he surpassed his record by 10. He should have passed out behind the wheel, but somehow he made it home.

Now he is deep in slumber, passed out. He only succeeded in kicking one shoe off before he fell onto his bed, facedown.

Tao wasn't alone. The shadowy figure of an entity filled the room. It's insistent grunting, yapping, and growling wakes Tao from his slumber. His leg twitches. His spirit was at war in his dream realm. Tao's fingers move across the bed as they pry at the dark shadows swirling around him in his dream. He can't see it, but it feels like time and space are closing in.

He struggles to fight the malicious presence. Martial arts skills do nothing in this spiritual realm. Half of Tao's willpower is reluctant to fight back. The face of the woman he once loved is attached to the evil presence. Tao's mind revolts against the fight.

No, Inyoku, don't do this, don't I don't want to fight you...... no!

Inyoku stands in the corner of the darkroom. Her nine tails squirm and writhe as they surround Tao's body. Her fox-shaped face and large slanted eye stare down at him with disgust. Inyoku smiles as she raises her dagger-sharp claws in the air, preparing for a one-strike kill. The fox demon cackles at the idea of Tiana being charged with the murder and Yolanda as an accomplice.

Her demon claws come swinging down, but they're stopped by an even stronger hand. The nine-tailed demon yapps and snarls into the dark fiery pits of Bounty's eyes.

"*Bounty*.... This is not your business," she growls, its voice monstrous yet feminine.

"Oh, he's definitely not mine, but Tiana is."

Before Bounty can cast his incantation to pull the demon from this realm, she coils two tails around his neck and throws him into the wall. Tao wakes flustered by the noise and freezes. Bounty's fury boils. He grabs the two tails gripping his neck and rips one right from her body.

The demon shrieks!

Out in the lounge, Tiana wakes too. She crawls over to where Yolanda is passed out on the sofa. She rouses her. Yolanda opens her eyes, asking, "Where am I?"

"She's here—" Tiana barely whispers, her throat tight with fear.

"Who? What?"

"Inyoku—" Tiana says, and scrambles toward the entrance. "Get up, we have to go!" Her heart plummets to her stomach. She hears a crash and gasps, "Tao—"

Yolanda scrambles to stand behind her, eyes wide and lips trembling.

"What's happening?"

Tiana looks at her and realizes Yolanda still doesn't understand the true danger that Inyoku poses. The grey walls in the hallways are filled with a miasma of black smoke. Specks of red glowing embers drift in the air.

Bounty?

"He's here—" Tiana mutters.

"Who?"

Tiana takes Yolanda's hand. She looks at her face. "Can you see the smoke in the hallway?" Yolanda frowns and shakes her head at the hall. "Are you alright? There's no smoke in here."

"Good. But something terrible is happening right now, and I think Tao is in trouble. We have to get to the bedroom and help him. Either come with me or hurry and leave from here."

Yolanda takes Tiana's hand and grips it tightly. "I'd never let you fight alone!" With one stiff nod, they head for the bedroom.

Tao scrambled to the corner of the room, eyeing the open doorway. Fear petrifies his legs to the floor. The horrid tails wave about, thrashing into everything they collide with. He rubs his eyes as he watches in horror.

Is that a nine-tailed fox?

The fox demon sees him in the corner and tries to pin him against the wall, with the spike on its tail. Bounty phases and reappears in front of Tao. He rips off the poisonous spike, then hauls himself at the demon, grips its neck, and lifts her off the ground. One of her tails sweeps his feet. Sending Bounty crashing through the window with the demon in hand.

Tao gets up and sprints for the door. Bumping into two bodies, he readies himself to strike them with deadly force when he realizes who they are.

"Tiana, Yolanda! We have to go—"

"Wait, where is he?" She runs past him. Yolanda trails behind.

Tao follows, asking, "Who, there's no time now?"

A stiff breeze rushes through the broken window. Tiana runs over. Out on the lawn, she sees the demon and Bounty, both in a tight battle. The demon screams in pain as Bounty brings his elbow down on its neck. A loud crunch echoes into the night.

Tiana turns to Tao.

"That's her true form, Tao."

Tiana rushes past him again and heads for the lounge, where there's a side is a door to the lawn.

"That's her out there. That's Inyoku fighting Bounty."

Tao runs beside her to the lounge, peering through the dark at the battle outside.

"Inyoku is a nine-tailed demon." Tao shakes his head in disbelief.

Bounty raises his hand to deliver another blow, but the nine-tailed demon escapes his grasp. In a flash, she's in front of Tiana, her tail raises, ready to strike her through. When a powerful force knocks her sideways.

Tao grabs Inyoku by her demon neck and grips tight. Energy rolls off his body as scale-like armor encases him. His short hair has lengthened, falling down to his side. Muscles ripple and pop as a mighty roar blasts from his unhinged jaws. Her tails stab and jab, chipping away at his armor. One dagger-like tail succeeds in breaking through the scales and cuts Tao deep. With a roar, he falls over. His other form dissipates as he hits the floor.

Before Inyoku can make another attempt towards Tiana, Bounty rushes over, snapping her neck with one quick punch. He plunges his clawed fist into the nine-tail's chest. Black blood shoots up into the air as her vessels burst. He twists his hand to the side, ripping her heart from its tethered chords, and pulls it free. In his hand is the still-beating heart of the demon.

Bounty staggers back from its corpse. His beast growls in satisfaction as it bites into the heart in his hand. He chews the last morsel and looks up as Tiana and Yolanda stare with wide-open eyes.

Bounty clambers to his feet. Yolanda runs over to Tao's side, checking Tao's pulse to make sure he's still alive. Bounty grunts at Tiana, placing his blood-soaked hand on her shoulder.

"Are you hurt?" his deep voice booms.

"No, I'm fine." Tiana looks him in the eyes and smiles. Bounty's nose twitches, surprised by the pride radiating from her scent. He then looks at the semi-conscious Tao and Yolanda and grunts. An awestruck Yolanda shyly waves her hand and says:

"Hi."

22

Chapter Twenty Seven

Jeff Zuken is the former owner of the Zukenburg Clearing Ventures, located near the South Branch of Chicago River's curve on the lower Westside. The property was bought off him a few weeks ago by a lesser-known company called Fenrir Enterprise, a company operating out of England. At least that's the information stated by the company's letterhead.

Zuken didn't get a chance to meet the new buyer. It didn't bother him much. He was happy to let the property go at three times the market price.

Stacia Rustivich was never that great with incantations and traversing realms, which was surprising for any female demon. But she never behaved like most of her kind. Her mother blames it on her mutt-blooded lineage that Stacia was dimwitted due to her father's genes. Stacia would just roll her eyes at her mother's disturbing ability to forget that she is the one that fucked the lesser demon, not the other way round.

Stacia doesn't gripe about her shortcomings. Where she struggles with guns, she masters with knives; where she lacks in womanly charms, she overcompensates in badass bitchiness. It felt like an even trade. So, where Ishtan and Keanu mastered jumping realms and chanting spells, she used the power of money. Instead of using the Versa mirror realm, she just bought the actual property. And with that, Stacia became the businesswoman of the family.

Tao Sun Ikeda looks nervously at the speedometer from the passenger side of Stacia's Alfa Romeo. The gauge reads 132 miles per hour, but it feels like she is racing them both straight to hell. Tao prides himself on having nerves of steel, but is feeling a bit cowardly as they drive along the river to the property.

Stacia looks over at her passenger, his face looking a bit pale. "You don't look so good mate, I know you'd probably not believe this, but I'm gonna say it still—"

"What is it?" asks Tao, while grabbing the hand rail above his head on the passenger door.

"I am sorry about your wife." She says while throwing him a weak smile. Something she is clearly not used to doing because it feels awkward.

"She wasn't my wife," Tao replies, jaw clenching tight at the thought of the betrayal.

Stacia glances at him and frowns. "Is that right?—Ishtan said she's your wife."

Tao pulls down on his sweater. The mere mention of her makes him hot around the collar.

"We were set to get married in a few months. But I was never gonna marry her."

Stacia shrugs, looks away, and says nothing more. She was used to being alone, a she-beast that did as she pleased, so small talk wasn't her forte.

"So how about you?" Tao replies while sneaking a quick glance at her face. He rubs his palms on his jeans. For some reason, his hands are damp with a light sheen of sweat.

Stacia looks at him and grunts, "Me? What?"

"Are you maybe—you have someone?"

Stacia grins, her nose slightly twitching as she sniffs the air.

Inner she beast: Mine – grrrr Mate now- strong -pheromones

Stacia grins, her teeth perfect pearly white, with a small gap between the front one. Tao stares at her and coughs in his hand as his manhood twitches in his pants.

Damn, she's attractive with her long ash blonde hair and striking green eyes.

"I'm a demon," Stacia says, "A real demon, from the deep dark places of hell itself, dating for us doesn't come easy."

Tao chuckles; he says, "I noticed. But maybe you have a demon lover or something."

Stacia smiles again. "Are you hitting on me, dragon boy?"

Tao felt flustered. "Oh no. Just making conversations is all."

Dragon boy... is that some Asian joke?

The road up ahead goes from tar to dirt. Dust billows behind them as the car goes through a narrow path and then comes out again. The river is on the left, and a white-sand yard spreads before them. Stacia parks her car beside an old semi, stretches her arms above her head as she says, "We're here!"

Tao asks, "What is this place? A shipyard?"

"Used to be. But I bought it for times like this."

The property's only structure is in the middle; a two-story with a warehouse below, its paint has gone from a red to a shabby brown. There's a truck in the warehouse; behind them sits a wrecked speed boat.

Tao's nose turns up as he eyed the place with suspicion. "Why buy this?" he dusted his hands off after touching the rusted rail. "Why not a proper house?"

"What's a proper house?" she asks as she goes up a stairway. Tao cautiously follows her. They come into an apartment that's well furnished even some of the décor were pieces Tao couldn't afford.

Well, color me impressed.

Considering the condition of the exterior, the interior is downright extravagant. Everything felt new. Stacia turns around and declares, "And here we are. Make yourself comfortable."

The long hall is re-fashioned into living quarters. There is a huge bed in the center of the room, then an area for sitting, where two couches face each other. Next is a lounge screened away by glass doors. The bathroom is behind a door in the lounge. Stacia calls from behind him and stands before an entryway that Tao missed.

"And here is the kitchen. Should you want to make yourself meals?"

Tao walks back in. He enters one of the most tastefully built kitchens that he's ever seen. It's like the rest of the apartment; modern and sleek, a long wide hall, two stoves on the right, and a huge refrigerator on the left. Sunlight floods the place through a window on the opposite side. Tao smiles at the white walls, at the flowerpot with aloes on top.

"You like it, I see. Is this proper enough for you?"

Tao sighs. "Yes, I apologize for my inappropriate judgment." He bows slightly in regret.

"Don't worry, lover boy. You have time to make it up to me, yes?"

"Yes," he asks quickly, "but I can't be a lover boy without a lover?"

"What do you mean?" Stacia's eye shimmer, as her inner beast stands at attention

Tao stammers. "I-I-I mean, look at you, you are beautiful. Very attractive. Maybe someone—"

"Do you want to see what I really look like?"

"What?"

"Do you want to see me? The real one, the demon I am? Your ex hid that part from you, correct?"

Tao shakes his head slowly, no longer feeling as flirtatious as before.

"Good, so let's drop this topic," Stacia says glibly. "Now do you want to cook?"

Tao nods slowly.

"Good, because I can't cook for shit.

23

Chapter Twenty One

Bounty sits alone on one couch. The wood moans and creeks as it struggles to bear his weight. Tiana, Yolanda, and a half-out-of-it Tao sit on the opposite side, facing him.

Yolanda stares at the *big man... beast... demon*. Right now, she wasn't sure what was what.

Tao swallows, still shaken by what occurred but more concerned about what he became. He rubs his palms together, trying not to look directly into Bounty's eyes.

Tiana tugs at the coils of her hair, not sure how to start this awkward introduction.

"You ate Inyoku's heart," Yolanda mutters.

Bounty nods slightly.

Tao says to himself, "If she was a nine-tail demon, then what the fuck am I?"

Tiana sighs and whispers to him, "I'm sorry, I never knew you had those.... powers... abilities.

I'm not sure what to say." She glances over at Bounty, who doesn't seem much inclined to share what he may know.

Tao nods, lost in thought.

Bounty sits very still; he looks like a big sculpture. The room falls into an eerie silence, with no one knowing quite what to say. "They will come looking when she doesn't show up," Bounty cuts in suddenly. His eyes fall to Tao. "She belongs to a very vengeful clan. They'll send more demons to avenge her death."

"Wait, are you saying the Nikaro clan are all kitsunes- fox demons? This can't be true. These are Onis from legends, things our oba-chans tell us, so we'll behave as children."

Bounty snorts at Tao's ignorance. "Ah, it all makes sense now." Bounty pushes his beast forward. His head shifts from a handsomely rugged man to Lycan.

Yolanda and Tao lift from the couch, preparing to flee. With a simple incantation, they both freeze. Stuck in place by his power. Tiana stands by his side and rubs his fur-covered arm, hoping to sway his attention away from them. But Bounty persists.

"Show yourself ancient one, arise from your slumber within." Bounty calls out into the room.

All three of them look around, confused, until Tao falls forward on all fours. His chest heaves as he struggles to catch his breath. Then, just like before, his skin darkens. Patchy black scales emerge on his skin, sharp talons extruding from his fingertips. He lets out a pained cry.

"Bounty, stop, you're killing him." Tiana slaps at Bounty's forearm, pleading for him to not hurt her friend.

"You dare summon me half beast!" A powerful booming voice silences the room. Yolanda and Tiana look at Tao in puzzlement. Tao stands to his full posture, eyes glowing bright green. Bellows of smoke rises from his reptilian-like snout.

"You have some nerve to question me, you latent Dragon! When you've been putting your scent all over my mate," Bounty growls.

"Yessss," he hisses. "She was mine before you ever got to taste."

Bounty steps forward, but Tiana beats him to the punch, swiftly slapping the smug look from Tao's face. As fast as his dragon came, it left. Tao stood there dazed, unsure of what transpired.

"Tiana? Did you just hit me?"

Bounty beast growled, proud of his mate's violent nature.

"Oh shit, you two have been holding out on me. I can't believe it." Yolanda folded her arms but quickly shut her mouth when all three turned to look her way.

"Wait, wait, what did I say? I swear, Tiana, I'd take our secret to the grave." Tao held his cheek with one hand extended to the other in submission. "No offense, big guy, I only see her as a sister now."

Tiana rubbed the knuckles of her hand, regretting punching Taos demon, dragon, lizard, whatever the fuck he was. She turns to Bounty, who still has a smug look plastered on his face.

"We have to leave this place," states Bounty. "We only have a small window of time before they find out about her death."

Yolanda raises her hand like she's next to be called on in class. With a grunt, Bounty looks her way.

"Sir, what is your name?"

"Ishtan Rustivich."

She nods. A big, fat, know-it-all grin spreads across her face as she turns to Tiana.

"It's nice to finally meet Tiana's mystery man—Tiana has told me so much about you."

Bounty growls out a laugh. "No, she didn't."

Yolanda shrugs, flustered. She nudges her friend in the rib, whispering, "Sorry, bitch I tried."

Tiana shakes her head at Yolanda's lightheartedness. "So what do we do now?"

Bounty assumes an air of authority. His eyes leave Tiana's face and focus on the group as one. His feral manner is dialed down, and he starts from the beginning: "I am Ishtan Rustivich, but I am also known as Bounty. I am a hell hunter.

"The woman you knew as Inyoku Nikaro was nothing but a demon in disguise. Her entire clan consists of demon assassins, just like the realm of men. Demons consist of various races. Be it land, water, air, or below, we also have territories and regions. Inyoku belonged to the Japanese faction, of which I don't know much. But I'm not authorized to hunt them down. Her family will seek vengeance. They are vindictive and extremely aggressive beasts. They don't forget. They don't forgive. And they will come for us all... especially you."

His eyes rest on Tao.

"They will stop at nothing until they complete their mission. You were never meant to marry. She was assigned to you for one thing, and that was to kill you."

Tiana worries for Tao, who appears to maintain his cool, regardless of the gut-wrenching news. He simply nods that he understands perfectly. Bounty continues, "It won't be long before they learn of the demise of one of their own, and they will regroup, prepare and come here—"

He rises up. "None of you are safe."

"What about my place?" Tiana asks.

"Out of the question."

Yolanda raises her hand. "Is my place safe? How about there? They don't know me, do they?"

"They do. Anyone close to Tao will be considered a Target. None of you are safe here or in your separate houses. We have to split. It's best we all go in separate directions." He chants something under his breath and turns his head slowly to the right.

Tiana and her group follow Bounty's gaze. Two figures appear by the wall near the hallway. Yolanda grips Tiana's arms so tight she winces. Tiana squeezes her best friend's hand, attempting to ease her uncertainty.

A male and a female step away from the wall. The moonlight illuminates the male's face. He has the same hair coloration as Bounty, but his hair is shaved on the sides with a top knot secured high into a bun. He looks like Bounty—they're similar but different. A coarse beard hangs down to his chest. He's shorter but seems to have a more muscular frame.

The female sticks to the shadows. From her silhouette, you can tell she had muscular curves. She has to be no less than six feet. Her long, ash blonde hair is the only thing Tiana could clearly see. They both wear dark leather jackets and boots, like they've just parked their Harleys outside.

"They're my brother and sister."

Yolanda raises her hand to ask, but Bounty cuts her off: "Yes, we are triplets."

"See, I fucking knew it!" Yolanda punches the air. Everyone looks her way, causing her to look down and pick the imaginary piece of lint off her sweater.

Bounty looks at Tiana. A strange scent of unease lingers from his mate. She notices him but averts her eye.

"The ugly one is Keanu. The pain in my ass is Stacia."

Stacia takes her time to look Tao over, assessing him from head to toe. She takes less time looking at the two women. When her eyes meet Tiana's, she bends her head with a short bow. The guy, Keanu, nods, and grunts a brisk, "Yo."

"Stacia, you'll take Tao away into hiding; Yolanda will be with Keanu," Bounty commands. He looks at Tiana. "And of course, you're coming with me."

"Wait, we have to be at work tomorrow. We can go to work, right?"

Bounty doesn't answer the question but gives Stacia and Keanu a growl to go on. Things happen quickly after that.

Yolanda says she needs to go by her place to get some stuff. Keanu tells her it's okay with him. She glances at her friend one more time before they embrace each other.

"I hope this shit ends soon," Yolanda whispers

"Me too." Tiana gives her best friend a love-filled hug.

They smile at each other one last time, and Keanu takes Yolanda by the arm. They walk out of Tao's house through the backdoor in the kitchen. Tiana takes Tao's hand. The sound of Bounty growling in the distance makes her roll her eyes. She squeezes it and tells him she's sorry again. Tao nods, reassuring her he'll be fine.

"This is a lot to process. I'm sorry my drama has caused this for you. As soon as you're settled, call me."

Tiana replies that she will.

When they're alone, Bounty comes to her and touches her face. Tiana's skin flushes at the fire in his hands. But this isn't the time for sex, she tells herself, as her body begins to react to him.

"What now?" Tiana asks Bounty for the umpteenth time.

"We leave Chicago."

"What? No, I can't leave—"

"We have to get out of the city," he repeats. "It's what's best."

"You don't hear me; I can't leave." She steps to Bounty. "I have to stay in Chicago."

"Why?"

"My Nana's here in the city. She needs me. She's the only family I have left, and she's old. If they can't find me, that's the first place they'll go."

Bounty stares at her face for a long time. Concessions aren't something he's used to making. But she belongs to him now. She was more than just some female asking for a favor: she was his mate. Even though he wasn't quite sure what that meant for them, he could do whatever he wanted to do with her—with a snap of his finger, he could even take her away into another realm.

Bounty finally blurts out, "Tiana, you don't understand what's coming."

"What's coming?" She puts a hand on his massive chest, her expression full of pride. "What's coming that the great Ishtan Rustivich, the Bounty Hunter, can't handle? You just killed a nine-tailed demon, ate her heart for dinner like it was nothing. And before this, you killed another demon to protect me. I trust you with my life to defend me from anyone and anything."

"One man cannot stop a legion,"

"A man, no, but we're talking about you."

She kisses his soft, full lips. Her tongue grazes over his protruding fangs.

"Fuck 'em!" she whispers.

Her hands go down to his hard-on and rub it.

"Don't start—"

"I can't help it. My adrenaline is pumping?"

"This is not the time, woman."

"Then fuck me quick!"

Bounty yanks her up into his arms and carries her into Tao's bedroom. With a quick swipe of his claws, he rips away Tao's sheet and removes her clothes, then ties her hands behind her back and pushes her butt in the air. With one hard yank, he pulls her to the edge of the bed, and with a forward thrust he roughly sticks his cock in without any sort of foreplay.

Tiana hisses at the rough intrusion. He fucks her harder, not even giving her time to adjust to the size of his shaft. In record time, her inner walls start convulsing.

Dark entities descend on Tiana's apartment Loft, just as he and Tiana leave from retrieving clothing and supplies. Bounty summarizes there must have been at least six of them. Their shadowy figures dissipate and reappear like miasmic mist. The moonlight shrouds their silhouettes: fukumen partially obscures their Asian faces, medium heights, and black clothes. Their blades sparkle in the low light of the approaching dawn.

Three come around the building, their vigilant eyes surveying each room. They get to the back. One stations himself below while two climb up the fire exit. There they wait with weapons at the ready—shuriken, glinting from the low light in the alley, unaware their prey has come and gone.

Bounty grips Tiana's arm as they walk down 24th Street, away from the sunrise. Tiana squints from the morning light. Chicago is slowly coming back to life as they round the corner on Canal.

Bounty stops by a parked Oldsmobile. He touches the rusty yellow top, and the car horn chirps once as the door unlocks.

"Get in," he snaps.

Tiana pulls the passenger seat door open; it smells like moldy earring backs. She enters the car while Bounty goes round. Almost yanking off the door to get in. He looks like a bull stuffed in a tuna can behind the wheel of the car. Tiana smirks, trying to laugh. Bounty rubs his finger over the ignition, and the car starts.

Cool, Tiana muses. He drives past "Food For Less Takeout" on 51st Street, turns the corner and heads onto Interstate 50.

"Do you have a destination in mind?" she asks.

"Nowhere just yet."

"So, we're just gonna drive around all day?"

"We'll drive until we throw them off your scent," he mumbles.

Tiana drops herself lower into the seat. Her eyes grow heavy as she watches the electric wires crossing from pole to pole. When she rouses from her sleep, the exit ahead says North Branch Chicago River. The car stops; Tiana looks out the window at the heavy foliage and trees on the right. The musky stench of the river makes her scrunch her nose. For the first time since last night, Tiana feels the pains of hunger.

"I'm hungry. Do you eat, like me?" she asks Bounty, just realizing that, besides sex, they really don't talk much. He looks at her as his meaty fingers scratch at his scruffy beard.

"I eat you, don't I?"

"But that's..."Tiana giggles. He asks her why she laughs, and Tiana squints up at the mellow sun.

"I'm really starting to notice just how different we are. I have so many questions, but I don't want to burden you with them all?"

Bounty says nothing. His hands grip on the steering wheel, his eyes set on the road. Cars zoom past them, heading in various directions. A semi-truck roars by, and Bounty glances at its taillights. Then checks the rearview vigilantly, staying alert of their surroundings.

"Ask away," he finally answers.

Tiana turns to him and folds her legs under her knees, her thick, coily hair lazily running over her shoulders. "I was just curious about you. I didn't even know you had siblings or that you're a triplet. I was just surprised. I know you're able to fuck, but do you do other things, like go on dates, get married, have children, you know, the works, the whole marriage/mate thing. I just don't understand what it entails for us!"

Tiana laughs, attempting to lighten the mood.

Bounty looks at her face, expressionless. He could smell the scent of her uncertainty. But he was also uncertain himself. *What does this all mean?* His inner beast chuffed back in reply.

Tiana continued, "I just have so many questions? Can you even have families if you don't age? Your kids would grow old while you stay young forever, or would they not age too because they have your genes? See, I'm rambling, right? I just don't get it."

Bounty nods slowly, not confirming or denying any of her questions. Tiana bites her lips then asks, "Have you been... you know, mated before — do you already have children?"

"No," Bounty grunts out.

"Do you want to?" she asks in a small voice while intentionally looking out the window.

Bounty glances at her then looks away. "No, I haven't been mated. I never wanted to be, nor do I want kids." His answer shouldn't hurt her, but it does. Tiana isn't ready to face the reason why it stings so much to hear it.

"Alright, enough questions. I'd really love to get some breakfast. Let's find a place we can eat."

Bounty grunts and starts the car.

The parking lot looks empty, except for three cars parked by the Laundromat a few doors down. Bounty parks the Oldsmobile close to the street, handing Tiana a wad of money, instructing her to get enough food to last her until the end of the day.

Tiana walks to the entrance with her hands tucked into her pocket, her eyes darting side to side for anything that seems out of place. She glances back at the Oldsmobile; it sits empty. He isn't on the road or anywhere on the lot. She shrugs, somewhat use to his sporadic disappearances. She walks into the restaurant, confident that, if trouble lurks, Bounty won't be far off.

Rows of stools line the front of the counter. A lone man in a white shirt wipes his hands and whistles along to a song on the radio. The clock on the wall behind the man ticks aloud; it says 11:53.

"Hi," the man calls as Tiana shuffles onto a stool.

"What can I get here?"

"You from out of town, huh?" the man asks.

Tiana considers her response for a second.

There's no need to lie, but I can't be certain who's who right now.

"Yes."

"Aww, really, from where?"

"From Up North, Milwaukee?" She frowns, hoping he'll stop asking questions.

The man gives Tiana a lopsided smile and tells her it will be about five minutes for her cheeseburger and cheese curds to be ready.

"Meanwhile, do you want some coffee?"

"Coffee will be just fine," she says, and looks out into the street through the windows. The car sits in the lot, still empty. Tiana half expects that Bounty will leave her for a bit to handle whatever he has to do.

"Miss?"

The man at the counter is back. He puts a steaming cup of coffee before Tiana and begins to mop his hands on the apron at his waist. Tiana stares at his movements over the tip of her cup.

Tiana looks from the man's hands to his face. Something about it isn't right. His forehead is funny shaped; his mouth seems too broad, his neck too thick. His arms are covered in thick hair. Tiana swivels around on her seat; there are no other patrons. Everything just feels unusually still... *It's too quiet.* There's a knobless door at the far corner behind the man. She leans forward and peeks over the counter—it's bare, no utensils, no condiments.

"Traveling the road, traveling the gravelly road, traveling the road, the long way home, gravelly with stones," sings the man on the radio with a Texan twang.

The man behind the counter whistles along, wiping his large

fur-covered hands. Their eyes meet. Tiana's blood runs cold. His eyes have green rings around the irises, his canines look unusually long. Tiana stops drinking the coffee. She asks for her cheeseburger.

"I'll go check now," says the man, and he breezes away.

Tiana slides off the stool and heads for the door.

"Miss?"

She looks back.

"Where are you going?" the man asks. In his hand, he is holding an oil-soaked brown paper bag.

"I, I, just wanted to—"

"Here."

He grins, puts the bag on the counter. His teeth are a combination of white jagged knives and shards... sharp and glistening. A black tongue flicks over his canine. He winks.

Tiana reacts fast. She grabs the door handle and pulls with all her might, but the door doesn't open. The man behind her comes from around the counter; he knocks the brown bag to the floor as he lifts the slat. Tiana trembles, staring at his approach in horror.

"You know, miss, you give off such a mouth-watering smell." He snarls, spittle flying from the side of his wide-faced lips.

Tiana's throat constricts. She tries to scream, but nothing comes out. Her back pushes against the door, but there's nowhere to run. When she finally finds her voice, he's the first name. She screams, "Bounty!"

The man laughs. "There's no Bounty here, little lady; no one can save you now! Don't worry, I'll go slow; give you a bit of pleasure before I rip your guts out?"

"Get away from me!"

"Come on, don't be shy. Think of me as a big puppy that wants to play?" The man's fly opens, and a horrendous-looking thick phallus extrudes out.

Tiana shrieks.

****

The moment they drove into the parking lot of the diner,

Bounty knew their enemy was waiting. He watched Tiana enter as he chanted, a spell of invisibility cloaking him from the human eye.

Bounty could smell the Hell beast from here. Due to its level, it is able to hide its true self from an Empath like Tiana. Bounty isn't surprised she can't detect the man's dark nature. In turn, Bounty pulls forth his demon beast from the depths of the shadows.

He hurries out the car and sweeps across the parking lot. Two more demons slither out the alley of the building, blocking his way.

"There's a Bounty on the Bounty," the twin krakens sing, yellow tentacles hang down their faces, like wet mopping locks. They have orange-tinged skin and opaque green eyes, their clothing soiled and torn as they hide under the guise of homeless beggars.

They were no match for Bounty, but these water demons seemed intent to start a war. They circle around him, their venom-covered tentacles elongated and swelled. But Bounty stands ready.

They leap at Bounty. He catches the closest one by its slimy neck, and the other one circles to the back. Bounty rips an oozing wet tentacle off the demon's head. It screams in pain as the green pus bubbles out of the wound. Bounty tosses him to the floor and kicks the other one.

It tries to sweep Bounty at the ankles. As usual, these soggy fuckers depend on sneak attacks. Before the demon's teeth can sink into his hamstring, Bounty grabs its neck.

Tiana's blood-curdling screams sounds out from the diner. Bounty's anger blazes red hot. He looks at the writhing demon in his hand and rips its jaw clean off. With a quick whip of his hand, he plunges his fist down into the demon's chest and rips out its beating heart.

He tosses the demon aside, throws the heart in his mouth and chants a spell, burning the corpse with ether.

The glass of the diner explodes as Bounty barrels through, tackling the demon off Tiana. They crash against the counter, smashing it into splinters. The Hell beast's eyes twitch and spark as Bounty tries to choke him.

"Amaruq!" Bounty growls. "Who sent you after me?"

The demon wheezes. "Come now, old friend. Who would send me after you? You are the one they send after others—"

Bounty pins Amaruq on the wall and asks Tiana, "Are you hurt?"

Tiana picks herself up, stumbling over debris. The restaurant is decimated, and so are the windows when Bounty crashed in. Tiana picks some of the splinters out of her hair and dusts some of her clothes.

"Watch for the glass!" Bounty warns.

He redirects his attention to the demon within his grip and growls, "I'm going to ask you one more time. Give me a wrong answer, and I'll break something you can't replace. Who sent you?"

"I don't know their name?"

Bounty slides his left hand into Amaruq's fly while extending his claws. There's a popping sound, and Amaruq screams. A thick vein pumps across his forehead. He shrieks at the roof; red tears pour out of his eyes.

Tiana grunts in pain and limps across the floor to a stool that's still standing. Blood leaks from the shard of glass jutting out over her left calf. Several crimson drops hit the floor.

Bounty's face turns feral. His beast's nose flares as smoke billows from his nostrils.

"Now or never, Amaruq!"

"Bounty p-p-please," the demon chokes.

Bounty beast grows bigger, Amaruq's bones crack and pop as he loses circulation.

"Bounty, please, let him speak!" Tiana pleads.

"No, he's too little too late!"

"We need the information! For all our sakes!" she begs him.

Bounty relaxes his hold. Amaruq falls on his knees and tumbles over to his side, hands around his neck as he hacks and coughs to catch his breath while dragging his body to lean against the broken wall.

"Talk!" Bounty snaps.

Amaruq waves his hands in the air, asking for more time to get his voice back. Tiana limps past Bounty, sidestepping the sharp jutting edges of the broken wood. She crouches in front of the crumpled demon.

"Amaruq. Bounty here is ready to rip your heart out of your chest and eat it. So why don't you give him what he wants?" Amaruq leans over, losing consciousness. Tiana gives his face a harsh slap.

"Tell us, Amaruq!"

He sputters, "Bounty's gonna have to promise to let me go if I tell him."

"I can't make him do that."

"Information is currency. I need my life in return." Amaruq looks at Bounty and gives him a ghastly grin. "Deal?"

Bounty nods.

Amaruq glances at Tiana and coughs at more bloody goo. "I don't know much. But I know the Nine-tail family wants the Asian guy for a reason. Something about him makes him valuable."

"Inyoku wasn't going to kill him?"

"No. They want him alive. And they'd stop at nothing to get him," Amaruq grins. "And you too. They definitely want you."

Tiana looks up at Bounty; she swallows the bitter bile that races to her throat, and to Amaruq, she says, "How did you find us so fast?"

"We can fucking smell you from ten miles away; we knew you'd come this way."

Tiana rises and walks to the place where the door used to be. She folds her hands across her chest and sighs.

Bounty takes one last look at Amaruq and says, "She saved your life. It won't happen again." He grabs Tiana's arm, and they walk out of the diner.

Amaruq calls after Bounty, "You've found yourself one hell of a bride, Ishtan Rustivich. Does she know her own fate? "He shrieks in laughter as the Oldsmobile drives away from the parking lot.

"Hahaha!"

24

Chapter Twenty Two

Detective Terrance Slaton stares at the wreckage of Philly's Diner and shakes his head. The place is crawling with cops, medical personnel, and nosey pedestrians craning their necks over the police barricade. There's a TV truck across the street; a female reporter kept pestering him for a statement but was met with silence.

"Detective, do you think it's more than a gas leak?"

He frowns at the reporter, shakes his head, and walks away. Reporters never understand the words, no comment, no matter what you tell them, they'd put words in your mouth, anyway.

He walks through the wreckage, carefully investigating the scene behind the door, at the back of the shattered counter. It was terrible in there when they opened it. Apparently, someone killed Phil Thompson, the owner, skinned him alive. There was a foul stench in the air. His gut instincts tell him the scene was riddled with clues; he just has to find them. His hard sole shoes crunch through the broken glass as two forensic agents collect blood samples from the smears on the floor.

"I want the results on that ASAP," he tells them on his way out. He walks back to his car. From there, he watches the crowd gathering. Most of them live across the street. People are attracted to death, like flies to a carcass. And sometimes, the predator comes back to the scene of the crime.

Someone in this crowd has to know something.

He watches the mouths move, their gestures as they talk about the incident. Some of these people are likely regulars to this diner, too. Terrance's eyes go to the edge of the crowd, and a Hispanic male catches his attention. A worn black hoodie hides his face, but something about him looks familiar. He isn't talking with anyone; his eyes are narrowed at the broken window. The Detective starts his car and drives out of the parking lot.

Soon the young man walks off too, strolling down Main Street. His sneaker leaves imprints in the light dusting of snow. He crosses the street and stops at the pawnshop, looking back to make sure he wasn't followed. He comes out of the shop's back and walks through the snow-covered backyard of another building. A chained dog barks and charges at him. He gives the German shepherd the middle finger and saunters on. He steps over a kid's bicycle with a twisted training wheel, then passes the side of that house whose owners are on holiday in the Maldives.

He tells himself he may come back that night to check the house for something he may need. He even takes a peep through the window casing the place for later tonight. He keeps walking along the sidewalk and faces east towards 8th Street, where he takes two more cuts about a block away from his ramshackle home.

An unmarked car suddenly pulls up beside him. Marcio takes off, instantly knowing the black guy in the car is a cop. Either that or a nark. So Marcio bolts down the street, the back of stumbling from the shagginess of his jeans.

Detective Terrance Slaton steps on the gas and pumps it. He crosses Marcio on 7th as he tries to dash into the alley side of an apartment.

"Freeze!"

The lad ignores and scales the low wire fence and over the

twisted hull of a kid's airplane in the patchy brown grass. Terrance goes after him, cocks his gun and screams again, "Stop, or I'll shoot!"

The male stops at the fence behind the house, bending over out of breath. Marcio would have gone up the fence if it wasn't so high. Plus, a pit-bull is waiting at the other side. Marcio puts his hands on his head.

"I didn't do nothing," he spits.

"Then why'd you run?"

Terrance takes Marcio's hands and cuffs him. He drags him back to his car in the street and pushes him into the passenger side. When Terrance is seated, he flips the hood off Marcio's head.

"You were at the precinct, weren't you?"

"That wasn't me."

"Look at me!" Terrance slaps the lad's head. "You passed me at the door two days ago. I remember you. Tell me what you were doing back there at the restaurant."

Marcio gives him a confused look; he shakes his curly hair making it fall down his face, hiding his guilty eyes.

"I was just passing through, that's all," he grumbles, his eyes shifty.

"Tell me what you know."

"I don't know nothing," Marcio insists.

Terrance takes his phone from his pocket. "Alright, let's find out." He dials and listens, then he says, "Katherine, tell me; Hispanic dude, curly hair, and a scowl. You had him leave a statement the other day."

He listens. The male stares at him, his eyes huge and expectant. He adjusts himself, anxiety setting in.

"I have rights," he murmured. "Fucking pig!"

"Yeah, that's him," Terrance says. "Marcio, right? Loony piece of shit, yeah."

"What? Me? Looney, what she gon call me looney for?"

Detective Terrance puts his phone away and looks at the lad. In a soft tone, he says, "Marcio, I could take you in and stamp something on you. I'm sure I can find something in your record; I'll make it stick like glue. Trust me. But we can talk about this right here, right now."

Marcio throws his head back, purses his lips. He hisses.

"What's it gonna be, man? Here or the precinct?"

"I already told the lady cop; she didn't believe me—"

"I'm listening."

Marcio lays it all down again. He tells Terrance about the drop he and his friend Ace did with some white guy named Harvey. And how this big guy jumped down from the roof and killed everyone except them.

"And you think he was at the restaurant too?" Terrance asks him.

Marcio looks at him and nods, pure terror in his brown eyes.

"He's not human."

"What do you mean?" Terrance inquires.

"I saw him pull these guys apart. And those other mother fuckers, they just like him. They're not human, maybe aliens or something. I don't know."

After a few seconds' thought, Terrance says, "I'm gonna take you in for more questions. I need you to tell the artist at the precinct he'll make a photo of this so-called alien guy you told me about. We need to catch him. I'm not arresting you; I just want you to help me catch this guy, alright?"

Marcio nods.

Terrance takes off the cuff from the lad's hands and drives away.

****

Tiana rises from the hotel bed reluctantly. Bounty has been shuffling her around Chicago all day and night. Her thighs are sticky from the residue of their earlier passion. She waddles to the toilet after making sure not to disturb Bounty, who's fast asleep. She runs the tap filling the tub midway, timidly dipping her feet into the water before stepping all the way in. She imagines him bathing with her.

That would be a disaster, she giggles. *His oversized body would overflow the tub.*

She closes her eyes, imagining round two of their lovemaking; for some reason, she is quite insatiable these days. She runs her soft fingers over a nub, imagining his tongue in her slit. Her nipples harden as her fingers explore the still tender places Bounty bruised from their last rendezvous. Her head falls back over the edge of the tub as she rubs her engorged nub faster. Her back arches, hips jutting out of the water as she fucks her own hand. She jumps and stops. Bounty is standing there, leaning on the bathroom wall.

No words are spoken. His erection pointing towards Tiana, telling her he already knew exactly what she demanded of him. Bounty walks her over to the bed. Turning Tiana slightly, so her head falls over the side. She sucks his cock between her thick, wet lips as Bounty leans across her body. Dragging his fingers through her pretty pink slit. He rubs it slowly; it's sticky with the combination of their essence. The sight of his seed dripping from her core makes his cock fatten. Tiana sputters and gags, startled by his sudden growth.

Fuck, I love that sound.

He thinks as his ass cheeks tighten. Bounty fucks her throat rigorously. Bloodshot, teary look up at him. He tries to pull out of her mouth, but she grabs his ass and sucks him in deeper.

Bounty throws his head back and exhales, struggling not to prematurely release his seed. He rolls her over and spreads her leg. With one hard thrust, he enters and gives her a deep, probing.

"You like it?"

She bites her lower lip, refusing to reply. His cock throbs inside her.

You like it when I bite my lip, huh?

So, she bites her lips some more and looks into the dark eyes of her demon. Bounty starts to thrust into her faster. His eyes are transfixed on her lips; his massive hand reaches forward, gripping her neck. But Tiana pushes him off just before he's about to finish. Bounty holds back a growl. Furious, he raises his hand to strike her thick thighs, but she catches his hand.

"Ishtan, let me fuck you," she moans.

He grunts and reluctantly takes her place. Tiana straddles him, taking his huge cock in her hands, and strokes the shaft. She turns around, giving him a clear view of her forbidden flower. He growls and grabs her ass, dragging it to his face, and begins to kiss her core.

Tiana swoons, the feeling so intense she can't help but cry out. She rolls her waist and shakes her big ass saturating his beard with her juices. Bending forward, Tiana takes his cock in her mouth and sucks it hungrily. With fourplay out the way, she turns again. Taking his stiff shaft and burying it deep within her. She rocks back and forth. His manhood slips in and out of her tight wetness. He raises his head, watching their flesh slap and meet rhythmically. Bounty bellows coming first; his hot spurts send her tumbling into an orgasm right after him.

****

The next morning, Tiana goes down to a nearby food truck and purchases eggs, vegetables, and pastries. When she comes back to the room, Bounty is sitting watching the news. Tiana looks at the screen. Her jaw drops open. She rushes to the couch where Bounty sits expressionless.

"The CPD is investigating the destruction at the diner. We have an eyewitness account, and we assure the public that the suspect will be apprehended."

The screen switches to the hand-drawn photo of — Tiana glances at him. "That's you, Ishtan. They have a picture of you. How is that possible?"

He leans forward; his eyes remain on the TV.

The news continues, *"There is evidence to suggest that the suspect is also responsible for the killing of three men whose bodies have vanished from the scene on the Southside. The body of the owner was found skinned, tied, and gagged."*

Bounty's photo appears on the screen again with the announcement that he's on the run, armed and dangerous. If he is sighted, citizens are to call the police immediately. Tiana picks up the remote control and clicks off the TV.

"Fuck," she says, flicking hair from her face. "It doesn't bother you?"

"Should it?"

She sighs and takes a look at the bag of eggs and pastries. The food makes her nauseous.

In the bathroom, she stares at herself in the mirror. A zit below her left eye is now ripe and ready to pop, and she touches it.

Bounty hasn't moved from his seat, somewhat curious about how the news channel is portraying him, so he clicks the TV back on.

There was no telling the troubles that await them now, with Bounty's picture broadcasted all over the news. Tiana looks at her reflection and fidgets with her hair, lips poked out, because Bounty won't allow her to call Yoyo, and definitely not Tao. Her phone rang nonstop the previous day. Christy called, then the head of the CHD, Aaron Lett. Even Toppence called and left a message, worried about her not coming in.

If I don't get back to work soon, I'll be out of a job.

Tiana rubs her temple, the familiar ache behind her eyes starting to return. *The whole world could burn for all Bounty cares. All he seems to want to do is fuck, fight, and vanish into the air.*

Tiana walks in the TV is playing again. The news anchor that Yolanda likes is giving his report; there's a confidence in his voice and efficiency in the way he gestures at the building behind him — Bounty reacts, sitting forward as if he can't hear the TV. Detective Slaton points to the dilapidated factory somewhere around Chicago. The street in the background of the live feed seems deserted. She comes around to look at Bounty.

"You know that place?"

He nods.

The report states that several people were killed after a drug deal went wrong. They are looking for the suspect in the picture. Tiana rises from the couch slowly, her eyes on Bounty's face. He turns to look at her, blazing green eyes like gemstones.

"Did you kill the people they are talking about?"

"No. I killed demons, not people."

She glances at the TV again. The camera pans into the wreckage of the diner. Highlights of the paramedics rolling a body out of the restaurant keeps replaying on the feed. The camera flips back to Detective Slaton.

"This suspect must be made to pay for these crimes—"
then he nods to the camera "they're claiming you killed
people! Demons are one thing, but humans are another!"

Bounty rises to his feet. Tiana feels doubt enter her mind.

"Bounty's big and powerful. He's more than capable of killing; would he really discern between friend or foe? The detective on the TV said he's a cold-blooded killer. I saw him kill Inyoku and other demons. What's stopping him from hurting me, too, besides us fucking."

"This is all a mistake. A terrible, terrible mistake. Maybe it's best we go our separate ways!"

Tiana panics, clutching the couch cushion near her hand.

Bounty grunts. "You won't last an hour alone on the streets, Tiana."

"I'll take my chances. I may be worse off being with you." Tiana points a stabbing finger at the TV. "They're gonna have my face on the TV soon. They will call me an accomplice, and they'll lock me away, oh God, my job." Her nervousness shows through her cracking voice.

"You can't leave my side," he growls, his lips pulled up in a snarl.

Tiana continues to back away. She hits her heel on something, glances at the floor to see one of her shoes.

She paces the suit. "Ishtan, please. Let's turn ourselves in. Let's go to the police. You can tell them everything you know about those guys. You can—"

"I can't. And you know this already. If you stop making things hard, I can take you to the mountains — hell, even another realm."

"Mountains... what realms?"

"A hideaway or something." He shrugs, and his massive shoulders barely move.

"No!" she yells. "Don't you get it!? I'm about to lose my entire existence, everything I've worked for! I can't go to work, can't see my friends, can't see my Nana! She's the only family I have! The cops are going to think I'm a murderer when they find my prints in the restaurant and wherever else!"

Her face breaks and tears spill from her large brown eyes. She crumples against the frame of the door. Bounty holds her, carries her to the bed. She begins to protest, assuming he just wants sex. But Bounty caresses her face, cradles her stomach and kisses her forehead.

Rocking her gently against his hard, muscular chest. Tiana is taken aback, never imagining a brute like him capable of compassion. Still unable to resign herself to fate, she weeps for everything she's bound to lose.

Bounty can do nothing more than rub the muscles in her shoulder until Tiana falls asleep.

****

-Sunday morning-

Sunlight peeks through the gap in the blinds. She squints, looking through the window at the people hurrying past on the sidewalk below. She finds herself alone in the room. Bounty must have done another one of disappearing acts. She pulls the blinds close and sits on the couch, contemplating her next move.

"Come on Tiana, what Nana would do in this situation!" she yells into the silence. *Nana will probably call the cops if I don't visit or call soon. Maybe it is best for me to stay away. Until things have settled down.*

In the shower, her mind goes through various scenarios, struggling to make right everything that has gone wrong. A smile forms at the corners of her lips, at the memory of Bounty holding her all night, waking up to find herself in his arms, his eyes wide open, watching over her. Just felt right. His breath warming her neck and his hands rubbing the muscles of her shoulder was one of the most intimate non-sexual interactions they'd shared.

Her eyes rove over his body; he's chiseled to perfection, like living rock molded by masterful hands. His thighs are two thick logs of timber.

Tiana grips his penis, sliding her soap-sudded hand up its length and back. She strokes it round and around, as Bounty pulls and thrusts his hips forward. She kisses his nipples, one, then the other. In silence, they wash and worship each other's bodies.

Tiana sits on the couch towel, drying her thick, coily hair. Since Bounty came back, he's been fascinated with her every move. She gives him a weak smile as she dresses and puts on her clothes.

"I need to say goodbye to my Nana, no matter what. I owe her at least that."

Bounty growls but nods in understanding.

There's a man standing ten feet from the Oldsmobile with a black bushy beard and a cigarette sticking out his mouth. His shirt's grey and his pants are black. He rubs his hand in his long dark hair and looks up and down the street. He removes the stub of his cig and tosses it on the ground. Then he walks off into the distance.

"Scout," says Bounty. "Harmless." He crooks Tiana's arm into his and they walk towards the car.

"Are we in danger?" Tiana asks, her voice rising in fear.

Bounty doesn't say anything until he's behind the wheel. "That's just a low-grade demon sent to monitor us," he explains. "They just watch. They keep to themselves mostly, just keep track of the checks and balances."

"What is there to check?" Tiana asks as the car heads back downtown.

Bounty looks her way, then replies, "The pact between heaven and hell, a treaty that keeps us out of each other's way."

"Are you serious?"

Bounty nods, checking his review periodically to make sure they aren't being tailed.

"So is all that stuff in the bible true, like the book of revelation?" Tiana leans towards him in fascination.

He glances at her, shrugs. "That comes later. If the balance fails."

"And if doesn't?"

"Things remain the same."

"Are you kidding me?" she exclaims. "How about heaven? I mean, going to heaven, does that even happen when humans die?"

Bounty starts to speak, but Tiana cuts him short, unsure if she is ready to hear the truth. He frowns and gives her a curious look. "I don't think we're ready for this conversation."

"Oh, fuck it, this is too much—" Tiana slumps in her seat. Bounty chuckles at her frustration and continues to drive.

25

Chapter Twenty Three

Nana lives in Englewood, in a grey stone two flat with two crabapple trees on both sides of the house. Bounty and Tiana pull onto the block, find parking a few houses away. It is already dark, but Nana Debbie is a night owl, always willing to stay up to watch her favorite TV show, MASH.

Bounty shivers, his hackles raised. He peers up and down the street before poking his head in the window and frowns. "It's clear."

What the fuck is this feeling?

Bounty's beast is on full alert. He didn't like this one bit, but knows Tiana won't leave without doing this. As soon as Tiana steps out of the car, Bounty stiffens and grunts. Across the street stands a dark figure. Tiana begins to back away to the sidewalk behind her. She looks over at Bounty, who appears eerily calm. The figure steps into the light and Tiana relaxes.

"Keanu, brother."

"Ishtan," Keanu says, and pats Bounty's shoulder.

Tiana lets out a loud exhale and bends over to lean on her knees. Fuck, these guys are creepy. She joins the two men, anxious to hear the news that Bounty's brother has about Yolanda and Tao.

"Tiana." Keanu gives her a small nod and smiles. "Is this brute treating you well?"

"Yeah." Tiana whispers, finding his extroverted personality quite unexpected.

Keanu looked like Roman Reigns had a baby with a biker, but he still favors Ishtan slightly. Despite his size, he exudes sweetness that warms Tiana's heart. Keanu reaches out and shakes her hands like they're old business partners.

I like this dude, demon or not. I wonder how Yoyo's taken to him?

He looks at Bounty and becomes all business again. "There's more watcher traffic lately, Ishtan. What does it mean?"

"I've seen them, means nothing," Bounty grumbles, rocking on his feet. "How are Tao and Yolanda keeping up?"

Keanu's eyebrow arches up. He shoots Ishtan a look that Tiana doesn't notice. "Our two wards are adjusting... to their circumstances."

"When can I see them?" Tiana asks. A slight glimmer comes to her eye at the mention of their names.

A car drives past, and they all fall silent until it rounds the corner and exits the block.

Keanu smirks and says, "When Ishtan says it's safe."

Tiana bites her lip. Bounty reaches over and tugs on her chin, dissuading her old habit. Keanu silently watches their interaction.

"Ishtan," Keanu interrupts, you're sure about the watchers?" Telepathically he warns his Brother, *News of your mating must have reached the old man. He'll keep sending watchers to confirm if it's true. Be smart, brother.*

Ishtan nods, then tells him, "Keep an eye out; if it looks like you're being followed, let me know."

"I'll keep her safe. You just worry about yourself for a change. I can smell her friend's scent all over you."

After a bit of silence, the sort that Tiana assumes of older male siblings, Bounty asks, "Any other news from home?"

"The usual."

"Which is?" Bounty cocks his head to the side.

Keanu shrugs. "That Grandpa wastes his time letting us half-bloods live, especially you. The amount of demons being sent back is way too few. Blah blah and so on. If he wants more souls, his old ass can come up himself and catch them. Those are Stacia's words, not mine."

Bounty's lips quirk slightly at the sides, like a smile, and his eyes shimmer green. "Stacia's still a fireball, huh?"

"Oh, don't you, and I know it; she even has that Asian guy sparring with her in the ring."

Bounty belts out a full belly laugh, "She'll eat him alive."

Keanu agrees. "I'm betting on it."

Keanu glances up at her Nana's house and his playful nature fades from view. With wary eyes, he peers at Tiana again, as though there is something that he'd like to tell her, but can't quite bring himself to say it.

Both men look hard at each other. Keanu asks him telepathically, *Are you sure about this?*

Bounty nods.

Keanu swallows and says, "So long, guys. Tiana, try not to give this lug too much of a hard time, will you?"

Nana's door is illuminated by a lone bulb hanging over it. Tiana thumbs the doorbell twice. There is a rumble in the house, then heavy footfalls.

"Who's there?" Nana shouts. Her southern drawl is unmistakable.

"It's me, Tiana."

"Baby girl, that you?"

"Yes, Nana Debbie, it's me and a friend."

Nana cries out in laughter when she recognizes the affectionate nickname Tiana's called her for decades. She removes half a dozen bolts that held the door in place; they clack and crackle until the last one is pulled away. Tiana quickly whispers to Bounty, "She probably has more locks than Fort Knox?"

Bounty stares at her blankly, as if he didn't hear her joke.

"Tough crowd," says Tiana, doubting Bounty's taste in humor. "Ouch."

The door opens a crack. Nana's face is there: reddish mocha skin with a faint trace of wrinkles. Her beautiful smile pulls apart, revealing pearly white teeth.

"Come on in, baby." Nana starts walking off as Tiana and Bounty enter a dark hall.

"I seen you with someone. Who's that?"

"My friend—"

"Your friend, huh? Well, come on let me get a gander at... him." Nana stops suddenly in her tracks and turns slowly. Her frame shakes and bends, then straightens. She peers through the darkness and her eyes narrow at him. She walks closer until she's beside Tiana, cocking her head at the hulking figure of Ishtan Rustivich.

Her voice trembles. "Abomination, you are not welcomed here!"

"Hello, old timer, now it all makes sense?" barks Bounty.

"Nana?" says Tiana. "What's wrong?"

Tiana grabs her Nana by the hand. Nana Debbie ignores Tiana; she takes one more step, her back straightens a little more, removing the hump that crumbled her with age.

"You don't belong here, boy! Best you leave while you still can!"

Tiana stands in front of Bounty. "I am sorry Nana, but he's just a friend, okay, I know how you feel about whites—" she pleads.

"Shut up, child. This ain't bout his skin, I know evil when I see it!"

Nana storms up the stairs towards her private quarters. Tiana tells Bounty in hush tones to wait. Bounty stares mutely. He watches as the old woman trudges up the stairs, a faint smile on his face, but Tiana doesn't see it.

Nana's house is big; two bedrooms on the top level and four rooms below. She sleeps on the top floor, in the bedroom to the right. The other she reserves for Tiana and Yolanda whenever they come to visit. Nana sits at the dining table and sulks, her small frame trembling with anger. Tiana pulls up an old, worn chair and joins her.

There is a bowl of fruits in the middle—apples, grapes and

peaches. But Tiana does not have much of an appetite left after the incident downstairs.

"Nana, it's because he's white, right?"

Nana glares at her. "No child, I know times have changed."

Tiana's brows go up. "Then what?"

"You don't—"

Bounty walks in. Dark and hulking. He stands there and says nothing, just stares in silence. The old woman stares back. Tiana feels the energy waves swirling around her, not exactly maleficent, but strong enough to frighten her.

"He is a demon," Nana hisses, slapping the table with her time worn hand. "A half-breed."

Fuck, Tiana thinks. "How can you see it? Nana, I can explain this. Please let me—"

"Ain't nothing you need to explain, child. I know what he is, a hell hound from hell. A reject half-breed wolf."

"You would know a thing or two about rejection, old timer," Bounty growls.

Nana's mouth snaps close. Her eyes shift from Bounty to Tiana, an apologetic expression drifting over her face.

"Why don't you tell Tiana what you truly are before attacking me? Doesn't she deserve to know your truth?" Bounty pulls a chair from the table, turns it around and straddles it. His emerald eyes stay pinned on Nana's face.

"Don't you talk about the truth to me? Ask yourself: what's the real reason you're here?" she snaps back.

Tiana's mind is reeling. Her head snaps back from Nana to Bounty. She wipes her sweaty palms across the thigh of her jeans. "Nana? What's he talking about?"

The old woman sighs. "I guess it's time."

The house is quiet; the clock over the china hutch reads 11:52pm, five hours after the usual time Tiana visits. Somewhere in the house a radio plays, the music sounds distant and foreign. On a different day, maybe Tiana would have recognized the tone. But tonight, the mood is solemn.

Bounty remains where he's been sitting, arms folded across his broad chest. Tiana refuses to budge. When Nana tells her to get some leftover ginger cookies from the oven. Tiana heard the request but her legs felt heavy. Like if she moved from the chair, her whole reality would crumble away. Nana sighs and excuses herself, her chair creaking as it scoots back. She has placed the cookie tray on the table, then sits and looks Tiana straight in the eye.

"What I'm about to tell you will flip your burgers in the air, Tiana. But I want you to understand what I did, and why I did it."

That familiar tension starts throbbing behind Tiana's eyes. She wants to turn to look Bounty way, but her nerves won't allow her.

Has everyone been lying to me this whole time?

A bitter stench perfumes the air. Bounty's beast growls, sensing its mate's distress.

"Go on," Tiana says, trembling with trepidation.

"That fellow here can see my true nature—" Nana says, her voice hard as steel. "And before I go on about who I really am, I need you to know that I love you. Do you understand?"

Nana touches Tiana's hand across the table. "Don't be afraid, child, you're getting his beast all worked up from your scenting."

She chances a look towards Bounty; his face softens as he nods his head for her to listen. The chandelier over their heads gleams brighter. Its light goes from a dull yellow to a fluorescent wash. All the colors in the room seem to hum. Even the white table cloth shines with such radiance that Tiana has to avert her eyes.

It was like the sun lowered itself from the heavens and was placed into the room. Tiana watches the older woman hover from her seat, suspended in the air over the table. Her skin peels back, reversing its aging. Her hair morphing from tangled matted grey to lustrous silky black tresses. Her shoulders straighten, no longer hunched over by the burden of age. Her old holey moo-moo falls off, replaced with a silky white remnant. Her breasts sit high, her face touched by a youthful sheen, skin smoothed like creamed chocolate.

Tiana stares up at the perfected version of herself, an almost complete replica of her younger years. She staggers back, knocking over her chair. Nana's voice comes through the bright light:

"The fact that you can gaze upon my radiance is proof that you are my child, Tiana. You are my daughter, from my womb you came. I am what some call a light bringer, a Harold of the heavens of men; I am not a mixed-breed like you or Bounty. I am one of the original fallen clan."

Nana spreads her hands; wings shoot from behind her back, eight in total, Large-tattered feathers lined with gold. But they are not what they used to be; only some look healthy while others are tinged grey. Many of them look burnt and bruised. The light bringer regards her wings with regretful eyes. She tries to beat them, but her attempt falls short, only a feeble flap. Her feathers fall back to her side. She settles in her seat, looking beautiful, young.

"This is who I really am, Tiana, and who you are too," she reveals.

The house has regained normalcy. The electric bulb overhead burns dull and low. Tiana silently picks her chair up and pushes it under the table but refuses to sit. Her hand grips the top of the chair so hard her knuckles turn white.

"How's this possible? So are you a demon, yes or no?" Tiana snaps. A single tear runs down her cheek.

"I understand, but watch your tone. I raised you better than this."

"You raised me... or is that a lie, too?" Tiana's tongue clicks in disgust.

"I ate of the flesh and took pleasures from the realm of men, some three hundred years ago. I fell in love with a man... a human, your father. But my kind... are hunted. When we rebelled against heaven, many of us were forced to pick a side. I didn't.

"I'm a dark angel, not a fallen. However, there is a price to pay for living among men. There's always a price: angels, demons and even fae came after us, me and my man. They hunted us across the seas, over land, everywhere we went. I wasn't aging, but he was. Soon the humans took notice. It wasn't safe for him to be with me. But he loved me still; through it all, he stuck with me. He sacrificed himself for me. When they weren't looking—both enforcer angels and hunter demons—he let me hide. I wasn't beside him the day he died. They tortured him to get to him. You see, they use people you love to get to you; they use your pain to make you vulnerable."

She looked at Tiana with teary eyes, "When he died, my only concern was to keep you safe. And I did. I taught myself to age like the rest of the humans around me. It was difficult, but I learnt. The more I practiced, the better I got. So, I have died many times from old age, only to surface again to another country, another town, another name. But I carried you in my womb hundreds of years until I felt it was safe."

Tiana felt her legs weaken. Wearily, she pulls out a chair and sits. Bounty continues to watch silently. "I'm an angel. You were pregnant with me for... years?" Tiana takes a deep gulp of air, unable to fathom what she was hearing.

"Half-angel. The correct term is Nephilim." Her mother adds, "Your father was human."

"And he sacrificed himself to save us?"

Her mother shakes her head slowly.

"But... I was raised in a foster home. You came and got me when I was twelve years old—?"

"When I had you, I still hadn't mastered the art of growing old. I couldn't keep you with me, so I left you in a foster home, worked there for a while but had to leave again because I was drawing attention to myself: I didn't age, never got sick, hardly ate, and I never tired. I maintained my angel powers; except for my wings when I rebelled. Do you not wonder why you rarely took ill, and why you have certain gifts? And most importantly why he chose you—?" Tiana's mother looks at Bounty.

"He chose you because he's drawn to your scent. When you're near me, I'm able to cloak you somewhat, but not fully."

"The fuck! Ishtan? You knew about me too?" She glares at him, her heart racing.

"Not at first, but it became clear later on. It wasn't my responsibility to tell you. It was hers."

"What! Fuck you, Ishtan! Fuck you, so this wasn't love, huh?"

"Language, child—"

Tiana turns on her mother. "No, mom—fuck, should I call you mom now? Or just plain Nan? I've lived all my life thinking you are my Nana, when you're really my mother. And to think that you've lived for centuries? And you, Bounty, you knew who I was, and you used me! You know what, was it fun watching me struggle, fun watching demons chase little ole Nephilim down—"

Bounty's face tightens. His inner beast howls, tearing at their soul, seeking to explain to its mate.

Tiana sighs and walks away from the room. She stomps back moments later.

"Wait, there's something else I want to know: do you guys know each other? Did you meet in the past; maybe have these little prep talks about me? Was this all a fucking set up? Hell, maybe you two have even fucked!"

Bounty gets on his feet, growls. "Watch it, Tiana!"

"Or what? Tear my heart out and eat it just like you eat everyone else? Or maybe haul me down to hell brag about claiming yourself a Nephilim?"

"Shut up, Tiana!" her mother bellows.

"Thank you, mom. Thank you very much." She begins to cry, her lips trembling. "Thank you for taking away the only thing that would have made the greatest difference in my life. Thank you for taking me to that foster home, for letting me grow up without the love of a mother! And thank you, Bounty, for showing me there's no such thing as true love!"

Tiana stomps out of the dining room. She swiftly made her way to the spare room, banging the door shut behind her.

The dining room quiets for a moment, except for the rhythmic chorus of crickets outside. The atmosphere grows awkward with every passing minute. The angel and demon stare at each other.

"What now, isn't this what you wanted?" asks Tiana's mother eventually, snapping the cord of the silence.

The demon stares in Tiana's direction, motionless, like a rock. He turns his head slowly. "Why don't you stop pussyfooting and tell me what you want to say?"

"I want you to leave my daughter alone."

"She's my mate. I need to protect her."

"She's my daughter," the woman counters. "I can protect her far better than you, hunter."

"What don't you understand? We've already been mated."

The woman slaps the top of the table suddenly, anger brewing in the pits of her eyes. Her face glows with unnatural light. Her eyes become the size of quarters. Her tattered wings open up behind her, and she doubles in size.

"She is my daughter! And I order you to let go of her. You will be the death of her. She's not as strong as you think — ,"

"Well, maybe you should get to know her better. She has power, she just needs to invoke it. I will not leave my mate."

"You brought the trouble that she's in now on her?"

"I didn't. It's in her nature. She will invite attention. Surely you understand this more than anyone else."

Their eyes blaze against each other, dark angel and half-breed demon almost at each other's throats. Both powerful, and both rejected by their own kin. Tiana's mother's eyes glow white, like the sky of heaven where she once called her abode. Bounty's glows green, bright as hell-fires and shrouded in endless darkness.

"Ishtan Rustivich, I rebuke thee."

Bounty gets off his chair and walks out of the house in silence.

26

Chapter Twenty Four

When she wakes, Tiana feels different. Perhaps yesterday's revelation was impacting not just her mind but also her body. It was like something ripped the veil from over her, like she is seeing the world with brand new eyes. Tiana rises from the bed, still clothed in the attire she arrived in. She swings her feet off the bed and looks at daylight streaming in through the window at the far end of the room.

Even light has a different texture to it now. She reaches out towards the ray, curious to see if it will become something malleable, and it does. She rubs her eyes, thinking it must be a trick. She walks slowly to the window, parts the blinds, and looks from the top of the buildings up into the sky. There, nestled in the grey-blue clouds, is the sun itself, a radiant ball of fire. Tiana looks directly at it, training her eye on its image. She can clearly see thousands of volcanoes spewing out of the sun's surface, red rivers of fire shooting upwards. Then crashing back into the river of molten lava.

My God, It's beautiful.

A tear runs down her face as the truth settles over her. She lets the warmth caress her and fill the pores of her skin. The sun's energy flows through her and around her. Tiana attempts to take in more.

-Knock knock-

There is a light rap on the door. She looks at it, hesitant to see whoever stands on the other side. A denim shirt, brown with dust and age, rests on the top dresser near the door. She had put it there some months ago when she slept over in this very room. She turns around, looking at the posters and trinkets and small reminders of her teenage years, when she stayed here after leaving the foster care system.

The knock comes again.

"Tiana? Can I come in?" asks her mother's voice, pleading, no longer sounding brittled with age.

She trudges to the door and pulls it open.

"Can you go through walls, too?" Tiana asks. "Bounty can. I was thinking instead of knocking. You could just slip in through the cracks or something."

Her mother laughs. It is like looking at a slightly different version of herself in the mirror. She's dressed in a pair of jeans, a Black Sabbath shirt rolled up to the elbows. And she's barefooted, just like Tiana likes to do when she's alone in her apartment. Tiana looks at her for a long while before letting her into the room. Her mother sits on the edge of the bed and Tiana joins her.

After a bit, her mother asks, "Do you understand the seriousness of this situation?"

Tiana sits back and hugs a pillow. "You've been following the news?"

"Yes. And that demon of yours told me everything—"

"Everything? Did he tell—never mind." Tiana's shoulder sags.

"Whatever you're doing with him is your business," her mother says. Waving her hand in disgust, she adds, "You're grown, and what you do and who you do is on you!"

"Did you just read my thoughts?"

"Not exactly. I read impulses, expressions, and with you I've always been accurate." She laughs, smacking the back of Tiana's hand.

Tiana sighs again, this time deeper.

"And don't worry about him. He left. He'll be back to see you. He has business to take care of."

"I need to get to work. We have bills to pay. I worked hard getting my Ph.D. I can't just walk away from everything I've accomplished." She slumps forward.

I'm losing everything. It's like nothing is real.

"Your days in the CHD may be over, Tiana. You're in danger from the nine-tailed clan. They are not to be played with. For now, you'll stay here. Where my aura can cloak you. And if you must go to work, be vigilant and careful, nothing is as it seems. Some of the people you see on the streets aren't really people. You can't see the more powerful beings because your full powers haven't awakened."

"Did you really love my father?" Tiana asks abruptly. Nan smiles. "Yes. I did my best to learn what loving a human man meant. Love is a difficult thing for an immortal to understand, but I think I did it. Not one day passes that I don't think about him."

"You think maybe he's in heaven now? Is that even how things work?"

"It doesn't really work that way, Tiana, but I do know his soul is at rest."

The two women are quiet for some time, each with their own thoughts.

"Do you have a picture of him... maybe not because it was so long along?" Tiana asks shyly.

"Yes, I do have something with his image," Tiana's mother replies.

They walk to her mother's room. She rummages through an old silver colored box lined with a red cloth. It's filled with old things, memorabilia, old Polaroid photos, seashells and ancient coins. She sits with the box on her lap, Tiana sitting beside her. When she finds what she's looking for, she falls silent, sullen.

She stares at an old drawing. It looks dog-eared and slightly torn. The drawing is dated 1721. Fort Mose, Florida. Age has blurred the colors. The background has weathered to a dull grey. But the people in it, mother and the man next to her, supposedly Tiana's father, are visible. Tiana gently takes the drawing from her and looks at it. He was a strong-looking man, broad shoulders, with a wide nose. Her mother Debbie looks just like she does now, but more innocent. Tiana can see the love and pride in his eyes as he looks at the woman he loves. The woman he later sacrificed his life for.

The missing piece fell into place — last night, Tiana met her mother, this morning she finally met her dad. Tiana smiles at the strong, handsome black male in the picture. She can see her curly hair must come from him too.

Tiana gives the photo back, but her mother doesn't accept it. Nan pushes back her hand.

"It is yours to keep now. So you can someday show your children."

Tiana rolled her eyes at the last part and sighed, "You look not a day over twenty."

Nan smiles. "I feel so old. Looking this young doesn't match how I truly feel. I tell you when you've spent as much time living as I have."

"Will I be like you, live forever?"

"That's something for you to find out by yourself."

Tiana snaps a photo of the drawing and saves it to her cloud, then puts the photo away in her dresser drawer.

27

‹✥✥›

Chapter Twenty Five

Christy Marlow stands at the end of the corridor, in front of Dr. Tiana McGuire's office. Her head cocks to the side, surprised to see Tiana standing by her desk. Her wide smile beams from ear to ear as she embraces her old friend.

"I have covered for you for almost two weeks now," she fusses as she shuts the door. "Toppence vying for your position to Aaron, but the rest of us were against it. Toppence is an asshole, can't trust him."

Tiana puts her bag on her table, where a thin film of dust has settled.

I'm going to need the cleaner to come in here.

Christy asks about Tao. Tiana tells her Tao is in Japan to see to family matters. After Christy leaves, Tiana takes some time to read through the 316 unopened emails.

-Knock, knock- Someone knocks on the door.

Tiana pauses, unsure whether to invite the knocker in. She and her mother talked about it that morning, warning her that some fae and demons couldn't hurt you if you didn't invite them in. Tiana goes to the door and asks, "Who's there?"

"Cleaning service, please," says a soft female voice.

She looks back at her dust-covered desk, and the files scattered around the room. Then pulls the door open. The woman is of medium height, with black hair tied with a flower printed bow. She's wearing the usual janitor's uniform. Tiana inquires, "I've never seen you in this building?"

The cleaner smiles shyly and confesses that she's new. She breezes right in and starts cleaning. Tiana probes the woman with her mind; her vibe is good, she's pure hearted.

"I'll be just ten minutes, Doctor."

"Call me Tiana."

She smiles politely as she walks out of the office to attend an early meeting. As she walks through the building, Tiana makes sure to stay vigilant, making sure to utter the prayer of protection her mother made her memorize.

Tiana finishes her meeting, uses the toilet and goes to wash her hands. The air freshener in the bathroom is evergreen fragranced. The thought of Bounty crosses her mind. He hasn't been around. Not that Tiana cares one way or the other—at least that's what she wants to believe.

She wants to see him, just as much as she wants to see Yolanda, also Tao.

Dammit, I miss him.

Her mother told her, "Look, you have to stay away from Bounty. Nothing good is gonna come out of it."

"But I'm a Nephilim; I'm not really an angel." Tiana shrugs, not understanding why heaven would even care.

"Angels and demons cannot mix." No matter how small your light bringer genes may be, they won't let you mate him. It would be seen as treason against the treaty. It's not worth the unbalance."

"The balance." Tiana mutters to herself as she dried her hand under the vent.

The fuck? The balance? Who even makes these rules? God or the devil?

At night Tiana sleeps comfortably in her childhood bed at her mother's place, the overhead fan on high. One sock on, the other lost within the sheets. She dreams of Bounty standing by her bed, watching the drool slide down her cheek. The moment she wakes she feels the family ache from his fullness in her core.

She smiles now at the memory of that dream as she walks back to her office, secretly wishing him to appear. But he hasn't shown up. He hasn't contacted her since he left her mother's place.

When she gets back into her office, the cleaning woman is gone. Christy sticks her head in the door.

"She's gone, huh? I'm going to need her number. She did one hell of a job cleaning."

"Who's gone?" Tiana asks.

"Your cleaner, of course. She says you brought her in—"

"What?! But—"

Tiana chuckles. *Mom.... That had to be her!*

Christy gives Tiana a questioning look.

"No, never mind. Yeah, I brought her in, the cleaner," Tiana stammers. Christy shrugs and leaves.

****

The autopsy reports arrive from the cook county medical examiner. Detective Slaton looks it over twice and another time for good measure, but it still doesn't make sense to him. The evidence doesn't add up. The suspect has either holed up somewhere or has somehow escaped the city. The APB the Detective put out has yielded nothing.

He shuts the door of his office against the humdrum of the precinct lobby, so he can think through the pieces of information he has. It's all disjointed, each clue leading him in opposite directions, like a gathering of jigsaw puzzle pieces that don't match.

The suspect leaves no trace: no prints, blood, or hair. He's like a ghost. Even the bodies of his victims go missing. Terrance sits back and wonders why he even cares so deeply. He thumbs through the forensic report again. Evidence shows that some of what Marcio said was true: the number of people at the factory matches the shoe prints found. There's even a print so large that the forensics team estimates the man's weight to be about 440 pounds, seven-eight feet tall. But that makes ab-solutely no sense. Someone that big would stick out.

Terrance doesn't want to believe it, but if he puts stock in Mar-cio's story, then that is the only plausible way any of this made sense. Someone strong and big did come down from that factory roof. The fiber that forensics dusted from the glass and floor proves that to be true. And then all the bodies of the missing girls, with their faces ripped off, hearts taken, and wounds cauterized, fit the M.O.

Maybe Marcio was really on to something.

He thinks about it again and shakes his head in denial. He tosses the file back on his desk. Until the diner incident, the precinct had kept the murders out of the press, but those snoopy reporters kept getting wind of them.

By mid-afternoon, Terrance tries, the monotony finally getting to him. He drives around the streets of Bronxville and Central Boulevard, eyes the guys on the street doing small time dealing, the skimpy dressed girls propositioning men around 4th and 45th. These are consequences of a system that consistently fails its people. They watch his black Buick and eye him with suspicion as he drives by and stops at the Pheasant Tail Bar on the end of the block to catch up with his good buddy Herbert Alsen.

Terrance loved to come here. Drinking to get away from the guilt-tripping of placing fellow blacks behind bars. *I'm just a cop, a detective doing my job. I can't carry the weight of the world on my shoulders!*

Olsen owns the Pheasant Tail, and he's always behind the counter serving drinks, seven days a week. Terrance walks up to the bar and slides on a stool. He looks back at the tables where a few white guys are drinking. The bar's clientele is a mix of all races, but the Germans seem to congregate here.

"Hey, my friend," Herbert says, grinning with his big brown teeth. There's some grey in his sandy crew cut hair. He's looking about sixty these days despite him being 53. He shakes hands with Terrance over the shiny black counter.

How's business, old chum?"

"Business is good, except for the blueback's. They want me to pay dues."

"Pay it."

Herbert's face falls. "Come on, you're a cop. You're supposed to help me."

They laugh at the joke. Herbert pours Terrance his bourbon and tells him the first glass is on the house. Herbert leans forward and, in a low tone, whispers, "I'm hearing things."

"I'd like to hear it."

"Yeah. It's still on the fresh list but a high ticket. They are saying there are new guys in town doing good numbers in the organ business."

The skin around Terrance's neck chills. He asks, "Whose saying?"

"Whispers, unknown faces. Toneless voices. But that's what I'd heard. I have two daughters, you know. They take faces and hearts, these freaks. They sell them at drops like it is dope. Some black dude spilled the beans in some bar and it filters down here. You look like you're in the know, Terrance."

Terrance nods, swallows the rest of his drink and is about to slip off again when Herbert says something else.

"They say it started in Berlin."

"What?"

"My cousins got a friend in this hotel, he's a security guard there. Said they found some girl with a missing face and heart some weeks ago. That's like three weeks before I heard it here. Terrible thing, I'm scared, man."

Terrance asks Herbert for the name of this hotel and the man tells him, "The Berlin Honors." He thanks Herbert and sends his regards to his girls. Herbert asks him if he's got himself a girlfriend yet.

"I'm too busy." Terrance laughs back.

Herbert calls after him as he steps out into the sun, "You need a vice, man."

Back in the office, Terrance searches Interpol for anything about missing girls, or girls with missing faces and hearts.

Nothing...

Then he searches for The Berlin Honors Hotel. He finds it, but there's no report of a crime committed in the hotel. "Of course," he murmurs, slamming his fist on the desk.

Shit can never be easy.

He sits back, exasperated. *Another fucking roadblock.* He scratches the back of his head, then picks up his diary and checks his schedule.

I'm going to Berlin. He sighs; it's a shitty way to police, but I'm tired of grasping at straws.

28

Chapter Twenty Six

Nothing is as it seems. There is a mirror between this world and the one the human eyes cannot see.

The Norfolk Yard on the city's map is just one two-story building with a large space for parking in front of it. Twenty meters from the building are the train tracks. Beyond that is Canal Street, which leads to Roosevelt Road and so on and so forth.

What the map doesn't show is that there is another building, exactly like the Norfolk Yard; it has the same color, two stories, red roof and parking in front. The difference is there are no workers wearing white hard hats, blue jumpsuits, working nine to five. In the Versa realm, this alternate building stands behind the original one. It sits empty except for its only occupants Yolanda Prescott, age twenty-nine, fashion designer and hair stylist best friend to his brother's mate. Unlike his brother, Keanu tried to stay by his ward's side, only leaving to tend to personal matters from time to time. For the most part, he keeps her hidden away in the Versa realm. It's safer this way. The less time she spends out in the open, the less drama they experience. But Yolanda had a way of wrapping Keanu's pup around her finger.

"My shop is my baby, my livelihood. When this is all over, I have to have something to come back to. Haven't you ever heard of doing things in decency and order?" Yolanda chides.

But Keanu doesn't argue with her. He quietly drives her to her shop on Marshall Boulevard. The black tourmaline crystals above the door tinkle and clang as they enter Yolanda's salon. Keanu's eyes dart up and his inner beast growls as a brief snap of energy rolls over him.

"Oh shit now, who's this handsome jock you got coming up in here, honey? Thelmala Ray asks while leaning out the dryer catching herself an eye full.

"You're too young to even know what to do with all that. Send him over to me, girl." The women in the shop giggle and bat their eyes Keanu's way. The tall brute just smiles and nods.

Yolanda replies with a playful wink, "Nah nah, this here is my white boy, go get your own."

One customer asks, "You got yourself a white boy for real?"

"Uh-uh, you got a problem with that?"

Not one objection leaves anyone's mouth, and with a *humph Yolanda* wanders to the back and retrieves a few more of her things. It's all a guise, but that is something Yolanda can't tell them. Keanu has made it painfully clear he only wanted to keep his ward to be safe. Yolanda hurries over to the computer and clears her schedule for the next four weeks. After a quick chat with the salon manager, about which clients to split with the other stylist, Yolanda's salon business is squared away.

She cuts her eyes to where Keanu stands, his long dark hair sitting in a bun. If Yolanda didn't know any better, she would swear he was just a regular handsome man. Keanu can feel her looking his way, but he ignores it. Opting to silently check out her station instead, carefully looking at her crystals and trinkets. Until she announced, she was ready to leave.

It had only taken two days of being Keanu's ward, for Yolanda to find out where Keanu drew his bottom line. He can be playful at times, but when it comes to keeping her safe, he's all business. And in his eye Yolanda is just that. It is no secret that she finds him attractive.

But Yolanda's number one dating rule is no chasing. Plus Keanu made it clear he isn't interested, so she leaves it at that.

"If I'm going to be gone a while, I need to end things with my boyfriend too." Keanu nods and drops her off. Without uttering a word of complaint, he parks the car and just watches and waits.

"Do you guys sleep?" Yolanda asks him when he picks her up outside the man's apartment the next morning.

"Not like you do." His words are blunt and quick.

"So, what? Do you sleep upside-down like bats do, hanging from trees and shit?"

"I mean I'm trying to keep the conversation going, but I'm dead ass serious."

Keanu smiles at her, but says nothing.

"Are you guys vampires? You know the whole stake to your heart type of thing?"

"No."

They drive in silence for a while, then Yolanda bust out, "You can call me Yoyo, okay."

"Okay, Yoyo, if that's your preference." Keanu grunts.

"And you can talk to me any time you want." You know get to know your ward.

"Why would I want to do that?"

"Seeing as you don't talk much," she explains. "I know some guys are like that, all shut-mouth and shit. But didn't know y'all white. *Cough.* I mean, Demons were the same way, too. If you haven't guessed I'm a talker, I tend to ramble on and on sometimes. So we should get to know one another, right? That should liven things up a little bit between us. Ain't we gonna be living together for a while?"

"Yoyo, we are not living together. I've been asked to protect you, that's all, it just happens to mean we'll be in the same area or room for most of the time—"

"So that's the same damn thing. You just made it sound cold?" She rolls her eyes and shrugs her shoulders.

"I find you... and the way you word things quite odd, Yoyo." He sighs, stroking his long beard as he looks out towards the road.

Yolanda laughs, throwing her head back. She glances at the demon as he drives and says, with a posh British accent, "Pardon me, my friend, but I speak that way when I'm with my friends. It's called code-switching that certainly doesn't mean I'm dimwitted, might I disabuse that impression."

When Keanu looks at her again, it is with genuine interest. They drive the rest of the way to their hideout in silence. Yolanda's no longer interested in making friends.

29

Chapter Twenty Eight

Tiana pulls the cover over her head. It's hot—too hot. She rolls a few times, then kicks the cover off. Grabbing a pillow for support, she feels nauseous, then chucks that same pillow to the floor. No matter how much she tried, a good night's rest just isn't happening.

She goes to work, halfway presentable. With black slacks, a sweater, and no earrings, Tiana just feels off. She doesn't even attempt to tame her coils. Tiana is on autopilot, hurrying to complete the project for Pfizer. Working with several other multinational corporations means she is short on time, with an even tighter budget. Her career is on its way up, and her income, too. If she can just ace this, the board would approve her promotion, despite the Inyoku fiasco.

Tiana types on her computer. Her hands slow down as sadness suddenly engulfs her, a deep foreboding lingering deep in her chest. She shuts her computer down and sits back, silently watching as the clock ticks towards 4:30.

The house is quiet when she gets home, the whole world quieter. Mama Debbie turned in earlier. Tiana now looks at her mother in a different light.

Why does she sleep? Or eat like humans do? When she was pretending to Nana, she ate. But there is no reason to keep doing it now.

Tiana recalls her memories of childhood Sunday gatherings, how the folks from the church would come around, and there'd be some singing, dancing, and food. Tiana walks over to the window. The street is full of shadows, moving silhouettes, and shifting lights. Her car is down there behind a — There's someone standing there behind her car, just staring at it. It's a man, and he's dressed in a red, or brown, or wait, maybe it's grey—Tiana can't be sure—turtleneck sweater, black trousers. His hair looks black from here. Smoke from cigar bellows in the air. Tiana gasps, "It's the man... no, the watcher they saw on the street the first day Bounty brought her here.

What is he doing?"

The man continues to stand there, his deep-set eyes stare at Tiana's corvette. Hazy smoke leaves his mouth and nose, carried off by the wind.

Tiana hears movement from below. The man must have heard it too, too, because he looks sharply at the house. His jet-black eyes contain no iris, but there's fear. He stumbles backward, and as he attempts to run down the street, there's a whooshing sound before quiet returns.

Tiana scurries back, goes back to bed, like a naughty child hiding from their parents. The man must have seen Mama Debbie. Tiana is sure of it. Thinking that makes her feel safe here, she tugs up the covers and lulls her head as she dozes off to sleep.

The moment her breath slowed and eye closed. Bounty had already arrived in her room. This old song and dance was nothing new for them. For some reason, her subconscious always called to him when she fell asleep. He never came at the same exact time, but there was never a night he wasn't there. Some nights she would conjure him up in different scenarios. The night before, he appears with a tweed tuxedo, gold shoes, and blonde hair that fell past his shoulders. His face is leaner, his eyes blue instead of green. Other nights he is a beast, other times, he looks innocent.

Bounty stands at the end of the bed, breathing in her overly rich scent, a worried frown on his face. With every summoning, it seemed to get headier. Tiana's face scrunches up as she senses him come near. She can feel his warmth, even in the depths of her sleep.

"I can't stay away from you, Tiana," Bounty speaks into her dream space.

"Why did you leave me? Why can't you stay?" her voice chants out.

"We long for our mate," growls out Bounty and his beast, step closer. He touches her naked feet. Slowly trailing his sharp claws up her thighs, pushing them apart as he drew closer to his goal. Her physical face scrunched up, but her impassioned pleas resonate in the subspace.

"Ishtan, please, I need you."

Deep in her dreams, Ishtan begins to walk along the side of the bed. He glides his hand over her feet, rubbing lightly as he passes. His touch causes fire to erupt underneath her skin. The first thing she feels is her dark nipples pucker and tighten. A zap of energy flows from the tips of her finger to her toes; pleasure cascades off the edges of her body and converges at the juncture between her hips. She opens her mouth and moans, "Yes..."

"I need to be in you," Bounty growls into her ear. "Let me and my beast have you."

Tiana whimpers, "How do you want to do that?"

"Close your eyes let me show you."

Tiana leans back, imagining herself on a bed of soft pink and yellow rose. His finger leaves, plucking at the stiff points of her breast. "Ishtan," she moans, pushing her large breast deeper into his hands, seeking his warm touch. Then, all of a sudden, there's another set of hands, bigger and a bit more forceful.

"Who's there?" Tiana moans, unable to fight off the rough caresses.

"Shh... it's just me and my beast," coos Bounty.

Their touch comes back. Prickly hairs scrape over her pussy. As a long-textured tongue grazes her clit, her breath stops. Don't stop, please. Her thighs shake as a furred finger parts the puffy lips of her vagina, digging deep into the moistness of her core.

"Oh, Bounty, fuck me now!"

She reaches down, gripping and tugging on his thickly furred ears.

She opens her legs wider than his beast feasts upon her with passion. Another set of human hands caresses her shoulder. Tiana jumps, startled by the touch. She looks up to find Ishtan in human form. She looks down and sees his were-beast rubbing his furry muzzle over her clit. She looks back and forth, growing wetter at the prospect of having both, trembling with excitement. She rolls her hips against his were-beast face as Ishtan watches.

Suddenly she's flipped on all fours, and the probing of a fleshy knob sinks into her. She gasps at the fullness. The human Ishtan pumps deeper, forcing every bit of his dick into her quivering sheath. She opens her mouth and screams but is silenced by the beast ramming its thick cock in her mouth. As one pulls out, the other pushes forward. She rolls her hips, meeting Ishtan's every thrust while looking his beast in the eye as she gags on its cock. Her core clenches tighter as she feels both of their thrust getting wilder, no rhythm to their strokes, just spasmed pumps as they rapture. They both bellow, flooding her cunt and her mouth with seed. As they pull out, she falls deeper into her sleep.

****

Tiana's days start to blur together. Everything around her feels numb. The Pfizer project was starting to feel overwhelming; luckily, Tao popped back in to save the day. With him back, things are starting to normalize, at least for her career. Her personal life is another story. Tiana looks up. Stacia sits in the far corner of the office. Her eyes were glued on Tao, a schoolgirl smile plastered on her face. Tiana takes the earlier statement back. Things are as normal as they could be with Bounty's sister Stacia glued to Tao's side. Watching them interact left the bitter taste of envy on the tip of her tongue.

The sound of a cell phone ringing broke the slice of the office, and Stacia excuses herself to take the call.

"Tiana, I need to talk to you about something," Tao stated as he shuffled a stack of the manila folders before placing them in the cabinet on the far wall. He sits on the edge of her desk, his once pale skin now a healthy shade of dark peach. Even his muscle mass has returned, maybe even a bit more than before.

"Inyoku's family, and my family's elders have been calling nonstop, they've officially been made aware of her disappearance," Tao started, a bit of harshness in his tone.

"But wait, they've been known; they're the ones sending demons after us. Is this just a ruse to save face?" Tiana sat back in her chair, unsure about how to feel about it.

"My father's family wants me to come home immediately, stating if I return, the rest of you will be left out of it."

The weight of Tao's words hits Tiana like a brick. "What are you gonna do?" Tiana asks.

"I can't go... but I need to go, Ahhh none of this makes sense." Tao paces.

Tiana has never seen Tao so perturbed. His hands fumble through his full black hair in frustration.

"And if you don't go, what happens?" Tiana asked.

Tao rubs his face and sighs, "Stacia explained that the Japanese faction will see it as an act of war, despite saving you. Killing Inyoku was out of his jurisdiction; either I sacrifice myself and go, or they continue to hunt us all!"

"What do you mean, sacrifice yourself? dear God!"

Tao pushes off the table with both hands and stands behind the chair, head down, resenting his fate.

"If you go back home, they will kill you the second you step off that airplane. We know that for sure, Tao. You did what you had to. Inyoku was just an assassin. The person behind this is over there waiting for another chance to strike."

Tao nods but refutes her words, "Even if we all agree to keep living on the run, they'll eventually start going after our families; I'm afraid my mother is already in danger—"

"Goddamn, I hadn't even thought about that; I'm so sorry, you and Yolanda's families."

Tiana sighs and covers her face with her hand, tears burning the back of her eyes as she fights to hold them back.

Can Mama Debbie do something about this predicament? Tao is right. There will be huge repercussions for what happened; we didn't think this through.

"I have to talk to Bounty about it, okay? I'll let you know what he says. Until then, can you just hold off on following this through?"

"I'll try." With a solemn bow, Tao leaves her office.

****

That night, Tiana stands near her window. The streets are full of deep, dark shadows. Her eyes adjust to darkness faster than they used to. But Bounty figures they aren't among the things that lurk in the darkness. Her mind drifts back to the events of this evening when she arrived home.

"Mama, if they really want to get to Tao, do you think you can stop them?" she asked earlier that evening.

Her mother hesitated, unsure of how to explain it for Tiana to understand.

"I don't know...." she sighed while clearing the table.

"As I explained before, every region is different, just like there are demons that belong to the air, there are demons that dwell like fish in the sea, and there are different breeds, races and types. The Japanese faction is full of ancient beings, some only a bit younger than me. If the nine-tailed clan wants to get to someone, they don't need anyone's permission to do it. The only thing holding them back will be the treaty. We just have to pray that's not a gamble they'd be willing to wager."

"But a lot of demons are in opposition to the treaty, especially the ones Bounty has faced?"

Her mother frowns at the mention of Bounty's name. "I'm saying they wouldn't be rash; they will make it seem like a justified action."

Tiana tenses up; a strong urge to cry overcomes her. Mama Debbie reaches out, holding Tiana's hand, squeezes it, then does something else. Energy charges pass through her fingers into Tiana. Her mother gives her a worried look and a lopsided smile, the sort that means -what comes next is unavoidable.

Thinking about it now, standing there by her window, Tiana felt even more confused. She yawns, hugging herself tighter, wishing for the warm embrace of another's arms. She leaves her window and climbs into the bed.

"Bounty... Bounty!" Tiana calls his name into the void.

"I am here." His deep voice growls behind her.

She turns and finds him standing there in a tux. The one she imagined time and time again that he would wear if they ever married.

"I love that tux," she says. Smiling at the handsomeness of her man.

"I knew you'd love it. But you did request for me to wear it, don't you remember?" he asks.

Tiana grimaces. A sudden cramp in her stomach, but she ignores it.

Ishtan even looks beautiful, like an ancient sculpture molded from the finest clay. The suit sits well on his muscular frame.

Her smile soon fades.

"I don't remember a thing when I wake, Ishtan," she says in a rush. "Why is that?"

"Because those are the laws of the dreamscape, what happens here stays behind."

"But I remember some things; I can feel you...." She looks down. "What we've done when I wake."

Bounty looks her over slowly, assessing her. "You've changed."

"I change?"

"Yes, Tiana. Your powers are increasing; it's even changing what this is between us."

"But you don't want that... you don't want us?" Tiana bit down on her plump lip.

"Oh, I want it very much, Tiana. More than anything else in all the realms."

Ishtan's voice is soothing to hear. It's still rough like she's used to; that husky growl still turns her on.

The dream progresses, as usual, resulting in him mounting her. His warm shaft, pulsing, thick with need. His lips touch her cheek; she tries to lift her hands so she can grab his face and him, but her hands weigh heavy on the bed. His eyes are greener than ever, too, like leaves glowing in the early morning sun. With one powerful thrust, his cock digs deep into her, and her hips rise up to catch every plummeting stroke. Ishtan's flowing hair falls on her face, tickling her nose. The passion heightens, his thrusts become faster, deeper; Tiana's body follows along, pushing her towards completion. He stiffens, gasps, and pours himself into her depths, filling her to brim as she falls deeper into the void.

She will wake in the morning, wet down there with a feeling of fullness, but without a grain of accompanying memory to explain why she's happy.

****

Mama Debbie knew it would come to pass. She had hoped she separated them in time. But fate can only be delayed, not avoided. She looks at her daughter, saddened by the premonitions she foresees. There's malicious energy inside of her that hasn't been there before. It burns deep, shrouding the rest of her in a mysterious air.

Tiana catches her stare.

"Mama, are you okay?"

"I should be asking you that, child. You seem a little off these days."

Tiana grins meekly. "Come on, mama. With everything that's going on, I'm just happy I haven't gone crazy." Then Tiana adds, "I just wonder why Bounty hasn't been around."

"You sure about that? You always hear you moaning his name when I try to get some sleep," her mother teases from the stove where she's making oats.

Tiana's face reddens.

"Me? I moan—what fine man?" she asks, her mind questioning if Bounty was up to his same old trick.

Has he been visiting me in my dreams again? That would explain the way my body feels every morning.

Debbie turns around, swinging the ladle in hand sticky with white oats. "You don't remember, huh? Well, good, and he's someone you ought to forget."

"Mama, come on. Not this again."

But her mother turns back to the stove. "Better focus on getting your job done at the office. You have everything you ever wanted at your fingertips. Don't lose sight of your dreams for some good for nothing, demon."

Tiana stares at her mama's back, smiling. For her to be an angel, she sure has a mean streak.

"Mama?"

"Baby, what?"

"How old are you?" Tiana asks.

She looks at her and chuckles. "Why don't you guess?" Her drawl almost makes her sound Southern.

"Two thousand?"

"Not even close, Titi. Try again."

"Did you ever meet Jesus?"

"Maybe." Her mother turns and gives her a wink

"What!" Tiana's eyes open wide. "What does he look like? Is he black?"

Her mama shakes her head, laughs hard, and goes back to cooking. Tiana gets up, tiptoes to her mother, and embraces her from behind.

"I love you, mom; I know I was angry about you deceiving me before, but I understand now; it was done out of love."

"Aw... Titi."

30

Chapter Twenty Nine

Miyake, Japan.

The Ikeda Clan now owns almost half the village; the head of the family, Daichi Sun Ikeda, seventy-five human-years-old, stout, and stern-looking, picks up a red envelope that was just delivered to him through an envoy.

The envelope bears the great name of the elder: Izanami Sun Ikeda. The elders never interfered with the younger generation unless provoked. This could only mean the contents of the envelope bear bad news. Red is the known color of the Nikaro family; the Ikeda clans' is black. To receive this envelope is a warning. The Nikaro clan is ready to spill blood.

Daichi's heart beats faster as his calloused hand picks up a narrow knife to slit open the letter. He stops, puts the knife and the envelope back on the table. He sucks a heavy breath and rises from the kotatsu. Walking over to the wide-open shoji doors of his study overlooking the side of the hill where his property resides.

Lush trees form a thick green carpet, growing tall out of the abundant white sand. Daichi regards the blue roofs of the small houses scattered throughout his terrain. He eyed the people walking along the narrow roads like ants. This village had a history dating back to the Yayoi era, when the elder dragons roamed freely. Even now, their clan holds power fearsomely throughout the island as Yakuza.

Daichi collects his thoughts centering himself before reading the elders letter. He walks back to the table, retrieving the envelope and the knife, striding his way down short wooden steps into the wide hall with wooden beams for pillars. At the end sits a raised platform. He climbs the platform and sits on a short bench. Next to him is a short-legged table, over which hangs four samurai swords with golden dragon hilts. His narrowed slanted eyes focus on the swords. They are the special ones—his Ojisan told him they are meant for the great tribulation.

On the far right of the hall, there's another rack; seven swords, different sizes, three samurai swords, and four katanas. These are the tools of their highest trained assassins, the ones meant to be passed down to these Sons. Daichi sighed. He retired as an enforcer and became the boss decades ago. Now, his second born pure blooded son will rise to take his place at the seat of the empire. Despite the birth order, he hasn't spoken to his eldest in years. His first-born son conceived from a childhood human fling. The boy and his mother were exiled by the elders.

Daichi regards the red envelope in his hand, sadness shrouding him as he thought of Tao, his eldest.

He grips his heart after reading the letter in its entirety. The white envelope slips from his hand and flutters to the floor. Pain racks his chest. The Nikaro family seeks recompense. "But why?"

Daichi frowns. "What—?" Tao... Inyoku. What does it even mean? How can Tao keep her when they have not consummated a marriage? When did the Nikaro family agree to marry into the Ikeda clan? Daichi folds the letter and puts it away; anger seething deep to his core. His wife must not see it. Not just yet. Until he's certain how deep the betrayal lies.

The letter doesn't say much about the circumstances that led to their engagement. But the head of the Nikaro family is willing to take drastic measures, likely because they believe Daichi is aware of the marital agreement.

Deeply troubled, he turns around on the bench and faces the rack of samurai swords. There's more to the letter for sure. Daichi wasn't sure who was behind this. Was it his wife and second-born son, or was this the action of the elders?

"Tao, I will try my best to protect you?" his hoarse voice echoes in the hall.

"Ichi?"

Daichi turns in the direction of the voice. The only person that calls him by that name is his wife.

"Are you alright?" She nimbly steps toward him, her sky blue kimono shifting as she neared.

He grunts, "Hmm. Enter dear wife."

She bows and comes down the steps slowly; taking care to make sure the wraps of her bright blue kimono don't drag on the floor. She joins him on the bench. Her eyes go to the rack of swords where her husband is staring.

"What is it? Tell me, is it your son? Is it Tao? Is he okay?"

Daichi regarded her in silence.

Why would she assume the letter was about my eldest son?

"He is..." Daichi pauses, making sure to be calculating with his words

Knowing her husband, she looks closely at his face and asks, "Is he okay, is there trouble?"

The man doesn't have the words to say, so he stares on at the swords. His heart breaks at her unknown admission of her betrayal.

His wife sighs, plucking at the imaginary threads on her kimono.

****

Daichi Sun Ikeda boards a flight to the Nikaro family estate in Tokyo the next day, without an invitation. He considers this trip to be of special circumstances, so there is no need to wait for an invitation that may never come until it is too late.

He doesn't tell his wife of his plans but calls Tao on the phone before making the trip. He and Tao haven't spoken in fifteen years. This estrangement worried him in the past. Now it kills him to think of the trouble headed for his son.

The ring stops. A subdued deep voice answers, "Hello."

"Is Inyoku with you?" Daichi asks.

"No."

Daichi exhales. He doesn't know if he should be relieved or worried. He begins to tell Tao about the letter he received from Inyoku's parents, how they think Inyoku may have been harmed. "Your fiancée... is she—"

"Did you call me to ask about Inyoku?" Tao cuts him off before he could finish.

"She is someone's daughter, Tao. They are worried about her. She hasn't called or returned."

"And how about me? Aren't I someone's son?" he accuses. "For a moment there, I thought you called to ask about my life, how I am, how I've been keeping since mother and I were exiled from our home, our country. A home you and your family thought I don't deserve until it came time for you to sell your eldest off as a peace sacrifice between warring clans."

"Enough!" Daichi voice chokes. "Enough... you made your point. We will come back to this matter, but for now I am on my way to see Inyoku's family. I have to know you have nothing to do with her disappearance."

"She didn't disappear, Otosan."

There is a pause. Both men, father and son, are silent, each listening to the unsaid words of the other but finding more anger and resentment.

"What happened?"

"We broke up," Tao snapped. "I don't want to marry Inyoku anymore. Besides, I thought that's what you've always wanted—to help the family grow stronger. Is that not the duty of the first born Ikeda?"

Daichi groaned. *Who told him that this was demanded of him? Who tricked him into marrying into their clan? I would never do such a thing, not after all him and his mother endured. He decided to keep silent about the possible betrayal. Tao's younger brother was vicious. Daichi thought it best to play along.*

Daichi says after a moment, "Do you know where she might be now?"

"I don't know," Tao lies. "She said she's going straight home back to Tokyo. You're saying she's not back there?"

"They believe something terrible has happened to her and think you have something to do with it. I will learn more when I speak to the chairman of the Nikaro family."

Tao groaned into the phone. "Whatever you do, Otosan, don't stay in the Nikaro house; don't eat their food and keep yourself guarded—"

"Son, is there something you aren't telling me?"

"Otosan, for once take my word. Inyoku and I are not engaged anymore, and in my eye we never were. All you owe her family now is equal retribution for the action they set forth."

Tao's words light a fire in the old yakuza. For the first time he found a piece of himself within Tao. "Your brother.... have you two talked?" Daichi asks, hoping to gain more clarity of the carefully woven plan his wife and the elders spun.

"And why would he call me Otosan? He is no brother of mine?"

And like that, the call ended.

As the airplane dives into Narita International Airport, Daichi recalls Tao's warning. He calls forth his inner dragon for strength and makes his way off the flight.

31

Chapter Thirty

Tiana stares, frowning at her reflection in the mirror. Disappointed, ashamed, and excited all at once. She didn't believe it.

Could I be...? Her hand gripped the porcelain sink tighter.

No, it can't be, I can't be. How... were different species?

Am I pregnant? But how... wait. My mother was an angel, and he conceived me. But Bounty is different. He's not human. He just has a human form. That's not the same thing, right...?

She splashes water on her face again, looks in the mirror and sees a few changes, especially in her chest area. In the last few days, Tiana grows alarmed by all the clues her body is dropping. Most mornings she wakes up so highly aroused her wetness would be plastered to her leg, her large breast even heavier. Her already sensitive nose seems to be working overtime these days. Then from there, it's been on and off fevers and the uncomfortable urge to cry, throw shit and yell.

While in a meeting that morning, she feels so hot that she is ready to rip off all her clothes. Ten minutes after downing a bottle of water, she barely makes it to the restroom before she wet herself.

Tao stands outside the restroom door, worried Stacia is further down the hall, vigilantly keeping an eye out.

"Tiana, are you okay?" he calls.

"I don't know, Tao. I don't—she heaves, and bolts into the stall she just came out. She throws her head into the bowl and retches. Her insides lift, and she feels it all the way in her soul. She spills a half-digested pastry into the bowl. Tiana stares at what she did through a film of tears. Quickly wiping her eyes with the back of her hand, she struggles back up.

Tao must have heard her. He's standing near the sink where Tiana just stood.

"Hey, you look..."

"I look what, and you better not say nothing mean?" She points a spit-covered finger his way.

Tao chuckles, throwing his hands up in mock surrender. "Ok, I won't say what first came to mind. I'll just say, you look amazing, different."

Tiana laughs, too, and glances at herself in the mirror again. She does look great, given the predicament – her hair is fuller, her skin glows with an indescribable radiance and her chest is huge. Her stomach rumbles again.

God. I'm pregnant.

Tao reaches over to the paper towel dispenser and hands her a towel for the spittle running down the side of her mouth. Tiana slowly feels strength return to her feet and chest. She feels hollowness inside her stomach. But that, too, will change when she has had something to replace the food she's lost.

Tao asks, "You must be coming down with something?"

She agrees.

By the time she goes back into her meeting, Christy has already taken her place and closed out the meeting. "Tiana, are you sure you don't want to go to the hospital?" her friend inquires.

"No, I'm okay." Tiana smiles.

Christy's large Latin eyes widen. She grabs Tiana's hand and pulls her through the small crowd of investors into the hallway, where there are fewer people.

Christy grips Tiana's wrist, checking her pulse. "How many months?"

"What are you talking about?"

"I'm an Obstetrician do you really think you can fool me?" Christy probes. "How many months pregnant?"

The world spins as the acidic burn of bile rushes up her nose. Tiana pushes away from Christy as she races towards the toilet again.

Christy Marlow's shoulders sag. "Yeah, that's it. You're definitely pregnant."

****

Tiana and her mother sit in the dining room in silence, her plate of vegetables and baked chicken sits off to the side. Tiana can't touch her plate. Neither one of them makes a move to lift their spoons.

"Sooo... are you gonna tell me why you ain't eating?" Mama Debbie breaks the deafening silence, looking at her child with knowing eyes.

Tiana purses her lips. "I'm just not hungry." Which isn't technically a lie, because she was tired of retching.

"Not hungry, huh? You can at least drink something." Her mother pushes a glass of mango tea Tiana's way.

Tiana shakes her head.

"No, thanks mama, I feel full—" Her lips purse further. "Maybe I'm coming down with something."

"You full of something all right?"

Tiana nods.

It is her mother's turn to sigh. She picks up her empty plate and gathers the uneaten food belonging to her daughter, then places the dishes on the countertop. Debbie turns to marvel at how much Tiana looks like her: that long thick black coily hair, her peach-shaped face, and the way her eyes thin out when she concentrates.

"Have you been seeing him behind my back, Titi?"

Tiana shakes her head again, lips pressed together. "Nuh uh."

"You've been sexing in my house, little girl?"

It takes Tiana three seconds to process what *her mother* asked her. Through lips still tightly pressed together, she says, "Nuh uh."

Exasperated, her mother closes her eyes. Tiana gets up suddenly and races out of the kitchen, covering her mouth, praying she made it to the restroom. Her mother covers her face with both hands and curses. "Shit, it all... *My baby is pregnant. Dammit to hell.*" She throws the wash towel on the counter, then frowns.

Debbie waits for Tiana at the door. Her daughter is hunched over the toilet bowl, shoulders shaking, her head bobbing over the toilet bowl. When she rises, Mama Debbie hands her a clean towel to wipe herself. She puts her arm around Tiana, leading her into the living room where she proceeds to sit on the couch.

"I've sensed a change in your energy for a while now," her mother whispers.

"But how, mom? I haven't seen Bounty in weeks. If I got pregnant before coming here, I would be further along...right?" she whispers in a hoarse voice of uncertainty.

Debbie takes her hands and caresses them. "Tiana, sweetie, I'm not human, but I still had you. I carried you in my womb for years. With us, pregnancy is different."

Tiana grimaces and sits up. Her brows furrow. "But I haven't seen him in weeks."

"Weeks, please. Child, I've sensed him here often."

Tiana glances at her with unusually wide eyes. "Ishtan? When was the last time he was here?"

"Just last night I felt his presence. He can't come around me because I rebuked him. I'm surprised he found a way around heaven's law to see you."

"Mama, you did what?" Tiana stands to her feet, anger cracking her voice. "I wasn't sure why he wasn't coming around. Why would you do that and not tell me?"

"Well, look at you now; it's not like it stopped much."

"If he comes at night, why don't I remember seeing him?"

Mother and daughter stare at each other, both seeing where the pin in the compass turns, but waiting for the other one to go there first. Tiana exhales and bows her head, taking her place back on the couch.

"He's done this before... he must be coming into my dreams."

"Don't tell me he knocked you up while you were sleeping," her mother blurts out.

"I don't even remember us doing it?" Tiana shakes her head in disbelief.

Hell, if I was getting some I would have preferred remembering it.

"Well, however it happened..." Debbie rolls her eyes. "We won't know for sure until we find out how far along you are. Maybe you were pregnant when you first got here. Even now I'm having a hard time sensing it. Your energy just feels different."

Mama Debbie rises from her place on the couch. She walks slowly to the window and looks out at the lonely street.

"The other night, I saw a man out there; I thought it was Bounty at first. Turns out it was a watcher, and they were here for him. Even they knew he comes here often."

"Yes, I saw him, too. He's been following us for a while," Tiana says. "Do you know why?"

"Bounty may be a Halfling, but he's strong," her mother says, glancing back at her. "Neither Heaven nor hell trusts him much. They can't send another demon to follow him around, because Bounty would kill them, but neutrals can't be touched."

"What's a neutral?"

"They are what results when angels mate with demons. Either they are killed at birth or made into immortal slaves that do the bidding for both realms here on earth. They don't interfere, and they only report what they see."

A worried look blankets Tiana's face, questioning the genetic makeup of her unborn child.

What exactly will my child be, a human, angel, demon... wolf? The picture in Tiana's head only made her more confused.

"Will this child be considered one of those things... a neutral...? Will having it upset the balance?"

Tiana's heart pumps hard with anxiety, her maternal instincts kicking in.

There's no way me or my child will become some type of slave, just because of some fucked up balance. Maybe Bounty can hide us away. But what about my career? Oh God, well maybe I can take off, have the baby and come back. Will Bounty even want this child? He said he didn't want children. Will he hurt the baby? Do the watchers already know I'm pregnant?

"I've been hearing reports about rogue demons buying human parts from the hospitals." Her mother's soft voice cut in, snapping her out of her negative thoughts.

"It's a known fact that the water demons and fae have been working with humans, seeking to overturn the balance. If what I hear is true, this will be their power move."

"Wow," Tiana said while nodding. "I'm mean, it's not surprising. Humans are capable of great evil, but what does that have to do with the pregnancy?"

"Come on now Tiana, follow along." Debbie snaps her fingers. But Tiana still looks confused. Her mother sits next to Tiana and explains better.

"In regard to the balance." Mama gestured with air quotes.

"At first, heaven looked away, no one really honored the treaty, it was just an imaginary line that no one really wanted to cross. Neither side really wanted war. Peace was profitable. You know—allow some decadence, live, and let live. Both sides reaped the benefits from the human realms. The Heavens harvested power from the humans worship and prayers; while demons glutted themselves on your fear, flesh and evil energies.

"The fae are creatures that are somewhere in the in-between. They rely on the earth and nature just as much as humans do. So with all the pollution and overpopulation, humans became the fae's enemy.

Now throw some know-it-all humans in the mix that find a way to do what they do best, and that's capitalize off misfortune. Now we have all the sides, ultimately trying to out-trick one another to see who can benefit more."

"Mom, how do you know all this?" Tiana looks at her mother, puzzled.

Debbie sighed. "What I'm saying is we don't know what this child will bring, nor can we predict how the fates will react. But the powers that be will be. A war will come no matter what. So let them busy themselves with other matters. We will keep this child and be fine."

Tiana sits back, pondering her mother's words.

Debbie studies Tiana for a while, her eyes boring through her soul, attempting to sense the life growing within. A dark film clouds her foresight, hindering her ability to see the nature of life growing inside Tiana. Debbie long suspected Tiana was pregnant long before today. And last night and many nights before, she smelt the demon but didn't see him.

Debbie reaches out and touches Tiana's belly... nothing. She frowns, moving her hand upwards, placing her palm on Tiana's chest. *Thum, dum, thump, dum.* That heartbeat is too strong to be hers alone. Debbie stills her expression, not wanting to alarm Tiana to her concerns.

"First things, we have to find out what's inside you, and find out how far along you are."

"How are we gonna do that?" Tiana takes her mother's outstretched hand and stands up.

32

Chapter Thirty One

Meanwhile, Detective Terrance Slaton hunts Marcio down to a trailer house all the way to the suburbs of Steger. This is after the detective had broken into the ramshackle apartment where Marcio had been living with Ace and found nothing.

Marcio sat groveling on the shag carpet of the dirty ass trailer floor, shaking and crying like a baby. Detective Slaton is pissed, tired of the bullshit and games. The place smells of weed, rotten food, and human shit.

Just a few minutes ago, Marcio was on the John trying to light one, with his jeans on the floor around his ankles. His hands trembled as his meth high wore off. *Zeet-zeet.* The old Bic lighter couldn't spark a flame. He finally gets his joint going when the door bursts open, the hinges ripped clean off.

"Oh shit, oh shit man, what the fuck! I didn't do nothing! I didn't do nothing!" he screams.

"Shut up! Wipe your ass, wash your hands and get out here!"

Marcio silently whimpers, sitting himself down on the dirty trailer floor. The detective snatches the stick of weed from his mouth and tosses it in the dirty sink.

"What do you want? I already told you what I know! This ain't even Chicago. CPD can't come out here!"

"Don't worry about where I can and can't go! I have been checking your background, Marcio. Seems you know more than you told me."

"What? What are you talking about? I'm alone in the whole wide world, no family, no nuttin."

Terrance pins Marcio against the floor and pulls his gun. He puts the barrel on Marcio's scrawny, tanned cheek. His breath smells like the south street sewers.

"Reynold Ash! That name sound familiar?" Terrance hisses in Marcio's ear. The lad freezes.

His eyes shift, and he shakes his head. "No, no, no, please don't mention that name," he pleads. "Don't say that name again, you don't wanna—"

"Shut up and listen. Something is happening in this city, and I want to know what it is. You told me you saw demons. Reynolds will know, he will have answers."

Tears spill from Marcio's eyes.

"Fuck..."

****

Reynold Ash lives in the basement of an abandoned building in Riverdale. The building used to be a part of the collection of structures that belonged to Bakersfield Elementary School. He parks his car outside the school gates, dragging Marcio through the back of the dilapidated building into a narrow-weeded road littered with trash from a nearby dumpsite.

It smells terrible. Terrance turned his nose up, wondering how it is humanly possible to survive like this. The building is dark, dirty, with smelly puddles of water mixed with urine and shit. A stray dog appears from behind a cracked pillar, barks once at them, and scampers off.

Marcio hesitates. The detective prods him forward.

"You sure he lives here?" he asks.

"You ain't seen shit."

Marcio continues to grumble. He walks to a place in the building where the foundation has caved, leaving a gaping hole in the floor. Marcio stops at the edge.

"What?" Terrance asks.

"This is it."

Terrance takes a look over the edge into a dark cave and steps back. He asks if Marcio is sure. The lad says he is, that he lived here with his cousin Reynold Ash until he got tired of all the things he did.

"What things?" the detective asks him.

"You won't believe me if I told you. Best you see for yourself."

Terrance pushes him forward. "After you, then."

Marcio stumbles down the surface of a slab. Terrance follows him down; he holds on to protruding steel rods, poking out of the sides of the fallen concrete. The floor levels out, leading to a long dark hallway. The walls are green with algae. The floor is filled with craters of different sizes. It's even fouler smelling than before. Terrance holds his breath at first but soon gives up, opting to bring out his mouth instead.

The terrain changes after a while, the walls are better; the foul-smelling puddles disappear. The hallways bend left and enter a hallway with electric bulbs dangling from the cracked concrete of the roof.

Marcio stops at a door and points at the handle.

He whispers, "That's his door."

"Open it."

"What? Why don't you just shoot me, huh?" Marcio shakes his head in refusal.

"Open it, dammit!" Terrance hisses.

Marcio glares at him as his frizzy curls dangle over his face. With a hard shove, the door swings into a long hall, it's smoky, dark, and smells of weed, spices and an assortment of other odors. Terrance's eyes adjust to the gloom; leaves from hanging tree stems hover from the ceiling, flower pots full of maturing weed plants with light sit off to the side. Towards the back, there's a mess of cars in different stages of deterioration. Terrance spots a Camaro, its engine hatch empty, some sort of shrubbery growing in the engine's place.

What the fuck is this dystopia?

"Who goes there?" a thick voice calls from a place at the end of the hall.

Marcio stops walking. He's trembling in fear.

"Stay here," Terrance whispers.

He goes on, cautiously walking forward. Green light shines behind a black curtain that runs the entire width of the hall. He flicks his safety off and checks the chamber. "This is Detective Terrance Slaton. I'm here to ask you questions. You are not under arrest. I repeat, you are not under arrest!"

"Are you armed?"

"Yes."

The voice roars, "And you say I'm not under arrest, detective Terrance Slaton?"

"It's just a precaution."

"Who determines what to be cautious of in my house? You or me?"

"I am a cop; I have to carry a weapon. Why don't you step out let me see your face? I need to ask you some questions—"

"Marcio, is that you?" the voice calls. "You brought a cop to my house?"

Marcio mumbles something behind Terrance. He sounds pathetic.

"Marcio is okay. He only brought me because I made him. Can you come out, Reynold? I really need to ask you some questions."

"About what?"

"The bodies. The girls that are missing their parts, and the demons."

There is silence...before the long curtain parts in the middle and one of the thinnest individuals Terrance has ever seen walks out. He wears long black pajamas that drag on the floor behind him. If a strong gust of wind blew in, the detective is sure Reynolds would fly away. He has long matted dreadlocks on his head; his eyes are so deep set in his face he looks blind.

Through lips the size of sausages, Reynolds taunts, "Be careful about the questions you go around asking, detective."

Reynold waves Terrance over to come follow him behind the black curtain. Marcio stalks in right after. It's like a juju man's enclave; red candles line the top of shelves left and right, a bunch of skulls stare with empty mournful sockets from a pole. The floor is marked by white and red chalk. Terrance turns around as he walks past to see that it is the combination of triangles of the Star of David. There are sprinklings of cowries everywhere, and the smoke-filled air is heavy with incense.

"The world is filled with the unknown. They seek to harm us all, so I try to know as much as possible. To be able to fight back, you need voodoo," Reynold explains as he leads Terrance to a place further in the back, where there are deep puffy chairs facing each other.

He points at the chairs and asks Terrance to make himself comfortable. The detective hesitates, but Reynold sits anyway in the opposite one. When Terrance is sure there are no knives under the furniture that may impale him, he sits.

"People don't come here, no. For you I will make an exception, but you have to be fast before *they* come," the man urges.

"Who's *they?*"

"Please, proceed with your questions."

Terrance removes the drawing of the big guy that Marcio and his friend Ace saw and shows it to Reynold. "I'm looking for this guy."

Reynold's eyes are expressionless. He stares at the drawing for seconds without moving. His eyes move slowly from the paper to Marcio's face. Terrance feels the trembling of the boy through the chair.

"Where did you see him?" Reynold asks Marcio.

Terrance ignores the question and asks one of his own, "You saying you know him?"

Reynold's eyes roll back to the detective's face. "That's hell's

Bounty hunter. He got nothing to do with you and me, until you cross, or stand in his way. Don't go near him, or *his*."

"He's wanted for the murder of at least three people."

"He ain't killed anyone who didn't deserve it," Reynold says.

"Well, you let me be the judge of that."

Reynold smiles. Brown and green plaque stains his teeth, *maybe from all the green leaves here that he probably eats*, thinks Terrance.

The man shakes his head slowly at the detective.

"You don't know what you're mixing with, detective. You best stay off whatever you're chasing that dude for. You'd only find death, chaos and pain."

"Let me tell you what I think, Reynold: there's nothing like demons. And if this guy is taking people's hearts and shit, it must be for the same reason that you are cooped up down here in this dirty, smelly place."

The smile leaves Reynold's face, and he grabs the top of his knees with his big hands. His breathing accelerates; it looks like he may explode and spit fire from his flaring nostrils. His left iris turns blue while the other remains black. Terrance thinks it's an illusion of the light. Marcio shifts beside Terrance. His butt is already slipping off the chair, prepared to hightail it out of the place. Reynold's voice booms at Terrance, "Mind your words down here, detective."

Marcio begins to babble, "Sorry, Reynold. I shouldn't have—"

"Shut up, Marcio!" Reynold barks. He turns his attention back to the detective. "Now, detective. You asked a question now you got your answers, you may leave."

"You didn't answer my question. Where can I find this—hell, Bounty? He needs to answer for the deaths—"

"Did you find bodies?" Reynold asks.

Terrance's lips pressed together, resolute not to say anything.

"You know the thing about your kind, and a majority of the people up there—?"

He pokes a finger up. "You think you are better than people like me just because you carry a badge. You think you are wiser just because you've been to college, and I ain't. You think just because you drive around in cars, that's the only way to get around, by mechanics, a product of physical factories. This is your problem, detective Terrance Slaton. Yours and yours alone. Down here in catacombs of the crude, all you see is everything that defines inferiority, your fear of the other side. But I tell you something now, detective, your badge, your gun, and that wisdom you carry around doesn't mean shit down here, in the seedy underbellies of the other side. Whatever I tell you here, you either take it as I say it, or get the fuck out of my house—"

Reynold rises to his feet.

"I'm 'bout to have me some important visitors. Now if you'll excuse me—" He gestures at the curtain, and the entrance.

Terrance folds his paper and puts it away. He looks around the place, at the candles and the incense burners filtering particulate smoke in the air and says, "Reynold, let me tell you something, too."

"Shoot."

"You can't beat the system, up there or down here. You can't beat the system, the rules. You just may be seeing me soon."

Reynold's deadpan face doesn't change, still. The curtain parts and standing there is a white guy. The first thing Terrance notices is the man's shoes. Golf shoes, incongruous in a place like this. And there is something unnatural about the way he smokes, as if he'd die if he stops sucking the tar from the cigarette. His hair is white and his eyes are a tumultuous green. The skin on his face looks like an ill-fitting mask. As Terrance walks past the man, their shoulders brush—Terrance is sure of it because he wants to touch the man—yet he didn't feel the physicality of the contact. A malicious feeling overcomes the detective as he exits the curtain.

Marcio is ahead, urging him to get the fuck on, man. Terrance looks back at the curtain, then at Marcio, who's practically about to cry.

"Do you know that guy?" Slaton asks the boy.

Marcio's eyes are huge balls in his face. "What does it fucking matter?? Let's haul ass!! Please!"

Terrance turns around and goes in through the curtain again. Reynold is hunched over. The white dude is speaking in low tones; the men's faces are barely ten inches from each other.

Reynold looks up at the detective, a little surprised that he still existed in the space around his world. "Detective? What the fuck are you doing?"

"There's something you said—"

"Fuck it!"

Terrance rushes on, "You said about the big guy I asked you about, that I should not go near him or *his*. What did you mean by *his?*"

Reynold stares at the detective long and hard. The detective's eyes are on the white dude, checking for his reaction, although Terrance doesn't know exactly why he did that.

Reynold says, "He has a bride. A girl. You fuck with her, he'll fuck you up."

"Is she involved? The killings?"

"Once again, you are wrong. You assume he is a man. He isn't a detective. He's a demon. Only he's different from the rest — ,"

"How is he different, and who's the girl?"

"You're the detective. Why don't you figure that out by yourself, boy?"

The white dude still won't look Terrance's way. His roiling green eyes fixated on the patch of real estate between his white and brown golf shoes and Reynold's clobbered feet. Reynold notices this and asks Slaton if there will be anything else.

Detective Slaton asks, "What are you doing down here, Reynold? What are you hiding from?"

"I can live anywhere I choose, detective. Can you?"

Terrance considers taking out his gun, shoving the paper with the drawing on it in the white dude's face, and asking if he's seen the man in the picture before. He shakes the thought from his mind and steps out of the place, joining the terrified Marcio waiting for all the way out in the smelly hall.

"Why did you wait for me?" Slaton asks.
you were with me."

33

Chapter Thirty Two

The house on Trumbulle Avenue in Little Village isn't a hospital like Tiana expected. Mama Debbie looks over at Tiana's bewildered face, throwing her a smile so she can feel more comfortable. "These are unusual times, unusual places cater to unusual circumstances," she says, while looking down at Tiana's stomach.

It's the only brick house on Trumbulle, with the queer-shaped step in front that rises from street level up to a red door. In the foyer, there's an aquarium with a single goldfish in it and a table with a pile of nature magazines on top.

"Mom, there are no chairs to sit," Tiana whispered.

"I see that," her mother whispered back.

The foyer is empty, except for white walls and a window that doesn't look like it's ever been opened before. The lady that invites them in is a pretty girl in a bodycon dress, with Tiana's kind of hair, but longer. Her skin is lighter, and she has an athletic build.

She says through clenched teeth, "Mother Martha will be with you in a short while." She smiles, then plods off down the hall.

Tiana looks at her mom. "Mother Martha?"

"Shush."

Tiana gazes down the hallway and notices movement through-out the house. There are more women. They stroll about, doing nothing much besides standing around chatting. The walls in the hallway consisted of a myriad of picture frames. But Tiana couldn't see what was on them. There are doors on both sides; red carpet covers the majority of the floor. The house was a hodgepodge of gaudy Victorian decor mixed with a bayou creole style.

Tiana touches the wall in the foyer; it's smooth. She feels no ill vibe. She tries to relax.

It's been two days since she and her mother confirmed her pregnancy. Today, they want to find out if she's carrying an actual child or harboring something malevolent.

Tiana looks over to her mother. Mama Debbie looks calm, a little distracted, but cool.

Is this what it feels like to go to your first prenatal appointment with your mom?

Debbie smirks at her daughter.

"Did you come to her when you were pregnant with me back in the day?"

"Yes."

"Uh. That's comforting." Tiana smiled weakly, trying to reassure herself about what came next.

They hear the clopping sounds of shoes pattering down the hall. The woman returns, announcing that Mother Martha will see them now. They follow her down the red-carpet hallway. Where the frames adorn the wall. Each frame contains a time worn photograph. Historical photos of people of color. From as far back as—the 30s maybe even the 20s.. They were all retro-pictures of old women: kinky hair, corn-rows, and maid clothes. Some even had bare feet, dirt roads, and shack homes.

Tiana turned her head. The doors in the hallway were also red. The house felt more like a dorm house than a place for a doula.

The woman stopped at the last door, placing her hand on the silver knob.

"I hope you find your answers. Good luck."

She twists her hand, and Tiana's breath is struck from her chest. The door opens into an impossibly huge hall. Tiana looks back at the compact hallway, not understanding how the door led to this space. The woman just looks at her and smiles.

"Come on, Titi," her mother urges.

They walk in. Tiana gawks at the sheer space, the propitious white walls that stretch for at least fifteen feet. There's a long black desk with chairs set off to the side. A lone woman sits at the head.

"Hello, Dr. McGuire, welcome child," the woman calls in a hard, country voice. "Why don't y'all come on here and sit with me?"

The woman smiles and follows Tiana with her warm, crinkling eyes. She gestures at the chairs opposite herself. Mother Martha had warm tawny brown skin. With a tiny node under her right eye; she was dressed like the women in the photos. But wore a long housecoat wrapped snugly around her body.

Tiana stumbles into her chair, still flummoxed by the massiveness of the whole room.

This can't be real. It feels like an illusion.

Tiana eyes the woman with mistrust as she stretches her hand across the black leather table and says, "Give me your left hand, honey."

"Are you an angel, too?" Tiana asks.

"There's only one true angel here, baby." Mother Martha smiles.

Tiana sighs and gives the woman her left hand. Mother Martha's palm is dry, smooth like that of a child. She holds Tiana's hand in her right and places her left palm over it. She looks into Tiana's eyes and shakes her head.

"It all leads in one inevitable direction, child. You carry children, ain't no lie. Your mama, she knows it but just wanted to be sure—"

"Children? You mean I got more than one inside of me?" Tiana shrieks, unable to fathom multiple births.

"Yes, child. I see and hear them like they're already born. I don't know their sexes yet, or if they black and beautiful like you and your mama, but one thing I do know, you wanna keep 'em."

Mama Debbie leans forward and puts her hands on the table. She asks, "Why can't I see them, Martha?"

"He knew you'd try looking. He hid um."

"The demon—" Mama says, bitterness in her voice.

Mother Martha nods.

Curious, Tiana asks Martha, "Do you know how he did it?"

"I'm sorry, Tiana. I can't. He guards your memories with dreams and illusions. I would go permanently crazy if I tried to access them. But I sense he did it out of an alien emotion on his own part, even though he doesn't fully understand why he seeks to protect you. But do you understand what it means when a man does that.. Do you understand what it means to be that man's mate?"

"But he's not a man, Martha!" Debbie snaps.

"Easy, Debbie. The deed is already done."

Mother Martha opens her lips in a sweet smile again. "I am sorry I couldn't have the girls serve you tea. But come again sometime, I'll make it up to you."

At the door, the woman calls Tiana and says, "It will be hard for you. Just rest in the fact that you won't have to make the hard decisions... but still, it will be hard in the end. Great responsibility will come to you on account of the arrival of those babies. I hope your shoulders are strong enough to carry it." She smiles.

Tiana nods, even though she doesn't understand the depth of Martha's words. They walk past the photos in the hallway on their way out; Tiana sees in one of the photos a woman dressed exactly like Mother Martha. That node was unmistakable, too. She's sitting in the middle of about two dozen women. The photo has to be over 30 years old.

Back in the car, Tiana stares at the red brick house. The door closes, and it once again looks like a college frat house.

"Who are those people, mom?"

Mama Debbie looked up back at the house and said, "They go by many names, but they've helped me when I've needed it."

"Are they angels, too?" Tiana asks again.

Debbie glances at her daughter. "Martha found me in the street one cold night. I was broken, hungry, and terribly hurt after facing a demon. She brought me here and made me well. She helped me deal with the loss of your father and taught me how to hide amongst the humans. She says only what you need to know and never talks about herself or the other women in there."

As they pull out of the driveway, it strikes Tiana as strange that the girls in that house could be anyone on the street. Or even a patient at the CHD clinic. She shakes her head in awe that the world really is filled with supernatural beings.

****

After a few days, Tiana was already starting to show. Her stomach seemed to grow overnight. To her surprise, one afternoon, Keanu came knocking on her office door, informing her that he was instructed to pick her up so she could spend time with Yolanda.

"Titi..... Is this really happening? You're going to be a mom?" Yolanda squeaked out as she threw herself into Tiana's outstretched arms. Tiana hugged her best friend tightly, relishing Yolanda's positive vibes and pure soul.

"I've missed you; it sucks balls that we can't call each other or text. I can only go straight to work and right back home. Anything else is out of the question," Tiana replied reluctantly, unwilling to let Yolanda go.

A solemn air filled the room as the two friends released each other.

"What are you gonna do? Will it be safe to have the babies while we're all still hiding? Her face is a mask of concern.

"I guess I'll just wait and see what happens." Tiana shrugs; she truly didn't have an answer. Night after night, she would worry and cry into her pillows, unsure of how to keep her or her children safe.

Tiana looked around the hotel suite. The room felt like they've gone back in time, with gaudy white furnishing and blush pink décor. The whole suite screams money. And it most definitely didn't fit Yolanda's vibe. Instead of taking Yolanda to his home, Keanu opted for keeping her best friend in luxurious overpriced hotel suites. Whenever they weren't in some place Yolanda called the "Versa realm."

"So, how are you holding up? In the protective care of your demon?" Tiana gave Yolanda a small wink.

Yolanda sighs as she brewed some lemon ginger tea in her new amethyst crystal tea set. "Well, this is new." Tiana winks.

"Yeah, this was a gift from Keanu," Yolanda replies, without meeting the questioning gaze of her best friend.

"A gift huh,... "Tiana wrinkled her nose and oinked like a pig. Causing Yolanda to cover her mouth and giggle.

"Girl, yes, just a gift, and before you ask, it's not happening!"

Tiana eyes her best friend and smacks her lips. "Heffa, I know you way better than that; you already let him hit." Yolanda couldn't do anything but laugh.

"Titi... Look, I really don't know what all this even is. One day he's the sweetest guy I've ever met, then the next day. He's a complete stranger. He won't talk to me; he puts up this wall." Yolanda takes a sip of her ginger tea and asks Tiana if she wants another cup.

Tiana waves her hands, signaling that she has had enough. "Yolanda, I truly am sorry for all this. Because of me, you've been uprooted from your whole life. Your shop, your business now you're stuck running for your life." Tears threaten to spill from Tiana's eyes, but suddenly Yolanda boops her nose.

Boop-Boop

"Look, I know you're hormonal and all that jazz, but don't you do this. Those babies can feel all those negative emotions. Then you'll come blaming me when they come out all ugly and shit."

Tiana falls over, laughing. "If my babies come out ugly, it comes from their daddy's side."

Both the friends snorted and giggled.

"How did Bounty take the news?"

"I wouldn't know I haven't really seen him."

Yolanda opted to leave that comment alone, to just lean forward and hug a friend for what seemed like the umpteenth time.

Knock knock

Keanu pops his head in through the door. "Sorry to interrupt ladies but Tiana its time."

With yet another embrace and a kiss on the cheek, Tiana leaves her best friend.

The car ride back in Keanu's car is surprisingly pleasant. As before, Keanu just seems like a normal guy, so Yolanda falling for him isn't too shocking.

"How's Tao doing?" Keanu asks, attempting to lighten the mood. "I imagine you'd want to see him, too."

"I actually see him and Stacia a lot." She adds, "We see each other at the office."

"Everything's changed, I know. Having us around, this whole ordeal, is a lot, I know," he speaks over the loud Metallica song blasting from the car speaker.

Tiana nods and looks out the window, unable to look at Keanu for long because he looks so much like –him- but slightly different. It has been weeks since she's seen Bounty in full consciousness. Instead of talking face to face, he only visits her in the dream space, where he is safe from her wrath and anger. If Keanu knows of his brother's cowardly ways of doing things, he isn't saying it; maybe it is better this way;

The awkwardness of the situation is apparent as they both avoid the elephant in the room. As he drives back to her mother's place.

Keanu's car pulled up two houses down from her mother's home, and Tiana stepped out. Closing the door softly behind her. "Thank you for protecting my best friend; keep her safe," Tiana mentions while tapping the roof of his Silver Mustang. He doesn't reply. Instead, he shoots her a ridiculous wide-tooth grin and peels off.

Tiana stands on the curb of the street. The afternoon's crisp air bites at her cheeks. She knows her mother is watching from the shadows. Keanu stopped about ten feet away and the Mustang Shelby revved back to the spot where Tiana stood. Keanu poked his handsome face out of the car.

"Does he know yet?" he asks, his soft green eyes scan her face.

Tiana has expected that question and is a bit annoyed he asked so late. She swallows and composes herself, even before the last syllable escapes Keanu's lips. She forces a small smile on her face and Tiana shoves her hands in her pocket. "He put these babies in here; I'm sure he's aware."

She shrugs and kicks her boot heel against the crumbling curb. Keanu exhales, nods, and guns the car again. The mustang rounds the corner, vanishing from sight. When Tiana looks up at the house, her mother is there at the window, a white apron around her neck, with a large silver spatula in her hand. She offers Tiana a broad smile and a wave. Tiana gives back a tight grin. She points down the road, signing that she's going for a walk. Her mother waves her hand, gesturing for her to go *on and get some air.*

Tiana stops at a park. Quickly finding her favorite park bench under the ample bough of a Green Ash tree. She gazes across the expanse of the park. A little girl in a fluffy white coat and matching earmuffs plays with a puppy. Her mother watches and laughs from a small distance under another tree.

It is getting to be a breezy evening. The sun is sinking low over the top of the building. In less than an hour, it would be dark. Another night of him visiting, another night of her forgetting one morning came again.

Tiana tires of the quiet, secluded atmosphere of the park. She walks back up her mother's street and breaks out to the rowdier man street three blocks away. The wind whips her coily hair into her face as she pulls up the collar of her double-breasted trench coat, catching sight of her reflection in the reflective windows of the shops.

The coat hides her bump well; weirdly, she likes that and doesn't know why. She walks past a clothing store, sees pink jeans and black boots, both displayed on a black mannequin. She slows down to gaze at it. Thinking the pants might be cute with the sweater she bought a few weeks back. She tries to get a better look at the price tag but can't see it well on account of the streetlights glaring and the cars all passing behind her on the road.

She frowns and brings her face closer. There's a man behind her. He cups his hand around his mouth to get his cigarette to light up. He dons a flat cap, black jacket and grey trousers. The curb hides his shoes, but Tiana already knows who he is. The man raises his head after getting his cigarette to go. Inhaling it deep, he blows the smoke to the air. Cars pass behind him, and passersby flit past too. Tiana looks on, her nerves uncharacteristically still.

Her brown eyes stare into his deep black ones.

Breathe, Tiana. Breathe.

She strides toward the end of the street, hoping to break off at the intersection. There's a pedestrian crossing there. She could join the human traffic and hope to escape her tail. Tiana increases her pace. It gets darker and colder, and the traffic grows louder. The clipping sounds of Chicagoans trying to get home fill her head. The ponderous smell of vehicle exhaust and the stench of human essences all come together, hiding the scent of the being following her.

She blends with the moving sea of bodies at the intersection, making sure to blend with the fast flow of people, continuing until she looks up at the green sign above that announces the green line is up ahead—Tiana has traveled three blocks. Her toes hurt where they rub against the curved front of her boots.

Tiana bolts into the nearest restaurant she sees and picks an empty table. She eyes the door, and the girl behind the counter dressed like gothic Lolita. The girl's hand is screened off by the counter, but it looks like she is tapping on a calculator or a cellphone. Tiana counts four people in the café. A couple occupies the table near the door. The woman flips her hand in the air, her wedding ring catches the fluorescent light. Behind them is a man by himself; he wears a blue beanie and huge headphones. The last man — *Oh, God.*

—the fourth man wears a flat cap, puffs of white hair peek out from under the brim. A cigarette resting between his second and third fingers. He raises his head, winking at Tiana, flashing her a toothy grin. His teeth a perfect set of pearly white teeth. He grinds them together; the sound they make grates Tiana's nerves. It sounded like two pieces of rusted metal being scrapped together. Tiny cold pins erupt from the skin on the back of her neck. The man keeps grinning, mocking her...

Tiana looks on as the man's teeth elongate. White, sharp, jagged points poke at his thin lower lip. Drops of crimson spatter his jacket. He takes off his flap cap, and on both sides of his head are two horns. His finger is replaced with claws that score the white top of the table. He begins to rise.

Tiana looks about the restaurant; she's the only one that can see his demonic form. If she screams, the people will only think she's crazy; if she stays, there's no telling what the demon will do...

So, she stands her ground. Looking the demon straight in the eye. "What do you want?"

"You carry abominations!" he hisses out, flashing its sharp fangs.

Tiana gags at the putrid odor coming from its open mouth. A black tongue, like a serpent, licks its lips wet with thick green slime.

"Do you know whose children I carry? And aren't you one of these said abominations too? a half-breed?"

"I've been redeemed by the great Lucifer... your abomination shall birth abominations, heaven weeps for you, and hell cries." The demon laughs a haughty cackle. He staggers toward Tiana, raises his hands into the air, and brings down his sharp claws.

Tiana shuts her eyes and expects the world to go dark, but...nothing. She opens her eyes again, and the demon has changed back to his human form. His forearm is in Bounty's murderous tight grip. He grips the demon's forearm, the bones of his forearm splinter under the pressure of his hand.

Boop! Bloop!

Sounds the cop car that just pulled onto the curb outside. Two cops walk out and make their way into the café; they give the two men standing before the pregnant woman a curious glance.

"Is everything okay here?" the one with a black mustache asks.

Bounty lets go of the watcher's hand, shoving him off.

"Everything's okay, officers," says Bounty. "This guy was hitting on my pregnant wife here."

The two cops look from Bounty to the cap-wearing watcher. And then back at Tiana. They surmise from the look on her face that what the big guy says has to be true. The pregnant woman puts his arm around the huge guy hugging him tightly.

The cop with the mustache was pretty large himself, real pudgey around the middle. He waves the watcher off, "Come on, man. Get out of here. Can't you see she's pregnant? Are you blind or what?"

The watcher raises his hands up. "I am sorry, officers. I'll just go my way."

"Yeah. Scram!"

The watcher walks out, giving Tiana another one of his pompous smiles, before joining the flow of traffic and vanishing out of sight.

"Sorry about that big guy," says the cop; he pulls at his mustache, giving Bounty a quick glance. "Do I know you from somewhere? You look really familiar."

"I get around a lot," Bounty's voice booms.

The cop chuckles and calls to his partner, who is sipping on the coffee he just ordered.

"Larry, did you hear this guy's voice? Did you hear the bass in that barrel of a chest?" He laughs. Back to Bounty, he asks, "What's your name, man?"

Tiana's heart drops into her stomach; she hears it as it hits her diaphragm.

Oh shit. We're fucked.

Bounty smiles, "Ron Beglin."

"Beglin, huh?"

Bounty nods, smiles, and extends his hand for a shake. The cop took it. Tiana winces, afraid that the cop's hand will be crushed. But it isn't.

"Whoa, what a handshake!" The cop continues to stare at Bounty's face.

His partner strolls over. He's leaner, taller, has a narrow face, dark eyes, and an Italian accent. He points with his coffee cup. Referring to his partner, he says, "Jack, I bet you my check for this week you can't beat this guy at arm wrestling."

Jack says, "Aw, get out! Look at him. This guy's bigger than Schwarzenegger. What the fuck!"

Tiana squeezes her face and winces. Bounty glances at her, then to the cops; he says, "Excuse me, officers, but I have to take my wife home. You must forgive me."

The two cops fall on each other, apologizing. "Oh, sure. Can we give you guys a ride? Do you have a car?"

Bounty says his car is sitting down the road. He thanks them, and they quickly leave the café. They walk a block before Tiana looks back to see if they have been followed. The cop car is still in front of the café, but the cops are not in sight.

"Here."

They stood outside the Regalway Cinema. The lighted awning declares that *Tenet* is showing at 9pm. Bounty opens the door of a parked red Dodge Challenger. Tiana stares at the car for a moment, wondering where it came from, but remembers that Bounty isn't a man. He's a demon; conjuring up a car is probably child's play for him. So she shrugs it off and climbs in. He jumps right in after and drives her back home.

They made it all the way home before Tiana hit him with questions.

"Why are you staying away from me?"

Bounty glanced up at the house. From the street the faint light of the living room lamp could be seen. The other windows were dark. But Tiana was sure her mother was watching.

"You think she would have stopped you, because she rebuked

you from the house? But you could have met me anywhere like you did in the past! "

"Isn't this what you wanted?" Bounty snapped. "She takes care of you now. How long have you fought me about becoming my mate? The only reason you want this now is because of that?" He looked down at her stomach.

His harsh words hit Tiana dead in the heart. Without a reply or rebuttal, she opened his door and stepped out.

Tiana watches him drive away, just as she watched Keanu drive off earlier that evening. She removed her coat and shoes, then made her way to the kitchen. Soon after, she found herself eating some left-over Italian Fiesta pizza that her mother left on the dining room table.

"Are you okay?" her mother inquires.

"I'm just tired, mom."

Her mother scrutinizes her from where she stands at the door of the kitchen. She wears a white sleeping dress. Her hair was damp from recently washing it. She says nothing more and retires into her room.

****

Ishtan comes to Tiana that night and several other nights after. This time, it's different. He's like his normal self: short black hair with dashes of brown highlights and his domineering presence, unlike the dreamy version of him that wears a tuxedo.

"Will I remember?" she asks him as he kneels beside the bed rubbing her swollen belly.

"Do you want to, or is our mating still a hindrance? A burden to your plans?"

"Yes, I miss you; I want to remember."

He places his head on her baby bump, closing his eyes while breathing in their mixed scents. Ishtan isn't as brutish tonight. He behaves like a perfect gentleman. He opens his eyes and the flash green. His inner beast lets out a deep trill. "They are beautiful Tiana."

"You can see them?"

"Yes. They have your eyes, your hair, too."

Bounty rubs her belly, a sharp cramp shoots up her side, and she winces. Frowning, he asks her if she's alright. Tiana says she isn't sure; she feels a pull deep inside her womb. As if the babies are tugging at her innards.

He caresses her belly again, promising her it will be alright.

"To keep them healthy, the children must soak in my essence. Will you let me make love to you?" He looks at her warmly.

Her heart skips a beat at his gentleness. "When have you ever had to ask me?" Tiana grins.

He gets in bed with her without taking off his clothes. While lying behind Tiana, he lifts her leg up, and pulls his manhood from his jeans, rubbing his cock over her sopping wet core. She worries at first that his sheer size might harm the babies. But when he enters her, she feels herself wanting him deeper. Somehow, he's just the right fit for her at the moment. Not too big, not too small, but just right.

They rock together until she falls deeper into the dream void. His hands clenched tightly around her body, providing warmth.

In the morning, Tiana wakes up with the memory of Ishtan coming to her. She remembers everything they said to each other and all the things he did. It felt like a portion of her had been excavated finally; her memories were made whole.

Unfortunately, the tugging feeling from the night before seems to come back. This time, she can tell it is the babies—every time they fluttered, a sharp pain would shoot up her spine. A mother is her baby's source of food and vitality. Yet, her babies seem to be taking more than she can give. Tiana goes about her days with a constant need to eat and sleep, but even then, she can never give enough. The babies feel like six.

Christy Marlow pulls her aside during an all-staff meeting, voicing her concern about changes in Tiana's appearance.

"Are you drinking? Are you hydrated enough? Your skin looks way too dry?"

"What! Of course, I've already finished a gallon, but I still feel parched—"

Christy drags her into the toilet and settles her before a mirror. "What do you see?"

"Me, Christy. What the fuck!"

"Look at you. You look diminished; if I'm honest, you look like hype," Christy complains.

Tiana rolled her eyes. "Well, be honest, why don't cha!"

"I noticed that I'm pregnant, in case, to my dismay, I'm not cute pregnant; I look like I've been hit with an ugly stick; yeah, I get it."

"Titi, I have three boys. You can't tell me about a pregnant woman's life. I know, I've been there. But this right here, this is something else. You need to see a doctor. Have you done that? If not, I can take you as a patient?"

"Look, I'm fine, Christy. Really, I am."

Exasperated, Christy Marlow lets her be. While driving home, Tiana catches a reflection of herself in the mirror. She frowns at the change that Christy mentions, and that her mother has pointed too many times, as well.

She tip-toes into the house, trying to sneak up to her room, but Mama Debbie is waiting in the kitchen. She catches Tiana as she creeps up the step.

"Mom?"

"Titi. Why are you creeping around?"

"I'm not creeping around."

"Come get some dinner when you're done having your shower."

"Uh-uh."

Tiana never comes down for dinner that evening—and for many evenings after.

****

There were warning signs. But Tiana, Bounty, even Mama kept tip-toeing around them. Evading the obvious, because the truth is too hard to bear. Debbie could feel the babies leeching off her body. Their demonic energy surged higher after every full moon. Bounty could even see their true forms; they gorge themselves on his essence. Even with him transferring power to them every night, it wasn't enough.

The babies shared a physical resemblance to Tiana. But all three babies were carbon copies of him, his strength, his power, and all three had split wolf and beast natures. To put it simply, Tiana was being poisoned by the babies' dark energies tainting her human soul.

Most days she's forced to be on bed rest. Unable to go to work, barely able to stand. On days when it feels like the babies aren't tugging at her guts, she manages to sit up in bed and work on her computer, which Tao was sweet enough to bring to her mother's place. In her less painful, lucid moments, Tiana directs Tao, teaching him how to perform her duties.

But lately Tiana's become too gaunt. Her eyes are sunken; her dark skin is ashy and pale. But still she refuses to let Yolanda take her to the hospital.

Teary-eyed, her friend begs.

"What do you think the doctors will see inside me?" Tiana snaps at Yolanda.

Yolanda wipes her runny nose on the back of her cashmere sleeve. "But you are dying."

"Think about it, Yoyo," Tiana whispers, barely able to catch her breath. "They'll see my baby's true forms. They'll kill them, dissect them, or worse. And then they'd find Bounty. I'd be putting them all in danger."

Yolanda wipes her tears. "Why don't you think about yourself first?"

Tiana sighs and rolls over; she falls into a heavy slumber as the drugs mama Martha sent over begins to take effect. Debbie hovers around her, sitting with her daughter when Yolanda isn't there.

When Tiana wakes, her mother is beside her.

"I'm going to go get Martha. She'll know what to do. It seems like the meds are no longer working,"

Tiana nods weakly

Mother Martha frowns when listening to Debbie tell her Tiana new symptoms; the older woman swiftly goes into a room, switches clothes, and steps out with a red turban, a long white dress, and an arm full of dry herbs. "Hurry, take me to her."

"The heavens weep!" is all Mother Martha could utter when she saw what the babies have done to Tiana. She touches Tiana's belly, examines it thoroughly before declaring that this is beyond her skills.

"I am sorry, Debbie. Her body is too weak for the babies—you know what the babies are..."

Both women share grave, knowing looks.

"What's happening to me?" Tiana sobs as she falls asleep that night. Her mother stares at her, knowing what mother Martha told her might come to pass. Tiana may not be able to bring the babies to term without extraordinary measures. Debbie kisses her daughter's forehead, and then quietly leaves her to sleep.

Tiana dreams again after many days of sleepless slumber. Ishtan has enchanted her, forcing her to sleep in hopes of easing her pain, but the babies are growing too fast inside her. The bigger they grow, the more dark energy they emit.

"Make them stop, Ishtan..." she pleads. "Make them stop poisoning me. Can you communicate with them?"

Hot tears make her eyes bite with fire. Her throat burns with gas from her empty belly, and it tastes like baking soda in her mouth every time she coughs. The mixture forms a puddle at the back of her mouth, making it difficult to breathe.

Ishtan stands against the wall, hands in his pocket, rocking back and forth on his heels of feet. He's torn between having the babies and saving Tiana's life. He walks over placing his palm flat on her belly, frowning at the yapping of the babies inside her. He can see them. Their fiery green eyes are his, not Tiana's, as he had hoped. They hear him chant a spell of merciful death and try to tear out of her belly; deflecting the spell before it had a chance to take. Bounty staggers back, horrified in spite of himself. For the first time in over thousands of years, he feels true fear.

I can't lose her... not like this.

His inner beast howls and scratches. The beast wants to save its pups. Ishtan wants to save his woman. He paces the room; his feet making heavy sounds.

Debbie sits up in her bed, aware of Bounty's presence but keeps calm.

"We have to take them out!"

Tiana's head stops lolling. "No, you can't. I want them!"

"But they are killing you! If we don't take them out, you will die."

A feverish spell of strength grips her. She wakes from her dream, but Ishtan isn't there. She only feels his presence. "No, you can't, Ishtan. You won't touch my babies. You dare..." She screams into the silence of the night.

"I know you're still here, Bounty." The room is cast in shadows; the only illumination comes through the window from the streetlights. Bounty rises from the tail of the bed, where it's dark. He leans with his face into the semi-light across her chest, his breath hot. His eyes are earnest, the veins in his forehead strain against the furrowed skin. He doesn't have the words, only the anger to show for how he feels for her. He asks again for permission to rid her of the babies, to free her. "To keep you alive, for me, for us." Bounty pleads

"They're innocent, Bounty. They are powerful because they are just like you; they need to be saved."

"No, Tiana. You need saving, not them." He blows hot. "I can't live with myself if I lose you."

"Well, find another way, Ishtan."

The determination in her face seals it for him, too. Ishtan recedes into the dark corner of the room by the open closet, and from there, he dissolves just as Tiana's mother stalks up the step.

34

Chapter Thirty Four

Tokyo, Japan.

The Nikaro Steel Corporation building in the province of Pyongyang is a 27-story high rise.—the 28th story. Is a level known only to a select few. Like many things in the human realm that are hidden beyond the veil. Only a few could be trusted with that information. Even amongst the demon clans. The Nikaro Clan's possession and involvement with the hell gate was scarcely known. The ones among men and demons who knew of the gate were only the cruelest and most barbaric loyalist to the great Cerberus and Lucifer himself. And if any being not classified as such should venture onto that floor, they were either welcomed with oaths or destroyed with curses.

Daichi Ikeda is not one of those beings. The Ikeda's were born from the bloodline of Ancient Dragons, ruled not by heaven nor governed by hell. His clan once reigned over the land of fae. But over the centuries the mighty dragon clan had fallen.

Daichi sat alone in a room provided by the Nikaro family. It was going on the third night of his visit, with no one granting him an audience. His duffel bag sat beside him, as he sat contemplating the silence that the family has presented to him since he asked for details of their

SIGHT OF THE BEAST - 295

daughter Inyoku's disappearance and information on who approved a marital union between her and his son. No one was saying anything. And his request to see the head of the family, Chairman Uwais Nikaro, had been met with excuse after excuse. There was a knock at the door, and two female attendants pushed a tray of food into his room. Like clockwork, room service delivered his food three times daily, making sure to inform him that the hospitality was courtesy of the Nikaro clan chairman. The food remained untouched. Daichi's inner dragon couldn't scent any impurities within the food. But Daichi was uncertain just how far this tangled web of deception spread.

So he heeded Tao's warnings. Not to trust anyone or anything while in the
Nikaro residence.

The stocky man that brought him from the airport came into the room that evening instead of the Chairman. He sat on the sofa and crossed his legs. Giving Daichi a contented little smirk that never reached beyond his nose. He asked about Tao's whereabouts and why he couldn't be found.

"Is he working remotely from a new place?" the man asks and waits patiently for an answer.

"I don't know what you are talking about. I received a letter claiming Inyoku, my son's fiancée, is missing. This is why I'm here. Who agreed to this union and why am I last to hear of it. I've been patient to show my consideration to the loss of your clan's child, but I will no longer tolerate your clan dismissal—"

The man waved his hand. Treating Daichi words like fly covered shit. "One would expect your son to be here as well?"

"Who are you again?"

The man smirks and says, "I am a representative of the family in the capacity to question you, Mr. Daichi."

The routine goes on for two more days, after which Sun Ikeda decides he's had enough and would like to go back to his island. Requesting a meeting with the chairman was a waste of time.

He packs and walks to the door but stops himself again. "Am I making a hasty decision?

Am I not indebted to the Nikaro's, not by my own volition but through those who plot and plan for my prodigal son's demise? "

He goes back to the bed and sits, grim-faced and sad about the turn events. Daichi recalled he was the one that introduced Inyoku to his second son Dai at a gala organized by Asianic Conglomerate It seems the elders and his youngest son, Dai, were busy. Cutting underhanded deals and plotting traps. Placing the burden of responsibility on Tao instead of the pure-blooded second son Dai. Was this their way of ensuring Tao never threatened Dai's claim to leadership?

Daichi shook his head in confusion. Tao was rebellious and resentful towards the clan. How was he enticed or deceived into this sham of a marriage??

Since he and his mother's exiles from the island, Tao had never really cared about the family's business. Or so Daichi was told. Marriage into the Nikaro clan meant coming back to Japan, something Tao nor his mother ever wanted, especially when Tao enjoyed working for the gaijin. But that was Tao's choice: the family had no right to interfere in the boys' life after exiling him.

Daichi felt betrayed by not only his wife and son but also by the elders. He knew he failed Tao in many ways. So he refused to let him be hurt any further. The actions of his youngest son still puzzled him: Tao was no threat. Dai had proven his talent for business with his recent achievements in Africa, buying up companies in expansion left and right, closing multi-million dollar deals the elders were pleased. So why do this? Daichi struck the floor with his fist. Tao could have been more too. If the clan elders accepted his half-human lineage. But Tao was a Halfling. As the firstborn, he was considered a disgrace.

"I have to get to the bottom of this," he murmured to himself. "I have to know what everyone here is hiding. I'll go find the chairman myself."

He grabs his travel bag and exits the room. Quietly walking down the long corridor; he sees no one. His eyes narrow in suspicion.

When Daichi walks to the lift, he presses the button that says UP and waits for the lift to arrive. He checks his watch and frowns. His watch reads 11:56pm, the second-hand lands on 12 at the exact moment his feet step into the lifts platform. Daichi staggers, the energy shifts the higher the lift climbs.

He watches as the numbers flicker on and off the higher the elevator climbs. "The chair main should be located on the 27th floor." He stretched his hand to press the 27th button but pauses. "*What? 28? How?*"

Confused, he counts by himself, even though he is sure there is no way there could have been a mistake. This is a whole building, for God's sake. He stops counting at number ten when he realizes it is no use. Maybe it isn't a floor per se; perhaps it's just an added loft up there for the chairman. Such an addition is quite possible. So Daichi presses the red button, 28. He eyes the other blue buttons suspiciously. The lift moves from the 10th floor where he is, and up it goes to the top. It opens a minute after. He steps off the energy on this floor causes his inner dragon to surge forth "No, this can't be. I have come here numerous times over the years and it was never like this. What is this malicious energy?"

He glances around the corridor. Gold plated panels decorate the lower walls of the never ending hallway. He sees his reflection in its metallic sheen. His pear-shaped face stares back at him. He listens for sounds but hears nothing. Daichi decides to keep walking thinking the chairman's office must be at the end of the hall.

"Strange," he mumbles. "Where are the doors? *What is this place, a secret level??*"

At the end of the long hall is an intersection that branches left and right. The light shines from both corners. He gets there and stops to consider his position. He goes right and finds a door on the left side of the wall. He puts his ear on the door , listening to check if there is anyone there—*Ah!*

Daichi removes his face from the door and staggers back. The door burns hot. Nearly scalding the side of his face. He goes to the door and shakes his head. His eyes glow green *as* he hears voices from behind the door, people talking. Someone yells, and Daichi steps back. The yell sounds unnatural; definitely not human... His inner dragon lets out a soft growl.

From the other side of the door he hears a murmured inquiry. "Who's there?"

That voice... it sounded familiar, but he couldn't hear it well enough to make sure. It had a serpentine lisp. Like listening to a snake hiss instead of speaking; its tongue is out sniffing the air for its prey. Was someone of the dragon clan here in the Nikaro building? The door begins to hum, and the floor shakes. Daichi takes a few steps back just as the door creaks open; instead of light, a dark shadow stretches across the grey Italian tiles.

He vanishes around the corner in seconds. His heart pumps hard, the muscles of his thighs on fire. It had been dozens of years since he last used his assassin skills. Thankfully, the lift was still there. He could feel the dark energy behind him. His inner dragon trembled. Whatever or whoever it was made his inner beast cower in fear.

Chiiing!

The doors of the lift open, and Daichi dives in.

He presses the last button—1—with his fist and looks out the lift doors; what he saw confused him. There stood the Chairman Nikaro in his partially shifted fae form. Nine bushy red tails whip aggressively behind his back, with Dai, his youngest son, standing near him, and a tall blonde-haired woman standing to his left. His son and the chairman aren't aware of his presence, but the woman turned to meet his eyes. She was shrouded in pitch-black mist of pure evil, her glowing green eyes were boiling with hate; with the flick of her wrist, a harpoon of dark energy catapults towards the closing lift door.

Daichi hurled himself down to the ground floor in less than a second. Barely escaping the demoness' attack.

Instead of leaving out the front door, Daichi exited from the fifth floor and took the fire escape down quickly. Hailing a taxi from there to the airport. Daichi often naps on his flights, but on this one, there is no sleep to be had. He slams his fist against his thigh. The first-class attendant startled by his sudden outburst. He nods in apology.

Why was Dai there? How had he not known that the Nikaro clan were Kitsunes and the most important question of them all, who was the demoness?

35

Chapter Thirty Five

Somewhere in Chicago. West Loop, Madison Street.

Bounty stands on the top of the North Atlantic Company building. From here, he peers at the sun as it sinks into the back of Lake Michigan. From this vantage, he sees the street below; the people appear quite small for the human eye but not for Bounty. He can see every face as if they are standing before him. The streetlights are coming on; it's beautiful. His siblings, Keanu and Stacia, stand on both sides of him, coming at his behest.

He speaks without taking his eyes off the sunset. "Something is about to happen."

Keanu glances at him. It's Bounty's tone that gets him concerned. Not exactly his words. Bounty's voice is low, not his usual growl.

"Ishtan, talk to us," Stacia pleads

"What have you heard, brother?" Keanu turns to him and asks.

"Demons are off the street," Bounty says as he turns his attention to the street below.

Night falls on the city in seconds, traffic is building up at the end of the street. He watches as an ambulance turns from Grove Avenue onto Manor, where two police cars are parked in front of the club. After going through the Manor, the ambulance stops behind the police car, shunting the traffic off through the curb. Lives must be in danger. There's been some shooting down there. He heard it just as he dropped on this building.

"There was movement from Japanese faction yesterday. We must keep a look out for the Nine-Tails and the old man. We have too many enemies to not be vigilant. We can't allow anything to happen to her friends—"

Keanu nodded, "It may kill her..."

"Yes. We must protect her friends if we want to keep her alive." Bounty glances at Stacia and then Keanu, making sure they understand the demands of the times. "We must protect them, for her sake."

And for yours, thinks Keanu. He sighs. Of the siblings, perhaps it is Keanu who understands most of the far-reaching implications of Tiana's pregnancy. Keanu hears things because he's a demon of few words, but his powers lie in spiritism. He has heard how Cerberus, their grandfather, thinks of Ishtan's actions.

But this is not what bothers Ishtan.

"What do you suppose is going on?" Stacia asked. "Why are demons off the street suddenly?"

"Aurone."

"He called them in? Why?"

"I'm trying to find out."

Keanu affirms, "Yes. I have not seen a watcher in days now. And that's unusual. Grandfather does these things when something majors about to go down. You think it has something to do with us?"

Bounty glances at him and says, "I hope it doesn't."

Keanu sees a hardness on Bounty's face that's been missing from it since he told him and Stacia about Tiana. It's the fierceness of a demon enforcer, the unleashing of the beast.

"What do you want us to do?" Keanu inquires.

Stacia looks at him too, ready to support her brothers in any form or fashion.

Bounty tells the two, "Whatever happens, keep them safe. That's what I need you to do for me."

"You can count on me," Stacia promises.

Keanu says, "Me, too."

Bounty is pleased. But doesn't smile.

Before he goes down to Tiana's bed to be with her, he must find out what sort of surprises the old man has been cooking up.

Whoosh!!

He descends on the street, leaving his siblings behind. They will find their way back to their wards and assignments.

—**********

Detective Slaton could feel it; something was going to happen today. He could feel it in his gut. When you're a cop for so long, you developed what the guys in the precinct call the *seventh sense*.

Last night, Terrance called in a favor from a buddy of his in Prague, a Hungarian guy who went to the police academy with him back in the day; Gruber is the guy's name. Gruber has been with Interpol for five years now, overweight and graying.

Gruber says, "Yes, there's been some weird occurrences in Berlin, but it only lasted for two months or so, a spell of strange murders by what German detectives called the *Avant-garde murderer*. It was a coinage used in the departments to describe how the perp fucked the girls up, scraped off their faces, and cut off their limbs. We had to practically piece the bodies back together."

"This perp is real messy. He likes to splatter their blood, eat their tits, even the ladies' faces. He cuts them off and probably hangs them in his home," Gruber explains. "There's a different theory, the most plausible of them."

"What is it?" Terrance asks. The whole thing sounded a bit too familiar to his liking.

"He's a Berlin cop, and he's a taxidermist."

"Why do they think he's a cop?" asks Terrance. His hand trembles as he tries to keep the phone on his ear and makes notes at the same time.

The caffeine pumping in his system is enough to jump-start a car. His eyelids are pulled back. He is amped. Thoughts of sleep leave him as he gulps down liters of coffee to keep him going. After what he experienced while visiting the voodoo guy in that basement in Riverdale, Terrance is afraid to close his eyes.

"He leaves no tracks, no prints. And never gets caught by the camera. Except in the Berlin Honors Hotel this one time—"

"Wait, what did you say?"

"What? I said—"

"No, Gruber. What's the name of that hotel?"

"BHH. The Berlin Honors Hotel. They found some girls there. Well, one and a half the other was missing her limbs. Sometimes, their breasts along with their hearts are missing, which threw off the investigation for a while, because you know, what taxidermist wants to keep a heart, like what for?"

"Gruber, I need dates. Tell me when this happened? And what's the detective's name?" Terrance's heart is racing. Could this be the break he needed?

Gruber sends the information Terrance needs within the hour. He compares notes, and his blood freezes over when his fax machine whines and a camera image of a very tall, muscular man comes in. Gruber even sends a copy of the police artist's drawing.

It matches the Chicago PD's copy, with only a slight variation in the shape of the nose.

"This is it!" he yells. Heads turn in the office grounds.

Shortly after, Terrance decides on a stakeout of Reynolds's place. That's where he'd catch the big guy if he is ever going to make an arrest. Now he's sitting here in his car, thinking of many things. His thoughts kept drifting to the past.

With no woman in his life except some occasional hookup, the detective doesn't worry about much. But he worries about his dad. Bart Slaton of the New York police department is a typical alcoholic father. Terrance used to have his photo in his wallet, along with his mother. Until one day, when drunk, his father yelled at him, "She died!

Your mama died! And you will never amount to nothing, just like her!"

Terrance ran from that apartment in Manhattan and never looked back, never returning his father's calls. They hadn't spoken in five years. Terrance's eyes misted. He sighs and rubs his eyes.

'You will never amount to nothing, you piece of shit!' Those are the only words I remember him saying to me.

He's a detective now. He isn't sure if his father is aware of his achievement. And he doesn't care one way or another. It doesn't matter, really. Terrance is a fighter, just like his mom. Terrance picks his third cup of coffee that he pours from a silver plastic flask and gulps; his throat makes that slurpee trill as the fluid meanders down his throat.

His weariness leaves him again; his eyes brighten, and he looks over the steering wheel of a car that he took from the pool in the precinct. The car is parked beside an empty, broken building, and behind him is a dumpsite. The stench drifts into his car; it's the smell of death; Terrance has seen rats the size of cats in these areas of poverty like this. He can't roll up his windows because the AC doesn't work in the car; it will get too hot. Beyond the dumpsite is a wall that's lost most of its plaster, and the rough surface is covered with graffiti. The road on which he is parked leads on to an old park that's out of use. The wire fence is twisted, and most of it has been stepped on, so much they stay down. Opposite the park is the empty, dilapidated building, the basement of which Reynold calls home.

Terrance scans the area, watching as someone walks across the old park. The person crosses the park, jumps over the twisted, broken fence—it's Reynold.

He looks different. Dressed in nicer clothes from the last time Terrance saw him. His locks are tied behind his head under some funny-looking hat; it looks like an old top hat. His yellow trench coat flaps about in the wind. He looks like he may have been coming from a magic performance. He's holding a walking stick with a gold-plated tip. As Reynold nears his building, he stops and gazes around, his dark eyes hard and suspicious. Terrance scans the area, too; perhaps the man hears something or sees something.

There are other houses near Reynolds's building, empty, broken, or worse off. There are two broken-down vehicles covered with bushes and leaves opposite the spot where Reynold is weaving around suspiciously. Satisfied that he's alone, Reynold struts into his building, swallowed by the dark yawn of the broken doors.

Terrance relaxes again. He starts to stretch his hands over the gear shift to the passenger's seat, where his half cup of coffee is when something moves in the periphery of his vision. His hand freezes; he scans the horizon, around the place where those old cars are in the bushes.

There's an apparition that looks like the head of a man behind the bent top of one of the vehicles. Terrance's hand knocks his coffee cup over, and the content spills as he reaches for his gun.

Shit, fuck!

He ignores the spilled coffee and focuses on the dark hump behind the car. It begins to move. Adrenaline spills into Terrance's blood. He freezes.

You are one big motherfucker!

Terrance thinks. The man that steps out of the back of the ruined cars is built like a small car turned on its tip: brown hair, white, very good looking. He wears a jacket with a fur collar, dark jeans, and black boots. He stops walking, and his head turns slowly on the swivel of a neck the size of a beam.

Terrance ducks as the guy's eyes settle on his car's general direction. His heart beats violently in his chest. He clutches his gun, flicks the safety off, and waits to hear footsteps. It occurs to him that he has to see where the guy goes, so Terrance raises his head every second until his head is up in time to see the big guy disappear into that building.

The detective counts to ten and comes out of his car, then crouches and runs forward, making sure there's no one else hiding in those bushes behind the abandoned cars.

As Terrance approaches the open doorway of the empty build-ing, he notices the broken windows on the side of the building. He breaks his runs and falls in line with the side of the house. He picks his way along the side among fallen bricks, pieces of broken glass, chewed-up wood, and blown-about trash. When he gets to the target window, he steals a look inside. There's nothing but darkness at first.

The next time Terrance peeps, he sees clearer.

His eyes fall to a spot on the floor where there's a gap leading to the basement. He remembers the place. Terrance scales the window easily and jumps down. Stealing his way toward the hole in the con-crete floor.

Bounty stands before the black curtain. He can see the man be-hind it even before the man realizes he's standing there. Within sec-onds of his appearance, the man knows. He wheels around and calls out:

"Who's there? Show yourself!"

The man pulls the curtain aside, sees Bounty; his rotten-toothed mouth sags open in shock momentarily, but quickly recovers. "Bounty, man."

"Reynold Ash."

"What brings you to my home?"

"Information."

"Do you want to come in?" Reynold asks, gesturing at the couch at the rear of the place.

Bounty's eyes sweep the interior. He doesn't move. His eyes come back to the black man, watching his movements, his littlest re-actions, his mannerisms.

"Why did the watcher come to see you?" Bounty asks him.

Reynolds avoids Bounty's eyes. "Watcher? What watcher?"

A deep growl grows in Bounty's chest. Reynold falls back as the demon grows bigger; his eyes turn green, his breath smokes.

"Okay, okay—" Reynold blubbers. "I don't know much, okay? Just enough to stay alive during this bullshit game called the balance that your fellow demons and fae are working hard to bring down!"

Reynolds's chest rises and falls fast. He steps back and strips himself of his big trench coat. He spreads his hand.

"Can I offer you a drink at least?"

"No. Tell me what I need to know." Bounty asks again, "What did the watcher tell you?"

Reynold pitches his butt on a couch and spreads his hand over the backrest importantly. Smoke, rising from the assembly of candles in the middle of the Star of David, haphazardly drawn on the concrete floor, drifts around him.

"Your grandfather still loathes you," says Reynold. "And your mother doesn't fucking care. At least that's the undying news we keep getting down here. There's the matter about the girl—"

Reynold suddenly finds his nails attractive. He sits checking them out. Then pouts his lips, like a girl's, and mumbles about how his manicurist isn't the best anymore.

"Why are all the watchers off the street?" Bounty clenches his fist in frustration.

Reynold gives Bounty a sympathetic look. "Are you fucking shitting me? You don't know why? Whatever you did made hell leave you out of the loop."

Bounty knows the man is playing with him and biding his time. He has to let him think he has fallen for his gambit. Whatever Reynold is about to accomplish with his ploy, Bounty considers it beneficial to his own cause, too.

"What is the planning?"

"I don't know exactly, but I hear it is something major. But of course, you are here. You will see it when it happens. Now about the girl, why do you put yourself through the trouble?"

"Who runs the organ farms," Bounty asks him as a diversion.

"Organ farm? What's that?"

"I grow tired of your misdirection, human!" Bounty roars and attacks, blaring fangs and razor-sharp claws.

"No, wait!"

Ten feet from the curtain, fifteen from where Bounty stands, detective Terrance listens to the back and forth between Reynold and the big guy. Terrance's skin crawls with so much terror that his teeth clatter. What he hears astounds and shocks him beyond words. He looks back the way he came, wonders if what's happening here is above his pay grade, way up in the friendly skies.

Although he understands little of what is being said, he forms a fair conclusion based on the words of the big guy, whom he now believes isn't human.

My God, am I dreaming or what?

As he knows it, the world has broken down. His reality lies in ruin, just listening to these guys talking.

Fuck! Demons. Hell!

In the movies, he's seen the actors fight demons with a cross and holy water. Terrance glances at the service-issue gun in his right grip and shakes his head.

No. I can't just run away. This is the guy from the photo Gruber sent to me from Berlin. It was definitely him that went through the wall of the diner.

His attention is snatched back when he hears the big guy shout, and he starts choking. Terrance doesn't know what to do, so he begins to back away from the place behind the curtain, just in case things escalate. That decision saves his life, because just as the detective moves behind a pillar, he hears the footfall of someone who doesn't want to be noticed. Terrance listens closely and hears more people creeping in. The big guy hears it, too, because he flings Reynold into the corner where the guy strikes what looks like an altar with his back and rolls over, toppling candles, casks of perfumes and smoking incense burners.

Water Demons, two of them, dressed in seashell-colored suits and spiky pink and red-colored hair. *Sea Fairies,* Bounty says to himself. He snaps his finger and sparks ignite from the tips of his claws. Reynold's curtains burst into flames. The man cusses under his breath, scrambles to his feet, and begins to gather his belongings into a small travel box that he drags out of the bottom of the couch he was sitting on seconds before.

Bounty's eyes turn to balls of fire; his hands are like the wings of a phoenix when he waves them. The burning curtains fly into the air, landing on the rest of Reynold's belongings. The voodoo man's place is on fire; he's screaming profanities, thrashing about, trying to save his candles. His bag of clothes catches flame. He slaps it on the floor, where more fire has started to grow.

The fire burns blue like ether; water is ineffective. The two water demons bring out short silver-colored metal sticks, like a runner's baton.

Lucifer's Wand. So, Cerberus stoops this low.

Bounty experiences a nagging feeling that he's in the middle of some game—a dangerous one. The two demons whipped their batons; the sticks burst open and elongate. One-touch from the sticks and a demon is on his knees, writhing and vomiting his life's essence until the demon is down and powerless. Lucifer's wand is a priceless possession, rare, and only great demons have them.

Cerberus!

The demons circle him; calamitous blue fire swirls around. The first demon, with pink hair, bounds forward, twirling wand building momentum, Bounty tries to grab him, and the wand scrapes his shoulder, sending Bounty flying off his feet with a bolt of energy, enough to power four blocks of households.

The demons cackle like hyenas. Bounty gets shudders with rage. The demons attack in unison. Bounty parries the pink-haired demon's wand—speed is key with wand holders—knocks the wand out of the guy's hand, grabs him by the neck, and uses the guy's body to block the red-haired demon's attack.

Bounty and the demon in his hand are thrown off the ground, but Bounty regains his position. He's down to one demon, the red-haired guy. Turns out the red-haired water fae knows many tricks. He hits the end of his stick on the concrete, and the wand splits in two.

"One for the price of two," he laughs, eyes blazing. "You are not leaving here, Bounty. Not until it is done."

"What needs to be done?" Bounty asks.

The demon spins the two sticks in his hands in an intricate display of dexterity. He throws one of the sticks. Bounty knows this is his chance. He has to hurry and finish. Someone might be in danger; this is surely a distraction. He snatches the stick from the air as it zooms past him. The demon is shocked. His pink-haired companion is regaining consciousness. Bounty grabs the pink-haired demon off the floor, impaling the guy with Lucifer's wand, ramming it through his back until it pierces the demon's heart. Bounty raises the impaled demon in the air while glowering at the red-haired demon, which backs off, horrified.

"Why don't you go back to Cerberus? Tell him this attempt is weak. He can do better."

The demon cackles, but his eyes lose their confidence. "Doesn't matter, Bounty. He wins, still."

Bounty tosses the mummifying demon in his hand into the waning ether-fire that has now engulfed Reynold's house. The demon's body begins to roast and disintegrate. The red-haired demon collapses his wand back into a smaller-sized baton, cackling as he recedes into the shadow behind the pillars in the basement.

He screams, "It is done, Bounty! It is done!"

Bounty goes to the charring body of the dead demon. He pulls the almost indestructible stick out of the burning chest of the demon, collapses it, and stows it in the fold of his jacket. He looks around and sees Reynold escaping through the darkened rear of the basement. He begins to move but becomes aware of another body, a man, lurking in the shadows—the same one he'd seen sitting in a car outside the building, but he deliberately ignored. He ignores him still and stalks after Reynold.

Reynolds stumbles and feebly climbs out a broken window. Halfway through, his long trench coat is caught on the hook of broken glass that's still sticking out of the frame. He struggles to get through, cursing at Bounty, the invading demons, and the entire hell horde. He almost drops his bag of candles, his voodoo bits and pieces, and some clothes. Sunlight hits his eyes, snow-dusted grass on the edge of the roof pokes at his face. Someone is coming. He looks around and sees Bounty marching toward that window in the ground. Reynold tries to roll back into the basement, but Bounty grabs his hand and hurls him out of there. His precious trench coat is torn along the front.

Reynold screams for God in heaven. "God is not here, Reynold. It's retribution. Tell me, you son of a bitch." Bounty pins him against the dusty paint of the wall. "Why was I attacked?"

Reynold chokes. He winces. "Why don't you ask your grandfather? I-I-I am not him."

Bounty punches him a little below his diaphragm on his left kidney. Reynold's eyes bulge. Then he screams as agony hits his whole frame. He begins to wheeze as Bounty punches him again, this time in his stomach. Reynold vomits bile. It spills out of the corners of his mouth; his eyes roll back, and he begins to suffocate.

"Freeze! Drop him!"

Bounty turns his head slowly. It's the black man he saw hiding in the car. He ignores him as he lifts his fist to bash Reynolds' skull in.

"I said, drop him! I'll shoot you if you don't comply. Now let him go!" the man's gun is pointed at Bounty's head; his other hand disappears into his blazer and comes back out with his badge.

"I'm a cop; I'm a detective." He raises his badge so Bounty can see it. "Now, drop that guy and put your hands where my eyes can see 'em!"

Bounty looks at the detective, cocks his head to the side, a little surprised by the man's orders. Bounty shakes his head slowly and drops Reynold, who falls and slumps over.

"Hands up!" Terrance barks.

"Do you know who I am?"

"I don't fucking care who you are, man. Just shoot them hands up in the air right now and turn around—"

Reynold starts crawling away. Bounty leaves the detective and pins Reynold in place in the grass. He puts a foot on the back of Reynold's left leg and twists; there is a *CRACK!*

Terrance shouts. "What the fuck! Did you hear a word I said?!"

"Shut up!" Bounty quakes.

Terrance didn't see a man's face when Bounty screamed at him; he saw the face of the beast, his true form instead: eyes so green they glow, teeth long and curving inward and about a hundred in one row. And the face made for pure destruction. The detective staggers, and he falls on his butt. Bounty's quick show of anger surprisingly vanishes in seconds. Heaving with the rest of his annoyance, he goes back to questioning Reynold.

"What did Amaruq tell you?" he roared.

"They are taking her as we speak!" Reynold says, breaking down in tears.

Alarmed, Bounty grabs his neck. "Who?"

"The angel."

Bounty frowns. *The angel? Tiana's mom? But why? Why would they take Tiana's mom?*

Bounty puts the man down. He rises and looks at the detective.

"You have been chasing the wrong person," he says.

He walks past the shivering detective, goes across the road. He walks towards the park, his steps quickening.

"Wait! Hey!" Detective Terrance runs after him.

When Bounty gets to the middle of the park, he vanishes.

"Fuck me sideways—" Terrance says, awestruck.

Reynold starts coughing.

Terrance calls it in on his radio. He goes to the man and checks him. "Damn, you have concussions. Your damn leg is broken, man."

Reynold coughs, blood splashes out of his mouth, his eyes glaze over.

"And your stomach is ruptured," Terrance adds.

"Help me up, please."

Terrance helps him by getting the man to sit with his back against the wall. His breathing comes out of him in ragged raps. He asks Terrance to get him his bag, which he dropped as he was picked by Bounty. Reynold opens the bag, rummages in it, and comes up with a small bottle of colorless liquid. He opens it and swallows a mouthful. His face contorts like the skin of a squeezed orange. He tilts his head back and closes his eyes.

"That's the big guy from the photo I showed you, right?"

Reynold turns frightened black eyes at him. "Yes."

"Okay, stay here, alright? I called an ambulance already. They'll be here soon, have to go."

Terrance starts towards the place where he parked his car. Reynold calls after him, "Don't be foolish, detective. You can't stop him!"

I'm not trying to, he muses. *I'm trying to help him.*

The house looks like it's been hit by a tornado. The two crabapple trees standing in the front look charred and bent. Three of the cars parked in front—one of them, Tiana's—are now unrecognizable twisted scraps of metal, black, and charred.

The road is quiet; no one walks past, no cops, no fire service. The house isn't on fire but it's been charred and burned with ether flame. The front door is lying in the middle of the road. The windows are missing glass, and the curtains drip melting acrylic. Bounty scans the house and street to make sure he's not walking into a trap. When he's satisfied there are no demons, fae or watchers lingering about, he races like lightning up the steps. His shoes tear through what's left of the wooden floor beams. He slams through Tiana's already-damaged door like a truck, sending the rest of it crashing across the wall in splinters.

The bed where Tiana should be is empty. The bedclothes are bloodied, and the legs of the bed are bent in an unnatural position. The walls are blackened with soot; her clothes are now burnt embers floating in the air. The room smells like a slaughterhouse.

Bounty's beast roars with anger, shaking the house's foundation. He goes to the bed and pulls at the bedclothes; he kneels in the black ashes and buries his face in the bed. He screams, the sound of his voice breaking the rest of the glass in the building, cracking the wall and shorting out the electricity. Those who hear the scream miles away think they're hearing thunder.

Bounty missed Tiana's mother on his way up the steps. She was injured, bleeding out, but still alive. She lies near the back of the couch in the living room. Bounty caught sight of her as he made his way out of the house.

"Bounty," she whispers.

He dashes to her, gently cradling her off the floor. Bounty turns down the upturned couch and places her on it. "What can I do for you?" he asks.

"Tiana. They took Tiana."

"I will get her back. I will kill them all if I have to."

She coughs. Bounty waits for her to catch her breath. Thankfully, she's not too far gone. "What did they do to you?"

"Lucifer's wand."

He grits his teeth. "Cowards. They tricked me!"

"Take me to Martha. She can heal me."

Bounty carries her down the street, stops by a truck with the keys left in the ignition. He deposits her in the back and jumps in. As he starts the car, he sees people lurking behind windows, houses, and trees. They peep at him as he drives away.

"Fuck them all to hell," he grumbles.

36

Chapter Thirty Six

Hell.

Cerberus (Aurone) lumbered through his backyard paved with fire, brimstones, and the souls of the damned that fuel his eternal flame. Hot embers flew into the air as his heavy feet trudged through the floor of his home. His faithful Hell Hounds yapped and snarled as he pushed open his chamber doors.

Upon entering, his eyes immediately went to the large cube hanging from his chamber's rafters. He stepped closer assessing the being that was encased inside. He chuffed.

"I see the halfling loss his senses. His eye roamed over Tiana's unconscious floating figure. He placed his hands in front of his chest, mocking how large her breast would be on him. The guards and demons in the room chuckled. "It's a pity she's of tainted blood; it looks like her hips are made for a good thrusting." Aurone eyed her once again, then cast his attention to the newborn pups at her side. His eyes narrowed. "why are they still alive?" his voice boomed off the chamber walls.

Amaruq stepped forward. Bowing in reverence before speaking

"My lordship, when we attacked the home to kill the girl these pups actually killed more than half our men."

"How could newborn pups fight? Do you take me for a fool?"

Aurone's face reddens with rage as spittle slides down his chin. Amaruq's voice faltered as he tried to explain.

"My lord I speak the truth I can demonstrate if you please."

Aurone pushed past Amaruq and made his way to his head chair. Before sitting he called forth a Harpy to bring forth his favorite virgin blood mead. With a wave of his paw, he gestured for Amaruq to proceed.

Amaruq cleared his throat, then chanted a quick incantation, summoning forth a lower level ghoul. The undead being snapped and snarled; it had very little intellect. Amaruq snatched a short sword from one of the demon guards and thrust the hilt of the weapon into the ghoul's hand. With a stern voice he commanded the lesser demon. "Kill woman, kill children!" Amaruq repeated the simple command two more times before the undead ghoul understood the command.

Aurone held his goblet in the air cackling, "I say Amaruq, could you have called a dumber demon." Aurone hit his knee with laughter, the contents of his glass slouching to the floor. Amaruq groaned and accepted the insult in silence. The ghoul finally charged towards Tiana and the pups. Sword drawn high in the air, ready to slice them through. When at the last second a power burst of energy shot out from the pup's bodies, disintegrating the ghoul into millions of ashes.

Aurone rose from his chamber seat dropping his goblet to the floor.

Amaruq smirked at the great Cerberus reaction.

"I'm not sure if this is a protection spell placed on the pups by another or if they are indeed strong enough to ward off deadly attacks." Replied Amaruq. As Aurone studied the pups from afar.

"Amaruq. Good job. Maybe killing them would be a waste. I'm glad you have a good eye for perception Amaruq, Lord Lucifer will be most pleased."

Amaruq's chest puffed with pride. All he ever wanted was a position next to Lucifer, Hell's king.

"He will come here, you know—"

Cerberus wheels on Amaruq. "He dares challenge my decision? He is alive because I approve. His bitch and pups still live only because I allow it—"

He walks slowly to the cube; He timidly touching the cube's surface.

His face creases deeply. "One, two—" he grunts. "Three!"

He looks at Amaruq. "There is a spell of protection over them. But the great power you feel belongs solely to them,"

****

Yolanda can't believe how far over their lives have turned. And it doesn't seem like it will stop anytime soon. She honks her nose into the handkerchief that Stacia gave her, wiping her reddened eyes with the back of her hand. She looks at Tao and asks in a soft voice, "What are we going to do about Tiana's disappearance?"

Tao hunches forward on the couch silent; he rubs his palm together. Then He shakes his head.

Everyone has gathered at Stacia's place. Tao sits beside Yolanda, and Keanu sits opposite them, watching. Stacia comes with two glasses of cold lemonade and puts them on the table. She gives Yolanda a pleading stare.

"You have not eaten anything since last night. It's almost noon again. You need to feed."

Yolanda sighs.

Her short curly hair is tousled on her head; her face is a mess from so much crying when she first heard about Tiana, thinking her friend had died. Bounty had rushed to Keanu's place in the night to ask him to bring Yolanda to Stacia's. Safety in numbers is what they believed.

Bounty stood near the window, staring out over the Chicago River and the skyline. Tao joins him there. Most of the sun is hidden behind dunes of grey clouds. Suffused sunlight bounces off the reflective surface of the nearby structures.

"Beautiful, isn't it?"

Bounty glances at him and chuffs

"Can you get her back?"

"It will be hard. But I will risk my very soul to do it,"

Tao glances at the demon's face. He looks so human; his emerald green eyes don't seem like they've been crying. But his subdued disposition jutted out chin and measured breathing showed enough.

"I will go with you if you need help. She is my friend, more like my sister. She means as much to me as she means to you."

"Where she is, you can't come," Bounty says. "I have to go alone."

Tao's phone begins to ring.

"Tao?" his dad calls.

"Otosan, have you returned?"

Bounty turns his head and listens. He is telling Tao of a strange occurrence he witnessed in Tokyo, at Inyoku's place. When the conversation ends, Tao is disturbed.

He suddenly goes quiet.

Bounty peers at him. He asks, "What's in Japan?"

Tao shakes his head. "Just some family matters," he says dismissively.

"If he spoke to the clan head, we'll need to know."

Tao ran his fingers through his hair. Frowning as he asks Bounty if he thinks the whole family could be Kitsunes.

Bounty nods. "Usually, they will be."

"My dad, he just told me something." He frowns and shakes his head, "Something about the—"

Tao shakes his head again.

"Never mind."

Bounty backs off. He walks away from the window; Keanu follows him. In two hours, it will be completely dark. He stands beside Stacia's car, keys dangling.

Both brothers stand beside each other, silent men who do more thinking than talking. Keanu says, "I was in the city. I heard some things. Grandfather definitely has, which is good. At least with him it won't be an immediate death sentence. He doesn't want to kill her just yet. You know him: kill them and give them an express ticket to heaven. Better trap them, give them a chance to mess things up by themselves so they can come down to meet him."

"Cerberus has always been a narcissistic bastard."

"Yeah, that fucker."

Bounty looks at his brother and smiles a little. Keanu now imitates earthlings in his speech.

"We have to hurry and save her. The pups need my essence to ward them from draining her life force too much."

"I will go see what I can learn. Living humans aren't allowed in Hell's realm so there has to be a portal or a gate we just have to figure out where," says Keanu.

Bounty shoots him a nod and drives away.

****

Detective Slaton puts the photo Gruber sent from Berlin under a big magnifying glass. He peers hard at the grainy picture. There are things he missed the first few times.

After the encounter with the beast earlier that day, he came back to his office to see what he missed, forcing himself to look over every detail for hints and clues.

His Captain pokes his head in the door and asks him if he's working late. Terrance replies with a stiff face. He directs his attention back to the photo.

Terrance brings the photo closer. The big tall guy isn't alone in the photo; there someone else. He looks closer and notices a male in front of Bounty. The camera catches only his shoulder, flat cap, and the back of his shoes.

Are those golf shoes?

It looked as if the Tall guy was tailing a suspect. And in this photo, Bounty is following the guy wearing the golf shoes. He checks his watch, calculates the time difference between Chicago and Berlin. He dials up Gruber again.

From the noise in the background it was easy to discern that Gruber was at the shooting range, the gunshots in the background were a dead giveaway. He asks Gruber if there were any more photographs with the big guy.

"Ah, you're in luck," Gruber shouted from Berlin. "The detective that worked that case is here. Wait; let me get a hold of him."

Detective Jürgen comes on. He introduced himself politely. Terrance likes him instantly. He repeats his question. Jürgen takes a few seconds to reply. He walks away from the noise in the background and tells Terrance there are actually a few more photos.

"Do you think maybe he didn't do it?" Jürgen asks. "That he may have known who the true killer was?"

"Yes."

Jürgen says excitedly, "Exactly! My thoughts exactly, I surmised that that big guy may actually be law enforcement of some kind, but I couldn't verify him! Give me ten minutes, and I will email some of the photos that make our theory likely, okay?"

"You have the photos on your mobile?"

"They are in my email. I keep everything there so I can work from wherever I am."

Terrance ends the call, opens his email and waits. Fifteen minutes and a cup of coffee later, the photos pop up on his screen. With shaky hands, Terrance uploads the photos on his computer and blows them up.

His jaw drops open. There are seven photos of Bounty, and they have this dude in the golf shoes walking ahead of him, except two, where Bounty is ahead of him and looking sideways. Terrance scans the golf shoe guy's face and sends it down to the guys in tech downstairs, hoping they haven't called it a night. To expedite his query, Terrance runs down the hallway, almost knocking over the janitor who works night on his way down the steps.

The guys at tech have received the photos and have blown them up on their own screen big enough to span the whole wall. The instruments here were acquired recently; FBI standard and the computers are jacked to every camera in the city. They begin a trace of the face, and in ten minutes, produce matches of the same guy—a total of fifteen of them. Terrance begins to cross-reference the photos—three pictures come up where the guy with the golf shoes is seen walking on the street, riding in a car; another three, where he is walking behind a pretty black girl with curly hair and a butt that makes Terrance's dick jump.

The girl.... The girl Reynold told the big guy about?

Terrance begins another trace.

Minutes later, there's a face and a name. Tiana McGuire, MD, works at CHD, University of Chicago. Grandmother Deborah McGuire resides in Englewood, Chicago.

"Looks like the big buy has a thing for chocolate."

Terrance sits back and breathes. He finishes his coffee and picks up his jacket. He checks his time: 10:56pm. He sits in his car in the parking lot and listens to the rhythm of the city, its murmur and breaths. He chants a quick prayer, then starts his car.

"Let's go."

He pulls out and directs the nose of his car towards the Woods.

****

Bounty stands on the Clark Street Bridge and looks at the big clock's face on the side of the River North Capital Management building. It is 11:57pm. A vehicle flies past behind him every five minutes or less.

The city is going to sleep. But Demons never sleep; he wouldn't be much of an immortal if he did. It's a breezy night outside. Snow flurries drift from the dark sky. Bounty blends in with the darkness of night and fades into the wind. He stands on the pedestrian walkway, even though the lights in the trusses shine brightly.

The bridge here is one of the few small portals between earth and hell. Allowing demons to slide between the two worlds effortlessly.

The clock on the North Capital building struck 12:00am. Bounty jumped off the bridge. He plummets through the cold air like a comet. Vanishing just before hitting the surface of the River. Then quickly steps through the portal.

****

The Great Cerberus, the lord of all HellHounds, is waiting in his great chamber when Bounty appears. Bounty wears his rage like a suit of armor, growling at the guards. They stop him. His hands start to glow with the ether fire of his fury. Bounty eyes his mother standing beside his grandfather and softens. But on the other side of the great Cerberus is the ass kissing Amaruq.

Aurone directs his hound guards to give Bounty passage.

"Where is she?" Bounty roars.

Bounty sheds his mortal skin, letting his Hell beast stand free.

"Your insolence knows no bounds," Cerberus spits.

"She is mine. My spoil. My mate!"

Cerberus cackles. "Know your place, Halfling!"

Bounty stands before his grandfather. His mother won't even look his way. And that's okay; it's the way things have been for over millennia.

"She committed no crime!" Bounty snaps, "Return her and the pups to me."

His mother snaps back, "Oh, but a crime was committed... Bounty." She says his name as if it tastes bitter on her tongue.

Bounty turns his burning eyes on his mother. She has not changed since the last time he saw her. His mother used to be a neutral demon, but her bitterness has warped her mind.

"What is the crime?"

"In your own words—you took spoil, you mated that woman. That alone is a crime against heaven and hell. You violated the treaty, we are at peace with the human realm...and heaven, yet you took spoils for yourself."

Bounty fumes.

Amaruq yawns as if he is bored with the hastily put-together tribunal. He rises from his seat beside Cerberus and says, "Come now, Bounty. You know the rules. Of all of us, you have spent the longest time up there. You know humans are curious, stubborn, and fickle beings. Their women, oh, they'll fall for you if you can fuck well. You know better. What are you gonna do, mate her? We all know what happened when it happened centuries ago—apologies to you, my lady."

He bows to Bounty's mother. "I'm sorry."

Bounty's anger triples. It's a travesty. Even Amaruq speaks in defense of the prick of a grandfather that he has.

"And what of the women your underlings kill... aren't you and Lecrae harvesting their organs? Is that you declaring war or keeping the treaty?" Bounty asks.

Amaruq rolls his eyes. "You are grappling for straws, Bounty. All of hell knows me and Lecrae are at odds. Plus the organ harvesting... that's the humans, not me. It's been going on for years. I'm just one of the many beings that regulate it, making sure things don't get out of hand. That's all. He looks at the face of treacherous Cerberus for support. He finds it.

"There's a way for you out of this, though." Cerberus comes back. "You just have to prove yourself to me, half-breed, you pass, and you earn my respect. You can have her back, and you can do what you wish, half-breed."

"And what is it I have to do?"

Cerberus gives him a derisive glare. "Three tests. You fight three HellHounds without a weapon. Beat them; you will be told the second test."

As they speak, three HellHounds march into the place. The ground quakes, and the place spreads, turning into an arena. All three HellHounds have Lucifer's wands. They are each commander of the sins. Bounty would've had the upper hand if they didn't have the wands. Where things stand, Bounty might as well give up. Cerberus isn't going to give him an easy pass; his grandfather will always despise him.

The HellHounds encircle him, wands spinning, bolts of fire, and sulfuric charges radiate from them. They come at him with such speed that he is shaken.

These Demons are at least nine hundred years old; they have strength and experience. Bounty has everything to lose. They will fight to keep their honor. Bounty will fight to spite the grandfather he despises, more than his birthright as a half-breed, as one of the three bastards.

His beast roars as it fights for Tiana and its pup's lives. Bounty's strength is in his fists; every punch inflicts the same damage as three wands, so when the first hellhound tries to hit him with the wand, Bounty doesn't resist. He's hit by bolts that crippled his mind instantly.

He collapses, facedown.

The legion of demons begins cheering. Cerberus chuckles. He begins to raise his band to give the order for Bounty's immediate expulsion.

But Bounty rises, grabbing the nearest hellhound by the feet, rising from behind, burying his fist in his back. He breaks the spine, breaks into the rib cage to the heart and pulls it out. He devours the hellhound's heart menacingly and picks the fallen wand.

The other two are momentarily stunned. Cerberus's hand hangs in the air. "What..." he says lamely.

Amaruq mumbles, "It's not possible—"

Bounty charges again just as Amaruq sneaks out of the arena.

The resolves of the other two beasts are utterly shaken.

Bounty soon knocks the wand out of another hound's hand, picks the wand and digs them into the hound's heart.

Cerberus raises his hand. "Stop!"

No, Cerberus. We fight till the end, to the death.

"We fight, Cerberus!" Bounty shouts. "We fight to the death!"

He spins the wands so hard and fasts they become blades in his hands. The last hellhound is decapitated.

Cerberus growls, "You win."

"What's the next test?"

"Demetri, get me his heart!"

Bounty grunts, dropping the wands. He looks at his mother. "You approve of this?"

His mother raises her twirling eyes at him. She nods. "Find him, bring his heart, and you earn your place as a true son."

"You said Demetri died two hundred years ago."

"Well, there's news he's still walking the dust of the earth, dear Bounty. Go, find him. Your earthling has less than a day to live, and she fritters away like a butterfly whose days are done."

Bounty glances at Cerberus and sees that treacherous cunning that his grandfather is known all over hell for.

"Go half-breed. Go; find the man who made you invalid, who gave you the unworthy ancestry that now plagues your existence."

Cerberus cackles again.

His mother smiles. Bounty stands his ground. "I want to see her first."

"I grant you permission—"

Cerberus places guards around the cube. He could easily tear them to pieces, but what good would it do? Cerberus would kill Tiana before they had a chance to flee.

"I have a better thought, guards place her over the great abyss, just in case this hard headed halfling tries to spoil my fun!"

" What abyss?" Bounty snaps "where will you take them?"

Bounty roars in rage. If she isn't rescued soon, all of this would have been in vain.

" Tsk Tsk ... think of finding her as another plight to your quest."

Bounty spits on the floor and growls. "I will be back for you, Tiana...pups." Seething in anger, Bounty staggers out of the presence of Cerberus and his vengeful mother.

37

Chapter Thirty Seven

It's morning on earth. It is the middle of the week, two days until the weekend. For most, it's another opportunity to make things right on their jobs.

But there are also people like detective Terrance Slaton. Ones that never truly stop working or rest. He tried to drive out to Englewood the night before, but stopped halfway through Clark Street Bridge. Someone reported seeing a man jumping. After handling that, He drove out to Tiana's apartment last night. She wasn't there, of course. He just needed to make sense of it all.

Now he's in Englewood, driving through the narrow, tree-lined streets. He slows down and rolls the car down the road slowly. The street is mostly quiet this time of day; there are no little girls making snow angels or boys having snowball fights on the lawns. There are homeless people, criminals at rest only to begin foraging again when darkness falls. He parks his car off the road behind a U-Haul truck two blocks from the house. Four men dressed in orange-colored jumpsuits carry a long sofa between them up the step of a building. Terrance slows down as he nears the two-flat building where Tiana's grandmother lives.

Terrance looks back to the way he came. No one is paying attention to him. Tiana's Nana's home is in shreds, totaled. Terrance stands in the street, surprised no one cares or bats an eye.

They grabbed her here. They took Tiana here; they distracted the big guy so they could grab her here.

He steps over the fallen branches of crabapple trees and goes up the steps into the flat. The living room is a mess; photos on the wall are either broken or lopsided. Terrance stops by the stairs that go up and rights a bent photo of Tiana when she was a teen.

The frame bends again because the nail holding it in place is bent. He makes his way to the top. The blood on the bedclothes has begun to smell. Looking around, the detective concludes forensics won't be able to find anything in a place where demons have abducted someone.

On his way down the stairs, he notices the photo is hanging straight. He freezes; there's someone in the apartment with him.

Bounty is standing in the corner by the window, where the white curtains billow in.

"Did you find her?" Terrance asks him.

He nods. His eyes follow the detective as he approaches him. Bounty wears a dark shirt, black jeans, and brown boots. Terrance pauses; his gaze falls on the demon's hands buried deep in his pockets. The way he rocks on his feet, he looks like an ordinary man.

"Is she okay?"

"I guess. For now."

"What do you mean?" Terrance asks.

Bounty steps forward suddenly. "What are you doing here?"

"I think I know who killed those girls in Berlin and who took your girlfriend." Terrance opens the fold of his blazer and removes a large paper. It contains the photo grid, combining all the photos that detective Jürgen sent him from Berlin.

Terrance points at the images of two guys wearing the golf shoes. "Here, I think it's these two, they are the culprits."

Bounty takes the paper and peers at the picture.

"Lecrae and Amaruq."

"Le-what?"

"This ones a demon.. the other is a watcher. they're the kingpins of human trafficking One of them took Tiana."

"I can help you get her. Where is she?"

Bounty narrows his eyes at the cop. He glides past him and stops before the photo of Tiana that the cop tried to the right earlier. He stands before it, just staring at it.

"She's in hell."

Terrance stammers, "Y-y-you don't mean that literally, do you?"

"She's in hell, dying slowly. I have to get her back."

Bounty turns to the cop suddenly.

"How did you find them.. Amaruq and the other?"

"The cameras—"

"Can you find anyone that way?"

Terrance says, yes, almost anyone.

"There's someone I need to find," he says. "He's hiding. Can you find him?"

"Do you have a picture?"

Terrance finds paper and a pen in the house and watches Bounty as he makes the sketch. He marvels at how fast Bounty did it and how realistic the rendering is.

"Come on, let's get to the precinct."

"Good," Bounty says and joins the cop in his car.

The tech office guys give Bounty only a cursory look, asking Terrance who the breathing tree trunk is before they go ahead with his request. They run the artwork through a scanner that projects the image onto a computer screen. They developed a graphic image that is close enough for computer software to read and compare with a cache from the database of faces in Japan.

Terrance pours coffee, then hands Bounty a cup. Surprised that he takes it, sips it, and thanks him. He remains subdued, however. They wait in his office for twenty minutes before Terrance gets the call. Terrance listens on the phone briefly, then says to Bounty, "I'm sorry, man. No match."

"It's not possible. Tell them to run the check again."

"They've run it four times already; Interpol, the Japanese government, FBI, CIA, and even the Russian KGB. No match. Your guy is a ghost, which means he's either dead or changed his face or really skilled at lying low. Or maybe there's nobody like that."

Bounty exhales. "Are you positive?."

"When was the last time you seen this guy?"

Bounty takes a second to answer the question. "A very long time."

"Did you do business with him or something? how is he mixed up in this?"

Bounty almost blurts out that the Fae he's looking for is Demetri, his father. But instead, he barks out, "He's family."

Terrance exhales too, smiles, and tells Bounty he is sorry.

"Thank you, for trying."

"What are you gonna do now?" the detective asks.

"I have to find him."

"How about Tiana McGuire?"

"When I find this man, I'll have saved Tiana."

Terrance grimaces, his mind trying to connect the dots. "You want me to give you a ride?"

Bounty smiles as he goes to the door. "I don't need it."

"Oh yeah, my bad. Good luck, though."

Bounty nods and exits.

38

Chapter Thirty Eight

They've all gathered in Stacia's place again. Bounty struggles to keep his rage at bay; everyone can see it. It comes out in the way he rocks hard on the balls of his feet, the hardness in his gaze, even though he hardly frowns. Yolanda begins to ask about Tiana, but Keanu stops her.

Keanu gently tugs her arm and brings her downstairs to a different room.

Yolanda paces. Why, why can't I talk to him?"

"It is hard for Bounty already—"

Yolanda points a finger in the demon's face. "No! He brought this on all of us! What did he think was gonna come out of this? All of this is happening because Bounty wanted to get his dick wet. Tiana is sick and dying because of him! Now she's missing. He got her into this shit! Y'all better save her and make her well; I don't care, just make my best friend back!"

Keanu's inner beast howls, sensing her deep desperation. She drops her rear onto the only couch in the room and buries her face in her palms. When her shoulders begin to shudder, Keanu puts his hand around her to calm her.

"He will bring her back, I can assure you that..." he says, also without much faith.

Bounty can't find their Sire. It's rumored that the great wolf passed away many lunar cycles ago. Then why did Cerberus give Bounty the task? Did their grandfather know Bounty could never find Demetri, tricking him into forfeiting Tiana forever?

It must be so.

Keanu touches the back of Yolanda's ear. Applying slight pressure on her pressure points. Her eyes begin to droop. Her head lolls to the side, and she falls into a deep slumber.

"When you wake, you should feel better. Sleep now, beautiful one."

Keanu gives his mate one last look before phasing up the side of the wall, back into the upper lounge.

Bounty asks him how Yolanda is.

"I knocked her out."

Tao's eyes widened in alarm. Keanu notices and clarifies, "I mean, she's asleep. She is under too much pressure. When she awakes, she should feel much better."

Bounty steps to Tao.

He looks at the three half-demons warily—Bounty, Stacia, and Keanu.

Bounty raises his hand. "Do not be alarmed. I need you to tell me about your clan? Are they powerful enough to be allies?"

"I told you everything I know. You know more than me I didn't even know Inyoku was fox demon, I know nothing of her clan or mine—"

"I need you to tell me again, did your father mention anything?" Bounty demands.

Tao sighs and tells the triplets that even he doesn't believe most of what his father said. He tells them about Inyoku's family and then gives a brief description of his own family.Going into as much detail as he could about Daichi, visited the Nikaro building in Tokyo, the strange twenty-eighth floor that no one knew existed.

"They've been calling me seeking to make a deal, claiming that if I come home, they'll stop chasing us about Inyoku. My father went to talk to the head of the Nikaro clan head. It seems like my father wasn't even aware that the Nikaro clan had demon lineage, either. He was just as surprised as me to discover it. They kept that information hidden well."

"Stacia warned me that no matter what I did, they would still come after us. So I didn't go. But how is it even possible to keep their Oni... I mean demon lineage hidden all these years?"

"Easy, my siblings and I have walked the earth for millennia. Demons, and fae have always coexisted here on earth hidden from the eyes of men?" Bounty replies, "you couldn't even tell there was a being slumbering within you until I called forth your power."

Tao shakes his head slowly. "Yeah, I guess you are right... Wait, what do you mean inside of me?"

He continues to stare at the trio standing before him in confusion. Tao thinks about some of the strange things he's experienced. The inner voice in his mind, the vague memory of saving Tiana from Inyoku. "No... wait, those were only dreams or hallucinations... right?"

"Nothing is as it seems," Stacia replies.

Tao shakes his head, unable to wrap his mind around that just yet. "So, what's the next step?"

Bounty answers, "The longer we wait, the less likely Tiana is to survive this!"

Stacia hisses and begins to pace, too. She stops at the window. From there, she muses. "Why can't we all just go away after all this? Ya know, take everyone to another realm? Even if we save Tiana, grandfather will always see her and your children as pawns. They'll never be safe!"

Keanu cuts in, "you're right sister, we made him look bad to Lucifer. He'll hunt us down until we're all dead."

Tao snaps his hand , recalling a lost memory , "Wait, there was something my father mentioned, something about a blonde-haired woman she was covered in darkness or smoke something like that."

Bounty looks at his siblings. His eyes shine green with rage. The five o'clock shadow around his jaw appears darker. His inner wolf begins to show. He takes his hands out of his pockets. Tao steps back while glancing down at Bounty's clawed hand.

"Ria!" Stacia hisses and Keanu nods it has to be

"I'm going to Japan. To that building, I'm saving my mate. What happens after that will happen—"

Keanu frowns and asks, "Why Japan, why would grandfather make a hell gate there?"

" I'm not sure but if Ria was spotted, there that has to be the abyss where Tiana and the pups are being held captive."

"Cerberus is bound by the treaty—Tiana is... mostly human... meaning she still has to die within the human realm." Stacia voices from her place at the window.

"Yes," agrees Bounty. "It means a hell gate would be his only loophole around the treaty. Whatever touches the gate would be considered his domain."

Bounty explains, "This will be a battle. There will be powerful demons guarding her. I will need you to help. Unfortunately, I can't do this alone." Then Bounty pauses; he steps closer to Tao. "Take off your clothes!"

"What?!"

"I sense a benign power from you. I need to assess your true strength." Tao glances over at Stacia, how bows her need for him to oblige Bounty's command.

Tao raises his shirt and rolls it up to his chest. Tao's chest and belly are a canvas of tattoos; red, blue, green, and brown whorls, loops, and intricate patterns of the Yakuza tattoos.

He says, "These are just tattoos. They don't mean anything."

"You are Yakuza," says Bounty.

"No, I'm not. My family is. I left home to run from all of that shit."

"I guess you didn't run far enough," Bounty grumbles.

Tao drops his head and gapes at the dragon on his body again; he shakes his head in confusion. He had gotten them sporadically over time, and now that he takes a closer look, they all look like one artist put them there.

But how's that possible? "What's happening to me?"

"Nothing is happening to you; you were born half-fae!"

Bounty's demeanor falls. Looking over at his brother, Keanu, while shaking his head, then back to Tao. "You're not suitable for the mission. You have powers, but you're a latent dragon that refuses to surface. Spells will have counter-effects on you—"

"Dragon? I'm a dragon?" Stacia steps over to Tao rubbing his back as he takes it all in.

"But not on me."

They all turned around. Mama Debbie stands leaning on the door frame. Stacia gasps. The striking resemblance to Tiana is overwhelming. Tao rises slowly; he drops his shirt back over the tattooed belly. Mama Debbie looks trim, with her narrow waist in a fitted pair of jeans like Tiana, though her breasts aren't as big. Her hair is plated in long corn-rows from the front all the way to the back of her head.

Bounty is awestruck by Mama Debbie's beauty. Staring at her makes him miss Tiana even more. They stare at each other. No judgment, no malice. A once-powerful angel who lost a daughter and a hell-born half-demon whose mate has been taken away.

"I'll go with you to Japan."

"No, you can't do that," Stacia begins to argue. "We need to find another way."

"There is no other way." She says, "We are running out of time. I am a fallen light-bringer; I still have enough power to stand against lesser demons. Besides..."

She steps closer. Her skin, though dark, begins to glow; a faint halo forms around her head.

"She's my daughter. She will need me to survive; her time is almost due."

Tao looks from Mama Debbie to Bounty, confused.

"What are you talking about? Is Tiana about to deliver her babies?" he asks.

Bounty shakes his head the babies are already halfway out and half way in. they are still connected to her.

Mama Debbie says, "It is different for demon babies."

"Oh God," Tao gasps.

They begin preparations for the battle, making haste. Mama Debbie invites Mother Martha to Stacia's place, who commences building an ethereal outer wall around the property. Bounty expects that Cerberus will send demons over. When he finds out, Bounty now knows he's been tricked.

Mama Debbie makes some calls to her old friend, asking them to stand with her. Powerful allies — fallen angels, vampires, werewolves, and witches — come swiftly and stand around the property, on the river. With the building fortified, Bounty teleports with Mama Debbie from the attic of Stacia's house.

They arrive in the alley of a crowded street, ten blocks from the Nikaro building. It's Debbie's first time actually stepping foot in Japan. But she knows the country has breezed over it in her many years of living.

They eye each other mentally, preparing themselves for the great conflict. They leave that alley that looks like the back of a cinema—Debbie touches the rough wall and knows it is only a bookstore. She follows Bounty out into the street of hundreds of people bearing peach-colored skin and slanted eyes going in various directions. The aroma of food saturates the air; steam rises from open food stalls, selling roast innards, insects, and other local delicacies. They crossed the road from this small market filled with the babble of Japanese tongues and joined a bus going upward towards the city's high-end area. Bounty points at a group of buildings, skyscrapers with masts pricking the blue sky.

He asked Debbie, "Do you see it?"

She lowers her head to get a glimpse through the front, where the driver turns the wheels.

One of the tall buildings is different from the others—a dark cloud, with lightning flashing from the base. Sparks fly off the side of the building every time the lightning hits.

Debbie nods. "Dark matter."

"Yes."

They sit quietly until the bus drops them off a block away. They walk the rest of the way, channeling their inner strength with each step closer. The Nikaro property occupies about half an acre of the street, which is not less than two blocks of space, with smaller buildings attached to it. Bounty leads the way into the parking lot. Four unarmed security guards—humans—stand ramrod at the door. Bounty's figure reflects in the glass walls as they approach, adorned in a blue business suit, black shoes, and black sunglasses.

Debbie looks elegant in a long grey dress; this way, she's not so obvious. The girl at the clothes store downtown told her to go for the red equivalent of the dress, saying it better complemented the gentleman's—Bounty—color. The girl winked at Bounty as they stepped out of the store.

The security guy at the door pulls the glass door open without asking questions. His companions don't even seem like they see the huge man and the woman.

For Debbie, the evil in the building begins to manifest to Debbie when they pass the fifteenth floor. The lift becomes heavier with the two of them in it; it is as though the building repels them, rebuking them, not wanting them inside.

On the eighteenth floor, the lift stalls, the lights begin to blink and hum. The box shudders. Bounty presses the exit button, and the lift stops.

Chiiing!

The mechanism behind the works of the will grind to a halt. Bounty begins to change, and for the first time in decades, he chooses his wolfish abilities first. He herds Debbie to the blind side of the lift door, just in case they are suddenly attacked when the door opens.

"Prepare yourself."

Debbie asks, "Do you think they know we are here?"

He growls.

"It will not matter!"

The doors begin to open. The lights continue to blink and waver.

The door opens, and they are faced with an empty hallway. Bounty steps outside, and Debbie follows him.

"They know we are here," Debbie says.

"How do you know that?"

"Because no alarm is going off."

She's right.

Bounty finds the steps a short brisk walk from the lift. They begin their way up; this way, they hope to not be caught unaware by lurking attacks. On the twenty-fifth step, Debbie stops behind Bounty.

He asks her what the problem is.

"I hear something," she says.

"What do you hear?"

The shrieking sound comes to her again, this time louder than the first time. Tiana. Debbie glances at Bounty and realizes the demon doesn't hear it.

She grabs hold of her hands. "Tell me, is it, Tiana?!"

"Yes." She walks past her. "We are close. Come on."

Resisting the urge to warp again to make their approach even faster, Bounty runs up the steps at a speed four times faster than the average man. Debbie could beat that speed, but she knows her own limitations.

The demons who attacked her home were not lesser demons but seasoned ones: rebels, vile and cunning spirits, she wasn't strong enough to fight against them. Debbie wasn't a battle angel. She was simply a lightbringer before she fell.

Bounty reaches the twenty-eighth floor and stops. He puts a hand out to shield Debbie; together they climb the last batch of steps leading to the false floor where Tiana and the pups are held captive. Bounty leads the trudge. They reach the top and meet semi-darkness. a stiff whooshing past their ears; the lights offer very little illumination, it's like walking through an abandoned mine.

There are no doors, just grey walls that stretch out before them, biding them to take the journey to nowhere.

"Are you ready?"

Debbie nods, but she stops again, her hands on her ears. She can hear Tiana's faint cries.

"Tiana? Oh, my baby, I'm coming."

Bounty's eyes burst into low, burning flames. His muscles bulge through his business suit; his thighs swell and stretch the seams of his trousers. Claws out, fangs white and hungry for demon flesh, Bounty moves forward. Debbie follows. Bounty's hands are suddenly three feet long He walks in the middle of the hallway, as his claws gouge the walls as they rake pass.

"Amaruq!!" he screams. "Show yourself! I know you're in here!"

"Hahahaha," bellows the gravelly voice of Amaruq. "Wow, you surprised me for a half-breed, Bounty. You went and outdid yourself yet again."

The demon's voice is everywhere; in the walls, the roof, beneath the floor.

"You coward!" Bounty snaps. "Face me, Amaruq. Let's see if those balls you go deep in the girly boys with are of any use now. Show yourself. Don't hide, you fool, kiss-ass cunt. You will never be worth shit to Lucifer!"

Grrrrraaagh!

The floor shakes even more. The low burning lamps in the ceiling begin to go out after they burst into grains of glass. The wall floor is plunged into darkness.

"Yes, Amaruq. Show yourself," Bounty growls. "Come get me if you can!"

"Oh, looks like Lecrae was unable to stop you; I will come to you. I know you will see me, but will your female friend see me? She seems powerful, too. But we beat her once, and we will beat her again, probably kill her. Then after that, the lost souls will feed on the girl. Personally, I'd like the babies for dinner. What d'ya say, huh?"

The darkness doesn't affect Bounty. He can see perfectly well. But Debbie stumbles forward.

"Bounty? Where are you?" Debbie calls.

He takes her hand and waits. The walls begin to rumble, something is coming. Debbie braces herself in the hellish blackness. She shuts her eyes, opens her mind to what she used to be: an angel of the light. Visions of her hovering in the clouds, seeing everything with God's eyes and a million times sharper than even the most sophisticated telescopes in existence. She sees herself before Him, hearing the heavenly music as it spreads from the place of eternal light and fills her soul.

Debbie sees others like her, bright beings; their radiance is thousands of times greater than all the universe's stars put together. One glance, the slightest glance from a human eye, or the touch of that light in its undiluted form, would vaporize the hardest matter. Debbie sees herself as she is again. Her hands glow whiteness in the truest form.

She opens her eyes, and the light explodes from her body, plucking the world from the demonic darkness and plunging it into that glorious brightness she used to know.

Debbie screams. Power surges from her body.

The corridor is illuminated in holy light; she sees the demons hanging from the ceiling, crawling towards them along the walls. The brightness of the light is too great for them. They vaporize and flake into nothing, dying off in their numbers.

Debbie walks away from Bounty, who is shocked by what he beholds. He looks down at himself somehow unaffected by her heavenly light. She turns to look at his beastly form. His claws tear into every being that escapes her light. Bounty rips their heads off. Swallowing or stepping on them till they burst and spread reddish-grey ichor on the floor. He picks them off one by one. Plunging his claws into their chests and ripping out their beating hearts with no regard or care. His beast roars in the ecstasy of battle. While taking a bite from one of the fallen demon's hearts, then discards what's left over his shoulder before finding his next victim.

Bounty wrecks carnage, and Debbie's holy light burns all that stands in their way. Somehow, the light from Debbie restores the lights in the ceiling. They spark; they flicker and hum to life again. Debbie's light wanes; her work is done. Bounty wipes the blood off his face, belches, and staggers past Debbie. She takes his hand,

Standing at the end of the hall is a slim man; long white hair. His mouth, however, is what catches Debbie's eyes—it's unnaturally wide, disappearing into the corners of his face. He smiles with plenty of sharp, jagged fangs.

His hands are so long they float just ten inches from the floor, littered with the fleshless smoking bodies of demons.

"I'm impressed, Bounty. Or should I call you Ishtan Rustivich? That was an impressive trick by your girlfriend's mother here." The demon's head turns slightly at Debbie. "But now, You have to go through me to get to her, Bounty.—"

"I have not come to just beat you, Amaruq."

"Oh. Really? We are here to dance? Me and you?"

"I am here..." Bounty belches smoke from his mouth— "To kill you, and when I'm done, I'll eat your heart."

Amaruq laughs. He sounds like a bird caught in a bird catcher's snare. He flexes his fingers, his claws dart out, and scrapes the floor as he advances forward. Bounty's fingers crack; his muscles hum, and the back of his business suit rips from the neckline down to his torso. Spiky hair shoots from new pores on his back. Bounty combines his two beast forms half demon half wolf, a half-breed, but one with the powers of both races. He's going head-on with a pure-breed, a true Hell beast.

Amaruq flies from the end of the hall, shrieking as he comes, fangs open, spittle flying, and claws reaching. They meet halfway with a powerful bang. The shock wave pushes Debbie back, with only half her former angel's power now back; her feet are unable to hold. She watches the demons as they battle.

Every punch that Amaruq lands causes booms. The sound waves ripple past him and crack the wall. Bounty takes the blows, absorbing every claw swipe and bite. Amaruq's poison barely reaches past the top layer of the Bounty's hide.

Debbie hears Tiana's muffled cry; pain lingers in her voice. Barely an hour has passed since she and Bounty traveled in from that dirty alley.

By now, Tiana's counter is running down. She must find a way to get past the ongoing battle ahead of her. Bounty reads her mind instinctually. He grabs Amaruq by the crotch, squeezes, and the demon howls like a suckling pig. Bounty grips hold of his neck and stumps him against the wall; there is a loud crack as the wall begins to cave in.

Debbie sees her chance.

She bolts past the fighting demons like a charge of lightning and reaches the end of the hall. There's a giant door. Panting, she pushes it and doesn't move. She pushes harder, but it still won't budge even after she bumps the wood with her shoulder. Amaruq notices their ploy to distract him. He starts struggling out of Bounty's hands. Amaruq chants a short incantation begins to change; his shoulders pop as if something is underneath them. His inner beast form is seeking to escape its prison. The demon's back ripples and the muscles shiver. Amaruq's skin burst open, wings—spanning at least eight feet on both sides —fan out. The wings have sharp claws for thumbs and membranes like the wings of a bat.

"Now, Bounty. I'm about to show you why they call you half-breed." Amaruq grins;

"I am about to make you regret you were ever conceived by that worthless shifter father of yours!"

Amaruq jabs Bounty with his sharp wings, puncturing Bounty's back.

He screams.

"Yes! Scream, Bounty, Scream.—hahaha!"

Amaruq turns his head slowly towards the end of the hall; he winks at Debbie and laughs at her. His eyes are an insane green, with rings of black and red.

Debbie looks into those eyes and prays they aren't fighting a losing battle. Tiana cries out again, She's begging for help.

Bounty howls ; his voice filled with pain, His powerful howl cracks the walls. Dusting flakes of plaster begin to fall on his face and Amaruq's. Debbie feels a sensation like she's being pulled away from the door. She glances down and sees that it is Amaruq, pulling at her with his wings.

Debbie coerces all the strength in her hands and shoulder; she struggles to resist the pull. She rams into the door just as Bounty's head-butts Amaruq in the nose. Amaruq screams, as the door yields under her weight. She's thrown into darkness once again. She senses her body falling, plummeting down a cast hole. She calls on her past glory. Her wings pop out from her back; she floats up,as eternal light bursts from within her.

She's in a great cavern with rocky sides, spiraling from the roof and beyond. With the aid of her celestial light, she sees a body suspended in the abyss below.

"Tiana!"

"Oh, my baby, my baby is alive."

She flies down the pit and hovers over the splayed body of her daughter. She's naked. Floating around her weakened bloody form, are the three pups still connected by their umbilical cords.

"Oh God, she's still bleeding and they're still connected."

When she tries to go closer to her, something repels her; a wall of protective demonic energy is barricading Tiana. Chains protrude from her wrists into the side of the cavern. Debbie must find a way to break the chains without Tiana plummeting into the abyss.

As she prepares to free Tiana, Amaruq and Bounty break through the doorway above her; they fall towards her. Debbie flies out of the way as both demons crash into the energy barrier covering Tiana.

There's a bright flash.. Amaruq falls through the barrier, the energy charges rip through his body, eviscerating his right half. As he falls, Amaruq tries to grab hold of Tiana's leg, but misses; he snaps, growls, and roars, fighting to pull Bounty's with him, but misses again.

As Bounty falls he rips Tiana's body from the chains securing her body to the cavernous wall, clutching her and the children tightly against his chest as they plummet into the dark abyss.

"Gotcha!"

Debbie grabs Bounty's left hand with every bit of angelic strength she has left. With a grunt, Tiana's mother lifts them up through the cavern and escapes through one of the walls Bounty destroyed.

"You're safe now, Tiana."

"Thank you, mom," she whispers faintly.
Debbie looks down at her daughter and nods.

39

❦

Chapter Thirty Nine

Mount Takao, Tokyo, Japan.

Debbie doesn't stop flying until she's over forty miles clear of danger from the Nikaro building. She flies and flies until she sees the green bushes on the side of mount Takao in the distance. The foliage will provide plenty of shade and protection.

She called forth her old light-bringer powers once again; whispering to the trees in the language of the old fairies, too, and making them do her bidding. She will need the trees to provide protection from demons that are sure to come after them. The beat of Debbie's broad wings sends the birds escaping into the sky from their own twig homes on the crest of the tall leafy forest.

She lowers Bounty gently in a small clearing ringed by trees. It looks like a place where foragers may have settled to rest not long ago. There is a fading campfire in the middle of it: cold burnt wood, black charcoal. Further outside this ring of clearing are wild amaranthus in bloom, green leaves, bright red cones and droopy buds. It is beautiful to behold, and the scent of them aids in healing.

Debbie's wings vanish. She runs into the bush and comes back with three broad leaves. She wraps each baby with a leaf. After cutting their umbilical cords, she stares at them for a moment.

Their eyes are still tightly shut, with little pink lips. One of the babies takes her forefinger and wraps its tiny hands tightly around it.

Debbie looks at Bounty. "They are adorable and look perfectly normal, I can't believe they have so much dark energy" she says.

But Bounty hunches over the prone body of Tiana, mute. His full attention on Tiana.

"Is she okay?"

Bounty shakes his head, his eyes bloodshot and angry. He caresses Tiana's face and sighs. "She's in very bad shape. She's lost too much blood."

He puts his ear on her chest, gives it a few seconds to listen. Her heart barely beats. She may not be with them for long.

"No, it can't be..." Debbie takes Tiana's head in her arms.

Hot tears streak the side of Tiana's face, leaving a trail of salt, white and otherworldly. Her skin remains sallow, her breath barely there.

Debbie puts her fingers through her daughter's curly hair. Surprisingly, Tiana's hair. Debbie kisses her gaunt cheeks; she inhales the scent of her—spiced mulberry. Debbie raises her head up into the sky. She prays and pleads for her daughter.

She begins to cry, and her tears are like acid. burning off into the air.

"Please, save her, please..." she pleads with heaven.

Silence.

A loud, resounding silence meets her supplication. Debbie's hair is in tatters; wet with sweat from the battle won. Only now, it looks like it was all in vain.

"I will save her..."

Debbie looks up at Bounty. He has grown fives times his normal size, about the same height as the trees.

"You said what?"

"Give her to me." He barks as he calls forth every bit of his demonic energy from his Hell beast and his wolf.

Bounty takes Tiana and lays her on the matted grass. He takes her wrist and checks for her pulse; her wrists are scared and bleeding from the chains. He presses harder checking frantically, but there is barely a whisper of life.

Debbie looks at Bounty and sees a broken man trying to save the woman he loves.

"You may want to look away now, Debbie," he growls.

Debbie falls on her bottom, and crawls back on her hands. "What are you going to do?"

Bounty rips what remains of his tattered suit, and draws a deep breath. He bares the claws of his right hand. They elongate, and sharpen. Bounty stabs himself below the ridge of his muscular chest. He pushes deeper and deeper past his ribs.

"What are you doing?" Debbie gasps.

His chest swallows his hand to the wrist. He grits his teeth; his chest weeps blood from the gaping opening created. Bounty pulls his hand out. One of his three demon hearts lays beating rhythmically in his splayed palm.

"H-h-how..." Debbie stammers. Her eyes widen when she realizes what Bounty is about to do. *No, it will kill...*she reasons madly. She wants to stop him, but Bounty is fast. His hands slip into Tiana's chest.

Gently, like dipping one's hand into water. He pulls out Tiana's heart, tosses it aside, then tears his out. He cleaves the bopping part in two, dips half into Tiana's chest and slips the other half back in his gaping chest again. Exhausted by the extraordinary measures he just performed, Bounty sits heavily, panting hard.

"Oh God, what have you done?"

Bounty's heart seals before Debbie's eyes. He stands up, bloody hands and chest. "Tiana—" he calls her gently.

She rushes over to her daughter's side. She takes her daughter's face from his firm grip, rubbing her hand over the spot where she saw Bounty's hand go into Tiana's chest. There's no scar. She touches the top of her forehead and her face lights up with hope and warmth. Debbie looks up at Bounty.

"It's warm, her skin is warm..." she beams. "OH God, her skin is warming up again. Will she truly live?"

Debbie gathers her daughter in her arms, and a single tear squeezes out of the corner of her eye. She closes them and smiles into the watching faces of the trees. Bounty goes to the babies nearby, where Debbie left them. He picks them and brings them to Tiana's side.

She opens her groggy eyes and tries to speak, but her throat disobeys. Bounty says, "Water, she needs water." He hurries off into the bush and vanishes.

"Titi? You are safe now..." Debbie sings. "You are safe now. He gave you half of his heart, Can you believe that—?"

"Mom?" Tiana rasps.

Debbie flushes with sheer joy. "Hey, baby. You're okay. And your babies are healthy, too. Do you wanna see them? They are right there."

She points off to the right, where the children lay with their small arms and legs wriggling in the air.

She lays Tiana down and walks over to the babies, gathering them into her hands. Just then, Bounty appears out of the bushes, carrying a satchel of water.

"Bounty? You came for me?" Tiana croaks.

He kneels beside her and helps her drink. She gulps it hungrily. Bounty takes the satchel away when he's sure she's drunk enough.

Tiana's eyes glaze over again, her eyelids fluttering a little before she falls into a deep sleep. Bounty carries her in his arms.

"What's wrong with her?" Debbie asks worriedly.

"She will sleep. Mother Martha informed me that I would have to make the ultimate sacrifice to save her. and that it was I did. Her new heart will require a healing sleep."

"How long will this take? Did mother Martha tell you?"

Bounty glances at Tiana's still face, her slow breathing. Then he turns and eyes the pups held tightly in debbies arms.

"As long as it takes for her to heal. Her body must learn to synchronize with my dark energy. Her human form will die off, but her divinity and my demonic nature will be all that remains. We must wait to see how it takes."

Bounty walks away with Tiana in his hands. He blends with the gloom of the forest and vanishes.

Debbie takes the babies, two girls, and one boy, in her arms.

"Come children, we must leave this place."

****

"Is it over?" Yolanda asks.

Keanu doesn't say anything at first, knowing that, despite winning Tiana back, the war is still on the horizon. He stares out the window at the smooth surface of the Chicago River, silently watching on. Bounty has been away, attending to Tiana in her sleep. Where he is, he didn't say. Keanu understands it's better for them to remain hidden.

Keanu answers her, "This is only the beginning, but return home for now. I will come to you when needed."

Yolanda frowns at his cold tone. "I hope Tiana gets better soon and comes back home to her babies."

They both turn from the window. Tao and Stacia stand off to the side talking. It's time for them all to go; each carries their belongings as they walk down to the waiting cars, the silence between them pregnant with persisting questions. Stacia volunteers to take both Yolanda and Tao back home. Yoland looks at Keanu with pleading eyes but he waves her on avoiding her once again. As they drive off Keanu stands watching, as the car rustles dust and becomes a tiny speck in the distance.

Tao tosses all night until early morning when his alarm blares. He gets up, strolls to the lounge, and sits on the couch. From there, he gazes from the window of his new apartment upon the waking city. The sounds of early morning traffic drift to him. A cop car—or an ambulance—moans in the distance.

He gets on the mat and does some stretches; his muscles are sore from sparring with Stacia in the ring. He tires of the exercise and sits again. Then he picks up his phone to call his father in Japan. Despite Tiana's issues, he still has the drama of his own.

****

Yolanda calls Tao three months later still worrying over Tiana. But there hasn't been much change. Tiana is somewhere unreachable. There's nothing to do except wait.

"It has been months, Tao."

"Yes, I know I was told the less we know the better."

"Any news on your situation?"

Tao tells her there's none.

Yoyo chuckles. "Well at least that's good to hear. How about dinner tonight?" Yolanda asks.

"I've moved away...not too far though—"

"You what? Why?"

"I couldn't stay in that house. I can't sleep at night.... I have these—" Tao fell silent, unable to voice his concerns. Not to Yolanda, at least.

"Dreams, right? I have them, too. Only when I wake, I don't remember them anymore. But they scare the shit out of me. And I have trouble sleeping, too."

"I moved to the North River. A two-bedroom loft," Tao replied, hoping to steer the conversation away from his dark thoughts.

"Nice."

They are both quiet after that. Yoyo is in her stylist's shop. waiting for her early bird clients. The place is almost packed, her customers rushed back to patronize her after her long hiatus. She watches her salon girl's stock the shelves as she reflects on how Tiana used to come around the place. She gazes upon Tiana's favorite chair. reminiscing on how they'd both turn the place upside down, just talking and laughing.

Her eyes sting with tears.

"Are you alright, Yoyo?"

"Yeah, I'm alright. I just...you know, remember—" She begins to pour her heart through the phone, unloading her emotional baggage.

"How about we visit the babies, Yoyo? We promised we'd be there for our God children."

She says it sounds like fun. Tao promises to pick her up the next day.

* * * * * *

"He took them away," Debbie says as she serves her homemade cookies. She pours apple juice into the cups and serves her guests.

"You let Bounty take the babies away?" Yolanda asks. "How could you do that? How could you let him take the babies? He can't—" Her body slumps into the seat in sadness.

"Baby, that man gave Tiana half his heart. I think he done earned his place in all ours. He'll do fine, I'm sure."

Yolanda sags into the couch even further.

Tao is stunned. He stares at the wrapped gift box on the table that he and Yolanda brought over. Strangely, he's not disappointed. The babies are better off with Bounty. They talk about how life is now different for them all.

Yolanda brings up the strange dreams, asking if Debbie was having them too.

She nods.

While the women talked, Tao seemed silent and distant. After heartfelt goodbyes, Tao drops Yolanda off at her apartment, then pulls out his phone and makes a call...

"Hello?"

"Stacia, it's me."

40

Chapter Forty

TWO YEARS LATER.

A young man takes three kids for a walk every evening near the Loyola Beach playground. The man is at least seven feet tall, handsomely rugged, with green eyes. His hair is the color of burnt toast, with a hint of brown. He's very tan and stern-looking. He never appears with his wife, and the neighborhood wonders why. He says very little when talked to, and he never starts conversations.

Sometimes, he can be spotted sitting on a park bench alone, staring out at Lake Michigan, like a man waiting for someone. His eyes hardly reveal anything about his thoughts.

Bounty was headed to the park with his children. When a cop car pulled up to the curb. Two officers approach him.

They ask him where he lives.

He points at the red brick building opposite the tennis court. "There. Is there a problem, officers?"

"Not sure. That's what we're trying to find out."

The man looks from one cop to the other. One of the cops stoops before the children.

"Hey kiddos, how are you today?"

They chorus that they are fine.

"And where's mommy?" asks the cop with a fatherly smile.

One of them says, "She's not with us."

The cop looks up at his partner and back at the girl. "What do you mean, she's not with you?"

The tall man herds the children and begins to walk away.

"Hey, where are you going?" the cop calls and tries to catch up. "We just want to ask you a few more questions."

The man turns around.

Up the road, a black Buick turns into the street. It rolls past the cop car and stops by the tall man. Detective Terrance Slaton's head pops out of the window.

"Hello, Ishtan."

Bounty smirks. "Detective Slaton?"

The two cops who stopped him stare at Terrance curiously. The detective steps out of his car and shakes hands with Bounty.

"Officers, is there a problem?" He flashes his badge. "I am detective Terrance Slaton, Grove Avenue precinct. Ishtan Rustivich here is my friend—"

"Oh."

"I hope you guys treat him well. He just moved into the area. As you can see, he cares for his children alone." Terrance leans down to look at the kids. Gathering them up in his hands, he walks towards his car, ignoring the officer's gawking stare.

"If there won't be anything more, officers. I have to join my friend and my children. Thank you."

Bounty walks away.

"What's up?" Terrance asks him.

Bounty shrugs.

They sit on a park bench near the beach; look off into the distance as a straggling of vacationers and tourists dot the sandy shores ahead. The girls play in the sand and the little boy and build castles a safe few feet away. The children remind him of Tiana. They have her curly hair, dark skin color, too, except for the boy, the one with his disposition, reticent and less playful.

"How's she doing? She'll be back soon?"

"I'll know by the end of the week. It's been two years already; her body took too much damage."

The detective gives Bounty a long stare at the side of his face. It thrills the detective that he was actually sitting with a real live demon. But Bounty is cool. He tells Bounty that the voodoo man, Reynold Ash, is dead.

"We think it was a robbery. He was alone when it happened; I almost called you up to check the place out..... There's been more movement according to intel at Interpol this time in Japan."

"You think they're starting back up?"

"Yeah. Unfortunately, I can show you photos the satellite captured when you come downtown."

After a while of watching the children play, Terrance says, "You know you'd make a damn fine detective. A man with your skills."

"You forget I'm not a man; I'm a hunter."

The detective chuckles. "Yeah. So easy to forget that. And that's the point, right?"

"I am not who I used to be."

"What changed?"

"My *heart* changed. Literally," he says with a smile on his face.

41

Epilogue

On some weekends, Bounty would take the kids to Mama Debbie's place. She spoils them with candies and cookies. Telling them stories about a time when angels walked the earth and tells them about their mother, too.

Neveah, Athena, and Icarus listen attentively when the stories are about their Tiana. The children were already showing signs of giftedness; they'd listen and stare at Debbie with grownup eyes and ask questions far past their age "So, is mom still on earth?" "Are we Nephilim or Hell beast? " "Will I grow up to look like mama too?"

Bounty cleared his throat for his pups to settle down.

"One question at a time now, children," their grandmother chuckled. "She's closer than you think; I'm honestly not sure what you children classify as. And Yes, Athena, you will be just as beautiful if not more?" Debbie smiles at their sweet little brown faces. The children look at their dad. "Is it true?" "Uhuh." Bounty nods, ruffling the small puffy fro of his son.

Debbie whispers to them. "Babies, you won't be coming to my place next weekend. You'll be with your mother instead. How about that?"

The girls raise their hands in the air and dance around happily.

While sweet, Icarus just smiles from ear to ear. The children fell fast asleep after overindulging in cookies and mango tea. So Debbie and Bounty took a quick walk to the end of the street, making sure they didn't stray too far from the house. Due to the children's giftedness, they had to have adult conversations away from their inquisitive little ears.

They talk about Bounty raising the children alone these past few years. "Watching you with my grands reminded me of how it was raising Tiana.

If it wasn't for Mother Martha, I'm not sure I would have made it all those years ago. You've done one hell of a job raising these kids, young man. I'm proud of you. I hope you know that."

Bounty listened silently as Mama Debbie praised him. He didn't know how to reply. He had never heard anyone tell him that before. It left an unpleasant warmness in his chest. Similar to how it felt when the kids kissed him goodnight or called him dad. His inner beast chuffed softly, his chest puffing with pride.

As they reached the end of the block, Debbie looked around, making sure they were out of earshot.

"Do you feel it?"

"Feel what?" Bounty hackles rose as he scanned the area for threats.

"I've been feeling some dark energy these past few weeks. But my foresight has been blocked. Whatever it is, wants to remain hidden."

Bounty growled and scratched his chin.

"I've also been having dreams, but I don't remember when I wake up. Yoyo called me, saying she and Tao have had them too. It's tough not being able to sleep at night. I can deal with the dreams. But those kids, Yoyo and Tao, I pity them."

"My wolf gives me the power to traverse the dreamscape uninhibited. I haven't seen or heard about any dream walkers recently, but I'll keep an eye on everyone. Amaruq died. But that weasel assed Lecrae hasn't shown his face in years. Whoever it is may not be from the Hell faction."

"And that's what bothers me, Ishtan. Have you gone down there since?" Debbie asks about hell.

"No," he growls. "They attempted to harm my mate and my pups. We weren't much of a family anyway, so there's no need for me to keep in touch."

Debbie nodded her head understanding his point. "Perhaps this was a blessing in disguise."

"You mean me meeting Tiana?"

"Yes, and the babies. Only time will tell how this will all work out."

As they approach the house. Bounty listens for the children thumpum, thumpum, thumpum! Their demon hearts are strong.

Debbie looked up at her new house. The old one had been destroyed beyond recognition. Stacia purchased her a Tudor home on the upper north side. Near Bounty and Tiana's newly built home... Debbie stood on the porch as she silently chanted a prayer of protection. Not just over her home but wide enough to span seven city blocks.

She smiled as a shield of protection solidified into place. Slowly but surely, her light-bringer powers were coming back.

The pitter-patter of little feet snapped her out of her daze. "Bye, nana!" the triplets cried out in chorus. "Goodbye, my sweets babies, and just think in a few days, your mama will be home."

******

Bounty could feel his beast pressing close to the surface. Hell, even his wolf was howling in his inner mind. Everyone was excited; today was the day. Tiana was coming home. The whole family of friends wanted to be there, but Bounty declined the suggestion. Wanting this moment to be solely just for him and the pups until Tiana was up for visitors. Tiana was placed in a healing sleep for the last two years; Mother Martha cared for her in his stead. Feeding her a mixture of holy water with nutrient soil from the volcanic pits of hell to help balance out her new nature. Making sure to stretch and fold her legs and hands, so the muscles didn't wither over time.

"Welcome, Bounty. She's ready." Says Martha as he and the pups enter her home. "Everything is in order." Martha leads them down a red-carpeted corridor. The last door on the right stands ajar. The pups rush past them and burst into the room first. The room is large but warm. It's richly decorated, giving it a homey feel. The white walls; help brighten the room despite there being no windows. Tiana laid on a bed dressed in fresh clothes that Bounty had brought over the night before; a baggy t-shirt and a pair of black fitted jeans, and her favorite pair of Vans.

Her hair must have been freshly washed. It smelled of lilacs. It was even longer than Bounty remembered. Her shiny, thick coils seemed to stretch past her breast now. Bounty shook his head slowly. His inner beast whined desperately for his mate.

The children appeared to be glued in place as they stare at the beautiful brown-skinned woman on the bed. Martha walked behind them, giving them a gentle push, and says, "Babies, why don't you go closer? She's about to open her eyes."

Bounty picked them off the floor and carried them to Tiana's bedside. They stare at their mother with inquisitive little gestures; they touch her hair, nose, and lips. Bounty smiles—something he now does effortlessly ever since he's been caring for the kids.

Tiana's eyes slowly begin to flutter open; Bounty growls out loud, causing Martha and the children to giggle." Daddy thinks mom is pretty." Neveah giggles into her little brown hands.

"Yes, I do, honey." Bounty smiles at his pups. Tiana's eyes are no longer brown like they used to be. They're opaque, ringed with an intense shade of emerald green.

Tiana slowly looks over at the children. Their beautiful brown skin and curly hair looked exactly like hers. She smiles but winces as her memories rushed back, bombarding her mind with images and sensations.

"Are you okay, mommy?" the children ask. Bounty quickly makes his way to her side.

Martha touched Athena's head affectionately. "Give it some time, Tiana. What you are feeling is normal." Tiana smiles weakly, but she shakes the pain off quickly. She sits up and stares at the faces of her children, one after the other, two girls and one boy. She takes their little faces in her hands one after the other and kisses their cheeks lightly.

"How long have I been asleep?"

"Two years."

Tiana glances at mother Martha. 'Are you a saint? How could I ever repay you for all you've done for my family and me?"

"I am all I need to be, to be of help to others. Kindness is not indebted. Welcome back among us, Tiana."

With a teary smile, she mouths thank you.

She turns to Bounty after wiping her eyes. "Where's my mother?" Tiana asks in a worried, husky tone. Bounty informs her that Debbie awaits her at home.

"Children, your mama needs to get out of bed now," Martha says and carries them off the bed.

What happens next surprises Bounty and the pups. Tiana pulls the covers aside, removing the housecoat tied around her waist. As the housecoat falls, two large crimson wings sprout out from behind her.

Bounty's eyes widen

Martha nudges him. "Hahaha, boy, I was waiting to see how you would react. I say, y'all sure have brought some excitement into this old woman's life. Ya hear?" The old woman slapped her knee and cackled in good spirits. "You know what happened to her, don't you?" asks Martha.

Bounty shakes his head in confusion.

"When you put half your demonic heart in her, she became something ... something that doesn't even have a name. Tiana was always half-angel; it wasn't whole until you gave her half of yours. You gave her what she needed to reach her potential. She's a whole new being now."

Tiana looked just as bewildered as Bounty. Her wings flapped timidly, like a wild butterfly, trying its wings for the first time. Their red fluffiness attracted the children's attention. They raised their hands in awe, wanting to touch her wings, so Tiana gently scooped up all three of them, allowing them to touch and groom her wings with their tiny little hands. She lifts herself off the floor with a slight hop and flies around the room with the children tucked securely against her body.

Martha smiled as she and Bounty watched on. "You know that means your father had to be more than just a wolf shifter don't you?" Martha asks in her soft nurturing voice.

Bounty nods.

"But you don't mind?"

He says, "No, I don't; whatever it was helped me save her."

Bounty's lost some of his demonic strength after giving Tiana half of his beast's heart. But his wolf spirit remained strong. Tiana fluttered back to the ground, softly placing the children down before stepping to him.

"To save me, u gave me half of one of your hearts. Words cannot express how much I love you..."

"For my mate and my cubs, I would do it all again."

With wings spread out, she picks the children up again. "What did you call them?"

Bounty tells her the children's names; she smiles.

"Thank you for saving us?" Tiana whispers in his ear.

"I couldn't watch you die; you're my mate, the other half to my soul."

"Are you sure? Or did you save me because I'm such a good lay?"

Bounty chuckled, caught off guard by her crude humor. "Well, a little of both."

They both laugh. Tiana instantly fell in love with the sound. With a short lesson from Martha on how to conceal her wings, Tiana was discharged to go home.

Tao and Yolanda were already waiting when Bounty pulled the car into her mother's driveway. Tiana looked around, mouth ajar. "Well, this is new!" the kids burst out in giggles. "No silly mommy, Nana has been living here since you went to sleep." Tiana shook her head at how intelligent her toddlers were.

Before Bounty could open her car door, Yolanda was already pushing her way past him. Yolanda screamed and cried as she embraced her best friend.

"I am so happy you're back, Titi."

"Me, too. I missed you all so much."

"So much has changed since you've been asleep."

Tiana smiled, her eyes falling to Yolanda's swollen belly. Tao hugs her but releases her quickly when Bounty and the pups started growling. "Whoa whoa, now did my god kids just growl at me? I guess I'll keep these gifts then." The children all scream in unison, "No, uncle Tao, it's daddy's fault we just copied him." Bounty looked at the children with a mock expression of hurt. "Who me? I would never teach my pups to do such a thing." Bounty claps Tao on the shoulder, and they chuckle in laughter. Tiana looks at Yolanda in confusion. "Umm, when did that happen?

Yolanda laughs and whispers. "I told you a lot happened while you were sleeping."

"I see," Tiana whispered back. After Tao issued each of his God kids a gift, he presented flowers and cards from Christy Marlow, others from people from the faculty, and some of the women Tiana had once worked with. Tiana shed some tears, thinking about how much has changed.

Tiana looked over at her mother. "I'm really a mom now, huh?"

"You will be everything I was not. You will be more," Debbie says, kissing her forehead.

As Tao and Bounty play with the children on the front lawn, the three women sit on the porch and watch them play.

Yolanda looked down at her belly. "I wish things could stay like this, but I'm scared for us all; this peace may be short-lived."

Tiana grabbed her best friend's hand, as Mama Debbie replied. "We will do what we always do, girls. We will fight and survive for the people we love."

Warning

Content beyond this section is for adults only

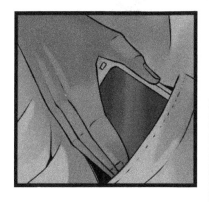

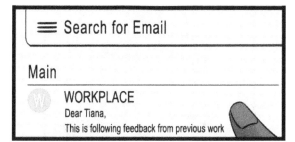

About The Author

T.M MCGEE

-Who am I …?

A mother, writer, advocate, and free spirit I have a passion for women's wellness and empowerment. My stories may contain some dark themes, even some unmentionable acts. But the women in my stories will always prevail and overcome their obstacles.

-Why did I start writing?

It all started from a dream. It was so vivid that I had to wake up and jot it down. It's been so much fun bringing my characters to life. Each one of them reflects a piece of me in some way, from their free spirits, their quirks, and even some of their trauma. Every story may not be your cup of tea. But my personality has never been one size fits all. So, here's to the people with more books than friends. May we always be different, and to ourselves forever true.

- As a novice writer, I hope to grow with grace and improve with time.

-More stories are on the way. So please follow me.

�Reviews are welcome�

Please follow @tm.mcgeeepub (IG)

Websites: www.tmcgeepub.com **&** https://linktr.ee/Neshailashes

YouTube: https://www.youtube.com/channel/UCOuQXBif-bopt7a8nqpYRgQ

Author Q&A

Q; now that book one is finished, how do you feel?

A: I feel exasperated; honestly, the book took so much out of me. It started as a dream, then kept building the more I dreamt about it. I'm just glad book one is complete.

Q: What do you love most about your book, and also what do you hate?

A: I love my characters; they're all different sides of me. Each one has a touch of my personality written into them. The thing I hate the most, I would say I struggled with proper editing for this book. I write how I talk. I always have. At one point, I was going to scrub the whole story. Only share it with family and friends, but they encouraged me to keep writing. I proofread and hired several editors, but things still slipped through the cracks. This tends to happen when you write in a conversational format. but you live, and you learn

Q: What do you want your readers to experience from reading your story?

A: I want them to be opened minded; whenever I read stories about mythology or science fiction, I couldn't picture myself as the character. So my goal was to paint/depict women of color in another light. Why can't we slay dragons, fly space ships or fight demons? The genre, language, and content may be uncomfortable for some, that's understandable. But I'm happy if at least one reader enjoys it.

Upcoming Books

Illicit- Taboo Series Book 1
Love Bites- Yolanda & Keanu Book2
Un-Taming The Beast- Tao & Stacia Book3

CPSIA information can be obtained
at www.ICGtesting.com
Printed in the USA
BVHW091532270521
608293BV00006B/1895

9 781087 960685